More Critical Praise for Michael Zadoorian

for *Beautiful Music*

"*Beautiful Music* thrums like a guitar riff and rattles like a bass drum. This soulful, funny, transporting, and often electrifying novel will resonate with anyone who's found their true passion—or is still on the hunt. It's not just a great Detroit story and a great American story; it's also a story about what it means to be human. I loved this book! In the words of Bob Seger, all I could do was turn the page."

—Davy Rothbart, author of *My Heart Is an Idiot*

"Like a song you can't stop playing, *Beautiful Music* casts a spell on your heart. With clarity and tenderness, Zadoorian sweeps us into a life that we recognize as our own. Remember when you were lonely, scared, unsure, and then somehow found your own kind of bravery and actual, genuine joy? *Beautiful Music* will take you there—and give you the soundtrack to get you through."

—Scott Sparling, author of *Wire to Wire*

for *The Leisure Seeker*

"Zadoorian's pace is deceptive, it's restful. But unexpected scenes jump out at you. Come to the end and you'll say, 'Oh my God.'"

—Elmore Leonard

"*The Leisure Seeker* is pretty much like life itself: joyous, painful, funny, moving, tragic, mysterious, and not to be missed."

—*Booklist*, starred review

"In this affecting road novel, an elderly married couple leave their Detroit home and take off in their camper for one last adventure together . . . An authentic and funny love story."

—*Publishers Weekly*

"A bittersweet fable of the golden years likely to offer consolation to readers who've ever known anyone old or have plans to get old themselves." —*Kirkus Reviews*

"Michael Zadoorian's bittersweet story about two runaways who are in their 80s and in failing health could be a lovely film." —*USA Today*

"I hoped for a book that would make me laugh during these tight times, and I was rewarded." —*Los Angeles Times*

for *Second Hand*

- An ABA Book Sense 76 Pick
- A Barnes & Nobles Discover Award Finalist
- Winner of the Great Lakes Colleges Association New Writers Award

"*Second Hand* may feel like a gift from the (Tiki) gods."
—*New York Times Book Review*

"A charming, comic novel." —*Marie Claire*

"Wonderful . . . a novel about finding value in the most unlikely places." —*Tampa Tribune Times*

"Anyone who has found delight in a thrift store, captured glee in finding that perfect scarf or that retro chair, will delight at this novel."
—*Booklist*

"How can one capture the spirit of this wondrous book in so few words? Marvelous observations about secondhand items and life in general . . . Readers will thoroughly enjoy this book and will be sorry when it ends." —*Library Journal*

"Astonishingly mandatory and compelling . . . frequent fascinating and insightful meditations on the nature of stuff."
—*San Francisco Bay Guardian*

for *Lost Tiki Places of Detroit*

"[The stories are] sometimes wildly funny and more than a little crazy, yet they have a heartbreaking affection for the battered lives they portray." —*Ann Arbor Observer*

"These newly envisioned stories of Detroit come at you without apology for the gritty language of the city, the racism, the madness of everyday life. The whiff of 'presence,' of being there, grabs at your throat."
—*Northern Express*

"These are stories that grab you, shake you and slap you upside the head." —*Lansing City Pulse*

"Zadoorian knows the streets and side streets and alleyways of his city and its surround; better, he knows the humor, the sadness, and the sometimes hidden beauty of life in the Rust Belt."
—Paul Clemens, author of *Made in Detroit*

Beautiful Music

Beautiful Music

Michael Zadoorian

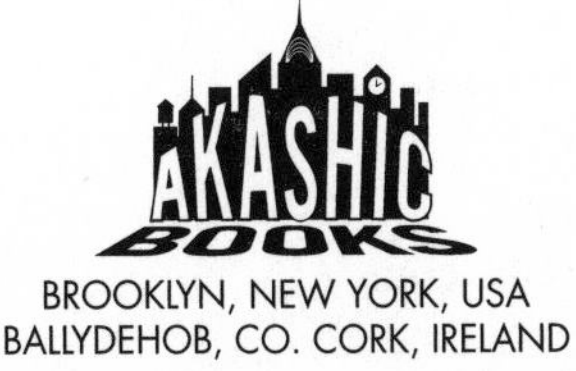

BROOKLYN, NEW YORK, USA
BALLYDEHOB, CO. CORK, IRELAND

This is a work of fiction. All names, characters, places, and incidents are the product of the author's imagination or are used fictitiously. Any resemblance to real events or persons, living or dead, is entirely coincidental.

Published by Akashic Books

Hardcover ISBN: 978-1-61775-617-7
Paperback ISBN: 978-1-61775-627-6
Library of Congress Control Number: 2017956554

First printing

Akashic Books
Brooklyn, New York, USA
Ballydehob, Co. Cork, Ireland
Twitter: @AkashicBooks
Facebook: AkashicBooks
E-mail: info@akashicbooks.com
Website: www.akashicbooks.com

In memory of Dave Michalak,
in lieu of the Epic Poem of Foghat

The last chord has died away. In the brief silence which follows I feel strongly that there it is, that something has happened.
—Jean-Paul Sartre

Don't you ever listen to the radio when the big bad beat comes on?
—Bob Seger

The Hits of '69!

A busy signal. That's all I hear, again and again. It's the fifth time I've called. My index finger starts to get sore around the cuticle from all the dialing. I'm calling CKLW's phone number. Luckily, it's not long distance or I'd be in big trouble with my parents. Though it could be long distance since CKLW is a Canadian radio station and I'm in Detroit, but I don't think it is. Either way, I don't know where I got it in my head to call them, but now that the idea is there, I can't get it out. My mother is in the other room and she hasn't started wondering yet what I've been doing on the phone for so long. She has one of her shows on and it's pretty loud. Lucky for me, but I still keep getting a busy signal. On the ninth try, cuticle red and aching, I finally get through. After three rings, a woman picks up and says, "CKLW request line. Can you hold for a moment?"

Of course I can. I'm thrilled. Over the line, I can hear the disc jockey, Ed Mitchell, announcing the song "In the Year 2525" by Zager & Evans. The song starts. It sounds tinny and staticky through the phone line, nowhere near as good as on my Kor/Sonic transistor radio. After a couple minutes, I start to panic, thinking that the operator has forgotten all about me, but then someone answers. His voice is so low and clear and deep that it seems to exist on a different wavelength altogether. There is nothing tinny or staticky about it. I'm actually speaking to the disc jockey himself.

"Okay! What do you want to hear?" he says, in a growl that sounds so very familiar to me.

I can't speak, having suddenly stumbled into a world where adults care about what I want.

"Hello?"

Is he mad? I don't want DJ Ed Mitchell to be mad. He's going to hang up, so I push out the words as best I can: "Uh, I want to hear 'A Boy Named Sue' by Johnny Cash," I say.

"Okay! Wasn't sure if anyone was there. Now look, I'm going to record your request, then we're gonna play it on the air later. Is that cool?"

I nod.

"So it's cool?"

"Yes," I say, realizing that nodding at the phone is not a good idea. Trying to make up for my mistake, I muster up my energy and yell, "Yeah!"

"All right!" says DJ Ed. He's an adult who likes it when I yell. "That's good. Say it just like that. Just say, *Hey, Ed Mitchell*. Then tell me your name, your age, and say the song you want to hear. Lots of enthusiasm. Got it?"

"I think so."

"Okay? Are you ready? And . . . go!"

I mess it up, of course. I forget to say, *Hey, Ed Mitchell*. And I forget to say my name too.

"You gotta get it right this time, or I have to go," he says, and I can tell that he means it. "Get ready. One . . . two . . . three . . . go!"

I take a deep breath and spit it out fast: "Hey, Ed Mitchell, my name is Danny Yzemski, I'm ten years old, and I want to hear 'A Boy Named Sue' by Johnny Cash!"

"All *righht*!" he roars. He is happy with me. I have pleased DJ Ed Mitchell. "Thanks, Danny. Good job. You'll be on the air in a little while."

Then the line goes dead.

I hang around outside with my Kor/Sonic for the next two hours waiting to hear myself on the radio. I hear the same songs, over and over again. "Crystal Blue Persuasion" "Choice of Colors," "Put a Little Love in Your Heart," "My Cherie Amour." I sit there on the glider in the backyard of our bungalow in northwest Detroit. Two years after the riot, my mother is finally feeling that it's okay for me to be outside again as long as I stay in the yard. She remembers, like I remember, the towers of black smoke rising into the sky down Grand River Avenue four miles away, the rumors of looting at Grandland Shopping Center just a mile from our house, the tanks rolling down Fenkell after the governor called in the National Guard, the news reports of snipers, and the hazy, frantic footage of people running out of and into burning buildings. She'd really rather I just stay in the house.

Mark and Jim, the closest I have to friends, come by to talk, but I've got the transistor pressed to my ear. "I'm going to be on the radio," I tell them.

"Sure you are, Tub-ski," says Mark, then the two of them go off to play curb ball.

Just as well, since I'm still not supposed to go too far off our property. Besides, it's important that I hear my voice on the radio. After an hour and a half, I start to worry that the *Ed Mitchell Show* is going to end without him playing me or my song. Or that the battery in my radio is going to die. I do hear one other kid request a song. It's a little colored kid who says, "What's happening, Ed Mitchell? I wanna hear 'Girl You're Too Young' by Archie Bell & the Drells." Only when he says the name of the group, he stretches it out so it sounds like the *Durr-ells*.

I worry that maybe since he got to request a song I won't hear mine. Yet a half-hour later, after a commercial for Gene Merollis Chevrolet ("*Gene Merollis, what a great, great guyyy*," sung by a man who sounds like he's got a cigar wedged in the side of his mouth), I hear my own voice squawk and boom over the airwaves. (My voice is lower than most kids my age because I'm husky.)

I'm so excited I can't even speak. I sit there on the glider in my backyard, swinging frantically, not even listening to the song, just letting the sound of my voice on the radio replay in my head. About the time when I do actually listen, the song begins to end. Johnny Cash is just about to shoot his dad for naming him Sue.

. . . But you oughta thank me before I die,
For the gravel in your guts and the spit in your eye . . .

A few moments later, Johnny Cash is done singing and the music fades. I know that even though CKLW will play this song hundred of times in the next few weeks, this is the last time I'm ever going to hear it in exactly this way.

My 1/25-Scale Life

Most mornings this summer, I'm awakened by the sound of the radio coming from the kitchen. It's tuned to WJR, *the Great Voice of the Great Lakes*. I lie in bed listening to "The Look of Love" by Sérgio Mendes & Brasil '66 or "The Unicorn" by the Irish Rovers until my father comes to wake me up. He knocks on the doorjamb, then grabs my foot and gives it a shake.

"Up and at 'em, Daniel."

"Okay, Dad."

Even though I just got out of bed, J.P. McCarthy, the disc jockey on WJR, is easy to listen to. He's like an uncle you didn't know you had. He says dopey stuff like "Good morning, world!" and "Remember my name in Sheboygan!" but I like him anyway. I notice the way my mother reacts to him. At the tiled kitchen counter, preparing a cup of tea for me, I watch as she pauses to listen to something he's saying. That moment, with her head cocked downward, half-smiling, I notice how pretty my mother is.

"What're you up to today?" my dad says. He asks me this every day.

"I'm just going to work on a model car downstairs."

"Why don't you get out and play some ball with your friends? How about that TV2 Swim-mobile? Isn't that around here today?"

"Oh no," says my mother. "Every kid in the inner city has swam in that thing. He'll get worms and god knows what else."

My father sighs. "Well, try to get some fresh air."

"Like there's any fresh air in this city," says my mother.

"I'm not all that crazy about fresh air," I chime in.

This is where my father gives up. He doesn't actually know that my mother barely lets me leave the house anyway. Not that I mind. It doesn't matter to me that it's summer. It's too hot and bright outside, the days too long, and my mother just wants me to be safe.

I even have my own special room in our basement. It was a coal bin before my parents bought the house, but now it's just a little narrow room where things end up, with an old red Formica drop-leaf kitchen table at one end where I build the model cars. I sit at that beat-up table, with the radio on and my X-acto knife and the squint of Testors model glue in the air. (I've heard that kids sniff it.) Under a dusty cone of light, I tinker together 1/25-scale replicas of pro stock racers like the Sox & Martin Boss 'Cuda or the nitro funny cars of Don "The Snake" Prudhomme and Tom "The Mongoose" McEwen. (Natural enemies in nature and on the quarter-mile!) While I work, the only sounds are CKLW and the trill of the dehumidifier, clicking on, drying and vibrating the stinging chemical air. I sing along to the 5th Dimension or the Cowsills. Sometimes I imitate the disc jockeys while I sit there. *"That's a little 'Keem-O-Sabe' for you, by Electric Indian. Coming up on four o'clock. It's about eighty-four degrees in the Motor City . . ."*

Occasionally, my mother hears me talking to myself down in the coal bin. She speaks to me from the laundry area. "Danny, stop talking when there's no one there to listen."

"Sorry, Mom."

"We don't need any more kooks in the family."

My mother doesn't want me to grow up to be a kook. Her whole family is full of kooks, according to her, which is why she doesn't talk to any of them.

I can easily spend the whole day building the model cars and listening to the radio, never leaving except to go upstairs to the bathroom or to make myself a sandwich. If my mother is in a bad mood, I just gulp back my hunger and swallow my spit. The washtub is my emergency place to pee.

During this third summer indoors, Jim sometimes knocks at the back door and calls for me, breaking my name into two parts. I sit there in the coal bin, ignoring him until my mother goes to the door and tells him that

I'm busy. She never asks why I don't answer him. Jim lives seven houses down from me and is moving away soon, away from Detroit, away from the idea of another riot that comes even closer to our neighborhood. His family is moving to Livonia, near the mall. I'm mad at him for leaving, so I sit there, ignoring him, building the model cars, staying out of my mother's way and trying not to be a kook.

The Sound of Everything

It's also the summer that my father and I go to the drag races. ("*This Sunday afternoon at Detroit Dragway! Gigantic Superfuel Funny Car Spectacular!*" say the commercials, echoing from my radio.) We take the long drive downriver in my father's Biscayne to Sibley at Dix, pay our two dollars, pull into the wide dirt lot, and park among the gray-primered muscle cars with bulged hoods and raised rear ends, the trucks with their empty trailers, and the family station wagons. We trek through a series of fences and fields to the bleachers, working our way toward the sounds of tires squealing and engines revving.

"Are you ready?" my father says to me. This is something he asks me every time we go.

I nod. "I'm ready."

"Okay. Because it's going to be loud."

We sit among crowds of lean, smoking men in white T-shirts, with blowsy, puff-haired women in pedal pushers, and grubby kids with Kool-Aid-stained mouths, all of us watching the homemade hot rods, air-scooped and cherry-bombed, that rattle in on trailers from Inkster and Allen Park and Fenton and even Brightmoor, near us. The cars pair up on the drag strip and take off, one heat every minute or two.

"When are the funny cars?" I ask my father over the sound of a new red-orange Pontiac "The Judge" GTO skittering off the line against a Bondo-patched Nova. The Nova wins.

"Pretty soon, I think," he says, taking the last puff from his Old Gold before dropping it to the dirt and stepping on it. In his beige sport shirt and neat mustard slacks, he looks different from the other men.

The funny cars are candy-colored, airbrushed, decaled fiberglass shells of cars, like what I would find in one of my model car kits, only full size, with giant supercharged engines, enormous black slicks in the back and much smaller mag-rimmed wheels in the front, all mounted on a spindly tubular chassis with a cage where the driver is strapped in. They have names like Motown Shake and Comet Cyclone. The crews roll the cars up to the starting line, where they start the engines—a thunder that ignites the air and causes my dad and I to turn to each other, our eyes wide with disbelief. He yells to me and though I can't really hear him, I know what he's saying.

"Are you ready?"

Grinning, I nod my head again. "It's gonna be loud!"

The crew pours bleach on the track and drivers spin their slicks till smoke billows, heating them against the asphalt for traction. Roar and squeal, steam and stink, all at an awful wonderful volume that makes my heart clatter in my chest. Soon the air is harsh with bleach and nitro fuel and I can barely breathe from excitement and fumes. Ears buzz and eyes tear, until finally a tall traffic light—the Christmas tree—counts down to a green light, and the cars explode off the line, tires scorching asphalt.

It's over so quickly you would miss it if you looked

away for seven seconds, but no one looks away. For those seven seconds, my father and I can see, smell, taste, feel, and hear sound. Sometimes my father brings earplugs, but we never use them. We crave that sound. We love how it feels, how it hurts. The sound fills us up inside. It seeps through my skin, between the bones and muscle, into the narrow spaces surrounding my heart, in those empty spaces that I hear when I beat my chest like Tarzan, the spaces that make my voice deep.

My Father's Beautiful Music

On the way home, our ears buzzing, our nostrils stinging, the pleasant stink of burned rubber and exhaust clinging to our clothes, my father lights an Old Gold and turns on the Beautiful Music station. It plays songs that I recognize from CKLW and WXYZ, but with no words and rerecorded by stringed orchestras. "Kites Are Fun," "I'll Follow the Sun," "The Windmills of Your Mind." Like CKLW, the station he listens to broadcasts from Windsor in Ontario just across the Ambassador Bridge from Detroit. What's strange about the station is that it goes off the air at sunset. When we are in the car together, coming home from the drags, and the Beautiful Music is on and the sun glows red behind us, the station will simply sign off for the evening, just like that. A song ends—say, "Both Sides Now"—then the Canadian national anthem starts playing. The announcer says, "*CBE is now ending its broadcast day. We will resume programming at sunrise tomorrow.*" The song faces out, then suddenly there's static. Gone.

This disturbs me in some deep, awful way, a kind of fear that I want to explain to my dad, but just can't. How can I tell him that hearing a radio station go off the air, hearing the music fade away like that, terrifies me somehow, drains me of all the good sounds and vibration from the drags? It's crazy. Maybe it's because music always makes me feel better. So the station going off the air, the static, the quiet—that's the opposite of sounds and vibration and feeling better. It's fear and emptiness.

Luckily, most of the time when the Canadian station goes off the air, my father right away punches one of the thick chrome buttons on the radio and switches over to WJR, where there's a baseball game on or more music. Whatever it is, it's a relief to me. The worst thing that can happen is that he just turns the radio off.

The Jams

I don't care much for rock music when I first hear it. I find this out in a classroom that fall, when one of the tough kids in my class brings in a record for show-and-tell. Before class, I hear talk between the desks that the record Barry Stegner is going to play has swearing on it. His plan is to trick our teacher Miss Ferlin into playing it in front of the class.

I have certainly heard swearing before from my mother and father, yet I somehow fear that having curse words spoken aloud in the classroom will cause some sort of disturbance, possibly even a riot. (But then I'm always worried about something causing a riot.) If that happens, I naturally assume that Barry Stegner and the other bad kids will take over the classroom, hold our teacher Miss Ferlin hostage, then maybe burn down the school for good measure.

I feel like it's up to me to do something since I'm the only boy in the class who has won a citizenship award.

(Me up on stage with dozens of girls, bursting with pride, not knowing that it will make me a target for every mean kid in the school—the tauntings, hat-stealings, book up-endings, and lunch-money muggings began shortly after that.) Yet I can't bring myself to tell Miss Ferlin that she's about to play an obscene recording. I don't want to be a tattletale, and besides, if there is a riot, what will they do to me? I have to keep my mouth shut.

An older, sandy-haired kid from the AV room rolls in a tanklike gray record player on a cart and plugs it in. The turntable silently starts to rotate.

Miss Ferlin looks out over the class. She has milky-smooth skin and a *That Girl* brunette bouffant, offset strangely by a slightly oversize and stationary glass eye. (No one knows how it happened, but it's impossible to not stare at it when you talk to her.) "Everyone, Barry Stegner has something for show-and-tell today."

Barry, sloth-eyed and loping, gets up before the class. Then he says, "I have a new record that I want to play." He holds up the album and I can feel the tension in the classroom.

Miss Ferlin takes a look at it, at the collage of images on the front, at the liquidy red, white, and blue letters across the top. "It looks very . . ." She searches for a word. "Patriotic" is what she settles on, spotting an American flag on the cover.

Barry pulls the album out of the sleeve and holds it up. The label is black and red with a large E at the top. He leers at the class, making a big show of placing the record on the ashy felt of the turntable.

"And what is this record called, Barry?" asks Miss Ferlin.

I sit at my desk paralyzed, feeling bad about how I am letting Miss Ferlin and her glass eye and the American educational system down by allowing this to happen. Yet I'm also fascinated, wanting desperately to see what's going to happen next.

"It's called *Kick Out the Jams*, Miss Ferlin."

Miss Ferlin seems not exactly sure what to make of the title, but she smiles pleasantly anyway. "And who's the recording artist?"

"The MC5," says Barry, grinning hard.

"All right then, class. Barry is going to play his record called—" She looks to him for confirmation. "*Kick Out the Jams*?"

"Yeah," he says, staring at her glass eye.

Barry places the needle on the record and with a lurid glance toward the class, he reaches over and turns up the volume all the way. The whole class somehow knows something big is coming. A sizzle of amplification fills the room. We hear the recorded whistles and hoots of an audience for a few seconds, then finally a man's voice booms out of the speaker, talking like he's being held prisoner in an echo chamber: "*Right now . . . right now . . . right now it's time to . . .*" There's a long pause, then the jangle of a guitar before the man screams: "*KICK OUT THE JAMS, MOTHERFUCKERS!*"

After that, a series of grunts and *ahh*s, guitar screeches, and drum beats that sound like gunshots. There is energy crackling in the air from the record, which reminds me for a brief, gleeful moment of the drags. "*And I feel pretty good—*"

Which is when Miss Ferlin, one eye shocked wide open, the other bored and noncommittal, rushes over to the record player, where her foot hits the bottom of the tank cart, sending it rolling across the front of the classroom. The record keeps playing: "*. . . and I guess that I could get crazy now, baby . . .*"

The music is raucous and angry and thrilling and scary. Even over all the noise, I can hear the sigh of approval from the class. Finally, Miss Ferlin pulls the plug from the wall outlet and the music grinds to a distorted halt. She pulls the needle from the record, grabs the record from the turntable, and hands it to Barry Stegner, who is very obviously thrilled with what has happened. Less so when she grabs him by the arm and drags him out of the classroom.

"You are going to the principal's office right now."

I'm happy when it's over, but there's something about the music, maybe just the volume of it, that haunts me for the rest of the day. I think about it later, when I'm in the basement building the model cars. It crosses my mind that the music I hear on my stations is not at all like what I heard today in class. Just as quickly, the idea evaporates and I continue to sing along to "Sugar, Sugar."

Stereophrenia '70!

It's 6:35 p.m. on a Wednesday and my father is still not home. It's not really all that unusual for him to work late. Sometimes his job requires it. He's the head keyliner for *Synchroscope*, the monthly magazine (or *house organ*, as he calls it, which is weird) for Detroit Edison, the electric company. The keyliner is the guy who cuts and pastes together the whole magazine. To me, it sounds more like he should be a type of car. (*Longer, wider, sleeker . . . Introducing the Ford Keyliner!*) When I ask my mother why he's late, she tells me that he was going to stop at Korvettes on his way home. I'm kind of peeved by this since it's usually my job to go there with him on weekends, when he buys cigarettes for him and my mother. At 7:10 p.m., he finally shows up, squeezing through the back door, carrying a large cardboard box.

"I'm home," he announces. I can tell he's in a good mood.

"What's in the box?" I ask.

"You'll see," he says. I look at my mother, but she just shrugs.

We follow him down the basement stairs into our rumpus room, which he's turning into a family room. I'm not sure of the difference, but he says a family room is more modern. His plans are to cover the cinder-block walls with paneling, then to build an Early American hutch with a mantle and shelves. He's already tiled the floor and put furring strips along all the walls. He also got an avocado-green electric fireplace on sale at Arlan's, which he installed with a wall of plastic stick-on bricks behind it, so it's coming along nicely.

Once we're downstairs, my father carefully sets the box down on the new linoleum. He slits open the top with his fingernail knife, rips back the flaps, and removes a couple blocks of snowy Styrofoam. He's really taking his time.

"You want to see what it is?" he says to me.

I don't know why he's being so mysterioso. "Yeah. Come on, let's see."

He reaches in and lifts out a brand-new Kor/Sonic stereo with a wood-grain and silver console, a glass-front radio dial, brushed metal knobs, and a record player with a smoked-plastic see-through dome.

"A stereo system," I say.

"You got it." Also from the box: two wood-grain speakers, fronts covered with tweedy cloth.

"I thought someone was going to wait until he finished the basement before he bought one," my mother says. She's smiling, but I can hear the sarcasm in her voice.

"It was on sale this week," my father says. "A really good price. A closeout."

"Oh." She's satisfied now. My parents love bargains.

It doesn't take him long to attach the speakers. Once he plugs it in and the wide eye of the receiver flickers awake with a golden light, I see a change in him. He keeps running his hand over the wood-grain console. "Pretty sharp, eh?"

"It's very nice, Hal."

"Yeah," I say.

My father twists a small knob to AM, then tunes it to CBE and the room is filled with a lush string version of "Eleanor Rigby." "Listen to that."

"We are," my mother says.

I look to the steps leading upstairs and to the sunlight shifting through the window of the back door. It's getting close to sunset. But I don't have to worry because he twists the knob over to FM, adjusting it to the first station he finds. There's the screech of a loud guitar, the bash of drums.

"Ugh, turn that jungle music off," my mother says.

He squints and searches until he finds an orchestra playing a song that I don't recognize, but both my parents smile.

"FM sounds great," says my father. "Listen to that."

We don't for long. He switches to *Phono*, then a velvety hiss fills the basement. My father picks up the left speaker, untangles the wire, and places it in the corner of the room. He does the same with the right speaker.

"Are you ready?" he says.

From a Korvettes bag that he must have carried in with the box, he pulls out an album called *Super Stereo Sound Effects!* As he slices the cellophane and extracts the record from the sleeve, my eyes are drawn to the designs on the cover—multicolored stripes, arrows, and uncoiled sound waves. By then, my father has the record on the turntable and we're hearing the sound of a jet airplane taking off. I've never been near an airplane, but it's got to sound like this. My father turns it up louder. My mother smiles, more strained this time.

"Listen to that," my father says yet again as he sits down. "Pretty good for a small unit."

Hearing my father use the word *unit* makes him seem different to me. I can feel the sound in my chest now, vibrating my heart. It goes to silence, then there's a noise that I can't quite recognize, a rolling, aching, reverberating rumble that grows louder until the room erupts with a low-pitched clatter.

My father holds up the cover and points to a listing on the back. "Bowling alley!" he yells over what I now recognize as pins dropping. He's still smiling.

When the pistol shots come on, my mother rises from the Early American couch (purchased on sale at Topps). "It's very nice, Hal," she says. "I'm sure we'll get a lot of use out of it."

My father jumps up. "Don't go yet. Let me put on some music."

"I should get back upstairs. I have potatoes on."

"One song," he says, raising the needle from the sound effects album with a tiny handle at the back of the turntable. He puts that album away then pulls another from the bag, the Carpenters' *Close to You*.

"Somebody went overboard on the record albums," my mother says.

"I wanted to get something you'd like," he says, carefully placing the needle on the disc. Gentle notes from a piano fill the basement as "We've Only Just Begun" starts to play. It's a favorite of my mother's. Karen Carpenter's languid voice flows through the speakers and my mother settles back on the couch.

"Ooh, that does sound nice," she says, a slight purr to her voice.

Just then, I realize that music has power. Vaguely sighing, my mother sits through "We've Only Just Begun" and even the song after that, "Love Is Surrender." She seems so happy. Then my father flips over the LP and plays the other hit, "(They Long to Be) Close to You." By the time it ends, we can smell the burned potatoes.

"Oh shit," says my mother, scurrying up the stairs.

In less than a minute, she comes back down clutching

the handle of a saucepan with a dishtowel. She holds it out for us to see. There are blackened, scorched rocks of some sort stuck to the bottom of the pan. "See what you made me do." She looks as though she's about to cry, which is something that happens quite a lot around our house. She turns and runs up the stairs.

"Eleanor, honey, it's okay," says my dad, chasing after her. "Let that soak. We'll go out to eat."

"Are you crazy?" yells my mother from the kitchen, sobbing. "I have round steak ready!"

I hear a pan hit the floor, then my mother's footsteps as she runs to her bedroom. I can follow the sound of the steps across the basement ceiling.

My father sighs, deflated, then says to me, "We can try it tomorrow."

Upstairs, my mother is having one of her crying fits. Downstairs, "I'll Never Fall In Love Again" plays along.

So begins my father's stereophonic period.

Pinochle Party

My father rarely drinks. It's a different story with my mother. My father has the occasional highball with their neighborhood pinochle group, but I can always tell when my mother is in her cups, because her voice grows high-pitched and giddy. I can hear it from my bedroom. I find the sound of my tipsy mother comforting. I enjoy the sounds of a party in our house—the jovial chatter of adults as they play cards, punctuated by bursts of laughter.

This month, for the first time in the history of pinochle group at our house, there is music. My father bought an extra set of speakers (my mother was not pleased), drilled through the living room floor (she was really not pleased), and wired the upstairs for sound. There's an orchestra version of "Knock Three Times" by Tony Orlando and Dawn playing when I come in to say hi to everyone. My parents like me to do this after the guests have arrived and settled in. Then I'm banished to the basement rumpus room for the night, to watch *Arnie* and *The Mary Tyler Moore Show* and *Mannix* on our portable TV, venturing up occasionally to pilfer leftover cheese cubes and crackers from the kitchen.

Once in a while, my parents let me hang around in the living room for a while. If I'm lucky, someone will talk to me like I'm an adult and not an eleven-year-old. Walt Brown, one of our neighbors, who is there with his wife Norma, does not do this. "Still got your baby fat, I see," he says, poking me in the stomach. I don't like it when he talks about my weight, but he's mostly okay.

Mr. Brown takes a pull off his pipe, glances around at the others, and says, "Whatdoyousay let's ask Danny? He's a young person."

I'm flattered that they want my opinion about something, though I have no idea what they've been discussing.

"Danny, have you ever heard of that rock group that started the riot, the Rolling Stones?"

I think for a moment. I know I've heard their songs on CKLW, but I don't know what riot he's talking about. Far as I know, rock groups had nothing to do with the riot in Detroit. Still, I nod like I know what he's talking about.

"What do you think of them?" said Mr. Brown.

There's something about the tone in his voice that tells me he doesn't care for them. I'm good at figuring adults out this way. I look directly at him and say, "They sound like Communists to me."

Roars of laughter. The adults are all amused by my comment, especially my mother, who laughs almost too long and too loudly. Mission accomplished. I don't really know what a Communist is, but I've heard my father railing against them during the news, so I know adults don't like them. Yet my comedic success doesn't have the desired effect. I'm not invited to join the group. No one offers me a highball and deals me in. In fact, it's as if all the laughter has just called attention to the fact that there's a kid in the room. After my boffo laffs die down, my smiling mother takes a drag of her L&M, looks at my father, and swishes her cigarette hand toward the hallway.

My father gets up, puts his hand on my shoulder, and leads me out of the room. "Okay, kiddo. Downstairs."

I look at him like, *Are you nuts? I'm killing here!* It doesn't matter. I have to go downstairs. For a while, I sit on the stairs and listen to the muted strains of music, the rhythms of their conversation, and the trill of my mother's laughter.

Voices of Night

Falling asleep to the sound of voices. This is something that I do most nights once I get a portable Kor/Sonic AM/FM radio with a cassette recorder for my birthday. I listen to the radio to soothe me as I go to sleep. The nighttime DJs seem to know that the darkness makes it necessary to speak softly. The music too has a quiet, soaring quality to it, like flying in a dream. "It Don't Matter to Me," "Easy to Be Hard," "Stormy."

My parents don't mind that I leave the radio on during the night. (Sometimes it helps drown out the sounds of them arguing. Not loudly, but with pointed voices that hiss and huff.) It's like an audio night-light to me, chasing away the bad dreams I've had since I was little. It's so low that even I mostly can't hear it, but I know it's there—music and whispered words that speak to me in some secret silent way, quelling my worries about school, quieting my heartbeat when I wake up panting and sweating, terrified of nightmares that I can't remember. *How can you be afraid of what you can't remember?* I ask myself. Yet I somehow seem to manage it.

Sometimes I wake up in the middle of the night, scared from the voices I'm hearing, thinking that someone is outside my window, planning to break into the house. This might be because my parents talk a lot about break-ins in the neighborhood since the riot, how Detroit is changing, how people are moving away and maybe we should too. Then I remember that the voices I'm hearing are just from the radio next to my bed.

If I sleep through the night with it on, in the mornings I just change stations and turn it up, so that the radio in my room is tuned to the same station my mother is playing in the kitchen. When I walk through the hallway of our house, I can feel the music from my room joining with the music coming from the kitchen. It's like I'm caught in the sound waves, floating in the broadcast as it takes place, as if I'm a part of the music and the words and the air itself.

Yet when I walk though that hall of sound into the kitchen, while we may be tuned into the same station, I don't know where my mother herself will be tuned or which one I'll meet up with—quiet Mom, sullenly standing by the stove, cigarette dangling from her lips, hair mashed on one side, rings under her eyes. Or maybe it will be the mom who won't get out of bed that day. (Then it's my father who's in the kitchen, there past his schedule, cheerily scrambling an egg for me.) Or maybe it will be happy, peppy, good-mood Mom, so glad to see me shuffle in.

That's today. Today, she greets me with a big hug and a kiss on the forehead, running her fingers through my hair, taming the matted tangles of my bad night's sleep. On our kitchen table, at my place, is a glass of grapefruit juice, full of pulp and seeds and a piece of burned toast. (I like it pale.) She's fully dressed in a striped turtleneck sweater and wool slacks.

"Guess what, Danny?" she says. "You're not going to school today."

"What?" Now I'm groggy *and* confused.

"I'm taking you out of school for the day," she says brightly. "We're going to go to the Art Institute. There's an exhibit I want us to see. But first, we're going to go have a picnic."

"What?" I give my mom a look like, *Are you kidding?* "No, Mom. It's winter."

"It's just weather. It's settled. We're having brunch in the park."

"I have a social studies test today."

"I'll write you a note tomorrow," she says, taking a bite of my toast.

"Mom. Just let me go to school."

"It's going to be really fun, you'll see."

"Mom."

Before I even get a chance to sit down, she hands me a cup of tea, turns me around, and pushes me toward the hall. "Now go get dressed. Be sure to bundle up. It's cold outside today. Wear your long johns."

I do as she says.

So my mother and I go on a winter picnic in Stoepel Park a few blocks away. It's a bright, sunny day, at least, and not too achingly cold. We sit on a thick woolen plaid blanket atop a picnic table where we've brushed off the snow. Out of the picnic basket that my mother packed long before I got up, we eat from waxed paper bundles—Olive Loaf sandwiches, Vienna Fingers, and apple slices sprinkled with sugar and cinnamon. My mother is in such a good mood, I even stop worrying about my stupid test. It's actually a lot of fun.

"Aren't you glad we did this?" she says. Her nose and cheeks are tipped with red and she looks so happy.

I nod and smile at her. "Yeah."

"Next stop, the Impressionists."

"Oh. I love the impressionists," I say.

"You do?"

"Yeah, those guys are great. Rich Little and Frank Gorshin?" I give her my best James Cagney impersonation. "*You dirty rat. Why I oughta . . .*"

My mother realizes that I'm giving her the business. She narrows her eyes at me like she's mad, but I can see her trying not to laugh. "Don't be a smart-ass."

I have to say, I'm pretty pleased with myself for being a smart-ass.

I brought my transistor radio along and we watch traffic pass by on Outer Drive and listen to the midmorning show on WJR. "Raindrops Keep Fallin' on My Head," "Something's Burning," "Which Way You Goin' Billy?"

Wherever we go, whatever we do, the radio is almost always on. I think, like me, my mother prefers things noisy. She needs to fill her self, her soul, with sound. And I think it drowns out the other voices.

Provocative Progressions '73

There are no middle schools in my neighborhood in northwest Detroit. There's only elementary school and high school. And going from one to the other scares me to death. I have no idea why my parents are letting me go to a place that I know will be full of drugs and hippies and racial unrest. Especially drugs. I'm pretty sure I'm going to fall in with a bad crowd and become a problem teen, then of course eventually someone will offer me a marijuana cigarette. I'll know I shouldn't take it, but peer pressure will force me. (I'm not entirely clear on what peer pressure is, other than it seems to be really good at getting kids to take dope.)

After my introduction to drugs, everything will change pretty fast, I assume. I'll probably take LSD and go schizo like that kid on *Dragnet*, paint my face blue, bury my head in gravel, and then die from getting too high, my dead eyes just staring at the wall. Or maybe I'll think I can fly and I'll jump off a building like Art Linkletter's daughter. Then again, it could be like what I've read in *Go Ask Alice* or *Reds*. I end up a heroin addict, living like a hobo, then overdose in some dirty back alleyway. Most likely it'll be one of these (unless it's a drug deal gone wrong), but I haven't decided yet. All because my parents insisted that I go to Redford High School. Guess they'll be sorry.

I worry about it all summer, but especially August, and especially at night. My fears are a leaky faucet, the drops coming closer and closer together, louder and louder, the dread pooling in my chest with nowhere to go. Even the songs on my radio annoy and scare me. Is

"Rocky Mountain High" about dope? Can I even trust John Denver? Besides that, I'm also concerned that the boys who tormented me in elementary school will all be there along with a whole new slew of Neanderthals gathered from all the area schools. I realize that when I'm not taking drugs or overdosing, I'll probably be getting beaten up. Looks like I'm going to have a busy schedule.

"I don't think I want to go to high school," I finally confess to my mother as we sit at the kitchen table two nights before school starts. She's in a pretty good mood, so it seems like the right time to bring it up.

My mother stubs out an L&M 100 in the hubcap-sized ashtray we keep in the kitchen. I make a note that it's due to be emptied. She looks at me, exhaling the last puff of smoke almost away from me, but not really. "Excuse me, what did you just say?"

"I don't think I should go to high school." This time I hear myself say it. I have to admit that it sounds a little unusual.

She peers at me, not sure if she should laugh. "What? What are you talking about? Not go to high school? Are you serious?" she says with a rasp of mucus in her voice. She very well may be where I got my deep voice. "Don't talk crazy."

"But I—"

"You have to go to high school," she continues. "There's no choice involved. You have to go." To make her point, she rattles the ice cubes in her glass, as if trying to will it full again. "That is crazy talk, Danny. Don't be a kook."

"I just don't think it's a good idea."

"You need your education, Danny. For when you go to college."

"I guess. I don't know. What if I just skip high school and go to a trade school?" I don't know where this comes from. What if they have drugs at trade school too? They may *make* drugs in trade school for all I know.

"Oh, you're going to college, young man."

This is the thing about my mother: she's crazy about me going to college. Her mom and dad wouldn't let her go, even though she had a scholarship and everything. All because they let her older sister go; then she quit after a couple semesters to get married. They just assumed my mom would do the same thing and get married. She's told me this story a few dozen times. She doesn't really talk much about how she actually did do the same thing.

Now she says, "Okay. What are you really worried about, Danny?"

"Nothing," I reply.

With the sharpened nail on her pinkie finger, she adjusts a strand of ash-blond hair away from her forehead. Then she crosses her arms. That's when I know she means business. "Come on. Out with it."

"What if someone forces me to take drugs?" I say, surprised that I'm confessing the actual thing that's worrying me.

She just stares at me for a few seconds. "Is that what we're talking about? For Christ's sake, Danny, no one's going to *force* you to take drugs." She uncrosses one arm and reaches for her cigarettes.

"Well, maybe not force. But drugs'll be there. What if I get involved with a bad crowd where everyone is taking dope?"

"You won't do that."

"How do you know?"

My mother bats the air in front of her, as if to say *pshaw*. "I just know. You're too good a kid."

What I am is the only kid in the world with a mother who is this sure that he's not going to take drugs. I've got a good mind to take drugs just to spite her. Except that they terrify me.

My mother looks at her watch, lights another L&M, and glances toward the stairs, I guess for my father, but he's down there putting magnet catches on the doors of our almost-completed Early American hutch which now surrounds our electric fireplace and holds our stereo unit. She grabs her glass and gets up to make herself another Canadian Mist and Uptown, which is her version of a 7 and 7. "You'll be fine." She walks back over to me, holding her drink. She puts her hand on my neck.

I slip my hands under the kitchen table and grab my knees, feeling slightly better having talked about my worries, but still filled with high school dread.

"Just watch out for the black ones," she says over her shoulder as she walks into the living room. I hear a *thunk* as the knob on the television is pulled out and a high-pitched whine as it warms up, then the theme song from *All In the Family*.

"Tell your father that Archie's on," my mother calls out.

Disorientation

It happens. I have to go to high school. It's a huge place, looming over me as I walk up to the front door that faces Grand River. The walk seems to take forever. I report to orientation in the gymnasium, which is filled with hundreds of kids, boys and girls, black and white, a lot of them looking as worried as me, a fact that I find comforting. We file in and are herded into lines, where we are registered, given schedules, books, and locker assignments. Then we're told to go sit on the bleachers. We all wait there with our books and papers, wondering what's going to happen next. I sit next to a thin black kid and a tall white kid with bushy reddish hair. None of us talk to each other. After everyone is registered and settled, a small man wearing a short-sleeve white shirt and a wide rust-colored tie gets up in front of us. He is bald, except for the sides, and for a wisp of fuzzy brown hair parted low and forced toward the center of his head like a bridge pushed over a river of skin.

"Welcome. Welcome, ladies and gentlemen, to your first day of fall semester at Redford High. I'm Mr. Koznowski. Mr. Koz, for short. For some of you, I will be your counselor. Some of you may have Mrs. Corbin." He nods toward a slightly overweight, middle-aged black lady off to the side. She smiles and waves and I like her right away, which is good since she's my counselor.

Mr. Koznowski raises his hand to encourage us to do the same. "So, are there any questions? About anything? Don't be shy, freshmen."

A few kids raise their hands with questions about changing lockers, finding their way around, and getting involved in sports. After that, some shy-looking spindly kid with a green and orange zip-up shirt raises his hand and says, "What if someone tries to get me to take drugs?"

I silently gasp there in my seat on the bleachers. I'm amazed that someone else is thinking the exact same thing as me. I lean forward, waiting for Mr. Koznowski to respond.

"That's probably not going to happen," he says. "But

if anyone does try to give or sell you narcotics at any time, just walk away and go immediately to your counselor and let us know what happened. We do not tolerate drug-pushing here at Redford."

It makes me feel better, this answer, though he is basically telling us to be snitches, which I know about from watching Humphrey Bogart in *Dead End*. Nobody likes a snitch. You end up with the "Mark of the Squealer," which is a knife slash on the cheek. Still, I'm glad just knowing that I'm not the only one worrying about drugs. I start to think that maybe high school won't be so bad after all.

This feeling does not last for long.

Gym or Swim or Death

After all the questions are asked and answered, Mr. Koznowski and Mrs. Corbin separate the boys from the girls. I'm not sure why, but that's when I start to get a bad feeling in my stomach. Once they split us up, we boys are on one end of the gymnasium, the girls on the other. Then two men approach our group. One is a dumpy middle-aged guy wearing a red nylon jacket that says *Redford High* in gray letters on one side. The other man is black and much younger and looks like he plays sports, probably because he's wearing a white short-sleeve nylon shirt with stripes around the sleeves and muscles underneath. He's also wearing a whistle, which leads me to believe that he's a coach. (Deductive reasoning! Sherlock Holmes movies on the late show have taught me well.) He's the one who talks to us boys. If my mother were here, I know she would say that he was very well spoken.

"I'm Coach Tillman, the swim coach. For physical education, all of you boys will be either in gym or swim. Coach Samuels and I will determine who goes into which class. But first, you'll all be taking a swim test."

This is not good. It's been a long time since I was in the water, Brighton Lake at summer camp during my father-imposed year of being in the Boy Scouts. (All because of my alleged need for fresh air again. Will his love for air ever cease?) Let's just say that when it comes to swimming, I do a lot of sinking. A lot. You know why? Because it's unnatural. I don't believe that humans are actually meant to swim. If we were, we would have been born with gills instead of lungs. My father does not agree with this theory of mine, neither do scout leaders, but I think I'm right on the money with it. The theory of evolution proves me correct.

Coach Tillman blows his whistle. A shrill echo bounces around the gymnasium. "Okay, boys, everyone single file into the locker room. Bring your books and everything else with you."

I search out the exit doors in the gym and consider making a run for it. Instead, I walk obediently in single file along with all the other boys. (I am cursed with being a rule follower.) When we get to the locker room, we stand there for a moment until the whole group is jammed inside. From the sheer crush of bodies, I get pushed up against a wall of puke-green lockers, scratched with names and swear words. The tile floor is worn to a dull finish from years of scrubbings. There is an ammonia smell in the air, but it's no match for the swampy odor of sweat, foot, and crotch.

"I didn't bring any swim trunks," says the shy kid who asked about drugs. Again, exactly what I'm thinking!

"You don't need any," says Coach Tillman.

"What are we supposed to swim in?" asks the kid, who I guess is turning out to be not very shy after all.

"It's boys only," the coach says in a way that tells me he's not used to anyone questioning him. "You don't need to wear anything."

So many different types of terror that I'm feeling. I have to take a stupid swim test? And I have to take this stupid swim test naked? I don't know how to swim. I don't like being naked in front of other boys. I can't make up my mind what to be afraid of first.

"What?" says not-so-shy kid. "We have to have swim trunks."

There are a few nervous laughs from the other boys. Coach Tillman leans over the kid, towers over him, so the whistle around his neck dangles into his face. "What's your name?"

"Fred Herrick."

Coach Tillman points a finger at him. "There are no swim trunks, Herrick. Got it?" He turns to the rest of us with finger still extended. "Now all of you pick a locker for your things, strip down, and head through that door—" he directs us toward a metal door with *POOL* stenciled on it in tall black letters, "—where you will take your swim test. *Understand*?"

Herrick nods his head, no more questions, spirit broken now. We will all do what we're told. I see boys already stripping down. Most of them don't seem terribly upset by the prospect of being naked, so I assume that's how I'm supposed to be too. I take off my shirt, then shoes and socks, then my undershirt. Finally my pants and underwear. I feel cold air coming in from somewhere, even though it's still summer weather outside. My testicles hastily retreat. I hear other boys going through the door, their voices rising as they head excitedly into the pool area. (They actually want to swim! They probably love air too. Idiots.) So with my eyes down, my hands and feet already numb from cold and fear, I file in naked behind them into a giant room of chlorinated echo and screech, where the walls are a brighter, tiled version of the rancid green of the lockers. Windows are mounted high along one side and sunlight streams in from them, making the water look artificially colored, the fakey blueberry blue of thawed Fla-Vor-Ice. The dark stripes of the lanes on the bottom are twisted and shimmering under the surface where there are already boys yelling and splashing around.

It's pretty obvious who knows how to swim and who doesn't. The nonswimmers are the ones who are not frolicking in the water. We're parked here on more wooden bleachers, and even though these are not as splintery as the ones in the gymnasium (all the humidity in the room, no doubt), the feel of damp wood against buttocks and scrotum is strange and unpleasant.

The coach's dark skin looks darker in the room. All the black kids in the class look darker and all the white kids look paler. I don't understand how the light can work this way. I look at myself, so pasty, and feel like I'm just barely there. Then I allow myself to peer about more freely. There are peters flopping around everywhere. I, of course, have not hit puberty yet. I'm not the only one, thank god, but it does seem like the majority of the hairless population is sitting on the bleachers with me. Is this a coincidence?

The coach blasts his whistle again. "Everyone out of the pool now!"

Dozens of dripping boys join us dry ones on the bleachers. Just then, there's a hiss in the air. I don't know where it's coming from, maybe it's just a sound in my scared brain or the ventilation system, or maybe it's the naked energy of sopping young boys so comfortable in their bareness, pushed against the ones like me, cold, shrinking, and shivering, that creates a vacuum in the tall-ceilinged room, like a high-pressure front moving in, something the weather lady would describe on the *Action News*.

The hiss dies down and "Mama Told Me Not to Come" by Three Dog Night starts playing in my head. I don't know why this is, because just the opposite thing happened.

Names are called alphabetically. Which means with my name, I'm going to have a long time to sit and stew.

The coach stands on one side of the pool's edge. In front of him are tall tiled blocks, which I think are for diving. Letters in the tile spell out *DEEP END.* I would say that these words give me the chills, but I can't really get any colder than I am right now. He calls out names of boys: "Alexander, Awrey, Baranski, Bennett, Blackmon."

Five at a time, boys climb up onto the tiled diving blocks and jump into the deep end of the pool when the coach blows his whistle.

Three of the first five swim all the way to the end of the pool. One of them flounders as he tries to get there. He makes it eventually. The one who's left sinks, comes up, and then sinks again. The coach holds up a finger, then points at the sinking kid. From out of nowhere, an assistant, a pimply white kid with a long bamboo pole, runs to the edge of the pool and holds the stick out for the sinker, who clasps it as if his life depends upon it, which I guess it kind of does. The sinker is led to the edge of the pool where he climbs out in shame. He's as hairless as me. I wonder: *Are kids who have gone through puberty somehow better able to swim? Does pubic hair somehow provide additional float and ballast? If so, does that mean all us hairless ones are aquadynamically doomed to flail around, then drop to the bottom of the pool?*

I watch as the process of names, whistle blasts, divings, successes, and failures is repeated. Some of the boys are strong swimmers, some are mediocre, and some look like they have spent little or no time in the water ever, like me.

They get the pole.

"Wentke, Wozniak, Wynneparry, Yzemski, Zaragoza."

By the time the coach finally calls my name, I'm so nervous I can barely even get up on the diving block. It's hard and slippery and I'm positive that I will fall off and crack my head open like a cantaloupe on the edge of the pool. Then I'll get an infection when I drop unconscious into the water which, after the endless line of diving naked boys, is most certainly half pee by this time. Is it just me or is the water more green now than blue? I think so. It will be like falling into a giant, tiled tureen of peter soup. As I continue to struggle onto the diving block, hopes are already not high for me. Boys are snickering and the hiss bumps up a notch in my head. "Get Down" by Gilbert O'Sullivan is playing appropriately in my head. I finally manage to get up on the block. A second later when the whistle blasts, I force myself to dive into that twelve-feet-deep side of the pool, which might as well be a thousand feet deep as far as I'm concerned, having never before been in water above my nipples.

I unintentionally execute a perfect belly flop. When I hit the water it sounds like a rifle shot. My stomach burns, and I go down immediately. The shock of impact opens my mouth and I swallow a few gallons of pee water as I gulp for air. I flap my arms and legs around. Even with my head three feet underwater, I can hear the air vibrate with the yells of the other boys. When I finally manage to rise to the surface for a quick breath, the volume of laughter is deafening. I go down again. The hiss gets louder in my head, along with the sounds of muffled glee and yet another whistle burst. No song is playing in my head at this point. The first thrust of the pole thumps my chest, the second one hits my arm, then finally, the third thrust wedges the pole under my armpit and pulls me toward the surface. Finally I grab the pole, rise slowly to the surface, sputtering for air as I let it guide me to the side of the pool. The pole disappears and I hold onto the edge of the pool, gasping. While I try to catch my breath, I notice a pair of wet footprints on the concrete. I watch them evaporate before my eyes.

"Yzemski," says Coach Tillman. "You're in swim."

I try to get my breath.

"Get out of the pool."

I try to get out of the pool, but I've never gotten out of a pool from the deep end before. I try to launch myself out of the water and don't even come close to getting my leg up to the lip of the pool. Near my head, water is being sucked down through the grate that runs the length of the pool. It's so loud I feel as though I will be sucked into the drain with it. I push up again and my leg slips and slides against the tiled wall, again nowhere near high enough.

"Yzemski! Get out of the pool!" repeats the coach. Laughter from the bleachers.

I lean forward against the side of the pool and pull myself up with all the strength in my arms and finally get my leg up, just far enough to wedge my testicles over the lip of the pool, with my own weight crushing them and causing me to scream in pain.

"Get him out of there," Coach Tillman finally says, shaking his head. With that, two assistant coaches grab me by each arm and pull me out of the pool.

Welcome to high school.

The Wonder of Korvettes

Since our family room is now mostly finished, my father has been enjoying the stereo more. Which means he's been buying records like they're going out of style. On Friday night, he and I go to Korvettes, where after buying cigarettes (a carton of low-tar Dorals for him, L&M 100s for my mother) we head upstairs and scour the remainder racks for Command hi-fi albums, which are his favorite. It's like Beautiful Music crossed with his sound effects records—wonky trombones, rat-a-tat bongos, spacey Moog synthesizers. The music bounces from one speaker to another in a ticktock beat with singers who sing instrumental notes instead of words—*zu zu zu* or *baah du bop baa!*

My father can't get enough of these albums with their glossy, bright-colored covers, full of dots and lines and sound-wavy designs that look like the music on the records. The discount racks at Korvettes are always full of them, with names like *Action!*, *Big Bold and Brassy*, *Spaced*

Out!, *Provocative Percussion*, and *Permissive Polyphonics*.

"Look at this," my father says, as he pulls out a copy of *The Age of Electronicus*. On its cover is an orange sky over a skyline of keyboards.

"That's a great one," I say.

"Here's a keeper." *A Latin Love-In* goes under his arm with the others.

They're only sixty-nine cents each, sometimes forty-nine cents. It's a way for him to get his hi-fi fix as cheap as possible. He usually buys me something too, maybe an old Smothers Brothers album, like *Mom Always Liked You Best!*

In the car on the way home, he punches in the cigarette lighter and turns down the radio. He shakes his pack of Dorals until a cigarette noses out of the pack, then raises it to his lips. By that time, the lighter has popped out. After a puff, he rests his arm out the window. "So how's high school treating you?"

"It's okay," I say.

"Just okay?" Another puff. "How's swim class?"

I look at him, not sure if I should say it. "I hate it."

He laughs, then gives my knee a pat. "I figured as much. Well, it's good exercise, Daniel. It doesn't hurt to know how to swim, whether you have gills or not." He peers over at me, brows raised. "You make any friends yet?"

"No."

He pats my knee again. "It'll happen."

I don't say anything to this. I turn and grab the Korvettes bag off the backseat to flip through the records. I pull out *Persuasive Percussion Volume 2*.

"That's going to sound good on the stereo," my father says, turning up the radio. "The fidelity on those records is exceptional. They're known for it."

I nod. I can barely hear "Winchester Cathedral" playing. I look up at the sky to see how long till sunset. I hope we make it home before the sun goes down.

"Daniel," he says, "I've decided that you're going to learn how to drive."

"Huh? What?" Where did this come from?

"Your mother and I have decided that it would be good for you."

"Why?"

"Just because."

I don't care for this idea at all. I'm fine with walking or taking the bus or my bike. I realize that this isn't usually the way that things are. On TV, it's the kid who wants to take driver's education and the parents who are hemming and hawing. I don't know why this is different in my family. "We don't need to do that. I'm not in any big rush, Dad," I tell him.

"Oh, I know you're not, Daniel," he replies, smiling at me in that half-laughing way he has. "You're never in any rush to do anything." My father will let me reason with him. He likes it when I clearly state my case and doesn't mind when I disagree with him. In fact, he encourages it.

"It just seems a little soon. I don't have anywhere to go. I don't *need* to drive yet."

He scratches the side of his head up around where there was once hair, but where there is now only freckled skin. "You know, someday you're going to want to go out on a date with a girl or drive somewhere with your friends." He locks his gaze on me. "Someday you're going to want *friends*."

What an optimist my father is. Girls. Friends. Dates. Driving. Good lord. "Still, it seems premature," I say.

"Let's hold off on this for a while. See how we feel in a year."

My dad smokes thoughtfully as he listens to me. "I see what you're saying."

"Good."

"And I'm ignoring it." He takes a final puff of his cigarette, frowns at it, then crushes it out. "I've already spoken to Mrs. Corbin and signed you up. You can take your time with driver's ed. You just turned fifteen and you can't get your official license until your next birthday, so you'll have a nice long practice period after you finish the course."

"But I don't want—"

"You and I will go out on the weekends early, when there's not a lot of people around. It'll be fun. And you'll be able to help your mother. Run errands and such when she's feeling tired. It will be good for you, Daniel." He clamps his hand on my shoulder for a moment. "And now we're done discussing it."

When we get home, *Persuasive Percussion Volume 2* is the first record my father puts on the stereo, but it doesn't sound all that great. Yet I don't think it's the record's fault. In fact, the instruments seem crisp, but when he turns it up for the fidelity, the speakers start to crackle. I can tell just by the look on his face that he's not pleased. Serves him right, I say.

Our Soon-To-Be Family Room

On Saturday, I'm still pretty PO'd at my dad. I end up sitting downstairs in the coal bin, building a Color Me Gone Dodge Charger funny car while I sulk. Though I am mad at my dad, it's pretty hard to avoid him. He's downstairs too, still doing the finishing touches on the basement. Our rumpus room looks different now that it's so close to being a family room. The paneling makes it kind of woodsy and with the Early American hutch around it, you mostly can't even tell that the brick wall behind the electric fireplace isn't real, that you could poke your finger right through it.

I can't hear the radio at all when he uses his table saw. He makes a cut, then turns it off to adjust, then turns it on again and makes another cut. It's not a good noise like at the drags, but it doesn't really bother me. Sometimes he leaves it on for three or four minutes at a time. I'll hear the beginning of "Dueling Banjos," then lots of sawing, then the end of "Neither One of Us (Wants to Be the First to Say Goodbye)." It's weird.

After he turns off his saw, he pops his head into the coal bin. "You should get outside," he says. "It's a nice day."

I decide not to repeat where I stand on the issue of fresh air. "Thanks. I'm good right here."

"Still mad, huh?"

I don't say anything.

"Okay. You'll see. But I'm going on record to say that you will love driver's education."

"I sincerely doubt it."

"We'll see."

He goes back to sawing. But it's not long before my mother starts yelling. "Jesus Christ!" she screams from the top of the stairs. "Please stop all that infernal racket, my head is about to explode!"

I hear a sigh come from my father's workshop, then finally, "I'll turn it off." I hear him sanding something after that.

Five minutes later, she's back at the top of the stairs. "What the *hell* are you doing now?"

Another sigh. I hear him put everything down and turn off the light. Shortly after is when I shut off the radio and head into the rumpus/family room.

That's where I find my father, sitting on the Early American couch, holding a smoldering Doral in his right hand, pinching the bridge of his nose under his glasses with his left. An old issue of *Arizona Highways* is spread on his lap, open to a photo of a car towing a house trailer driving down a long desert road.

"Want to go for a walk to the drugstore or something?" I ask him.

"Yeah," he says, not looking up at me, "I do."

Fitting In

At school, I master the art of not being seen. Even though I'm not so tall and slightly wide, I'm very good at working my way through all the different kids in the hallways without making any contact. While I'm weaving through the halls, the other kids are only blurs to me—white blurs, black blurs (more every day), pretty blurs who see right through me, smart blurs who do not recognize me as one of them, and older blurs who I work the hardest to avoid. I bend my body, weave and wiggle between them, like walking between raindrops, taking care to never touch or look at anyone. If I brush anyone at all, that's a point against me in my head. Touching or being seen also makes me more vulnerable to the mean blurs who torment kids like me. That's why it's best to keep moving. The faster I walk, the less they see of me. I'm a bat, flying low through the halls, using my sonar to find the spaces between the other kids, mentally sending out pulses and navigating by the echoes that return, all while anticipating someone's next step and the direction they're headed. The way their head is turning tells me where their body is moving. I make sure that it's moving away from me. I fill and unfill the spaces of the hallway with me. I may not be all that good at fitting in, but I do know how to fit in between.

The Dreaded Swim Class

My days start with swim. Even though we are now allowed to bring swim trunks from home, they don't make me swim any better. The good thing is that the other kids in the class are bad at swimming too. (Coincidence that at least three-quarters of the class hasn't hit puberty? I think not. More proof of my *pubes = buoyancy* theory.) Most days Coach Tillman has us do drills of specific strokes—breaststroke, backstroke, sidestroke, butterfly. The only one I'm even slightly good at is the one where you float on your back and kick like a frog. Lying there with my ears underwater shuts out the echoes of the room and the other boys. It calms me down as I float there, looking at the ceiling of the pool room. Sometimes in my head, I play the music that Dad and I play at night in the rumpus/family room. "Power House" by Sid Bass or "Lady of Spain" by Tony Mottola. I always float too long because I'm not listening for Coach to tell us to flip over and do the breaststroke. He has to blast the whistle and call my name. When I flip is when I have the problems. I just cannot seem to float. Today, one of the other boys calls me *water lard*, which would be fine if it was funny, but it doesn't even make sense. I feel better when Coach Tillman shoots him a look. The kid shuts right up.

The good news is, no one has forced me to take drugs yet.

Driver's Education

My father drives me to my first night of driver's education at Henry Ford High School. (Redford doesn't have it's own course.)

"I'm really proud that you're doing this, son," he says as we head up Evergreen Road.

"It's not like I had any choice," I answer, still peeved at him for making me do this. High school is bad enough, what with swim class and some of my elementary school tormentors starting their old high jinks with me, and now driver's education. I'm exhausted just thinking about it.

My father considers this with a nod, as if to say, *You've got a point there*. "Well, I'm still proud of you. I think you're really going to enjoy it. I don't know why you're giving me such a hard time about it. You love cars. I just want you to learn how to be more independent."

"I'm plenty independent."

Right here is when my dad laughs at me. "Ha! Daniel, you are not independent at all. You wouldn't go to high school if we didn't make you."

"That's not true," I say.

"Yes it is true." He looks at me the way he always does when he knows I'm fibbing. "Your mother told me you didn't want to go."

"She told you?"

"Of course she told me. What? You think we don't talk about you? She said that you were afraid the other kids were going to make you take dope."

"Stool pigeon."

He cocks his head at me. "Well, don't go giving your mother the Mark of the Squealer."

I'm still annoyed, though I can't help but smile. He's seen all the same dumb movies as me. I cross my arms, resigned to my fate. I look out the window. *Kinney Shoes. S.S. Kresge. First in Fashion.*

"Daniel, you know that if I didn't force you, you wouldn't do anything. You'd just sit in the basement and build your model cars or listen to your radio or read your hot rod books."

Instead of saying anything, that's when I just start singing like Julie Andrews, in a high voice with a British accent and all: "*These are a few of my fave-or-right things.*" I really ham it up, just like in that dumb nun movie that my mother made us all see at the Mai Kai when I was a kid.

My dad cracks up. He laughs for a good half-minute. He's got to wipe his eyes after. He thinks I'm funny. He's my best audience, to tell you the truth. "Wisenheimer," he says to me, still chuckling.

Finally, we pull into the parking lot of Henry Ford and his face gets all serious. "Look, I just want you to be able to drive and be able to take care of yourself. Your mother—" he stops to think for a couple seconds before he starts talking again, "—needs our help. She's got a lot to do. It's up to us to help. You understand?"

I know what he's talking about, because he's been taking care of a lot of stuff around the house these days, including cleaning and some of the cooking. In fact, Mom has been spending quite a bit of time in bed lately. I nod.

"So do this for me, all right?"

"Yeah, okay."

He pats my chest twice with the palm of his giant

hand, which is his way of hugging. “Good boy. I’ll be back in an hour and a half. Give ’em hell.”

Driver’s Ed Street Rod!

That night, at our first lesson, Mr. Sikes the instructor, a black man with horn-rimmed glasses and a parted Afro wedged high on the right side, lets us all take a drive around the test track. He takes three of us out at a time, in a green Plymouth Duster. He sits in the passenger seat while we take turns driving. He tells us all not to go over fifteen miles per hour. I watch the two other kids, a black kid and a white girl, both hit the gas too hard and end up on the curb of the track. They’re all over the place. They can’t control the car at all.

“No, no,” says Mr. Sikes, over and over to the kid. “Slow down. Focus on steering.” But it’s no use, we’re up on the curb again. The same thing happens with the girl, except she goes even faster.

Then we pull over and it’s my turn. At first, I try hitting the gas and I start to do the same thing as them, then I think about how the funny cars idle at the starting line at the drags and I wonder if a regular car will run without hitting the gas at all. So I take my foot off the gas and the car goes about five miles per hour. It’s really slow, but I can actually control the car.

“That’s the way,” says Mr. Sikes.

“Hit the gas,” says the boy in the backseat.

“Quiet, youngblood,” hisses Mr. Sikes, then turns back to me. “Don’t listen to him. You’re doing fine. You’re doing just fine.”

He lets me drive the entire rest of the course, way longer than the other kids.

Okay, turns out that my father was right. I love driving.

Melancholy Baby

Over the next ten weeks, on Mondays and Wednesdays, my dad takes me to driver's education, then comes back later to pick me up. At first, I assumed that he would go home, but then I started seeing bags from Arlan's or Topps and other discount stores in the backseat—square, flat bags, the kind that contain record albums. One night, he came back with *Afro-Desia* by Martin Denny, the next time it was *Twenty-One Trombones*, the time after that, *The Plastic Cow Goes Moooooog*.

A couple times before we leave for class, he tries to convince my mother to come with us, just to get her out of the house, but she won't budge. She seems content to just stay in. Maybe she's where I get it.

"You two go. I'll be fine." Then she kisses us both goodbye and makes herself a drink.

I notice days now when she doesn't even put on a dress or slacks or anything. She'll just have on her favorite flowered duster and an old pair of unlaced pink Keds, with her hair pulled back into a ponytail, the loose strands hanging lank around her ears and eyes.

"Are you okay, Mom?" I ask her one morning after Dad has left for work. She was scooping out grapefruit into a bowl for me, but then just stopped, like she lost interest. "You look tired."

"I think I have iron-poor blood, Danny. I should get something for it, I suppose."

I think of the commercials that I see on television for something that's supposed to help this, but I don't say anything.

When I ask Dad about it on the way to driver's ed, he seems surprised that I noticed. He's quiet for a few seconds, as if trying to figure out what to say to me. "Your mother's always been a little, uh, melancholy, Daniel," he finally responds.

While I sort of know what *melancholy* means (mostly from the old song I've heard my father sing), I'm not so sure in this case. And it's not really like my dad to use a word like that. "What do you mean?"

"She just gets a little blue, son." He reaches over to turn on the radio. It's playing an organ song that I don't recognize. He turns it down a little.

"Did I do anything wrong?"

He shakes his head. "No, you didn't do anything wrong."

"What can we do? Should she go to a doctor?"

"She's been to one, Daniel," he says, looking up at the rearview mirror, then over to me. He gives me a half-smile. "Don't worry. She'll snap out of it. Just be nice to her. Help her whenever you can."

And then one day, she does snap out of it. That Wednesday, she decides to join us when Dad takes me to driver's ed. She comes out in a nice green and yellow flowered dress with her hair all done. She looks better than she has in weeks.

"You look nice," I say. She really does.

"Your father and I are going out to eat at the Sno-White Dining Room once we drop you off."

She seems so excited that I'm not even peeved that they're not taking me. I'll have a can of Campbell's Chicken with Rice Soup and toast quarters at home. My dad is smiling like crazy too.

When they drop me off, my mom gives me a big hug and a kiss like she's sending me off to the war or something. Then they take off like a bat out of you-know-where, as my dad would say. I watch the tail end of my father's big light-blue Bonneville sway down the street.

I guess they must have had a good time because they're almost an hour late picking me up at driver's ed. I was starting to get pretty worried, especially since my dad is usually waiting for me when I get out. When they drive up, both of them seem, well, kind of drunk. Their cheeks are flushed and damp. My dad's tie is loose and one side of his shirt collar is flipped up toward his face. My mother's tidy dress is rumpled now, her hair is crushed on one side and a few tendrils are hanging in her face. She's way over in the middle of the front seat, shoved in close to my dad, and neither of them have their seat belts on. (I decide not to lecture them about this even though they pound it into our heads to wear them in driver's ed.) She leans to open the passenger door and pats the space on the seat next to her.

"Come on, honey. There's room for all three of us up here."

"I'll just sit in the back, Mom."

"No. Come on. I want to sit with my two fellas."

Luckily, there have been no other kids around for the past forty-five minutes. I don't mention that I was starting to get scared waiting there so long. I get into the front seat. My mother puts her arms around both of us. I wish she wouldn't because it's making her dress pull up way over her knees so I can see where her nylons are connected to whatever it is they're connected to. I can smell whiskey and sweat mingled with her Chantilly.

"Isn't this nice?" she says, giving me a kiss on the cheek.

Abandoned Waffles

Sunday morning, my mother gets up early to make breakfast for Dad and me. She is still in a good mood, making waffles and humming along with the radio as it plays "Love Is Blue." At one point, after she pours batter in the waffle iron and closes the top, I watch her as she walks back behind my father and puts her hands over his glasses while he reads the *Free Press*.

"Guess who?" she says, then swings around and sits in his lap.

"Hey," he says, annoyed, trying to pull his crumpled paper out from under her. "Come on. What's the big idea?"

My mother looks at him, her feelings hurt now. She gets up and walks into the bedroom.

"Eleanor. Honey," says my father. He sighs, puts down his paper, and follows her into the bedroom.

That's when I notice the waffle iron starting to smoke. I get up and open the lid. The waffle is a little brown, but not bad. Dad's still in there talking to Mom so I decide that this one is mine. As it turns out, I'm the only one who gets a waffle since they don't come back for a while.

Later, he and I practice my driving around the parking lot of Grandland because the supermarkets are closed. I drive his Bonneville, which is very different than the Dusters and Demons we use in driver's ed. It's gigantic. It feels like I'm piloting the *Hindenburg*. (I wrote a paper on rigid and semirigid airships in seventh grade and have been interested in them ever since.) Still, I get used to it.

It helps that there are no other cars in the lot besides us.

"Just stay calm and keep your eye on the road, Daniel," says my father, as I drive up and down the aisles of the lot.

"There's not really a road," I say.

"You know what I mean."

"I'm just trying to not drive into the light posts."

My father looks at me and nods. "Good plan."

The only thing that happens is that I hit a bumper block once when I don't quite stop soon enough, but other than that, I do pretty good.

Sonar Fails Me

At school, I lay low, use my sonar to slink between the other kids. I keep quiet and take the back stairways when I can, but even with all that, I have attracted attention. Tim Riggle is a former elementary school tormentor. I don't know what I did to him, but he's hated me since sixth grade. Anytime he had a chance to spill my books or steal my hat for monkey-in-the-middle (he needed the mouth-breathing Hollins twins for that and unfortunately they're going to Redford too), he would do it. Nothing has happened yet in high school, but I see him staring at me during second period when I go past his locker to get to English class. His locker is right next to the classroom, so it's hard to avoid him.

My father notices that I'm worried about it on our way to driver's ed that night. He turns down the radio, which is fine with me since he's playing the Beautiful Music station from Canada, which is also making me nervous. The days are getting shorter. It's going to be dark soon. Before long, we'll be practicing our parallel parking under the lights on the track.

"You okay, Daniel?" he says to me at a stoplight. He shakes his pack of Dorals until the tip of the last cigarette peeks up, then pulls it out with his lips.

"I'm okay."

"You're quiet tonight." He looks at me for a moment. "You still worried about Mom? She's fine." He punches the cigarette lighter.

"No."

"What are you worried about?"

"Nothing."

We take off from the light with authority, which is the way he's teaching me to do it. "I don't think I believe you," he says, smiling at me now.

The lighter pops out and he holds it to his cigarette. I don't say anything.

Finally he says, "So who is it this time?"

"No one."

"Daniel."

We're almost to Henry Ford by this time, so I'm hoping the conversation will end soon. "Just this stupid guy."

"They're always stupid guys. Smart guys don't pick on other kids." We've been through this before. "Okay," he says, "what's this stupid guy's name?"

"Dad, you can't go to the school—"

"That's not why I'm asking. Now, what's his name?"

I just gaze at the road, at the bowling alley on our left. "Tim Riggle."

Dad nods. "Okay. Now tell me: what do you do when Tim Riggle looks at you, wherever, in the hall or in the school yard?"

"I don't know. I guess I look away. I look at the floor."

He nods again, thinking. "All right."

We stop at another light. He turns to me, takes my chin between his fingers, and turns my head so I'm staring right at him. "Now listen to me. Here's what I want you to do: the next time Tim Riggle looks at you, don't look away. Look him straight in the eyes and keep looking. Don't stop. Let him look away."

"What if I run into something?"

"Well, don't do that. I guess when you have to look away, do it. But you look him straight in the eyes for as long as you can. You don't have to do anything else. You don't have to look mean. I just want you to look at him."

"Why?"

"Just do what I say."

"Okay." I don't know about this.

The Look

The next day at school, I follow my father's advice. As I come around the corner to get to my English class, I see Tim Riggle standing by his locker talking to some kid I don't know. As I approach, he stares at me, giving me that *I'm going to kick your butt* expression, but instead of doing what I always do, which is look down, I meet his eyes and stare right back at him. There's a brief moment of pants-peeing terror, but it's easier than I think. At the moment our eyes meet, I feel something change. He actually seems surprised by the way I'm looking at him. I'm scared to death, but I keep it up and then the amazing thing happens: he looks away. He looks *away from me*. It's crazy because all we did was look at each other, and no one said a word, but something happened.

Suddenly, a whole lot of things start to make sense. I realize now why kids like to pick on me. When I look down or look away, it seems like I'm not going to do anything, so that makes me a good target. Just by looking scared, I have been basically inviting Neanderthals to come push me around. It's like I'm wearing a big cartoon sandwich board that says: *Bullies Welcome*.

Of course, it's all bluffing. Both my father and I know that I'm not going to fight anyone because of my high moral principles and cowardice, but I realize now that it might not matter. Perhaps all my tormentors need to think is that maybe, just maybe, I might fight and that may be enough for them to leave me alone. Either that, or it will result in an even worse pounding later. We'll see.

So Many Questions

Dad works late that night and comes home tired, so I don't really get a chance to talk to him. He goes to bed early, which he doesn't usually do. Mom and I stay up and watch television. We watch *Adam-12*, *The NBC Mystery Movie* with Banacek, then *Kojak*. It's an evening of cops-and-robbers shows, which Mom isn't that crazy about, but she doesn't complain. She's quiet. She sits in her chair smoking and drinking Canadian Mist and Uptowns. Every once in a while, she rattles the cubes in her glass and I get up to make her another.

"Thanks, honey," she says to me. I'm beginning to wish she didn't drink so much, but it hardly seems to do that much to her, so I guess it doesn't really matter.

"You're welcome," I reply, bringing her the refilled glass. I sit back down.

Then, out of nowhere, she gets all talkative. "So. Has anyone made you take drugs yet at school?"

"What?"

"Has anyone made you take drugs at school?"

She says this in a way that almost makes me think she's kidding. I don't think she would kid about something as serious as drug-taking, but I'm not sure. I look at her. "No," I say. Then I add, "Not yet."

"That's good. You were worried about that. Have you run into any kids on dope?"

It makes me uncomfortable to talk about this. I just want to watch TV. Kojak's in a jam and I want to see what happens. But Mom doesn't seem to care.

"Well, have you?"

I turn from Telly Savalas to her. "I don't think so, but I guess I can't be sure."

"I think you'd know."

"Maybe."

"I'm sure you're fine. I told you that the good kids find each other," she says, taking a sip of her drink.

I don't tell her that the good kids are not finding me.

At eleven o'clock, I make the mistake of watching the Channel 7 *Action News* with Mom. There is a mayoral election going on and watching the candidates on TV gets her pretty riled up. Roman Gribbs, the current mayor, is running against a new guy named Coleman Young, who is black. I don't really care who wins, but my mother sure does.

"If that one thinks he's going to be the next mayor of this city, he's got another think coming," she says, taking a sip and sitting forward in her chair. "Who the hell does he think he is? Does he think the blacks are just going to take over?"

Bill Bonds, the newscaster, doesn't answer her question. He just goes on about a robbery that occurred in the east side.

"I don't know what's happening to this city," says my mother. "There didn't used to be crime like this." She stubs out her cigarette with enough force to make me think she's going to knock the big ashtray off the end table. "If this keeps up, we're getting the hell out of Detroit, I'll tell you that much."

I'm not sure what she's talking about. The news has never been anything but crime and bad stuff for as long as I can remember. (Except for the last story, when they report something good.) Either way, I don't like watching the news with my mother. She yells at the television, at Bill Bonds with his beige suit and his puffy, blow-dried hair reading the news, and at me, is what it feels like.

I pick up her glass for a refill, even though it doesn't really need it. In the kitchen, I finish up the bottle of Uptown and there's not quite enough so I pour a little extra Canadian Mist in her glass. Quietly, I place it next to her, then go to my room to read and listen to the radio and wait out the news. I'll come back later to watch Johnny Carson.

That night when I'm lying in bed with the radio on, I hear "Stoned Out of My Mind" by the Chi-Lites on CKLW. It's a pretty good song, but I can't tell if it's about drugs or not. At first I think it is, but then it just seems like it's about love. I think about what Mom said about leaving Detroit, about black people. Certainly at school, there are more black kids almost every day, but I notice that they mostly keep to themselves. They sit together at assemblies or hang out with each other in the hallways and even in the locker room. Then I think that maybe since I haven't made any black friends, I must be prejudiced. Then I realize that I haven't made any white friends either, so I'm probably okay.

In school the next day, I continue the terrifying program of looking back at Tim Riggle when he looks at me. I don't make a face or anything like I'm tough (because I'm not and we all know that), I just look at him neutral-like. When I see him before English, he actually turns away again. I try not to get too excited about this development, but it is encouraging.

That night, when we're driving to my driver's ed class, my father glances over at me and asks, "So, how's school going?"

Ugh. I'm beginning to wish that everyone would stop asking me about school, but I guess I brought it on myself with all my worries about drugs and my natural bully-magnetism, so I shouldn't complain too much.

"It's okay," I tell him, hoping to move on to a new topic as soon as I can.

"How's algebra?"

"Hard," I say, even though it's not that hard.

"Everything else all right?" He pulls a pack of cigarettes out of his jacket pocket (it's getting cooler outside) and then realizes it's empty. He crumples it and puts it back in his pocket. He doesn't say it, but I know exactly what he means, and now I'm afraid to tell him that his advice is working because I'll jinx it and things will go back to the way they were.

"It's going okay," I say, nodding.

He gives me a kind of sideways look, his eyes narrow, but not like he's mad or anything. He's just checking to see if I'm telling the truth. Or maybe neither of us wants to jinx things.

"How's swim class?"

"Still hate it."

"Well, at least you're consistent." He smacks my knee and smiles. "Anyway, it's good for you to know how to swim."

I shake my head like I'm disgusted. "Swimming's for suckers, Dad," I say in my best Humphrey Bogart. "You know it and I know it."

He laughs, which is all I wanted to happen. After that, we're quiet for a couple minutes.

"Dad, are we going to move?"

My father looks confused by this. "No, not as far as I know. Why?"

"Mom mentioned it. She's worried. I guess about black people taking over."

My father takes a deep breath, but he says nothing. He reaches for his cigarettes again, touches the crumpled pack in his pocket, then puts his hand back on the steering wheel.

"What's going on?"

"It's complicated, Daniel."

"Why is it complicated?"

"Well, we've lived here all our lives and things have been a particular way. Now everything's changing." He checks the rearview mirror, then glances at me. "We just don't know what's going to happen. We're concerned."

"So are we going to move?"

"No, we're not going to move."

"Are you scared?"

Again, my father doesn't say anything. Which scares me.

The next week, I only run into Tim Riggle once in a while. I don't know if he's stopping by his locker at a different time now or what, but I'm glad. In between classes, I put my head down (but not too far down) and glide between the bodies of the other students. While I do it, usually a song runs through my head. This week, it's "Pretty Lady" by Lighthouse. Still no sign of drugs, though I do hear the word *narc* now and then in the halls. I'm not really sure what it means, but I'm keeping my eyes open.

Parking-Lot Chicken

That Saturday, we get up early and head down Outer Drive to Korvettes, where the lot is bigger than the one at Grandland. After a couple laps around it and a half-hour of practicing my turning, backing up, and parallel parking, my father directs me toward the front entrance where he has me turn down the main aisle, facing away from the store. There's a clear lane ahead of us to the end of the parking lot, at least a city block long.

"All right," he says, pointing straight ahead. "Here's what I want you to do: I want you to drive straight down the lane."

"Okay," I say, putting the car into drive.

He grabs the wheel for a moment. "But I want you to give it the gas and really get some speed going."

"In the parking lot?"

"Yep. Really goose it."

I'm not so sure about this, but I do what he says and get the car up to about forty mph pretty quickly. It feels like the light posts are flying past me. We're headed toward West Chicago Road, which is deserted, but I would hit bumper blocks and sidewalks and curbs before I got to it.

"Dad?" I say, wondering what I'm doing this for.

"Keep going," he says, eyes alternating between the speedometer and the aisle ahead.

When I get it up to forty-five, he says, "Now hit the brakes. Hard!"

"Just stop?"

"Do it!" he yells.

I slam the brakes hard and both our bodies jerk forward. The tires shriek, the Bonneville creaks and shimmies. Something in the trunk of the car tips over with a loud *clonk*. Even with my seat belt on, I almost hit the steering wheel with my head. When we finally stop, we're only about ten feet from the end of the lot. My fingers are death-gripped on the wheel. The squeal of the tires is still resonating in my ears, but even louder is the sound of my breath and my heart throbbing in my chest. I smell scorched rubber like at the drags.

My dad takes a breath. "Okay. Now you know what happens when you slam on the brakes going forty-five miles an hour. *That's* what happens," he says, looking straight at me. "You have to be ready for anything, Daniel. *Anything*."

I am still shaking, but I manage to nod at what he says. I wish we had not done this. The car is idling gently now. My foot is still crushing the brake pedal. I finally take a breath and let up on it a little.

"Okay," my father says, "why don't you drive us home?"

"Really?"

"Yep. You'll be fine." He pats my chest with his hand.

So I drive us back home, my first real time on the road with other cars, and I do okay. Everything feels easier than what just happened in the lot. The only time Dad yells is when he wants me to take off faster from a traffic light.

"For Christ's sake, Daniel. Stop being so damn timid. Give it the gas," he says. "Take off with some authority."

At the next light, I give it the gas.

"Better," he says.

When we get home at about eleven thirty, Mom has just gotten out of bed, having her first Coke of the day. I tell her that I drove all the way from Korvettes.

Even all drowsy, she looks at my dad like, *Do you think that was a good idea?*

"He did great," says my father.

She turns from my father to me. "Well, good for you, Danny."

Dad spends the rest of the day doing touch-up on the Early American hutch in the basement. It's all stained and mostly assembled, but he needed to attach some trim, along with the mantle. By Saturday evening, he's finished.

The rumpus room is dead. Long live the family room.

Monday's Surprise

On Monday, my father is late coming home from work. My mother is lying down with a headache so I assume dinner will be whatever leftovers we can scrounge from the fridge. When he finally shows up at the side door, he asks me to give him a hand with something in the car.

"What did you get?" I ask.

He opens the trunk of the Bonneville to reveal four boxes, all marked *Fisher*. "I got us a new stereo," he says. "A good one."

"Where did you get it from?" I ask, stunned. "This isn't from Korvettes."

"Almas Hi-Fi in Dearborn."

Almas Hi-Fi is no discount store. I've been in there once with my father and we walked out floored by the prices. I'm a little disoriented by this extravagance. This is not where the Yzemskis shop.

We carry in the boxes and put them on the floor of the family room.

"Was it on sale?" I ask.

My father shakes his head as he slits open one of the boxes with his fingernail knife. "No, but they let me trade in the old one for a good deal."

He must've sneaked the old unit out of the house last night. It had been disconnected and covered last week while he was finishing the hutch. I just thought it had to do with all the staining and fumes being bad for a stereo. The whole house has stunk of stain and turpentine for the last few days. It still does.

Despite the fact that my father did get a deal (kind of) on this new stereo, there is no indulgent smile on my mother's face tonight as she appears at the top of the stairway. She's been looking drawn again lately, but tonight she seems half angry and half worried. She's holding a Canadian Mist and Uptown.

"Hey, Mom. Did you see this?"

"So you decided to get it after all," she says drily.

"Uh-huh," my father responds in a neutral way, obviously trying not to sound too excited.

She heads back up into the kitchen.

"Don't you want to hear it?" I yell up to her. Then I hear the *thunk* and hum of the television being turned on.

My father looks over at me sheepishly. "Your mother wasn't so crazy about the idea of a new stereo."

"But this one's going to be way nicer than the old one."

He raises his eyebrows. "That's what I told her, but she wasn't convinced."

My mother's reaction makes me wonder if we can't actually afford this fancy new stereo and if we'll end up losing the house or something, but since my father doesn't seem to be concerned, I figure it's okay. In fact, now that she's gone, he seems pretty excited, which makes me excited too. I watch as he carefully connects all the new components to each other, wires the new speakers, runs them behind the shelves of our newly finished hutch so they're just the right height and angle for the room.

"You ready to hear this?" he says to me, standing there with his hands on his hips. His voice is serious, but he's smiling.

I nod, all excited. My father presses the power button and the glassy silver face of the stereo glows like a dashboard at twilight. There is a brief burst of static that almost turns to dread in my stomach, but my father quickly switches a knob to *Phono*. A low-pitched hum charges the atmosphere of the family room. He then removes the dust cover from the turntable, places it on the couch, and grabs the nearest LP. In one fluid motion, he pulls out the paper sleeve inside the album cover and slides out the disc—balancing it between middle finger on the label and thumb against the glossy edge—and places it on the spindle of the stereo. He flicks the *Manual On* lever and the record starts spinning. Holding it by a tiny metal handle, he gently settles the tone arm, tipped with a real cartridge and a diamond stylus, on side A of *Genuine Electric Latin Love Machine*.

It sounds so beautiful. All those electronic *bleets* and *bloops* through actual high-fidelity stereophonic speakers. So clear and crisp that it's like Richard Hayman is playing "Windmills of Your Mind" on the Moog synthesizer right there in our new family room. We just stand there and listen to the whole song before saying anything.

Finally, I just say, "Wow."

"Yeah," says my father. The next song comes on.

"It sounds incredible."

"It sure as hell does."

We sit down on the couch at the exact same time. I should just want to shut up and listen, but I realize that I want to ask my father something.

"What do you like about music, Dad?"

At first my father laughs like he thinks I'm kidding, then he looks over at me like he's impressed by my question. "Well. I don't exactly know, Daniel. I haven't really given it much thought." He sits back in the couch, slings his hands back behind his head as "La Comparsa" plays.

I figure this is all the answer I'm going to get. I don't even know what made me ask the question, but before I can even think any more about it, he starts talking again.

"That's a really good question, son. I guess it makes me feel something that I'm not used to. I guess—" He grabs the pack of Dorals from his shirt pocket. "I don't know. I mean, I go to work every day. I come home to you and your mother, we have dinner, I putter around down here or we watch TV and go to bed and get up and do the same damn thing all over again. I don't even think about the days going by."

He lights his cigarette. "But when I'm here with you, like right now, listening to something on the stereo? Or just listening to it while I read the paper? Or work in my shop? I don't know, it makes me feel different. Almost like a different person. I know that sounds crazy, I mean I'm here listening to it, but it's like I'm not here. Does that make sense? It takes me somewhere, changes something, slows things down—Christ, I don't know. I'm not making sense." He glances over at the Early American hutch and squints for a moment like he's just noticed a missing piece of trim or something.

"It just makes me happy," I say, suddenly aching for my turn to talk about it. "All the stuff that bothers me, all the things that I worry about, it all gets replaced in my head by music. So I don't have to worry about that anymore."

He takes a puff and exhales. "You shouldn't worry so much, son. You're going to be fine."

My father and I look at each other and just listen to the music. We say nothing else because nothing we could say would sound better than us here, listening to music. We are hooked. Every night after dinner, or after driver's ed, he and I go downstairs to the new family room to listen to *Switched-On Bacharach* or *Sound in the Eighth Dimension* or *Bongos Bongos Bongos*, or any of the other albums he's collected over the past year or so. We take turns getting up to change the records. We play them even when he's in his workshop and I'm in the coal bin building the model cars. Sometimes I do my homework downstairs just to be near the stereo.

All the while, with all this music playing, my mother sits upstairs watching television, drinking Canadian Mist and Uptowns, getting quieter and quieter.

The Nutty Teacher

I'm pretty sure something is wrong with Mrs. Golonka, my English teacher. Seriously, she's a kook. She reminds me of Jerry Lewis in *The Nutty Professor*, except that he was actually pretty smart in that movie and I'm not so sure about Mrs. Golonka. She's a lot older than the other teachers and she never seems to know how to control the class. I get the feeling that maybe she was planning to retire, but thought she'd give it one more year. Then as soon as school started, she realized—*Uh-oh*.

A couple weeks back, the kids wouldn't quiet down at the beginning of class, so she started knocking on her desk with her knuckles. She did it once and nothing happened, so she did it again louder. I was sitting there at my desk not talking to anyone (the curse of the Citizenship Award continues), and I just watched the whole thing. A few people laughed and everyone kept talking, the white kids at the front of the class talking to each other in their seats and the black kids in the back not even bothering to sit down while they talked. Finally, she rapped on the desk one more time. All that happened was that someone at the back of the room yelled, "Come in!" A few kids laughed, then kept talking.

So what does she do? She just kept knocking. She was so flustered and didn't know what to do to get control. I wished I could help, but I'd just call attention to myself and end up getting pounded. (Both of those things go against everything I stand for.) So I just watched as Mrs. Golonka kept knocking on the desk as if it was a door to a house where the lights were on, but everyone in there hated her guts. Her face got redder and redder, until she started shaking her head all crazy and then she stepped into the wastepaper basket next to her desk and shouted, "You children treat me like trash!"

That's when the class finally stopped talking. Everyone was in shock. We just looked at our teacher standing there in the dull green wastebasket, the sides of it buckling as she shook her fists up and down like a wrinkled, rubbery-faced Baby Huey having a tantrum. She didn't start actually crying until she realized that she was stuck.

To her credit, she did get the class to quiet down. That is, until everyone *really* started laughing at her. That kept going until Mr. Acitelli from tenth grade English next door poked his head in the classroom and barked, "Quiet!" With one word from him, everyone shut right up. Then he scanned the classroom and said in a hushed voice to the kids in the back, "Sit *down*." Everyone standing slithered back into their seats. Then Mr. Acitelli walked across the classroom and casually gave Mrs. Golonka his hand as if that was what gentlemen did when a lady was stuck in a wastebasket. As he left the classroom, he stared at the whole class as if he was daring us to do something. Nobody did. Until he left, when a lot of the kids started snickering again.

Today, though, what happens is different. Mrs. Golonka is trying to get the class to discuss *A Separate Peace*. I would have rather been reading *Street Rod* by Henry Gregor Felsen, which a classic as far as I'm concerned, but I did read the book. I didn't really like where Phineas falls out of the tree and breaks his leg and everything else happens, but I liked it overall.

Mrs. Golonka, who seems less confused today, is trying hard to get the class to talk about the themes in the book. "The narrator says that he killed his enemy while he was at the Exeter Academy. Does anyone know what that means?"

I think about saying something, then decide it's too risky. However, Fred Herrick, who did all that talking on our first day, still hasn't learned to keep his mouth shut. "Does he mean Phineas?" he asks, raising his hand.

"That's not what I'm thinking," says Mrs. Golonka. "Though certainly it could be interpreted that way. How did he change?"

Just then, a wad of paper flies from the back of the room and lands at the feet of Mrs. Golonka.

"I saw who did that," she says, checking the seating chart, then looking up at one of the black kids sitting in the back. "James, there will be no more of that."

"I'm not James," says the kid. He points to the kid next to him. "He James." The one who isn't James is dark and stocky; the other is thin and light-skinned with a high natural.

Mrs. Golonka right away becomes flustered. "No he's not," she says, consulting the seating chart again. "According to this, you're James."

The two kids look at each other, then at her. "What you sayin'? We all look *alike*?"

"I said no such thing. All I know is James is supposed to be sitting where you're sitting."

"Well, I ain't James. I'm Curtis. He James," he says, pointing at the kid next to him. "Ain't that right, James?"

His skinny arms crossed, James nods dramatically. It's pretty easy to see that they're giving her the business, as my dad would say.

Mrs. Golonka lets out a little exasperated gasp and glances down at the seating chart again. "Well, I don't really care which one of you boys is James—"

Suddenly, the kid who's not James stops smiling. He shakes his head in an exaggerated way and looks at the other kid. "What I want to know is which one of us you calling *boy*?"

Then all of a sudden, I'm not so sure that they're kidding anymore.

Mrs. Golonka doesn't know what to do. "I just meant you . . . you young men."

James points a finger at Mrs. Golonka. "No, you call us *boy*. You hear that, Curtis? She just call us *boy*."

"What?" says Curtis loudly. "*What*?"

"You heard me. She call us *boys*. Like she own us or some shit. Like we her slaves."

Curtis stands up. "Ain't no one calling *me* boy."

James stands up too. "You a bigot," he says, pointing at her.

"I'ma report you," says Curtis, as he opens the door and rounds the corner out of the classroom, with just a hint of a smile on his face. They walk out.

"Ol' honky bitch," James mutters outside the door.

After they leave, Mrs. Golonka is near tears. She sits down and tells us to quietly read *A Separate Peace* for the remainder of the class. At least she didn't jump into the wastebasket again.

Sunrise Static

On the thirtieth of October, the Wednesday before Halloween, when I open my eyes, the whole house is quiet except for the low-pitched hum of static coming from my radio, which is stuck somewhere in between stations. I must have tried to turn it off during the night and just turned the tuning knob instead of the on/off switch. I'm about to put it on WJR, when I realize there's no radio coming from the kitchen. Instead I hear my mother, her telephone voice, calling my father's work, telling someone that he's picked up a bug somewhere and that he won't be in today.

I didn't even realize that he was still in the house, since much of the time he's gone before I even get up. I turn off my radio so as not to disturb him. The house seems so very quiet.

I pad into the kitchen after going to the bathroom. "Morning," I say.

My mom says nothing, she just gives me a half-smile and sits at the table with me as I drink my cup of tea and eat my toast. I think about what song they might be playing on the radio right at that minute. Then I get up and dress for school. Before I leave, I go up the stairs to my parents' bedroom to say goodbye to my dad. I whisper to him, but he's sleeping with his back away from me so I just let him rest.

I walk to school, which is about a mile and a half. I walk under trees messily cross-stitched with white toilet paper that's been thrown over the branches. I count the windows of the parked cars scribbled with soap, and the broken eggs dried on front doors, surprised by how many kids have gotten a head start on tonight's pre-Halloween activities. At school, I get in the building all right, past the smokers, the freaks, the tough kids, and the huddled groups of ignoring black kids, all without incident. I get to my locker (no sign of Tim Riggle) and drop off my books before heading to swim class. I enter the locker room and strip down to put on my always-damp pair of swim trunks, just like I do every morning. (I would not be surprised to find moss growing on the north side of my trunks some morning.) Today, we practice our breaststroke and backstroke, and then swim laps for the rest of the period. My eyes burn from the chlorine, my ears are clogged with water, my arms ache from the laps, and my stomach stings from my daily belly flop into the water, all as I fight off my body's natural inclination to sink. Yet at least nobody harasses me (or anyone else), because Coach Tillman does not put up with anything like that. He runs a tight ship, as my dad would say. Running through my head is "Honky Cat" by Elton John, which has been there since Mrs. Golonka's class.

After I shower, I head into the locker room. Just as I get my T-shirt and underpants on, Jesse, a quiet black kid from our class, comes up to me.

"Coach wants to see you," he says in a soft voice.

"He does? What for?"

Jesse shrugs. "He just said after you get dressed you should go see him."

At first I think it's a joke that he's playing on me, but Jesse isn't that way. He just tries to get through swim and mind his own business like me. Besides, sending someone to the coach isn't a good trick to play since he's sure to ask, *Who told you that I wanted to see you?* Then someone's going to be doing extra laps.

So I get dressed and head to Coach's office. Considering how much I hate the class and how bad I am at swimming, I'm pretty sure that I'm in trouble, though I don't know exactly what he can do to me unless I'm being sent to a special remedial swimming class for the aquatically retarded where we all swim in a rubber wading pool.

I've never been in the coaches' offices before and I don't want to be there now. It seems like everything there is made of metal or covered with tile, except for a wooden chair here and there. Along the back wall, there are partitioned bins filled with sporting goods—basketballs, bats, soccer balls, bases stacked for baseball, as well as the red rubber balls they use for slaughter-ball. (Not having to play that game is the one great consolation of being in swim instead of gym.) When I walk in, all the other coaches leave. Coach Tillman motions me over to sit down on one of the wooden chairs. It's hard and splintery, probably because a lot of people in swim trunks sit on them, wearing off all the varnish and swelling the wood.

"Mr. Yzemski," he says. He calls all the boys by *Mister*. It's one of the things that he does. "I need to talk to you. Something has happened."

Just his tone makes me stop thinking about the chair as well as everything else.

"I have some tough news."

I kind of stop hearing after what he says next. I sort of hear, but I sort of don't. How I feel is that I'm back in the pool again, trying to tread water, but it's not working. The water level is just over my mouth and nose, then my ears, then finally my eyes. I hear only distorted words, sound waves that try to vibrate the water but don't make much sense. Then I drop beneath the surface where everything is blue and quiet, but I can't stay there. The pole wedges itself under my arm and pulls me out of the water. I try to go back under, but the pole won't let me. And Coach is talking to me and I have to hear what he's saying.

"Mr. Yzemski . . ."

I don't know who thought the swim coach was the

person who was supposed to give me the news that my father had a heart attack and died this morning, but apparently someone thought he was the one to do it. He can't be telling me what he's telling me. I don't say a word. I don't want to say anything, as if by speaking or even acknowledging the idea of this might be enough to make it true.

"I don't believe you."

He shakes his head. "I'm sorry, Mr. Yzemski—*Daniel*. We just got a call from your mother, Eleanor. She wanted someone to tell you."

As soon as he mentions my mother, I think, *She would never do that*.

Coach Tillman is full of his coach talk, telling me that I have to be strong for my mother, that I'm going to have to be the man of the house and all the rest of the stuff that you might have heard once in a movie. I feel the breath squeezed out of me and I don't know what to do. I stand up and look around for the door since I've forgotten where it is.

"Daniel," says Coach, standing up as well, "we're going to get someone to drive you home."

This is when I run out of his office. Out in the hall, I pass the principal's assistant, who is probably supposed to give me the ride. She yells after me, but I shoot out the side door of the school onto Westbrook and start running home, never once stopping. Along the way, I tell myself that there's no way this could be true even after what he said about Mom, that this is Coach's idea of a joke and I'm definitely going to report him to the principal. I will get him fired, then I'm going to beat up Jesse for being part of the joke. I run and run, block after block, a different route than I usually take every day, cutting through yards, dogs barking at me as I jump fences, splitting the back of my pants scaling one of them, bloodying my hand on the spiky top of another. As I get closer to my house, I can feel how overheated I am even in the cold weather, how red my face is, my nose and eyes running into my mouth and onto my chin, the sweat leaking down my spine, my T-shirt soaked around the neck and under the arms, the tingling in the tops of my ears, the pounding in my temples and chest, but I keep running just to prove that it's all a lie. I arrive at my house to find a Detroit Police car in front, a blue and white Fury. From its radio, I hear a muffled voice, then a blast of static.

I don't remember anything in my life worse than seeing that car.

Vibrations '74!

Everything is different now, as you would kind of expect. I find out that even after a horrible, horrible thing happens, other things happen. Your eyes keep opening, your ears keep hearing, your lungs keep breathing, even though you're not sure why and you wish they wouldn't. Songs still play in your head, especially when you wish they wouldn't. Winter comes. Days still pass and you somehow slog through the slush of them. When you can sleep, and sometimes you can when the radio does its job in the right way, when it plays songs of a certain type that are not full of meanings, quieting your mind out of its own awareness, lulling you to a place of blankness, where for a moment or two, your thoughts of him don't crush the breath out of your chest. When you can sleep, and sometimes you can, you awaken to a still house, with only the murmur of your radio to let you know that you're awake and alive. Once in a while, your eyes open to the sounds of your mother rattling around in the kitchen. This does not happen often. The kitchen radio is rarely on. Everything is different now, as you would kind of expect.

Grief turns you into someone entirely new. I no longer even feel like Daniel Yzemski. I am now someone who completely ignores Thanksgiving and Christmas and New Year's, who is never hungry, who barely has the energy to walk to school in the mornings. Yet my body completely ignores how I feel. It does whatever it wants. I hit puberty and lose weight and grow two inches taller. My face and body darken with hair. I don't recognize myself in the mirror after a shower anymore. My body tells me to be another person and I have no choice but to be one. My voice changes and gets deeper still. This is the only thing that makes sense to me. All the hollowness makes my voice resonate more.

Strangely enough, the only place I do feel at all like the person I was is at school. I go back to looking at the ground anytime anyone looks at me, bully threat or not. It's hard to talk to anyone, much less look them in the eye. Teachers leave me alone, some know what has happened, but it doesn't seem to matter to Tim Riggle and a few others. No one gives me a hard time in swim class, though. Coach Tillman doesn't let it happen. He has also stopped problems in the hall for me with a well-aimed glance at a potential tormentor. He and I don't talk, but I can see that he's keeping an eye on me, which should make me feel better, but it doesn't. I do my laps every morning and say nothing. I'm still not a good swimmer, but I don't mind it so much anymore, especially Free Swim, when we are allowed to do whatever we want. I welcome the dull hiss in my ears when I'm far under the surface in the deep end of the pool. The world above my head finally makes sense. It looks and sounds as it feels to me, muffled and warped, silent and suffocating. I stay down as long as I can, but always end up rising to the surface, flailing my arms and coughing like a donkey, eyes red from chlorine and the tears that no one can see in swim class, my body betraying me with its stupid need for air. Coach looks at me, a flash of worry in his eyes, then he turns away and blows his whistle.

In the hallway now, my sonar has petered out. I am no longer able to walk between students, much less raindrops. I bump into the other kids and they scowl at me. In biology class, a couple kids have started calling me *narc* right to my face. I still don't know what it means, but I suspect it has to do with short hair and an overall lack of bell-bottom pants. I am lucky to have clean clothes as it is. My mother doesn't get to it often, so I've started doing the laundry myself and have learned all the washing machine lessons you would expect, including that pink shirts do not go over well in high school hallways. *Fag* has become a pretty close second to *narc*. There are sympathetic eyes that follow me in the halls too, with their sad-for-me glances that linger longer than they should, followed by a turn to a companion and a whispered comment. Somehow, those are the worst of all.

As for Mom, Dr. Hadosian has got her on Valiums to calm her down, but now she's so calm, she's like one of the zombies from *Night of the Living Dead*. When she's not sleeping, she's drinking or watching television. In the evening, the television is always on. Often I watch it with her, but a lot of the time I just play the radio in my room while I do my homework or read hot rod books. No Beautiful Music stations, just Top 40. Livelier music is better, but it doesn't really help. "Seasons in the Sun," "Love's Theme," "The Way We Were," "Show and Tell."

It was my mother who started playing the stereo again. The Carpenters' "Close to You." J.P. McCarthy played it on a morning when she actually got up to try to make some breakfast for me. She dropped the spoon and ran into the bedroom. I had to turn off the stove. When I got home from school that day, she was downstairs in the family room, on the Early American couch from Topps, crying, playing that record over and over and over. I didn't know what to do, so I lay on my bed listening, thinking about that night when he first brought home the stereo. But after about the tenth time she played "Close to You," it truly started to annoy me. Then it made me sad again, then angry, then I didn't really even hear it after a while. I went down and sat with her for a bit, but it didn't change anything. Her crying would stop when the song ended, then there was a pause while she put the needle back on the record, then the song and the crying would start over again. I had liked the song when I first heard it on the radio, but that night I realized it was a horrible, sappy song. The playing of that song went on for two nights straight, then it just stopped. I never heard her play "Close to You" again.

I never want to hear that stupid song again.

Yet a few days after Mom is done with the Carpenters song, I find myself in the basement too. I put on a stack of Dad's Command records—*Provocative Percussion Volume 2*, *Strange Interlude*, *Dimension 3*—then go into the coal bin to build the model cars. For a little while, I feel better. Somehow, with his music playing, I can make believe that he is still in the house somewhere, tinkering with something, putting the final touches on the hutch, or just sitting there on the couch reading the *Free Press*. It's the only thing that makes me feel better.

I build lot of model cars in the months after my father dies.

Noisy Quiet People

Once we start playing the stereo and radio and turning on the television, the noise never seems to stop. It's like we're afraid of the quiet. We walk numbly around the house, Mom and I, the air swollen with sound. Yet for all the noise, she and I don't talk all that much. When we do it's just about nothing, what we're going to eat for supper or what to watch on television.

One night, the two of us are sitting in the living room, silently eating Campbell's Chicken with Rice Soup that I heated up, with quarters of buttered toast. We're eating from trays in front of the television while we watch *George Pierrot Presents*, a travel program where people show movies from their trips all over the world. You'd never think that George is some big-shot international traveler since he weighs about three hundred pounds and looks like a seventy-year-old walrus in a suit, but he is. Sometimes he shows his own movies. It's my mother's favorite program. She used to always say, *Isn't that beautiful?* or, *I'd love to go there someday*, when one of his guests would have movies of some exotic place halfway across the earth. She doesn't say it much these days.

Today, George's guest is some guy with movies from his trip to Tahiti. Everything there is sunny and tropical and beautiful. In Detroit, it's already dark outside at five p.m. Branches are slapping the side of the house and the wind is so thick with frozen flecks, the view out our front window looks like the reception between TV channels. I suddenly understand why they call that *snow*.

"Do you miss him?" I say to my mother. I don't know why I ask her that. I should be pretty sure that she does, for all her crying at records and the way she collapsed at his funeral, but it's a way to start.

Mom doesn't say anything. She just looks straight ahead at the TV, her eyes large and liquid.

"Mom."

It's like we avoid talking about him. Yet I want to talk about him. She's the only person I have to talk about him with. His only living relative, his sister, who never got along with my mother, didn't even come in for the funeral, she just sent a flower arrangement that said, *Loving Brother*. Mom didn't even tell any of the "kooks" in her family about him dying so they weren't there. She hadn't talked to them in years anyway. The men he worked with in the graphic arts department were full of kind words, quick to tell me that I'm the man of the house now, but I can't talk to them. The pinochle group hasn't been around for years, since they all moved away to the suburbs.

She puts down her spoon and starts to light a cigarette, but then puts the lighter down. The cigarette trembles between her fingers.

"Mom, did you hear me?"

"Yes, I heard you."

"Do you miss him?" I repeat, just trying to make her say something.

My mother stares down at the table. "This is very hard on me, Daniel," she says.

I don't know if she means talking to me now or the fact that Dad is gone, yet I don't want her to stop talking, so I don't ask. She doesn't say anything else.

"I miss him." I don't know what else to say. I guess I just want to say it out loud.

"I know you do," she says.

"Do you miss him?" I ask, like a broken record.

"Goddamn it, Danny!" She turns to me, her face red, her lower lip quivering. "What do you want from me? He's dead. He abandoned us and there's nothing we can do about it."

"I'm sure he didn't mean to—"

"Leave me alone, goddamn it. I don't know what I'm going to do."

Slowly she turns back to the television, trying to swallow. By now, the guest is talking about Paul Gauguin, who lived in Tahiti a long time ago. I recognize some of his pictures from our trips to the Art Institute. I have a couple spoonfuls of chicken soup.

"Mom."

"*What*, Danny? I'm trying to watch this. This man was a great painter. Look at those colors."

"Why won't you say it?"

"I don't *want* to say it." She doesn't turn away from the television, from the coastline of Tahiti, from stupid Gauguin's paintings of women in colored dresses, from George Pierrot's blubbery voice.

I stare at the soup in my bowl, at the bright yellow globules of fat floating on its surface. My throat closes up. Tears roll off my face into my soup, which is already pretty salty.

"Mom," I say when I catch my breath. I guess I can't shut up now.

"Jesus Christ, Danny."

"Are we going to lose the house?"

Without looking at me, she shakes her head. Her voice is quiet again. "No. We have your father's pension and his insurance policy. We'll be all right. For a while, at least."

"How long is a while?"

"I don't know," she says, getting annoyed with me again. Then she takes a breath and turns to me. She doesn't look mad now. "Stop worrying, honey."

My mother doesn't say anything for a long time. She

just sits there holding her unlit cigarette. I want her to say something more, but instead she places her cigarette on the tray and turns her head toward the kitchen. I'm guessing she's looking for her drink, which she left on the kitchen counter. I go up and get it for her. I put it down on the tray in the space where she has pushed away her soup. I kneel down beside her and give her a hug. At first, she just keeps looking at the TV screen, then eventually she leans into me. We stay like that until it gets uncomfortable for both of us. Finally, I have to pull away, which is when she gets up.

"I'm going to bed," she says, putting her hand on my neck for a moment. Then she picks up her drink and leaves the room.

"It's only five thirty, Ma," I say.

"Good night."

I can't tell if this helped or not.

I Save Us from the Poor Farm

I decide that I need a job. After a couple weeks of checking the want ads of the *Shopping News*, I see one for a part-time job in a shipping room, afternoons at a place on Grand River. I could catch the bus there after school. At $1.75 an hour, it's not going to pay the mortgage, but I can make some dough and get away from the house. I only have so much homework and can build only so many model cars, and sitting around just makes me sad. I'm hoping it doesn't involve too much fresh air.

After school, I take the bus straight down Grand River to a place called the Haus Shoppe. It's not far from the shopping district near Greenfield where I used to go with Mom and Dad before they built the mall in Livonia.

When I walk in the front door, there's a girl sitting at a desk. She's a little older than me, with a wide, blank, pretty face and the straightest brown hair I've ever seen. I tell her that I want to apply for the job in the *Shopping News* and she gives me a clipboard with an application attached to it. I sit down on one of the white fiberglass seats by the front window, next to a giant plastic plant in a turquoise fiberglass pot, and start to fill out the form.

From hidden speakers somewhere I can hear Beautiful Music playing and start to feel sick to my stomach. It's not like it is when I listen to it at home to trick myself. I take a deep breath, keep my head down, and fill out the form—name, address, phone number, work experience. Even though I've never had a real job, I write down that I used to mow the lawn of Mrs. McCoy across the street until she moved away. I also delivered the *Shopping News* for a year when I was thirteen. I forgot my Social Security card, so I just leave that blank.

I give it to the girl. "Will someone call me if they're interested?" I ask her. I'm not sure how this works. She gets up from her desk and tells me to wait.

I sit back down and in less than a minute, a hardy-looking guy in a short-sleeved cream-colored shirt and a brown striped tie comes out to greet me. Like my dad, he hasn't got much hair up top, but he's got a friendly smile.

He looks down at my application, then up at me. "Danny?"

"Yes sir," I say. We shake hands.

"I'm Stan Switala. I'm the office manager."

I just keep shaking his hand and smiling until it starts to feel uncomfortable. Finally, he pulls away from my hand, which is good since I was starting to get a cramp.

"We can talk in my office," he says.

I follow him down a hall where the walls are alternating panels of avocado green, harvest gold, and rusty orange. The floor is really shiny like it's just been polished. I feel my shoes sliding on it a little as I walk, so I'm careful not to slip. On the walls are framed color drawings of swoopy, slanty-looking houses. He leads me into an office with gold-colored walls, with more house drawings hung on them.

"Park it," he says, as he sits behind a desk.

I sit down on another fiberglass chair, a turquoise one in front of his desk.

"So, you're interested in the job in the shipping department?"

"Yes sir."

"Call me Stan." He looks down at my application. "I see that you delivered the *Shopping News* for a while. Why'd you stop?"

"My dad was afraid it was interfering with my studies," I say, which is the truth. "But that was—I, I was a lot younger then. I'm in high school now and I only have class about four hours a day."

He considers this. "Still, wouldn't your dad be concerned about this job doing the same thing?"

My throat squeezes shut. I don't like to lie, but I don't want to tell him the truth either. I don't know what to say, so I just say something: "He died, sir."

Stan Switala looks shocked. I'm shocked too. I haven't really said it out loud much. Still, I'm pretty sure that I'm doing a good job hiding how I feel. That is, until Mr. Switala hands me his handkerchief. I'm so embarrassed for being a big baby. I start to get up to leave, but I feel a hand on my shoulder, lowering me back into the scoop of the chair.

"It's okay, son."

I wipe my face with his handkerchief. I notice the initials on it: *SAS*. "Sorry about that, sir."

"I'm the sorry one. Call me Stan."

"Okay. Stan."

"You all right?"

I nod yes. "I have plenty of time to do my homework now, sir. Stan. I have too much time." I hand back his handkerchief. I actually need to blow my nose, but I'm not going to get snot all over his nice hankie, for crying out loud.

"I understand."

"What exactly is the job?" I ask, trying to divert his attention from my blubbering.

"It's in the shipping department. You'd be packaging up books and blueprints to be mailed. That's the gist of it."

"That sounds great. I'd really like to have a job. I'm a hard worker."

"That's good to know," Stan says, smiling again. He stands up like the interview is over, so I do the same. "Okay, Danny. We've got a few other applicants. If you get the job, we'll give you a call in the next day or two."

"Thanks, sir. Stan."

We shake hands again (shorter this time) and I leave. I head back out onto Grand River, toward the bus stop, feeling like a complete moron for crying at a job interview. I just want to go home and lock myself in the coal bin with the radio and a model car kit. I take the bus to where it stops at Stout Street by Mr. Tony's Sub Shop. I walk the five blocks to my house from there, a Pig-Pen cloud of embarrassment following me all the way.

When I walk in the side door, my mom greets me at the stoop, holding an L&M and a highball in the same hand. She's very efficient that way.

"Some man called. Did you apply for a job somewhere?" She raises the glass to her lips, but takes a puff instead of a sip.

I nod at her as she exhales, not sure how she's going to react.

She pulls a dampish receipt out of the pocket of her housecoat and hands it to me. "He says you got it." There's a phone number scrawled on the back, and beneath it: *Stan*. "You're supposed to call him tomorrow."

I'm surprised by this. Turns out crying at interviews isn't such a bad idea.

Mom squints from the smoke as she takes a sip of her drink. She looks at me and I'm not sure if she's angry or not, but she puts her free hand on my cheek. "Good for you, Danny," she says, her voice cracking, as if I'm about to leave her for a place where she won't be allowed to follow. "Good for you."

Whereby I Encounter Hippies for the First Time

The Haus Shoppe sells five different books with detailed floor plans for five types of homes—*Split-Levels*, *Two-Story Houses*, *Colonials*, *Vacation Homes*, and *Affordable Homes*. People order the books and if they see a house they like, they can buy the blueprints to give to a contractor or to build themselves. This is what Stan tells me on my first day as I get a tour.

When I first step into the shipping room, I notice

right away that the radio is on. It's not on the stations that I listen to and I don't really like what I hear. All conversation stops between the two guys standing there at a long counter. They're both hippies with long hair, both in their early twenties, both wearing flannel shirts and jeans. They give each other a look when Stan leads me over to them. I've never talked to hippies before. All I can think of is, *Are they on drugs?*

"That's Dale," Stan says, pointing at the one who has hair down to the middle of his back. I hold out my hand, which he halfheartedly shakes.

Dale lifts his head slightly. "Hey," he says.

"That's Mitch." Stan gestures toward the other one, who has small dark eyes, a beard, and slightly shorter hair. I hold out my hand, but he's far enough away to avoid shaking. He raises his hand and grunts at me.

"You guys, this is Danny. He's going to be helping us out back here."

The counter they're standing at is stacked high with blueprints. In front of them is the rest of the shipping department, which has a couple different stand-up work desks, all of them stacked with the five books Stan mentioned.

"I'm starting Danny on combos," says Stan, grabbing a stack of labels off the counter and leading me to a Masonite-topped desk. "Okay, Mitch?"

"Sure."

At the desk, Stan holds up one of the typed address labels. He points to a pair of numbers at the bottom under the address. "Just grab the books that correspond with these numbers." He slaps them down on one of the flat cross-shaped pieces of cardboard stacked on the desk, then folds the top and bottom flaps over the books. He folds the side flaps over those, then pushes a button on a tape machine that shoots out a sixteen-inch length of wet paper tape. "Throw a piece of tape on it, flip it over, and slap on the label."

After Stan shows me how to identify the number of the postal zone from the zip code, he writes it on the package and stacks it at the end of the desk. "Think you've got it?" he asks.

I look up at Mitch and Dale, who are laughing about something. "Uh-huh," I reply.

"Everything we do here is a different version of this," Stan says.

He has me try it. I figure out the postal code, even though the radio is so loud. There's a man is singing in a weird voice:

But I still did destroy her
And I will smash
Halo of flies . . .

After that he starts screaming. I try not to be distracted. I do a couple more packages, look up the zones and mark the numbers.

Stan seems pleased. He claps a hand on my shoulder. "Good job."

I kind of want to hug Stan right then, but I know that would be a bad idea.

"You have any questions, just ask the guys. I'll stop by later to check in."

I nod, hoping I won't have to talk to anyone. Once I start, the music ends and the disc jockey reads off a long list of strange songs and groups, all in a deep, quiet voice. It's not at all like the DJs I know. A commercial for a car-stereo store comes on.

One of the hippies, I think it's Mitch, says, "Hey, what do you like to listen to? I could put on something else."

It's nice of him to ask, I think. Maybe I was wrong about hippies. "I like CKLW and WXYZ," I respond.

"Cool," says Dale, the other hippie. "What bands do you like?"

"Um, I like the DeFranco Family and Bread . . . Terry Jacks."

"Oh," says Mitch. "That 'Seasons in the Sun' song?"

"Yeah."

"That song fucking sucks," says Dale.

"All those people you mentioned are bogue," says Mitch. "They suck donkey dick."

Mitch and Dale enjoy a long laugh. I look down at the two books I'm packaging, trying to concentrate, face burning.

"Put on W-4, Mitch."

He changes the station to another very loud song. I have to concentrate to ignore the grind of the guitar and the singer who seems to be screaming at me. After the song ends, another quiet-voiced disc jockey comes on. While the music was loud and nervous, he's relaxed, his voice trickling from the radio in a way that I find comforting, even after being tricked by hippies.

"*'All Right Now' by Free on WWWW. Before that, 'Uncle Remus' from the new Zappa, Zeppelin's 'When the Levee Breaks,' and we started out the set with Bowie and 'Moonage Daydream.' Gotta pay the bills, but we'll be back with some Manfred Mann.*"

"Fuck! Another commercial," says hippie Dale, spinning the knob again on the stereo. After he settles on a station, there's some spacey, meandering piano music. I can't say I like it, but I don't really dislike it.

"Hmm. We'll see how long I can stand this jazzy shit."

This is jazz? I think. The only thing that was ever called *jazz* in my house was the big band music that my parents used to play once in a while. This is not it. Another song comes up right after that's completely different. *Where is the disc jockey?* I wonder. After a song ends, there's supposed to be talking.

Mitch turns it up. "I like this jam."

I lower my head and tape books into boxes. I'm not sure what a *jam* is, though this song isn't bad. It's got guitars, but the singer isn't screaming at me.

You're my blue sky, you're my sunny day . . .

"You like the Allman Brothers?" asks Mitch.

"I don't know," I say, surprising myself a little. "Maybe."

"Not as good as Terry Jacks," says Dale.

"Or Bread!"

More laughing. I don't know why, but I keep talking. "I've never heard them," I say. "Are they a group?"

Dale and Mitch look at each other, just shaking their heads.

"Fuck," says Mitch. "You are fuckin' weird. Are you some sort of retard?"

Dale holds his hands up, as if he's trying to keep things civil. "Now, Mitch, while I agree that it is indeed fuckin' weird that our young friend here has never heard of the Allman Brothers, it does not necessarily indicate that he is a retard."

"I guess so," concedes Dale.

"But then, it doesn't mean that he's not one either."

I don't like this debate over my mental capabilities. "I am not a retard," I say, loud enough to be heard over the music.

Dale turns to Mitch, as if impressed. "Hear that? He says he's not a retard."

"Seems like just the sort of thing a retard would say."

"True. True. But we could *choose* to believe him."

Mitch shrugs. "Do what you want. I'm betting on retard."

So this is my new job, I think. *Listening to screechy music and putting books into boxes while being insulted by longhairs*.

"Time to learn how to collate CCs, Terry Jacks," Mitch says to me after I finish all my combos.

I have no idea what he means, but I follow him over to another table that's laid out with the same five books, only stacked very high.

"What's a CC?" I ask.

"A CC is a complete collection of all the books. Just watch."

I make a note of the word *collate*, which I will look up when I get home, though it seems to mean putting things together.

Mitch grabs a flattened premade box from a big stack next to the counter. He manipulates it into a rectangular cylinder with flaps at the top and bottom, then turns the two bottom flaps down and over each other, and staples it shut.

"There's your CC box." He slaps one book from each of the five piles into a stack on the table. "There's your books. Put the books in the box. Fold down the flaps and staple it up." He drops it on a stack of others just like it.

"That's it?"

"That's it. If you want, you can make a bunch of boxes first, then do all your collating at once. There's more books in the storage area up front marked with the numbers. Get them when you need to restock. Got it?"

"Yeah, I got it."

"Okay. Try not to fuck it up, retard."

After that, Mitch and Dale leave me alone and I make complete collections. Quickly, I realize how boring and repetitive my new job is, so to pass the time, I see how fast I can go, stapling empty boxes and collating books, until the CCs start to pile up behind me. As I speed through them, I imagine all the people who will receive the books I'm packing, them in their tiny old living rooms, dreaming of fancy new houses. I think of vacant lots slowly filling with lumber and shingles. I think of the men who will fasten it all together to create a house. I start to think of my father putting up the paneling in our family room, but I make myself stop thinking about that. It would be unprofessional of me to cry in front of the hippies. So I just decide to listen to the music. Some of it is not bad. I like the disc jockeys, even though they don't talk as much as I'd like and by the time they say the crazy names of the groups (Hawkwind? Hot Tuna? *Frampton's Camel?*), I can't remember which name goes with which songs. On top of that, Dale keeps changing the station. The piercing guitars, screaming singers, and pounding drums annoy me at first, but I notice that they help me to make complete collections faster.

At the end of the afternoon, Mitch comes over to see how I'm doing. (They've been ignoring me, so I don't think they've noticed the trips I've made into the back to refill my books.) When he sees the stacks of CCs that I've collated (I staggered them like bricks to eliminate tippage), hundreds stacked up behind and around me, he just stares at them.

"Jesus fuckin' Christ," he says.

After-Work Encouragement

My mom greets me when I come in the back door at about five forty-five p.m. I wish she'd change her housecoat once in a while. I make a note to wash a couple of her other ones and hang them up on the back of her door.

"How was your first day at work?" she asks.

I put down my books and hang up my jacket. I'm not entirely sure what to tell her. "It's okay. I just put books into boxes all day. It's pretty easy."

"Well, that's good."

I don't know exactly what she means by that. Does she mean that I need it to be easy because I'm so dumb? "Stan is great, but my co-workers are jerks."

"They always are."

"Why do you say that?" I ask, taking off my boots.

"It's the truth. People are shits."

I sigh at her. "Come on, Ma. Jeez. Why do you say things like that?"

"It's true. You're always going to have to kiss someone's ass in a job."

I love my mother, but I'm pretty sure this is bad advice.

"It was that way for your father."

It kind of annoys me that she brings him up now. "How do you know?"

"He told me."

It feels like she's already telling me that I have a crummy job. I know it's a crummy job, but I don't need to hear it from her.

She points two fingers at me, a smoldering L&M 100 between them. "This is why you need to get to college. I couldn't go, but you have to."

"Maybe I don't want to go to college. Why don't *you* go to college if it's so important to you?" I don't really mean for this to sound mean, but it does.

"Never you mind. You're going if I have to go turn tricks up on Eight Mile to earn the money."

"Well, it would be nice if you got a job."

"Very funny." She picks up her drink and heads for the living room to watch the six o'clock *Action News.* "There's beanie weenies on the stove," she says over her shoulder.

Lately, dinner has been hot dogs chopped up in a lot of things that come in cans: German potato salad, SpaghettiOs, even beef stew. I would actually prefer just plain hot dogs and have told her so, but she says you can't have just hot dogs for dinner. I tell her that buns would be nice too, but she ignores me.

I fill a bowl with beanie weenies and head into my room before something on the television gets her started.

Life at the Haus Shoppe

I settle in pretty quickly at work over the next couple weeks. I can do my job without really thinking about it. To keep my mind from going to bad places, I concentrate on the music on the radio. To my surprise, I hear rock bands that I actually like. After a while, I can count back songs from when the disc jockey announces them, so I can tell who sang what. I like a song by Ted Nugent and the Amboy Dukes called "Journey to the Center of the Mind." The guitar reminds me of the sound-effects record where the plane is taking off. I also enjoy a song by a group named Deep Purple called "Woman from Tokyo" and a song by Jethro Tull, where he plays the flute. I like Alice Cooper too, even after I learned that she is a he.

The worst thing about the job is Mitch and Dale. It's not like school, where I can get out of a situation pretty quick just avoiding a certain street or hallway. I'm trapped at this place. Here's a list of my nicknames so far: *retard, tard* (to save time?), *dorkus, straight guy, nurdosaurus rex, dimski, Terry Jacks* (I still like "Seasons in the Sun," no matter what they say), *bunghole, asshole, asswipe, shit-for-brains, dipshit, dick, dickweed, fat ass, fat fuck, fucknut, fuckwad, fuckstick, dildo, bilbo, dildo baggins*, and let's not forget *needledick* and *numbnuts*. Oh yeah, and *whooping crane* (I have no idea why). I can't really say why the names don't bother me. They're just words, I know. And even if they're words that are meant to hurt me, they can't really hurt me, not the way it hurts when someone punches you. At school, if I have a choice of calling myself a *pussy* (*chicken* is also popular with tormentors) and getting hit, I will always choose the name. I mean, wouldn't *you?* So after a while, the names just don't bother you. (Or maybe my nuts aren't the only things that are numb.)

Mitch and Dale also enjoy playing practical jokes. They intentionally jam my stapler. Or put a box of tacks on my desk with the bottom cut out so when I pick it up, the tacks scatter everywhere. Or rig the water bottle on my tape machine so when I push the button to extend the wet tape, the bottle spills all over my mailing labels. After any of these, they both yell, "Sab-o-tage!" And then they laugh.

So far, hippies are not my favorite people.

Life After Dark

The good thing about the Haus Shoppe and making CCs and even Mitch and Dale is that it all keeps me busy. It keeps me from thinking about my father all the time. It's not that I don't want to think about him. It's just that I can't stop thinking about him. Which means that school, work, listening to the radio, even getting insulted is better than what I'm feeling the rest of the time. I still can't sleep and a lot of the time even the radio doesn't help. I go up to his room and touch his clothes, go through his box of cuff links and tie tacks that he kept on his dresser, the place where he kept his keys and wallet and fingernail knife. There are still white shirts folded up from the cleaners in one drawer, even though he had gotten more casual in the past few years, wearing turtlenecks and sport coats. I know it sounds crazy, but even the smell of athlete's foot powder in his closet makes my chest hurt.

Building the model cars doesn't really help, but it's still something to do. Right now, I'm building an AMC Ambassador, a car that I think Dad might have liked. It's big, like his car, which is still in the garage. No one has driven it, but I've opened up the garage and started it up a couple times and backed it up and down the driveway, because I know he would want us to take care of it. It's bad for a car not to run it once in a while. I think I might try to drive it soon, but for right now, just being in it is hard.

Some nights, I sit there in the coal bin, listening to the nighttime FM DJs, who are even more quiet and calm than the daytime FM DJs. I like the sounds of their voices, even if I don't always like the music they play. It calms me down. You can tell that they love to talk about the songs and the albums and the groups. Sometimes they play music that reminds me of my father's *Switched-On* Moog albums, from crazy-named groups like Tangerine Dream and Soft Machine and Kraftwerk with synthesizers that soar and *dweedle* and *bleet* and go on for seventeen minutes and put me in a musical trance, making me feel like I'm dreaming or outside my body watching from above, there in the coal bin. Sometimes the music is just quiet and pretty, like one song called "Nights in White Satin."

Letters I've written, never meaning to send
Beauty I'd always missed, with these eyes before . . .

This new music is a relief to me. The music I liked before just reminds me of the way things were then. I need new things to think about. The old things are wearing me down.

A Talk with Mrs. Corbin

At school, while blindly bumping my way through the halls, my hair still wet from swim class, heading to my second period, I'm approached by someone, a middle-aged black lady who looks familiar, who even smiles at me, but I can't quite place her. She walks up to me like I should know who she is and it's then that I realize it's Mrs. Corbin, my counselor. She spoke to me shortly after what happened with my father, but I don't remember much of that time. I recall that she said she had spoken to my father, what a nice man he was, and how sorry she was to have heard of his passing. I remember those words she'd used: *his passing*. They struck me at the time. It seemed like if someone passes you, shouldn't you still be able to see them? Aren't they still there, but just up ahead? Guess what? They're not.

"Daniel," she says to me now, touching my shoulder, "how are you doing?"

I've discovered that a lot of people ask you how you're doing after someone dies. The only answer to give is, *I'm fine.* Of course, no one believes you and you don't believe it yourself, but it's the only answer. Trust me on this.

"I'm fine," I say. I can tell she doesn't believe me. I don't care, to tell you the truth.

"I was wondering if we could talk?"

We pause in the hallway, while kids slide along either side of us. When you're speaking to a teacher, the air around you suddenly expands and all the pushing and elbowing eases up. It quiets down too.

"Am I in trouble for something?"

"No, not at all, Daniel. Of course not."

"I have to get to English class."

"It won't take long. I'll write you a pass."

When she says that, I think of *passing* again and wonder why she's always using that word. I guess it's probably hard not to if you're a teacher. *Hall pass. Passing grade. His passing.*

I follow Mrs. Corbin to her office. Even though she says I'm not in trouble, it still feels that way. She leads me away from where all the kids are rushing to their classes. It's in a quieter part of the school, with more teachers walking around than students, an area where I don't belong. I follow her into her office. She has me sit down on the chair across from her desk and then shuts the door.

I turn around for a moment and can still see blurred images of people walking by in the hall through the pebbly glass of the window. Mrs. Corbin sits down herself.

"What's going on?" I'm sure I'm in trouble at this point, even though I've been told I'm not. That's just the way my mind works. For someone who never gets in trouble, I think I'm in trouble all the time.

"I just want to talk, Daniel," she says. She smiles and then I believe her. "What's going on with you?"

"Nothing's going on. Everything is fine."

The smile fades just then. *Uh-oh.* I'm getting the feeling that she wants to talk about my father. And while I wanted to talk about him with my mother, I'm pretty sure I don't want to talk about him with my guidance counselor.

"I just wanted to see how you're doing."

"I'm good," I say. "I'm fine. I told you." I feel panic surging through my body. I'm not sure why.

"How did driver's education go for you?"

"Fine," I say. "I finished it. I got my learner's permit. I can get my license on my sixteenth birthday."

"That's good. You can help your mother. How are things at home?"

Why does everyone assume that my mother needs so much help? I mean, they're right, but how do they know? I stare at some plaques on the wall. There are framed photographs of Mrs. Corbin with students.

"Daniel?"

I look back at her. "They're fine."

"How is your mother handling things?"

If Mrs. Corbin thinks I'm going to tell her that my mother sleeps all day and drinks herself into a stupor every night, can't even get to sleep without her Valiums or Libriums, and can't even talk to me about my father, except to get mad about him dying like he did it just to spite her, she's got, as my mother would slur, another think coming. I just nod my head like a madman. "She's great," I say. "Well, not great, but okay. Fine. Good."

"Are you sure?"

"Yes. Absolutely."

"How are *you* handling things? This is a very difficult thing that you're going through. I know it must be a very hard time for you."

"I have to get to class, Mrs. Corbin." I stand up from my chair.

This is where Mrs. Corbin stops being so nice and starts acting like a teacher. "Daniel, sit down," she says sternly. Then she adds, "Please."

I want so bad to run out that door, but I sit down. I can't help myself. Why am I so obedient? I need to be a problem teen. I need to be a rebel.

"Thank you," says Mrs. Corbin.

Winter Sab-O-Tage!

Winter gets wetter and sloppier. When it's not that, the cold makes the half-melted snow by the bus stop hard and jagged and edged with soot and grime. At the Haus Shoppe, business is booming. I have made thousands of complete collections by now. Stan has also hired a pair of brothers who go to St. Mary's Catholic school down the street. The Finney brothers, though not hippies, seem to get along great with Dale and Mitch. The older Finney brother, Matt, is a loud, tough-sounding guy, who likes to hold up his hands on either side of his shoulders, then snap his fingers and point down to his peter, while saying out of the side of his mouth: "*Lick.*" He thinks this is hilarious.

I don't find it all that funny, probably since I'm the one he's usually saying it to. The younger Finney brother, Andrew, is small, thin, and kind of sissyish, even by my standards, and I get called a sissy a lot. What's interesting is that he talks constantly about all his girlfriends at school. If he does it too much, his brother will say something along the lines of, *Shut up already, you little faggot.* I feel bad for him, but it's actually a good thing when the Finney brothers fight, because it takes the attention off of me.

Mostly, I am settling in well, getting more jobs from Stan every day, which I am happy to do. ("Jesus, you little fucking brownnoser," says the older Finney brother to me. "I think you might have missed a spot on Stan's ass that you didn't kiss." It's not really like that. Anyway, I notice he doesn't say anything like that when Stan is around.) One of my jobs is to police the outside of the building and pick up after the customers of Dooley's Bar next door; they tend to throw up on the sidewalk or chuck beer bottles against the wall of our building when they come out drunk. If it snows, it's also my job to go out and shovel the giant sidewalk that borders Mettetal Street and Grand River.

Which is what I am doing one afternoon after a big midday snowfall when I get brutally snowball-attacked by Mitch, Dale, and the Finney brothers. Yes, I know it's just snow we're talking about here, but this is not a couple snowballs playfully chucked at me, like a fun, impromptu snowball fight. This is a well-planned attack.

They must have been making snowballs in the alley for days, then leaving them out there to freeze up. One minute I'm shoveling snow, the next I'm getting clobbered by ice balls from every direction.

"Kill the Crane!" I hear someone yell, possibly Mitch, but it's hard to tell after the first ice ball in the ear. I get hit in the head a couple more times, plus the stomach, the back, and the ribs. When an ice ball hits me in the testes, I go down.

I hear chanting. They're all yelling, "*Kill the Crane!*" as they circle around me, like something out of *Lord of the Flies*. (A good book, but again, it's no *Street Rod*.) Someone runs away and comes back with a pail of slush, which they dump on me. That's when I find out that it's not so much slush as snowy gravel and dirt from a pile behind the building. When I yell at them to stop, I get a mouthful.

Obviously, I'm pretty good at ignoring when people are mean to me, but this is hard to ignore. I am on the ground, flailing around, unable to see from all the slush in my eyes, still getting pelted by ice balls in the crotch even while I'm down. They're all laughing, until Stan comes out and breaks it up.

"What the devil is wrong with you boys?" he says to them, helping me up, trying not to slip on all the snow and ice. "Get the hell inside, all of you." They disperse quickly back into the shipping department.

"Good lord." He shakes his head like he's fed up. "Go get your things and knock off for the day, Dan."

I do what he says. Since my face is wet, and my hair is plastered against my forehead, I tell myself that no one can see that I'm crying when I go back in for my school stuff.

On the bus, I sit at the back, away from the few people

who are on it at this time of day. All the way to my stop, I can hear the water drip off of me onto the floor.

Mom Puts Her Foot (and Drink) Down

At home I hang up my still-soaked coat by the back door, take off my galoshes (which everyone in high school loves, by the way), and try to head to my room without attracting attention. I hear the theme to *Match Game* coming from the living room. Then the volume turns down.

"You're home early," my mother says to me as I head down the hall.

I put my books down on my bed and stomp back to the living room. I stand there under the doorway arch, my anger confused now, teetering over into wanting to run to my mother and wrap myself around her legs, blubbering like the time when I was watching television when I was five and a *PLEASE STAND BY* message came on. It was a scary skeleton-like stick figure leaning against a cartoon TV with jagged lines behind it. It terrified me so much that I didn't know what to do but run around in hysterics until I found my mother. She let me cry myself out, while trying to figure out why exactly a little cartoon had scared me so much.

That's not what I do today. Mom is sitting in her gold-flowered armchair holding a smoldering L&M in one hand, and her small greenish bottle of Coke in the other. There's only a little left in the bottle. It's around four o'clock, which is usually the time when she goes from Coke drinking to Canadian Mist and Uptown drinking. She looks me over, but doesn't say anything about my clothes being soaked, the scrape on my forehead, or my swollen lower lip from an ice ball to the mouth.

"I don't like my job anymore," I say, trying to keep my voice from quavering. "I'm quitting."

She puts the little bottle on the end table, just missing a green straw coaster, then takes a drag of her cigarette and stares at me dully. "No you're not," she says, very matter-of-factly.

"Yes I am. What do you care?" I don't mean to sound snippy, but it sounds pretty snippy.

She stubs out her cigarette in the hubcap ashtray. The smoke seems to trail right up to her face, where she waves it away. "I said, like hell you're leaving that job."

I'm getting angry now. "What difference does it make? I'll find a new job."

My mother picks up the small plaid snap purse that holds her package of cigarettes. "It makes a lot of difference. Listen to me. You're staying at that job. You're just going to ignore those idiots. You're not going to talk to any of them unless it's about work. You're not going to joke around or try to get along with them, you're just going to go there and do your job and come home. Do you hear me?"

Stan must have called her. "No, I'm quitting."

She stares at me, her eyes clearer than they've looked in months. "You are not quitting your job, do you hear me?" She points down the hallway, then unsnaps the plaid purse and plucks out a cigarette. "Go get cleaned up."

I guess I have no say in this matter. "Why?" Now I just sound bratty.

"Because we're going out."

I'm ready to yell, but I don't. I realize that I feel better getting bossed around by my mother. No one has bossed me around at home since Dad was here. Maybe me needing my mother has helped her to act like a mother again. So I go into my room and get cleaned up.

That night, we go to Bet & Jessie's on Grand River for Scottish fish and chips. She even lets me drive the *Hindenburg*. It's the first time I've driven anywhere since Dad died, so I'm a little rusty, but I do fine, and it weirdly cheers me up to drive his car. At the restaurant, Mom doesn't really eat much, she just tops off her ginger beer with Canadian Mist from a plastic flask, but I am surprisingly hungry. I eat all my dinner and most of hers. We come home and watch a Banacek on NBC's Wednesday night *Mystery Movie*. I make sure to go to my room just before the news comes on at eleven. Ever since Coleman Young got elected mayor a few months ago, I've been trying to stay away from my mother when the news is on. At least for a while, until she gets used to the idea that Detroit now has a black mayor.

Attempted Breakfast

When I open my eyes in the morning, the pain is there like always, yet it feels different today. Maybe it's because I hear music playing on the radio downstairs while my mother cooks breakfast. This has not happened much since my father died. Hearing WJR from the kitchen makes me feel a little better about having to go back to work this afternoon. On the other hand, I'm not sure how I feel about hearing "Sunshine on My Shoulders" playing along with the song on my radio, which is "Smoke on the Water" by Deep Purple.

"Morning, Danny," says my mother at my doorway, in a singsong voice that worries me a little. It's a bit too cheery, but I guess I'll take it. "Rise and shine!"

I walk into the kitchen, drowsy from lack of sleep, the events of the previous day slightly muted but still smarting, along with my cuts and scrapes, the bruises on my side, not to mention the dull ache in my crotch. Despite the movie of revenge that reeled continuously through my head all night long, I have decided to do exactly what my mother has advised: I will ignore them. Anyway, it's not like I would really take a box cutter to Mitch's jugular or staple the Finney brothers in their stupid faces, even though that all sounds like a lot of fun.

In the kitchen, Mom is filling up the kettle. She's got a freshly laundered (by me) housedress on, with her hair pulled back so tightly, her eyes look bulgy. She seems so very awake, I'm wondering if her doctor has prescribed something new for her. She's been going to Dr. Hadosian for ages, long before everything happened with Dad. Mostly, he gives her stuff to help her sleep, but he has occasionally prescribed what she calls *a little pick-me-up*. If that's what's going on, then it seems to be working. She is officially *picked up*.

"What's going on, Mom? You didn't need to get up. I can make my own breakfast."

"I know you can, dear. But I wanted to make it for you today."

Sitting on the kitchen table is a moldy half-loaf of bread which I've been meaning to throw away.

"Oh. Okay."

"You go get dressed. I'll take care of this."

"All right," I say.

When I come out dressed for the day, she brings over a plate of scrambled eggs with bacon and toast. Even though the toast is almost black (which is actually the way my father liked it, but not me—still, it's probably a good thing since now all the mold has been carbonized), there are shells in the eggs and coffee grounds in my tea (I don't know why), I feel the weight on my chest lighten by a few ounces. "This is nice, Mom. Thanks," I say. And I mean it.

"Don't forget what I told you," she calls out as I leave.

At work, I do exactly what my mother told me to do. I answer all questions "Yes" or "No." I do my job. I don't try to talk to Dale and Mitch or the Finney brothers. I speak only when spoken to. I give them the silent treatment. The effect is interesting. They actually notice that I'm not speaking to them.

"Are you pissed about yesterday?" says Dale, slyly.

I shake my head no.

"He's pissed," says Mitch. "The Crane is pissed."

"Whoop!" yells one of the Finney brothers. They like to do this because of my mysterious nickname.

I work on a big stack of combos and concentrate on the radio. It's WWWW and I hear the DJ announce a song by Black Sabbath. I'm surprised to find that I'm really enjoying it. The guitar is loud and cutting and the words are about pain and suffering and misery. I like it.

It's not the way that the world was meant
It's a pity you don't understand
Killing yourself to live . . .

"Whoop!" says the other Finney brother.

I get through the day without speaking to any of them

except about work. I can tell that it annoys them and I like that too.

I come home that night, feeling pleased that not talking worked so well, to find my mother asleep in front of the television. When she wakes up a couple hours later, she doesn't even ask how things went at work. I think about telling her anyway, but I decide that I don't feel like talking about it. Instead, I do some homework that I've been meaning to get to.

The Stupid Letter

I'm doing this under protest. I'm only doing it because Mrs. Corbin, my counselor at school (you talked to her when you forced me into taking driver's ed), told me that it would be a good idea for me to write down some things in a letter to you. I don't honestly understand why, but she says that it will be good for me. That it's a way to talk to you, to say some things I might not have gotten a chance to say to you before. I didn't tell her that I thought it was a stupid idea because, well, you're not here anymore. I also didn't tell her that you would have thought it was stupid too. You would have called it a load of malarkey or BS and told me not to bother, but Mrs. Corbin made me promise I would do it, and even said, "Cross your heart and hope to die?" Then I could tell she felt bad right after she said "hope to die" because you are dead and that made me feel sorry for her. It didn't matter anyway. She had me trapped in her office so I really had no choice. I know she's nice and she's just trying to be a good high school counselor, but I really wish she'd just mind her own business. So I'm writing this stupid letter under protest. I don't have any idea where to start so I'm just going to write down some stuff so I can tell her that I did it without being a liar. You know I have rules about that sort of thing.

So here goes. I'm here in the coal bin, Dad. I'm at the old table where I always used to build the model cars. I've got the radio on.

Right now, the DJ is playing a pretty good song called "Ooh La La" by a rock group called the Faces. I'm sure you and Mom would probably call it jungle music, but I'm starting to really like rock and listening to it here somehow makes me feel less dopey about doing this.

I still can't believe you're gone. I walk around in a daze most of the time. I keep thinking there was a mistake and you're going to somehow come back, even though I know that's crazy. (I saw the police car in front of our house, but they wouldn't let me even see you until the funeral.) Yet none of it stops me from all the time thinking, "Where is he today? Why isn't he here?" Then I remember: "He's dead." I have to tell myself that about a hundred times a day. Every time I have to say "He's dead" to myself, it's like an X-Acto knife cut in my chest, so quick and so sharp and so deep. That kind of cut where it all happens so fast, even the skin is confused and doesn't even know to bleed at first. Then it won't stop bleeding.

Just writing these words down on paper makes me miss you. I miss talking to you. I miss seeing you come home at night. I miss driving around with you, shooting the bull, sneaking off to get a slice of square pizza at Angelo's up on Plymouth and not telling Mom about it. I miss you giving me driving lessons, even when you ended up yelling at me. I knew you were yelling just because you wanted me to be a good driver and not get myself killed. I even miss not seeing you. I miss coming into the kitchen in the morning and smelling your aftershave in the air after you've left for work. I miss the sound of you sawing something in your shop or pounding nails or drilling. It's not like we were actually together, but we were both down in the basement, building our stuff, and it felt like we were doing it together. In between sawing or drilling, I could yell out something to you. "How's it going over there?" And you'd yell back, "It's really coming along. How about you?" "Good." Then we'd just go back to work with the stereo playing something like Enoch Light and the Light Brigade.

I miss going to Korvettes with you. I'm sorry now that we used to go there to buy cigarettes for you because they probably helped make your heart attack happen, but I'm still glad we went. Is it dumb that I miss going shopping with you? It wasn't really about buying stuff, even though finding bargains was fun. I just liked hanging out with you, looking at records. Walking through the aisles of a store was just an excuse to talk.

I miss you pushing me into things for my own good. I have no idea what my own good is. I'm just guessing. That's why I got a job. I think you would have encouraged me to do it. It's a place down Grand River that sells home plans and books. I work in the shipping department. I'm making money, but what I like best is that I have to work hard there and it keeps me from thinking "He's dead" so much. I'm around other people so I can't be bawling all the time. Especially around the hippies I work with who are real jerks. I'm trying not to bawl right now while I write this stupid letter. I know you didn't like it when I cried, and when I would, you would just tell me, "Come on, knock it off," and usually I could do that. So I'm imagining you telling me that right now. It's helping, but hearing your voice in my head telling me not to cry is also kind of making me cry, so maybe it's not. It doesn't really matter because I've written enough of this stupid letter. Now I can tell Mrs. Corbin that I did what she asked.

Dangerous Food

Despite my mother's help with the Mitch and Dale situation, it isn't long before everything goes back to normal. I begin to realize that my mother can no longer be trusted in matters involving food. I'm tired of asking questions about what's on my plate: *Is that the pot roast we had three weeks ago? Is this some sort of exotic cheese? Should this be furry?*

I know the fact that she's still trying to keep me nourished means she loves me and she's doing the best she can under the circumstances, but it's hard to remember this when she's serving me something she was scraping over the sink two minutes earlier.

"Here, this is still good," she says, handing me a plate of gelatinous chicken.

"There's green stuff around the edges."

She shakes her head wearily. "That's nothing. It's fine. That just means it's fresh still."

"Mom, mold is not a sign of freshness."

"Don't be a smart-ass. Just eat it," she says, walking back to the living room with a fresh drink. (She never seems to eat her own meals, I notice.) "It's dinner."

"I'm not so sure about that," I yell to her.

After the first couple of wincing, retching nights on or over the toilet, I lose my taste for blue food. That's when I begin going to Mr. Tony's Subs after I get off the bus. I eat my sandwich as I walk the five blocks home. I hate spending the money, but I hate diarrhea even more.

Now if she gives me anything that looks hazardous, I just pick up my plate and tell her that I'm going to eat it in my room. A little while later, I flush it down the toilet. She never notices. By that time, she's usually into her fifth highball and curled up in front of the boob tube.

At this point, I start to remember just how much my father had done around the house, how much laundry and shopping and making food he did. I'm doing a lot of those things now. I realize how much time she spent napping and watching television. Dad was always telling me how tired she was.

Most of the time when I get home from work, she's in the same place on the couch where she was when I left. Or else in bed, the sheets gathered on the floor, with a book about the Cubists or something like that tented next to her. It makes me think of some of the stuff Dad would say to me, when she would decide to stay home when we were going to the movies. Stuff like, *Your mother is having one of her sick headaches, so she's just going to stay in bed.*

I start to understand that my mother had a lot of sick headaches when my dad was alive. And now with him gone, it's like one long sick headache.

The Silent Treatment

Not talking to anyone at work helps in ways I never would have predicted. I discover that if you decide someone doesn't matter anymore, they no longer matter. As the weeks go by, I get better and better at ignoring them. I turn up the volume on my silence. The small part of me that is still paying attention to them sees that they are mystified at my new abilities. It's like my sonar has been restored, only now I'm sending out pulses of silence to navigate. They still insult me but it's like I'm able to slink in between the words so they don't touch me. It's as though they aren't really even talking about me.

"Mitch, is it just me or does Danny look more like a dildo today than usual?"

"I don't know. He always looks like a dildo. But then, sometimes he doesn't. Sometimes he just looks like a faggot."

"I vote retard."

"Whoop!"

The hilarity keeps coming. So I just stand there at my desk, taping singles and combos into their boxes, making complete collections by the hundreds, focusing on the DJ who is talking about an album by a new band called Bad

Company, which has people from two other bands, Free and Mott the Hoople.

I don't even notice when Mitch and Dale and the Finney brothers lose interest in harassing me and go back to work.

The only time that's difficult for me is when everyone talks about what's playing on the radio. It's only then that I'm tempted to talk. Or when they play Name That Tune to see who can guess the song in the first few notes. I'm beginning to recognize more of the songs on FM radio.

Man of the House

Since last year, I'm pretty sure at least a thousand people have told me that now I'm the man of the house. I really wish they'd stop saying that. (They also tell me I need to take care of my mother, but they have no idea what this involves.) So I decide that in my official capacity as Man of the House, I'm going to Korvettes this Friday night. Though I still just have my learner's permit and am technically only supposed to drive with a licensed driver, I decide to take my father's car anyway. Obviously, this is a big deal for me. It's one of my first steps in my new program to become a rebel, so I'm pretty pleased with myself. Even though I'm not sure I have anything to rebel against. Or maybe I have *everything* to rebel against and I just don't realize it yet. I guess we'll see.

On the road, my main goal will be to not get stopped by the police, which shouldn't be that hard since I'm a very safe and conscientious driver. I will buckle up my seat belt, abide by the posted speed limits, make full stops at stop signs, keep my hands at ten and two, and look both ways before turning into traffic. (I know this is not very rebel-like, it's not how the boys in *Street Rod* would drive, but it will have to do until I get my license.) Those weekend mornings driving around with my dad taught me well. I'm still a little nervous since it's been awhile since I drove (other than Bet & Jessie's on the night of the snow attack), but I tell myself that I will be fine. Besides, I need to keep practicing for when I take my driver's test and I can't count on Mom to take me out.

When Friday comes, I don't lie to Mom, I say exactly what I'm going to do. She should know that I just have my learner's permit. She should also know that I'm not supposed to be driving by myself. She *should* know. It would likely be a problem for most parents, but not mine. Instead, here's what she says to me after I tell her where I'm going: "Korvettes? Oooh, could you pick me up a carton of cigarettes?"

I sigh. "Maybe you should think about quitting, Ma."

"L&M 100s," she says, completely ignoring me.

"I know what you smoke. I've only seen you do it about a million times."

She ignores me. I also notice that she doesn't give me any money for cigarettes, but since she doesn't make a fuss about the rest of it, I decide that this will simply be the price of a night of rebel freedom. I'm just surprised she didn't ask me to pick her up a fifth of Canadian Mist.

I Was Born a Ramblin' Man

The *Hindenburg* starts right up and I let it run for a few minutes. Smoke billows out of the tailpipe as I rev the engine. It has been a long time since it's been driven more than a couple blocks. I loosen the moorings and guide it out of our garage, extra careful not to scrape the fence or the side of the house. I doubt Mom would even notice if I scraped it up, but I don't want to find out. Most of all, I just don't want to hurt it. Dad loved the Bonneville.

I know it's just a car, but it still smells like him, like his cigarettes, like his aftershave lotion, spicy-sweet and familiar, the Avon Tai Winds that he used to splash on from the thick blue glass Polynesian bottle that I keep in my room now. Awhile back, Mom was throwing out his stuff in the bathroom (it seemed so soon and she was throwing out everything) and I managed to grab it out of the wastebasket. It doesn't make any sense, but smelling his smell is like magic to me. I can feel his freshly shaven cheek on mine like when I was little and he would say, *Give your old man a hug*. These smells kind of make me happy, but also make my chest ache. I tell myself to concentrate on driving and nothing else.

As I back out onto Stout Street, I see a little black kid on the other side of the street on his bike. Even though I'm nowhere near him, I stop completely until he goes by. Then he waits and watches me back out onto the street.

The seat belt digs at my stomach, yet I can't help but to wear it. This rebel is still afraid of going through the windshield. Even though I know they showed us all those gory *Death on the Highway* movies in driver's ed just to scare us, they worked on me. I don't want to be like that guy who gets thrown out of the car and impaled on the telephone pole. So gross, though I could hear a couple people in class snickering at it.

I cross Fenkell, passing Pete Madzik's Standard station, where Dad got the cars maintained, both the *Hindenburg* and my mother's Tempest. I look for Pete, but he's gone for the night. I check my gas. There's about three-quarters of a tank. It crosses my mind that my dad was the last person to put gas in this car. I tell myself to concentrate.

I take Stout past the houses where, according to my mother, the hillbillies live. That seems mean, but I do notice a few houses that have cars parked on the lawns and inside furniture on the porch. I've also seen kids running around in front yards wearing only underwear and church shoes. I notice a couple new *Keim Sold Mine* and other real estate signs on the lawns. There are more and more of them popping up in our neighborhood.

At the end of the block, I turn right on Outer Drive, a wooded boulevard that never seems to begin or end, it just runs in a circle around the city. Since it's six thirty on a Friday night, it's deserted. I take it four miles to West Chicago Road, which will get me to Korvettes. This is the same route my dad and I used to take on Friday nights. Again, I feel the tightness in my chest, but it also feels so good to be out by myself, away from school, away from work, and away (this is a little harder to admit) from my mother. At the traffic lights, I can hear my father's voice telling me not to be afraid, to give it the gas and to take off with authority. So that's what I do.

The Remainders

After I buy Mom's cigarettes down in tobacco and sundries and drop them off in the car, I enter the main store, which seems different tonight, all bright turquoise and white, gleaming with chrome and floor wax. On my way to the escalator, which leads to the record department, I walk through the ladies department. All around me, women are shopping or stationed behind cash registers.

There are women mannequins on platforms on top of racks of dresses, looking down at me in their wigs and pantsuits. I feel like I'm the only man in the place. I pass the undergarments section, where there are racks with pictures of women in bras and pantyhose. My pants tightening against my legs, I ride the giant escalator in the middle of the store up to the record department.

Once upstairs, I linger around the periphery, browsing through the cutout bins. Of course, the first thing I see are remaindered Command and 101 Strings albums, even a couple that my dad owned. I'm tempted to stop, but instead I walk on by. Tonight I have a mission.

I have money in my wallet that I earned myself at the Haus Shoppe by putting up with the hippies and by making complete collections faster than anyone in the world. With it, I'm going to buy my first rock record. I can't really say why I waited so long to do it, except that maybe I was waiting to hear the right one.

When I get past the cutouts and into the middle of the record department, the first thing I think is, *How did I come here so many times and not notice all these rock albums? They're everywhere*. I see names that I've been hearing every afternoon on the radio—Allman Brothers, Steely Dan, Santana, Queen, Eric Clapton, Pink Floyd, Aerosmith, Yes, Wishbone Ash. Even though there are at least a couple I wouldn't mind getting, none of them are why I'm here. Then, there by the cash register, I see it. It's hard to miss since there's a whole rack devoted to just this one record, its gaudy (my mother would say) orange, yellow, and green-tinted cover repeated four times across and three times down. It's quite an incredible sight, really.

I pull one of the albums from the rack and hold it

in my hands, examining it, gently turning it around and over, enjoying the feel of it, the sharp cellophaned corners digging pleasantly into the heels of my hands. Through the plastic I touch the thick paper band that's wrapped around the record. It spells out in strange exotic-looking elongated letters:

LED ZEPPELIN—HOUSES OF THE HOLY

I look at the cover, at the naked little shaggy blond-haired kids climbing the craggy sides of what, at first glance, appears to be a kind of mountain or volcano. Then I look again and see that it may just be a pile of giant stones, pitted with holes. Whatever it is, it makes me nervous to think about naked children climbing something steep and dangerous. I fear they are about to fall between the rocks, never to be seen again, or at least never to be the same.

"Have you heard it?" says a voice next to me. I didn't even realize I wasn't alone. I turn to see a gangly kid in overalls next to me, a faded blue Nazareth T-shirt under them, his forehead and cheekbones swollen red with acne. (*Pizza face* is what Mitch and Dale would call him, I'm sure of it.)

"Yeah," I say. "Well, not all of it."

"Get it, man. It's excellent. The whole album is fucking monumental. One great jam after another. Just excellent."

"Okay. Great. Thanks," I say, holding my copy even tighter. "Excellent."

"Later." When he walks away, I notice the *Led Zeppelin III* album tucked under his arm.

This little exchange surprises me, makes me even surer about the choice of my very first rock album. I guess I could feel like I'm just one of the nameless, faceless herd of kids who are buying it, but that's not at all how I feel. Instead, I feel a sense of community. I glance around at everyone in the record department and I think that they don't look all that different from me. Their hair is longer, their clothes are patched and baggy and different from mine, but they're still just kids. For the first time, I feel like I'm one of them. I belong. *You like Zeppelin? I like Zeppelin too!*

I place the copy of the album that I've been holding back in the rack, then pull out the one behind it. I don't know exactly why, but it's as if my own sweaty-palmed desire has somehow soiled the album. I hold the new one under my arm, carry it as I would a schoolbook, only here at Korvettes, no one will flick it out onto the floor.

Suddenly I feel calmer, yet my senses are amplified and everything seems sharper and clearer. I hear now the ding of cash registers, the squeak of my Topps sneakers against the polished floor, the syrupy tones of a Beautiful Music version of "My Cherie Amour" by Stevie Wonder suddenly loud in my ears. In my hand, the album now feels different, heavier, like an object of many meanings that will make amazing things happen.

Rock and Roll Will Set Me Free

I drive home feeling more comfortable in the giant car now, not dwarfed by it as I was before. I keep glancing over at the flat, square Korvettes bag on the seat next to me. When I have to stop short at a light, Mom's carton of cigarettes slides onto the floor, but I catch the record in time.

At home, I announce myself at the back door. There's no answer, only the sound of the television in the den blasting *The Odd Couple*. I hear a laugh track, but no laughter from my mother. She's always watching comedy shows and not laughing at them.

"I'm home," I repeat, raising my voice just slightly.

There's no answer. I put her cigarettes on the kitchen counter, then slip downstairs into the family room. I turn on the lights, settle on the arm of the Early American couch, press the power button on the stereo, and watch the console flicker awake behind the glass. I turn the knob to *Phono* and the vague little hum of feedback excites me. Is my hand shaking? I slip the album from its bag, then pull out my keys. On the key ring is my father's fingernail knife (stolen by me from his dresser box). I drag the blade though the cellophane a couple inches till I hit the thick paper band around the album. I rip away the cellophane and drop it on the basement floor where static electricity wilts it into the glittery linoleum. I slip the band off the LP, then flip open the gatefold to reveal a picture of a castle on a mountaintop with a glowing blue sky. Near the top of the mountain, a man holds one of the blond kids from the front cover over his head: a sacrifice.

I breathe in the chemical musk of ink, new cardboard, and plastic. I guess I'm prolonging this moment, savoring it. As I bend the cover back, the spine of the album stretches and creaks in a satisfying way. I slip my thumb and index finger into the slit on the right side of the cover and grab the record, encased in more of the thick embossed paper. I hold the large white square in both hands. The title of the album is printed in large letters at the top. I start to read the lyrics, but I'm too excited. I upend the sleeve, letting gravity slide the disc out, holding it the way my father taught me—middle finger suspended on the center label, thumb firm at the glossy edge. With my left hand, I remove the smoked Plexiglas turntable cover from the stereo and set it on the counter. I place the record on the turntable as if it were a gift.

I'm not exactly sure why, but I decide to play side B first. (I've heard "D'yer Mak'er" a lot on the radio.) I grab my father's headphones from one of the shelves, plug them in, and place them over my ears. I turn up the volume. I flick the *Manual On* lever and the turntable starts revolving. I raise the cue lever with my thumb, move the tone arm over, then lower the needle gently onto the shiny lip of the disc.

A click and then a whisper of hiss before the opening chords of "Dancing Days" boom into my ears. Jimmy Page's razor riff is so crisp and so loud and so satisfyingly off-kilter that I'm stunned by it at first. There is something about this riff that just makes me happy. Then Robert Plant comes in, so clear and casual, a kind of laughter to his voice:

Dancing days are here again
As the summer evenings grow
I got my flower, I got my power . . .

In that moment, when Robert Plant stretches the word—*pow-wur*—my heart swells. It's a revelation, a word I just learned from listening to Dale the hippie, who I'm finding out is pretty smart when he's not being mean. I'm sitting there on the arm of the Early American couch in the family room that my father built, my eyes closed, smiling so hard that my face aches.

Is that the way it should start?

Tonight everything feels different. I feel free. Free of my grief, free from the pain of my mother, free from the meanness of everyone in the world. I just want to stay in this moment with this couch and this stereo and this record.

I Discover the Fade

Something happens. I hear a slight fade in the music and I look at the record on the turntable, the Atlantic label spinning redgreenredgreenredgreen, and I can see that "Dancing Days" is almost over. As the song gets closer to ending, I panic. Then it ends and there's silence. I know there will be only a few seconds before the next song is on, but I jump up and lift the needle and play the song over again. It's still incredible. Yet before I know it, I hear that fade again. I play "Dancing Days" over and over and over. Each time, the song makes me feel so good, but when it starts to fade, it hurts in my bones. Then it starts to make sense to me after the sixth or seventh listening.

At first I decide that when you can hear a song start to fade, it makes you realize it'll be over soon and you'll never have that feeling again of hearing it for the first time. Though that doesn't quite make sense. I'd heard "Dancing Days" on the radio before and had no idea of how excellent it was, so I have to adjust my theory. I decide that sometimes it takes time before you really *feel* a song. Maybe you never do. Or maybe it's the tenth time you hear it that you finally, truly *feel* it, and something snaps in your heart and a jolt of pure happiness shoots through you better than all the dope in the world that anyone can force on you. That's when you know you love that song and you don't want it to go away.

Yet you also have to know that you only get so many listenings to a song before the love of it, the joy of it, the specialness of it, starts to trickle away. (Like when you hear a Top 40 song for the hundredth time.) So when you hear that fade start to happen, you know you can't ever hear that song in exactly the same way. Knowing that is like an ice ball in the nads. Because you're never going to feel the same way until the next excellent song comes along. And who knows when that will be?

Turns out, not very long with this album. After listening to "Dancing Days" at least a dozen times, I'm halfway through "No Quarter," going crazy over it too, when suddenly the earphones are pulled off my head. It scares me at first, then I see my mother standing over me, yelling. Her face is red and shiny, probably from Canadian Mist.

"What the hell are you doing, Danny?" Her voice is high and harsh. "I've been calling you and calling you!"

"What does it *look* like I'm doing?" I shout back. "I'm listening to *music!*" The tone and volume of my voice surprises me, but it surprises her even more.

"You're going to go deaf listening to it that loud."

I can't hide my anger like I usually do. I grab the headphones back from her. I don't hit her or push her or anything like that, but she seems shocked that I would dare to snatch them away like that. She looks at me for a moment as if she's not sure who she's talking to.

"Good," I say, spitting the words at her. "Being deaf would be better than listening to you."

She smacks me across the face, which she has never

done before, but I just sit there glaring at her, my face burning where she hit me. She doesn't know how much tougher I've gotten since high school and the Haus Shoppe. By tough, I just mean being able to take everyone else's punches and mean words, but I think that counts. I keep staring hard at her.

"I'm sorry, Danny."

I want to tell her it's okay. I want to say that I miss him too. I want to say that we're going to be fine. But I can't because I don't think we're going to be fine. I just stare at her. I put the earphones back on, but the song has ended.

I Go Free-Form

I spend less time down in the coal bin. I still build the model cars occasionally, but my room is my new sanctuary. I barricade myself there with the radio and my music magazines. I have to buy them all—*Creem*, *Circus*, *Rolling Stone*, *Crawdaddy*. I go crazy over FM radio. Every night, I fall asleep listening to the WABX disc jockeys playing whatever they feel like playing. Little Feat segues into Gil Scott-Heron which segues into Foghat which segues into Sun Ra which segues into Black Merda which segues into Canned Heat which segues into Tim Hardin which segues into Muddy Waters which segues into the Firesign Theatre which segues into the New York Dolls. (I also learn what the word *segue* means.) The sounds fill me up, the music nourishes me, gets me ready for the next grueling day at school and work.

I no longer listen to the Top 40 stations or anything on AM radio. I listen only to laid-back FM jocks—Mark, Dennis, Paul, Dave—Air Aces who talk slow, sometimes slurred, who don't care if they flub a song title or allow ten alarming seconds of clanking semisilence to go rustle through the stacks to find an album cover so they can read you the personnel. They play whole sides of an LP if they feel like it. I make sure to listen at around nine forty-five, when the evening jock makes way for the nighttime jock. *The Changeover*, they call it. Sometimes they rap for a half-hour. Most of the time, they talk about music, but one night the two jocks get in an argument about the difference between progressive FM radio and commercial radio. They talk about how AM is the worst kind of radio—the screaming DJs, the loud commercials, and worst of all, the awful popular music. I look up from the copy of *Creem* that I've been reading (an in-depth profile on post–Velvet Underground Lou Reed by Lester Bangs) to nod my head in agreement.

"*What's more important to you, man?*" says one of the jocks. "*A paycheck or the freedom to play anything you want on the air, anytime you want?*"

"*Obviously, I want to play anything I want. That's why I'm here.*"

"*But you get a paycheck, right?*"

"*And you don't?*"

"*I do. But we get to play what we want. We're not at the mercy of program directors or station managers.*"

"*No, but still, since we're both getting paid, and this radio station is funded by businesses and we still have to play commercials, it's a cop-out.*"

"*You mean I'm making this bogus salary and I'm still copping out?*"

"*Right on.*"

"*All right then, man. I quit.*"

"*Okay. Me too.*"

I listen to them both quit their jobs right there on the air. I just lie there on my bed staring at the radio, my mouth hanging open.

"*I hereby resign from WABX, the radio station formerly of your dreams.*"

"*Not responsible.*"

"*Not insane.*"

While the two of them quit, some other staff members of the station make their way into the studio to take over. Someone plays an entire side of Dylan's *Blonde on Blonde*.

First, I can't believe they actually quit their jobs because playing music on the radio sounds like the very best job in the world to me. Second, hearing them talk about working in radio makes me realize that if this is a job you could quit, it's also a job that someone could hire you to do.

I feel the direction of my life shift.

Autumn Contrasts '74

Fall term begins with another naked swim test (yay!), which I manage to pass, though I haven't gotten near the water for all three months of the summer. I do the full two laps, only faltering halfway through my second, but getting my stride back when I see the assistant start to reach for the pole. As I pull myself out of the pool, Coach Tillman glances at me only for a moment, but he seems pleased that I pass. Or maybe he's just happy that he won't have to look at me for another two semesters after what he had to tell me last year.

Of course, gym class won't be any better. From what I hear, it's a little football, lots of basketball, with occasional "free days" where we play slaughter-ball, the game of choice among tormentors and other mouth-breathers and knuckle-draggers.

Yet even after my triumphant swim test, I walk wet-haired to my classes with the song-ending, bummed-out feeling of the fade twisting around in my guts. The season of fall is cursed to me now. I think of last year and starting high school and my father coaxing me into driver's ed and the family room and the records and everything else. The air smells the same as it did then, and I recognize the way the sun shimmers both dark and light through the trees, the turning leaves closing like fists, fighting but still falling. Everything is the same. Except for me.

Sometime over the summer, my voice settled to its final timbre. It was already pretty low and then it just got lower. I sound like my father now. I know this because my mother has told me so. Sometimes it confuses her when I say something to her from another room, but these days a lot of things confuse her. I try to take care of her as best I can. I love her, but I now understand why my father disappeared into the basement so often. Other events of the summer include: full pubes, faint sideburns, longer hair, less chunkiness due to growing three more inches, erratic bonerism, and, oh yes, wet dreams. It would be more embarrassing were I not the one who does the laundry.

I'm taking a speech class this semester, which is being taught by one of our new teachers, a tall, lanky black woman by the name of Sherita Floyd, who is, well, beautiful. (I would say *foxy*, but this doesn't really sound right coming out of me, at least not yet.) So beautiful that I can barely speak to her at first. Which is not a great thing in a speech class, but luckily I get over it.

"Daniel," says Ms. Floyd (don't call her *Miss*) after I finish my very first class presentation, which is an extemporaneous speech about the zeppelin. (The airship, not the band.) "We're going to need to talk after class."

"Okay," I say, now absolutely convinced that my presentation was horrible and that I'm already in some sort of trouble. So stupid of me. When will I realize that nobody wants to hear about stupid Ferdinand von Zeppelin, inventor of the rigid airship, or the *Graf Zeppelin* (which flew over Detroit in the thirties) and its sneaky two-sided tail fin with a German flag on one side and a swastika on the other (after the Nazis became unpopular, it was mostly photographed on the flag side), or even the USS *Akron* being lost at sea, which was a much worse accident than the *Hindenburg*, just for the record.

After class, I show up at Ms. Floyd's desk. She is writing something in her class log. I stand there and look into her natural, which is lightish brown and round and perfect and just slightly glistening. Even filled with dread as I am, I'm also trying not to stare at the rest of her, wrapped in a shiny, clingy maroon dress. Finally, she finishes and looks up at me.

"Daniel Yzemski, you have an absolutely lovely speaking voice," she says.

This doesn't sound that bad so far. "Uh. Thank you," I respond. "Was there a problem with my speech?"

"No, not at all." She pauses for a moment to think. "It was very . . . *informative*. You certainly know a lot about zeppelins."

Looks like I'm not in trouble, though I do detect a certain lack of enthusiasm about rigid and semirigid airships.

"What I wanted to talk to you about was, are you aware that we're currently auditioning for someone to do the announcements on WRBG?" WRBG is our school radio station. (*Redford's Boys and Girls*, ahem.)

"No," I say. "I had no idea."

"It was right there on the speech club bulletin board. In any case, I think you should audition."

I've never tried out for anything in high school, but Ms. Floyd asking me to audition is like some sign from the radio gods telling me that I'm on the right track. I'm thrilled. My master plan is already working. Getting on the radio is why I'm taking a speech class in the first place.

"Okay. I'll do it," I say, amazed by the words coming out of my mouth. This is indeed a first. I have never exhibited anything even resembling high school pep.

"Auditions are today right after fifth period."

"Oh," I say, dejected.

"Can't make it?"

"No, it's just that I have to go to work then."

Ms. Floyd seems a little disappointed. "Well, it's up to you, Daniel. I just thought you should know. I think you'd be an excellent candidate." She starts flipping through her class log again. I guess I'm dismissed.

During my fifth period, I decide that work can wait, that it won't kill me to lose an hour's pay. I stand in line at the phone booth to call the hippies. Luckily, I get Dale, who's been laying off me a little lately, unlike Mitch.

"I have to stay after school for an hour, so I'm going to be late today," I tell him, making it sound like I have no choice. "It's pretty important."

To my surprise, Dale doesn't give me a hard time. Well, he gives me a little good-natured ribbing: "Uh-oh. Detention."

I appreciate that it's not mean, but I don't say anything anyway.

After the pause gets uncomfortable, he says, "All right, get here when you can. It's going to be a busy day."

"Thanks, Dale." I mean it. It's the first thing that I've said to him in months where I don't sound like a robot. I think maybe he notices.

"No sweat, Dan."

I'm amazed. No *dildo, crane, tard, fuckwad,* or *doofus*?

Dan.

Weird.

The Audition

I try to avoid reading aloud in front of the class because it calls attention to me. It's like a Boy Scout signal flare to tormentors: *I just realized I haven't slapped Yzemski upside the head for a week. I better get on that.* Yet the fact is, I'm quite good at it. I've been an excellent reader since kindergarten. My mother, for all her quirks, says that she read to me every day when I was a baby, then a toddler. Thanks to her, I could read well before I started kindergarten. At least that's what she tells me. I believe her, even though she does like telling stories where she ends up as the hero.

There are five other kids in Ms. Floyd's classroom after fifth period, three boys and two girls. I'm guessing that we were all encouraged by her to audition. We sit at desks that she's arranged in a semicircle, then she gives us each a mimeographed script with announcements on it.

"All right, everyone," she says. "I'd like you all to read the script that I've given you, one at a time."

No one mentions going in alphabetical order, but I'll still end up reading last (as usual) because I'm at the end of the semicircle. As the other kids read, I hear where the hard words are, where they stumble, so I make note of the same words when they appear in my script. I also hear what type of reading sounds good and what doesn't. I hear words that a newscaster would emphasize, so I decide to do that. Best of all, I have time to read over my script and become familiar with it. There are announcements about the chess club and the homecoming dance, and about a class trip. Nothing too difficult.

When we finally get to me, I make it through my entire script without one mistake. I am like a cross between Bill Bonds on *Action News* and an FM disc jockey, which is probably a weird combination, because Bill Bonds is kind of crazy and angry and an FM jock is spacey and laid-back, but I think it works.

"Now, I'd like you to exchange your script with the person next to you," says Ms. Floyd.

I exchange with a girl named Gina, who has never paid any attention to me in the past and manages to keep her record intact. She snatches my script and throws her own on my desktop like she's afraid of accidentally touching me and contracting some horrible nerd plague.

I read her script and only flub once. Other than that, I do it perfectly. I don't know why, but reading aloud calms me down. I'm conscious of the words coming from my mouth, but it doesn't matter. I can't pay attention to anything else when I'm reading aloud, which is good. The other kids are fine, but I can say with a certain amount of confidence (which is unusual for me, as you know) that I'm by far the best. From what I can see, my only real competition is a black kid named Alonzo, who is pretty decent.

After a few other reading drills, Ms. Floyd tells us that she will notify her selection for the announcer tomorrow. On the bus on my way to work, I can't help feeling a little excited. I try to tell myself that it doesn't matter if I get it or not since I did a good job, but I don't believe me when I tell myself that. Then I get to work and I have to focus on ignoring the hippies and making complete collections as fast as I can. I hear good songs from Argent, Steve Miller, Quicksilver Messenger Service, and cuts from the new Sparks and the new Fleetwood Mac, *Heroes Are Hard to Find*.

Shirts, Skins, and Me

The next morning, I am on my way to my second period, still recovering from the daily ordeal of gym class. (Is it a surprise that I'm not good at "Shirts vs. Skins" basketball? Perhaps this is due to the fact that I always end up being a Skin. Which leads me to the question: why does so much of boys' high school athletics involve nudity? Topless basketball. Naked swim tests. I'm afraid to think of what's next. Anyway, I'm walking down the hall with a really good Todd Rundgren jam called "Heavy Metal Kids" going through my head when Ms. Floyd corrals me.

"Daniel, I need to talk to you," she says, pulling me aside. Kids are passing by, looking at us. My first thought, as always, is that I'm in trouble. Second thought is how my hair is all wet and messy. I didn't really get a chance to comb it. Third thought is how Ms. Floyd's natural glows around her face like a picture I've seen of a saint or someone like that.

"Congratulations, Daniel," she says to me, reaching to shake my hand. "You're our new WRBG announcer."

"I am? I thought we'd find out later," I say, too stunned to be happy, but still shaking her hand.

She raises her eyebrows, confused at my comment. "This *is* later. You're finding out *now*." She puts her hand on my shoulder and it feels cool and smooth. Her fingers are long and shiny and bronze-colored, her nails glossy maroon. "Come on, you're going to be late for second-period announcements."

"We're doing it right now?" I say, quickly going from stunned to nervous. I try to swallow, but I can't.

"Yes we are, Daniel. I've already notified your second-period teacher and told her that you'll be late coming to class every day. After the announcements, you'll proceed *directly* to your class, understand?"

I nod. We start heading to the WRBG studio. She

takes off with authority, talking to me as she walks.

"You're actually going to be a music director too, so if you can, you should provide music to play as an intro. I hope you'll play music that all the kids will like."

"Are you kidding?" I can't believe what I'm hearing. I had no idea. "I get to play records?"

She points one of those fingers at me. "A little music at the beginning just to get everyone's attention. No songs about drugs or sex."

My face starts getting hot. I run up to a water fountain and take a quick drink.

Ms. Floyd looks at me, concerned. "Are you okay, Daniel? I know this is sudden, but I thought you'd be pleased."

I wipe my face with my sleeve and nod again, amazed at the fact that my master plan is actually working.

"I am pleased," I say. "I really am."

My Life as a Radio Personality

My first day on the air goes okay. At the beginning of the show, Mr. Beckler plays the Redford fight song from a scratchy old record. Then I read all the announcements without messing up once. Ms. Floyd and Mr. Beckler, who co-manage the station, are watching me and they seem pretty impressed.

"Well done, Danny," says Mr. Beckler.

"Very nice," adds Ms. Floyd.

"Especially since you had no time to prepare."

Ms. Floyd gives Mr. Beckler a little glance, then turns back to me. "That's radio. Come on, let's give you a tour of the station."

This doesn't take long. It involves me standing in

the middle of the tiny studio while they point out the turntable, a small beat-up cassette recorder/player, the microphone, two sets of headphones, potentiometers, patchboard (so many cords sticking out of it), and other controls. I notice a shelf with sound-effects albums that look like they're from the 1950s. I don't mention that while I'm happy about doing the announcements, the fact that I get to choose the music to *intro* and *outro* the show (new words, along with *pots*, which are potentiometers for short) makes me really excited. That, and the fact that I get to sign off with my name. I decide to go with Daniel Yzemski. A good choice, I think. The only thing I didn't like was today's music. That's got to go.

When I walk into class late, I feel different. A couple kids look at me as I take my seat and I wonder if they know that it was me they just heard on the radio. And yes, I know that it's actually a PA system and not radio, but still.

Good Times, Bad Times

When I get home, the first thing I do is find my mother. She's in the living room watching the Channel 7 *Action News*.

"Guess what?" I say from the doorway.

My mother is talking to the newscaster Bill Bonds, who is reporting about some sort of busing decision that was made over the summer. "Oh, for Christ's sake, this again?" she says. "They are *not* shipping our kids to these black neighborhoods. When are they going to stop this nonsense?"

Stupidly, I keep speaking: "I'm on the school radio station."

"Between this and that son of a bitch Coleman Young telling all the whites to get out of Detroit, I don't know what the hell is going on. Good Christ."

I look at the glass of Canadian Mist and Uptown sweating on the end table next to her. "Did you hear me?" I say.

She's still looking at the TV. "What?"

I walk into the living room, turn the sound down, and stand in front of the TV.

"What are you doing?" she says, peeved, trying to look around me.

"Something good happened today. I got chosen to be on the school radio station. They chose me."

Finally, my mother is listening. "They chose *you*?"

I don't like the way she says this, as if there must have been some sort of mistake.

"Yes. I'm the new voice of WRBG. I do the second-period announcements. I'm music director too."

She actually smiles at me. As if she has just realized, *My son has achieved something and this reflects well upon me*. "Well. That is good. I didn't even know your school had a radio station."

"They do and I'm on it."

"Who chose you?" Again, that mistake sound, but less of it this time.

"My speech teacher, Ms. Floyd."

"She's one of those *Ms.'s*, is she?"

"Yeah," I say. "She's nice. She encouraged me."

"Well, I can't believe you actually tried out for something."

"Neither can I," I say, kind of chuckling.

"I'm . . . I'm proud of you, Daniel." It sounds like it's

a chore for her to get it out, but she does it. Then I think it occurs to both of us who would have been the most proud. I watch sadness wash over my mother's face. I'm sure I look the same.

"I just did the first announcements today," I say, swallowing, trying to salvage the moment. "Everyone said I did a really good job."

"I didn't even know you liked to do that sort of thing." I watch her eyes flicker back to the TV.

"Yeah," I say before I think about it too much. "I think it's what I want to do."

She turns back to me, confused. "What do you mean?"

"I think I want to be on the radio, like a disc jockey." I don't mean to reveal my master plan so soon, but it seems like a good time.

"You can't go to college to do that."

"Why can't I?"

"That's not why you go to college. You go to college to do something substantial."

"Being on the radio isn't substantial?"

She's not looking at the television now. "No. Babbling into a microphone isn't substantial. You're a sensitive boy. You should be an artist. Don't you want to play music yourself? You could be a classical musician, instead of that junk you listen to."

"My music is not junk," I say, getting annoyed now. "Besides, I tried the violin. You forced it on me when I was seven. I was horrible at it."

"Because you didn't practice."

"You didn't like it when I practiced. It gave you a headache. *Everything* gave you a headache." This is what I get for revealing my plan too soon.

"That's beside the point. You could have stuck with it."

"I want to be on the radio and I'm going to be."

"This is ridiculous, Daniel. I won't allow it."

When she says that, I don't exactly know what happens, except that I raise my voice: "You won't *allow* it? Why the hell do you get to say?" I'm getting her attention now.

"You watch your mouth, young man."

"What do you even know about any of this?" I yell. "Have you ever even had a job? You could be working somewhere right now. Instead, you sit around here and mope and drink and complain about hippies and women's lib and black people."

"You be quiet, Daniel," says my mother, her voice breaking.

"At least they're doing something. They're trying to change things. You've just given up."

"I said be quiet!"

"I'm not going to be quiet. I know what I want to do and you're not stopping me. So *you* be quiet!"

I realize that I am now screaming at my mother. The sound of my own voice scares me. That's about when she starts crying.

"You don't know about anything," she says, sobbing. At least I think she says that—she's got her hands over her nose and mouth.

I look down at my own hands. They're shaking. I sit down next to her. "I'm sorry, Mom," I say to her in my softest voice. I put my hand on her back. There's hardly any flesh there, just bones and sinew and housecoat.

"I want to do something," she says between sobs. "No one wants me to work for them. There are all kinds of young girls out there who went to college. Everyone gets to do what they want."

"No they don't, Mom."

"I'm useless."

"You're not useless."

"I *am* useless. I don't know how to do anything. All anyone ever said to me was, *Get married. Have a family. Your husband will take care of you.*" She coughs.

"He did take care of us," I say, trying to keep from crying myself. "Nobody wanted Dad to die."

We're both quiet. "Sometimes I did," she says in a low voice.

I take my hand off her back. "Mom."

"Sometimes I just wanted to be able to leave, to go somewhere and be free of everything and everyone."

"Even me?"

My mother doesn't say anything. She just keeps crying. I notice the ring of grime around the collar of her housecoat. After a minute or two, she looks back up at the television. I stand and turn up the volume again. Then I go to my room and put on some music.

The Green Manalishi

Despite all my worries about us running out of money and losing the house, we didn't end up in the poor farm over the summer. In fact, I actually spent some money on clothes and albums. (The first four Zeppelin albums, among others.) I figured it was okay since I was working so many extra hours. Even though I have a few LPs now, I know I can't rely on my collection to use at the station. I'm also afraid to take them to school. So after work on Saturday, I head to the public library on Fenkell. I spent a lot of time there over the summer when I wasn't working, just to get out of the house. It was cool and quiet and a good place to read, but they also let you take out record albums. So I take out as many rock LPs as they'll let me. (The librarians know me so they bend the rules a little.) They have a decent collection, though most of it is a few years old. Still, I can't be fussy.

I also start using my cassette recorder at home to tape music from the radio. I record whole blocks of music. This gives me a chance to study the style of the disc jockeys and the things they say. Mr. Beckler teaches me about bringing in tapes *cued up* to the songs I want to play. I'm only playing about thirty seconds of music at the beginning of the show and thirty after I sign off, so it almost doesn't matter where the music comes in, but it matters to me.

About two weeks after I start doing the announcements, I record a block of songs on WABX when they play "The Green Manalishi (With the Two Prong Crown)" by Fleetwood Mac. It's a rare song to hear, from when they were a blues band. So the next day, before the announcements I play almost the first minute of the song—those great, chugging, repetitive guitar riffs, all with this eerie ambience of evil about it.

Bustin' in on my dreams
Makin' me see things I don't wanna see . . .

I'm bobbing my head along with it and it's such an excellent tune that I read the announcements better than I ever have. For the outro, we let it play out to where the guitar gets jangly and distorted and there's a creepy ghoulish sound that whines through the fade, and that's where we pot it down.

Mr. Beckler, who is always in the studio while I'm there, doesn't say anything except, "Good job, Danny," so I guess it's okay with him.

After second period lets out, I'm at my locker when I see someone coming toward me. It's John Tedesco, a kid I knew from elementary school. We used to say hi to each other then, but when we got to high school he grew about a foot, acquired an air of coolness, and stopped acknowledging me. (Which leads me to ask: Is height proportional to cool? If so, is this correlated to pubes, buoyancy, and aquadynamics? Discuss.) He swaggers through the hall, at least a head taller than most everyone, but not self-conscious about it. He's the exact opposite of me; I pudgily, invisibly lurk the halls, sliding through the bodies (I am slowly regaining my sonar), avoiding eye contact, trying to stay clear of tormentors and everyone else.

Today, John walks right up to me. He's at least six five, with a frizzy-brown, white-kid Afro high in the forehead. My guess is that he needs to wear the army surplus jacket since he requires extra-tall clothes. His jeans are a little short like mine (I bought my first pair over the summer, and then promptly shrunk them in the wash), but perfectly ragged enough so you don't notice. He wears the kind of flannel shirt that even I'm wearing now, but better somehow.

"Hey, man," he says, flicking my shoulder with the back of his hand, "you play that music on WRBG?"

I nod, not sure where this is going. "Yeah?"

"Dig it. 'Green Manalishi.' Excellent song."

It takes me a moment to realize that he's complimenting me. "Oh. Yeah. It is."

"You like that early Fleetwood Mac?"

I nod again, excited that someone appreciates my musical tastes, especially someone who had previously ignored me.

"Peter Green, Jeremy Spencer. So excellent. Way better than that wimpy West Coast shit they're doing now."

I surprise myself by disagreeing. "Really? I like the Bob Welch stuff." Apparently, I have an opinion about this.

He makes a face. "Aw, man. You don't know what you're talking about," he says. "Come on. Christine McVie is a fox, but her songs are so girlie."

I am stung, but don't back down. I make a dismissive noise and frown at him. "You hear *Mystery to Me*? 'Hypnotized' is a great song."

He breathes loudly through his nose, almost snorting. "All right, that's a good song, but I still think you're better off with the old shit."

I think maybe he likes that I'm arguing with him. I like it too. We start talking about Danny Kirwan, the link between the two Fleetwood Macs. Just then, I feel like I'm a member of a club where I know the secret handshake and I didn't even know that I knew it. Neither of us want to end the conversation, but the halls are starting to empty around us.

"You ever go over to the Mouse House on Grand River?" asks John. "They got *Melody Maker* direct from England."

"Are you kidding?" I say, thrilled to hear someone be all excited about this kind of thing. "I've never seen one. I've just read about it in *Creem*."

"No shit, man. They got it. The British magazines are excellent. *Creem*'s good, *Crawdaddy*'s okay, *Circus* is a joke—teenybopper shit. But *Melody Maker* and *New Musical Express* are where it's at."

"Wow. Okay. Thanks."

"You want to go over there after school?"

I want to so bad, but I know I can't. "I gotta go to work," I say.

John looks at the watch on the wide leather strap on his wrist. "We could cut class and head over there right now."

"Really?"

"Yeah, sure. Why not?"

I shrug. "I don't know. We'll get in trouble?"

His *pffft* tells me that he's disgusted by the very notion of this. "Haven't you noticed? No one gives a shit around here."

"Yeah?"

"Sure, man. I do it all the time."

The idea of this both terrifies and excites me. I have never cut class in my entire life. I have always been a model of good attendance and student citizenship. Then it occurs to me: where has it gotten me? I became bully bait. Not only that, but who's going to punish me even if I get caught cutting class? My mother? The woman who wished I wasn't there? Who barely reads the mail? I've been writing the checks for our gas and electric and phone ever since I noticed the warnings coming in the mail. I have to drive her to the bank to put money in the checking account. I was afraid they were going to turn off our electricity and I wouldn't be able to play the stereo. We'd be living in the dark with even more rotten food than usual.

"Come on, Yzemski," he says, twitching his head toward the door. "Let's book."

Before I can think on this further, the period bell rings and John pulls me toward the side door, where we slip out onto Westbrook Street. We walk past the kids out there smoking cigarettes. I smell something else too; I think it's marijuana. I can see the 8th Precinct, half a block away up on Grand River. I want to say, *You're smoking marijuana and there's a building full of police across the street! Are you people crazy?* Luckily, I manage to keep this thought to myself.

"Step it up, Yzemski." I'm realizing that John is kind of bossy.

As we walk, I have a hard time keeping up with his long strides, so I pick up my pace. He narrows his eyes at me. "So what do you think of the new Tull?"

I haven't even read the reviews of *War Child* yet. I've been expecting my latest *Creem* any day in the mail. "I just heard a couple of cuts. 'Skating Away.' 'Bungle in the Jungle.' I like it. At least it's not one giant song, like their last two albums."

He takes this in. "You didn't like *A Passion Play*?"

"Not really. I liked *Thick as a Brick* okay. Least there was a couple of decent cuts from it." *Uh-oh*, I think. Here we go.

"Fuckin'-A. Concept albums are horrible. Ponderous. Pretentious."

I get the feeling that he's showing off a little, trying out those words on me. I mostly agree, but that's not what I say. "What about *Tommy*?" I say. "By the Who?"

"What about it?"

"That's a concept album. You hate that too?" I'm still trying to keep up. Man, he walks fast.

John looks at me like he's trying to figure me out. I

get the feeling he's used to everyone just automatically agreeing with him. I'm surprised *I'm* not automatically agreeing with him. He says everything with such authority, it's hard not to agree, yet I'm not. I'm just so happy to be talking about music with someone, I'm hardly even thinking about cutting class. Hardly.

"Right on. 'Pinball Wizard' and shit. But *Tommy*'s got actual songs in it."

I'm barely noticing where I'm going. I have to make sure not to trip. "So does *Thick as a Brick*."

John looks like he's almost mad, then he throws his hands up. "Yeah, I guess so, but with Tull, it doesn't feel like it. The songs all run into each other, all dainty, like one boring long-ass folk song. Where's the guts? Where's the balls?" He shakes his fists in front of him. "Where's the fuckin' rock and roll?"

I like how he's really getting worked up about this. It's making me the same way. "You're right," I say. "I like Tull when they play *rock*. Like on *Aqualung*."

John shakes his head real fast. "*Aqualung* is a fucking masterwork." He stops there in middle of the sidewalk just as we reach Grand River, midday traffic roaring in front of us, and starts singing in a gravelly British accent: "*Sit-ting on a park bench*—" Then he sings in the riffs through his teeth while windmilling an imaginary guitar in his hands. "*Eyeing lit-tle girls with bad intent!*"

"*Snot run-ning down his nose!*" I sing back to him, trying to keep from cracking up. "*Greasy fin-gers smearing shabby clo-o-thes!*"

We both start laughing there on the sidewalk like a couple of maniacs.

He stops suddenly and looks at me, real seriously, as

if to see if I'm ready for what he's about to say. "I'm going to write for *Melody Maker* someday."

"Yeah?"

"Yeah."

"Cool." It's the first time I've said that word aloud. *Cool*.

We jaywalk across Grand River and end up right near the police station. It occurs to me: Are there still truant officers? Could I get arrested for cutting class? I'm worried but John doesn't seem to even notice. I glance over at the goofy sculpture of the massive car horn with an eight ball on the bulb. There are giant blue Tiffany lampshades on poles next to it. I don't understand that art.

We keep moving until we pass the fire station, where a couple firemen are outside with the door open. They look at us. A short, heavy guy yells, "Shouldn't you two be in school?"

Oh my god, I think. *This is it. We're caught. My life is over*. I don't know what to do. Filled with panic, I turn to John.

He shakes his head and calls over to the fireman, "No school today, man. There was a mini race riot."

The guy frowns at us. We keep walking. Nothing happens.

I repeat: *Nothing happens*. This is amazing to me.

The thing about our school is we actually do have race riots. Little ones just every once in a while. Basically, some white kids will get into a scuffle with some black kids. Someone yells, *Nigger!* then someone yells, *Honky!* and next thing you know, there's a fight. Other kids usually don't join in, but sometimes they do. Mostly everyone watches. Except for me. I get out of there.

"I've already talked to someone at *Creem* about an internship," says John.

"Wow. That would be excellent."

"I know."

"You ever talk to Lester Bangs? He's my favorite writer."

John looks at me like he's wondering if he can get away with lying, then says, "Nah. Just their office manager."

"Oh."

"I've written a couple record reviews for them, but they're not out yet."

"For what?"

"One of 'em for an obscure Stooges import. You probably haven't heard of it. Pretty hard to get ahold of."

Even though I think he may be lying, I don't say anything. I don't really know that much about imported albums, only that they usually have glossy, desirably flimsy British cardboard jackets. We walk farther up Grand River toward an old house painted purple and pink and blue in a psychedelic pattern, which is now faded and peeling. I've seen it from the bus, but didn't know what it was. The sign has Mickey Mouse on it, only with a long warty nose and sharp teeth.

Mouse House
Head Supplies

I follow John through a peach-colored door. Inside, it's like someone moved the furniture out of an old house so someone else could start a store there. Lots of bare floor space, but the walls are full of posters—W.C. Fields, the Marx Brothers, Uncle Sam asking, *Have YOU had your pill today*? Also, crazy paintings of mountains and seagulls and a pair of shoes that look like feet. The air is hazy with incense like a church with BO. Off to the right, in a dark room which may have once been a bedroom, I can make out posters glowing blue and red and yellow on the wall. I see one with a cartoon of a melting hippie with a caption under it that says, in liquidy letters: *Stoned Agin!*

We pass an old-fashioned wood-and-glass display case with a guy sitting behind it, his worn-at-the-heel army boots up on the cracked, taped countertop. He's got frizzy black hair parted directly down the middle and a droopy mustache, and he's reading a little newspaper called the *Fifth Estate*. He glances up at John. I hear Iron Butterfly playing from somewhere in the room.

"Hey, man," he mutters, like he doesn't really want to say it.

"Hey, Donnie," John says. "What's happening?"

"Same ol' shit sandwich. Another day, another bite."

"Hey," I say, just to be friendly.

The hippie says nothing. He just looks at me in my plaid Kmart shirt and my Topps sneakers and my too-short Big Yank dungarees (as my mother calls them). I recognize the look. It's the look I get from the hippies at work and from kids at school. I'd hoped longer hair and new clothes would stop the look from happening. It does happen less at school now. Being on the radio station helps. Yet this guy, this hippie Donnie, he can tell I'm trying desperately to fit in. That's why he's giving me the look. The dreaded *narc* look.

Narc. Last year, I'd been called that a bunch of times and didn't understand what it meant, only knowing that it was interfering with my attempts to walk the halls unnoticed. Then, right before summer vacation, some long-haired kid threw a crumpled note at me in biology class. I opened it up and it said: *Die narc.*

"Why do they keep calling me that?" I said under my breath.

I heard a sigh from next to me. It was Jill Orr, the hippie girl who was my lab partner in biology. She wore feathered earrings and velvet jackets and patterned silk blouses and seemed to float around in a cloud of flowery-sweet musk oil. She was so beautiful it made my eyes hurt, but that may have just been her perfume. I was thrilled that she was forced to interact with me. She, unfortunately, was less than thrilled.

"You look like a pig, man," she said.

"A pig?"

"A cop. A narcotics cop. A narc."

"*That's* what that means?" At first, I was kind of flattered that I looked like a police officer, someone strong who no one picks on, then I realized I wasn't supposed to feel that way.

She nodded without looking at me the way she usually did, like on TV where spies meet to exchange information but don't want to look like they're talking to each other. "Yeah, dumbfuck. The police send kids into the schools to rat out the kids selling drugs."

"And they think I'm *that*?"

She finally turned to me briefly, eyes scanning me, head to shoes. "What do you expect? You got that short hair and them nerdy clothes. It's like the cops dressed you. You *look* like a narc." Then her eyes met mine. "Are you?"

"No," I said, half mad, half crushed. My face was burning. "I ain't no stinkin' snitch." She stared at me when I said that phrase, cribbed straight from *The Bowery Boys*. I wasn't sure if she was impressed or had just decided that I was an even bigger weirdo.

At that point, I knew I had the money to buy some new clothes and that my mother wouldn't care if I grew my hair. I just didn't think that stuff mattered so much. It made me mad to think that it did. Then I realized that no one cared what I thought. That was when I became determined to survive high school.

And now, here at the incense-and-BO-reeking Mouse House, run by a disgruntled hippie, I see the next logical step in my master plan to fit in (which I have folded into my master plan to become a DJ since I'll never get a job in radio if everyone thinks I'm a narc). Straight ahead, I see a rack of T-shirts with the names and pictures of bands on them. Bands that I like. There's a handwritten sign right over them lettered in purple ink: *Git yer shirt t'gether!*

Cool blue and yellow and cream-colored T-shirts with names of bands on them like *Blue Öyster Cult*, *Edgar Winter Group*, *the Kinks*, and *J. Geils.* I want to head there, but John directs me to a table where there are magazines and newspapers spread out in small stacks—*Zap Comix*, *The Fabulous Furry Freak Brothers*, *Weirdo*, as well as *Creem*, *Melody Maker*, and *New Musical Express*.

"Check it out, Yzemski." John picks up a copy of *New Musical Express*. The headline on the cover is about T. Rex, who I like okay, but know are really popular in England. I had read about them in *Circus*, but I don't tell John that.

I pick up the newspaper and open it. I see an article about David Bowie written by Nick Kent. I'd read his articles in *Creem*. I hear a cough from somewhere in the store.

Just then, John grabs the paper from my hand and refolds it. He shakes his head and whispers to me, "Don't read them. He doesn't like it."

Without thinking, I glance up at the hippie glaring at me from behind the counter.

"We're going to take this *NME*, Donnie," says John, holding it up.

"Fuckin' better. It's not a fuckin' library, man."

"We know." Then under his breath, he says to me, "Don't get me banned. The guy's apeshit about people reading the magazines and not buying them."

I nod my head like crazy. I don't want to get banned either, now that I've discovered this place. I look over at Donnie the angry hippie and try to smile.

"How much are the T-shirts?"

He stops scowling. "Four bucks each."

I walk over to the rack to look at a blue Led Zeppelin. On the front is the picture of the *Hindenburg* crashing that I recognize from their first album, which I love. I pull the shirt off the rack and hold it up on the hanger to examine it closer. It's a large. "I'm gonna take this one," I say, putting it on the counter.

"My man's got good taste. They're three for ten."

John pipes up just then: "Come on, man. Zeppelin? So bogue. Plodding, bloated, overhyped riff rock ripped off from American genius blues artists. Come *on*."

I turn to him. "You don't know what you're talking about. Led Zeppelin is excellent. Just because the magazines don't like them, you don't like them."

I surprise myself by summing up John Tedesco and dismissing him with one sentence. He knows I'm right too, because his face turns red and he looks back down at the cover of a *Melody Maker*. I pick out a Blue Öyster Cult T-shirt in yellow and a tan Who shirt. Smirking, Donnie packs them all in a brown paper sack along with the *New*

Musical Express. At this moment, I feel like I have the secret of coolness in my hand.

"Enjoy, man," he says to me, head nodding, almost smiling. I may have redeemed myself in Donnie's eyes, bloodshot as they are.

Now that I've made my purchases, I walk around the store a little more. I glance again toward the dark room where I notice a different poster glowing red, green, and orange this time, one that looks like a chart of men and women screwing in different positions of the zodiac. I'm a little scared to go into that room so I keep walking. Behind a different display case, I see objects that remind me of when my elementary school class took a trip to Greenfield Village, where we saw a demonstration of the art of glass-blowing. In this display case, there are long colored-plastic cylinders standing on their ends, along with an assortment of fancy tweezers.

"Need some paraphernalia?" says Donnie, walking over to me.

I've never heard this word. I look over at John, who is now checking out the T-shirts himself. He's holding up a Slade shirt, which surprises me.

"Paraphernalia?" I say, not entirely sure I can get it out the right way.

"Yeah, man. Smoking paraphernalia." He says it and I can hear the suspicion creep back into his voice.

"Right." Finally it occurs to me that this has to do with drugs. But instead of feeling scared about being near something drug-related, I'm actually more scared that I'm doing things a narc would do. "Nah, man. I'm cool," is what I say. It's something that I heard from a movie, or from Mitch and Dale, I can't remember where. Regardless, it seems to amuse Donnie.

"Oh, are you *cool*?" he says in a sort of *hardy-har-har* way. "Yeah, you're cool all right, man."

Suddenly the bag I'm holding feels a lot lighter. John joins me at the counter, holding a copy of *Creem* and an Amon Düül II T-shirt. I've vaguely heard of this band and from the look of the T-shirt, I don't want to know more about them. The front of it has gloomy-looking trees on it and the words *Phallus Dei*.

Now that we're standing next to each other, Donnie stares at the two of us together. Me, small and on the husky side, and John, tall and reed thin. "Look at you two," he says with a phlegmy laugh. "Fuckin' Mutt and Jeff!"

From somewhere in the room, I hear an endless drum solo.

I Miss the Bus

At the bus stop on my way to work, I am still buzzing with excitement over cutting class, over my victory on the school radio station, over my meeting a cool new friend who seems to bring out smartness in me that I'd never noticed before, over my purchases of clothing that may actually make me look like less of a narc. I am at the bus stop a little early, standing with my books and bag of treasures, not even minding that I'm going to work where I'm going to have to ignore Mitch and Dale while they make fun of me. I'm standing toward the back of the bus stop area, away from everyone else, just barely close enough to look like I'm waiting for the bus. Redford High has no actual bus shelter on Grand River, only an area by a sign where the grass has been worn away by generations of dazed, milling students, walking like lemmings into the bus that leads them to the suicide sea. (Okay, I didn't know what a lemming was until I heard some of National Lampoon's *Lemmings* on WABX. Amazing what you can learn from FM radio.) Depending on the weather, the dirt is either cracked and hard-caked or greasy and muddy, like it is today.

In front of me, there are a group of black kids talking loudly who I've never seen at the bus stop before. One of them is short and has a medium Afro and is wearing a black-and-gold dashiki with a turtleneck dickey beneath it. (Ms. Floyd offered an extemporaneous speech about her dashiki one day after we gave speeches. Mine was about the *National Lampoon*, which I had just coincidentally discovered.) He is obviously entertaining the others, almost like a comedy routine, or at least it seems that way to me. He's doing what I think is a caricature of a show-off and it's pretty funny.

"You *know* how bad I am," he says to one of his friends, a tall kid with a giant Afro with a red-and-green pick sticking out from the back, who is nodding and laughing like he can't stop himself. "Thomas know how bad I am," the kid says, bobbing his head now. "He know. He know I'm the baddest." Thomas is doubled over now, laughing so hard that he's not even making any noise as his friend struts around like a bantam. "I feel sorry for y'all. None of you sad motherfuckers can achieve this level of bad-a-tude." Then he leans back and presses his flared-out fingers against his chest. "I mean, damn, look at this. I'm *Black Belt Jones* bad!"

I'm watching and listening and I'm feeling like, *He's right. He is bad.* But instead of keeping my head down and quietly minding my own business like I usually do waiting for the bus, I find myself looking over at the kid and nodding and smiling, just like his friends. He's really funny. And when he glances over at me, I feel like I'm part of all of them, because I'm in on the joke. Then I see the expression on his face change.

"What you lookin' at, white boy?"

I don't know what to say to this.

"I said, what the *fuck* you lookin' at?" All his friends stop laughing.

I decide that I should probably say something. "I was just . . . I just thought you were being funny."

"You laughing at me?" His face is stern now, his lips tight against his teeth, his mouth just a slit. "Laughing at *me*, motherfucker?"

I halfheartedly point at his friends, my face now so red that it actually hurts. "We were all laughing . . ."

He walks up to me, presses his hand against my chest. "Look at this fuckin' white boy, standing here with his *lunch*." He makes a big show of staring down at the bag in my hand. "What, Mommy make that for you? That a big-ass lunch!" He turns to his friends and they are laughing again. The few other kids at the bus stop, both black and white, start to slowly separate themselves from us.

Before I can even correct him, he snatches the bag from my hands. "What the fuck is this shit?" He pulls out the *New Musical Express* and throws it on the ground. "Fuckin' newspaper?" Then he reaches the T-shirts. "*Aww*. Somebody been shoppin'."

Before throwing down the bag, he pulls out the Blue Öyster Cult T-shirt and holds it up to his chest with his pinkie fingers sticking out, and sashays around. "Look at this faggot shit. Blue Öyster *Cunt*. Fuckin' faggot white boy." He throws the T-shirt on the ground and stomps on it. Then the bus shows up.

"Fuckin' little pussy." He picks up the bag with the other T-shirts, throws it under the bus, then he and his friends get on. Everyone else gets on the bus too, as though nothing at all has happened.

I kneel down to gather up the newspaper and my T-shirt that is now filthy from being stomped into the muck of the bus stop. When I look up, the black kid and all his friends are in the bus, making faces at me with their middle fingers up against the glass. As the bus pulls away, I run into traffic to grab the bag with my remaining T-shirts. A lavender Metropolitan cab honks and almost hits me, but I get the shirts.

That night, with the deadly fade crushing down on me, I take them all home to wash, but I know that I'll never wear the Blue Öyster Cult. It will just stay in my drawer. While the washing machine chugs away, I tell myself, *Okay, at least you didn't cry*.

I've Got the Music in Me

I can feel it happening. Despite the setback at the bus stop, I can feel music changing me, though I'm not exactly sure how. Perhaps it's the way it has helped me at home, with the exhausting task of handling my mother. Or how it's helped me to know my future life's work as a disc jockey. Maybe it's the magazines and how they've shown me how to look less like a narc, how to talk cool, how to maybe someday get a girl to like me. I feel as though music is showing me the way, sharing its secrets with me. Apparently, it's also given me a friend.

The period after I read the announcements, John usually meets up with me. Today, he is not pleased.

"Yzemski man, why you playin' that Top 40 shit?"

I played "Smokin' in the Boys Room" by Brownsville Station for the intro to the announcements. I recorded it from the radio. It sounded great, and I sounded pretty good myself. One tiny flub in four minutes. Not bad.

I roll my eyes at him as one would to a parent. "It's a good song. I don't care if it's in the Top 40. I like those guys."

He shakes his head exaggeratedly. "No, no, no!"

It's actually pretty funny. This sort of thing is starting to become a routine with us. John tends to hate a lot of what I play on the school radio station. "You are such a snob," I say.

He loves to get all exasperated with me. "I just have good taste in music, turkey."

"Snob."

"What are you gonna play tomorrow? Chicago?" He holds his clenched fist up near his face as if it were a microphone, then contorts his mouth like some hokey lead singer. "*Feeling stronger every daaaay! Lord almightaaay!*"

I start laughing. He looks at me, trying not to crack up. "You're a fucking pussy, Yzemski."

This only makes me laugh more. We head down the hallway to the side door out of the school. It's Thursday, the day that the new issue of *New Musical Express* shows up at the Mouse House and needs to be purchased by one of us. That person gets to pore over it first, then pass it along to the other one. We cut class every Thursday. So far there have been no repercussions from cutting English class. I wonder if maybe Mr. Acitelli isn't reporting it because he doesn't want me to get into trouble. He was one of the few teachers who said anything to me after my dad died. Most of the rest of them barely know my name unless they're looking at it on the seating chart.

It's like John says: no one's really paying attention. The older teachers are skating by until they can retire and get out of Detroit like a lot of the white people. They don't say it aloud, but I can hear it in their voices, feel it in the looks they give to the black kids. *I'm putting up with you because I'll be gone soon.* As far as skipping class goes, sure, maybe I'll get caught if they call, if they send a letter to the house, but my mother's not paying attention either.

John and I walk in silence along Grand River for a while. "You hear the new Traffic?" he finally says to me.

"Yeah, they played a few cuts yesterday on W-4 at work. It's good."

"It's really good, man. 'Walking in the Wind'? That is a righteous jam."

"Not as good as 'Low Spark,' but pretty great."

"True. 'Low Spark' is a masterwork."

"Yeah."

More silence till we get to the Mouse House, where Donnie guffaws and calls us Mutt and Jeff. I think we may be the highlight of his week. All signs seem to indicate that Donnie is always stoned on marijuana. Yet I have not seen him go schizo, not even once.

Talking to Television

Mini race riot on Friday. Just a little skirmish out on the lawn of the school at the end of fourth period. I'm standing at the window in speech class with some other kids, watching from the second floor. There are a couple of white guys swinging at a couple of black guys, not much actual fighting going on, with some other kids, black and white, running around like they're going to kick each others' butts. I can't tell who's winning. I'm just glad I'm not down there.

"Oh dear. This is not good," says Ms. Floyd, joining us at the window for a moment. She then rushes out of the room, her platforms clonking fast against the linoleum.

It's hard to guess what starts them. Every so often, something just happens. Someone says something, bumps into someone, and before you know it—mini race riot. Generally, everyone gets along—kind of together, but kind of separately. The black kids hang out with each other and mostly sit together in class. Sometimes you'll see a white kid walking down the hall with a bunch of black kids, yet it's rare. Even when those black kids at the bus stop were mean to me, I didn't like it, but they were just being jerks. Usually, the black kids leave me alone. I'll tell you one thing: they never call me *narc*.

When I get home, I don't tell Mom about the mini race riot because it will just get her all worked up. This still happens most nights when she watches the eleven o'clock news. Everything that Bill Bonds says gets her so riled that she just ends up yelling at the television, cursing the new mayor, saying, *We're moving the hell out of this goddamn city, Danny, before they burn it down again.* She acts like I'm there next to her, even though I'm usually locked up in my room by this time.

Before my father died, they would both sit in front of the television talking to it, griping about what they thought was happening to Detroit. It was mostly my mother, but to be fair, it was my dad too. If I was still awake, I would just turn up the radio in my room. I didn't like it when they talked that way, though I kind of understood why they were scared. After the riot, no one knew what was going to happen, only that things were changing. Everyone was so afraid black people were going to move into our neighborhood. That was the worst thing that could happen. Now black people are moving into our neighborhood, and it doesn't seem to be making a difference. Except for all the white people moving away.

I will say this for my mom (and Dad when he was alive): I never saw either of them ever be mean or rude to anyone, black or white. I'd seen my dad with black co-workers when he would take me to the graphic arts department on the Saturdays he worked and he was courteous and friendly, like always. Same with Mom when we go to the grocery store or at the doctor's office, joking around with Dr. Hadosian's nurse, Mildred. (Mom's nicer to her than she is to the doctor.) Is it fake? Is it hypocrisy? Can you be a friendly bigot? Is it possible to have opposing sides of something in your heart? Can you believe that things are one way, but your actions reveal something else? Can you fear the idea of certain people, but not the people themselves up close? I simply don't know.

Maybe I just don't like it when people talk to the television. I mean, I love the radio, but I don't talk to it.

PB & Johnny

When I hear Bill Bonds signing off, I sneak into the living room to switch over to Johnny Carson. At this point, sometimes Mom is awake, sometimes she's asleep. She's awake tonight, sitting in my father's BarcaLounger, snuffing out a cigarette in the overflowing hubcap ashtray. Suddenly, she's in a good mood.

I grab the ashtray to empty it. She smiles at me. "Thanks, honey." She holds out a stubby green rocks glass. "Could you freshen this for me too?"

"Sure, Ma," I say. "Have you eaten anything today?"

She looks off toward the picture window where her eyes lose their focus for a moment, then she turns back to me. "I think so."

I take her glass with my other hand and head to the kitchen. As I dump the butts into the garbage, I can hear the theme song—*duh nunt nunt nuh nuh*—with Ed McMahon saying, "*It's* The Tonight Show, *starring Johnny Carson!*" while I tip the big bottle of Canadian Mist to pour a shot into the little glass that now never seems to leave our countertop. I go to the freezer for ice.

"Tonight, Johnny welcomes Charles Nelson Reilly, Freda Payne, comedian David Brenner, and a visit from the Mighty Carson Art Players."

Doc Severinsen's band ends with "Shave and a Haircut," while I fill the glass with Faygo Uptown and take it over to my mother, who already has another Eve lit up. (They were out of L&Ms at the drugstore, I guess.) It's an extra-thin cigarette and she's holding it with her thumb at the filter like a hypodermic needle, so the long narrow ash doesn't fall off. I put the ashtray in front of her so she can flick it off.

"Just in time." Mom exhales the smoke, then smiles at me. "Looks like a good Johnny."

Some nights, things work out this way. I hide while she yells at the TV, but it somehow gets all the fear and hurt out of her. Sometimes it puts her to sleep, other times we stay up and watch Johnny Carson together. It's the nicest part of the day when it works out this way, and it almost makes me glad that I have no rules anymore, that as far as my mother is concerned, I'm an adult now and I can do pretty much anything I want. Since I can still hear Johnny's monologue, I head back into the kitchen where I make her a peanut butter and jelly sandwich. I carefully slice the moldy crusts off it, then cut it into quarters the way she likes it.

I figure that with any luck, she'll be asleep after the show and I'll be able to switch channels back and forth between *In Concert* and *The Midnight Special*. There are a lot of good bands on tonight.

Venus in Leather

Everything works out as I planned. Mom's asleep and I'm watching *The Midnight Special*. It's toward the end of the show when Suzi Quatro comes on. I've seen her in *Creem* and thought she was a stone fox, but seeing her on TV, with her fluffed-out shag, playing the bass in her tight leather catsuit, singing with her band, is something altogether different. She's so beautiful that I feel weird having a boner there while my mother is in the room. I just try to pay attention to the song she's playing. "Glycerine Queen" is a great song, with a raspy lead guitar and a stomping beat. Mom has been sound asleep for some time, so I think maybe I can turn up the volume just a little. The second I do it, she wakes up and frowns at the television. I turn it down right away, but not so much that I can't hear it.

"What the hell is this?" she mutters, her eyes barely open.

"It's just a music show, Ma. Go back to sleep." I wait to see if she does what I say. Her eyes stay slitted, but they don't close all the way.

"What *is* this?" she says drowsily. "Is this acid rock?"

I hear that expression once in a while, but I'm not even sure what it means. I'm sure it has to do with drugs, like everything else. "I don't know, Mom. I don't think so."

"Who's that girl singing?"

She's asking a lot of questions, but she's not telling me to turn it off, so that's something, I guess. "It's Suzi Quatro. Those guys are her band."

She considers this for a moment. "They're her band? She's just a little thing."

"Yeah, I guess. She's actually from Detroit."

"She is? And she's on TV?"

"Uh-huh. I think the east side."

"Hmm. She's not bad. I like how she plays that guitar."

"It's a bass, Mom."

My mother turns and shoots me a look. "It's a bass *guitar*." Even sleepy, Mom can muster up the sarcasm. "These girls can do anything nowadays," she says.

We sit and listen and Mom keeps watching Suzi Quatro strutting around onstage in her leather outfit, playing her bass and singing.

Your lifestyle past is gonna get you soon
Spend a few years in a padded room . . .

Me, I think I'm in love. Mom, she's kind of nodding her head and seems to be thinking about something, yet she's not complaining, so I don't say anything. Before long, her eyelids flutter closed, but just before she falls back to sleep, she opens them again, looks at the television, and says, "Good for her."

A Visit to the Tedescos

After work on Monday, I use the phone at work to call home. When Mom answers, her voice is a little slurry, but okay.

"Hey, Mom. I'm going to my friend John's house for dinner."

Sigh. "All right, but I was going to make chicken."

"Sorry," I say, feeling bad, which is crazy since it's not like she actually made the chicken. The chicken is really just a hazy theory in my mother's head. If it even exists, it's most likely an iced-over lump that never even made it out of the freezer after a few drinks. Instead of feeling guilty, I decide that I'm doing us both a favor. "I'll see you later, Ma."

After I hang up, I catch the bus back up Grand River and get off near Evergreen and walk to John's house on Vaughn.

John answers the door. He's so tall that he practically has to bow his head in his own house just to let me in. They love John in gym because he's so tall. I don't think they'd ever put him in swim class, even if they had to fish him out of the deep end with the pole. They're always trying to get him to try out for basketball, but he won't do it. *Fuckin' jocks. I don't want to be on their stupid fuckin' team,* is what he says. I like that about him.

"Hey, man." John leads me down the hallway to a door. I can see his mom in the kitchen and I start to walk toward her.

He pulls at my jacket. "What are you doing?"

"I was just going to introduce myself to your mom."

John looks at me like I'm insane. "Fuck that," he says,

opening a door leading to the basement. "We're going to my room."

We walk down the stairs, where the light is dim and reddish. A stereo is on and I can hear "Spain" by Chick Corea and Return to Forever tootling away endlessly. I don't really like fusion jazz that much, but I don't say anything. Off to the right is John's room.

"This is cool," I say.

The place is carpeted in chocolate shag with walls covered in honey-colored paneling. Aside from the bed, which is draped loosely with a plaid blanket, there's not much furniture, except for a couple of beanbag chairs. What you really notice are the rock posters plastered everywhere. Ones that I've seen advertised in the back of *Creem* and the *Lampoon*—Lou Reed, Tull, Mahavishnu Orchestra, Can, Iggy and the Stooges. He's got his own Marantz stereo, a Wollensak eight-track recorder/player, and giant RTR speakers that are almost as big as me.

"Man, this is excellent. Where did you get all this stuff?"

John shrugs. "My old man. He and my mom got divorced a couple years ago so he buys me anything I want. Wants me to like him better than my mom. Trying to buy my affection. Typical divorce shit. You know the deal."

On the floor, there are at least a hundred albums lined up against the wall. At the end is Bowie's *Pin Ups*. I pick it up, turn it around to scan the song listings. "Really?" I say. "Your dad does that?"

"Sure. Aren't your parents divorced? I figured they were. You never mention your dad."

I flip the album and keep looking at the cover, at Bowie's airbrushed face, his neutral gaze meeting my own.

"He died last year." I peek up at John. He usually acts like nothing surprises him so I'm not used to him looking so stunned. I don't like him this way. I like him being cocky and boastful, the opposite of me. It's better that way.

"Fuck, Yzemski," he says, as if out of breath. "Man, I didn't know that. Fuck." Then finally, "Bummer."

I put down the Bowie and pick up an MC5 album. The cover looks like a collage of pictures that a kid might make in elementary school. In the left center is Rob Tyner's face, his eyes heavy-lidded, his mouth drowsily hanging open. I turn it over. The second cut on the first side is "Kick Out the Jams." I want to smile, but can't just then. Farther down the track list I see a song called "Motor City Is Burning."

"Yeah, bummer," I finally say, never having said the word before, yet I've heard Mitch and Dale use it a thousand times. I try to swallow. Does your dad dying qualify as a bummer? I guess it does. Maybe it overqualifies.

"You want to smoke some weed?" John says to me.

"Here?" I don't know why I say that. What I probably meant to say was, *Weed? You mean marijuana? Drugs? The very thing I've been so scared of in high school?* "What about your mom?"

He makes a *pffft* noise, which is one of his favorite noises. "She doesn't know," he says. "Even if she did, she wouldn't do anything about it." He picks up an album lying flat on top of the others, the Allman Brothers' *Eat a Peach*. Keeping it horizontal, John pulls back the top cover of the gatefold to reveal a drawing of a pointy pastel land of mountains, giant mushrooms, cute hippie girls, and a truck that's carrying a gigantic peach in its flatbed. Lying against the center crease are two twisted-up cigarettes.

"I've never smoked it before," I say.

John widens his eyes in fake astonishment. "Wow. There's a fucking *Action News* flash, Yzemski. What a surprise. What *have* you done?"

"I don't know what you mean." I put down the MC5 record on a flowered TV tray.

"Have you done anything?" he asks accusingly. "Have you ever smoked a cigarette?"

I shake my head.

"You ever fucked a girl?"

I shake my head.

"You ever felt a girl up?"

I sigh. "No."

"How much you whack off?"

"I don't know. I guess I don't."

John laughs, a choked half-guffaw. "*Fuck*, man. Dumbass. You're not even smart enough to lie."

I didn't know what to say to that. Just then, Chick Corea whoops in the background at me as he plays his electric piano. Even fusion jazz is laughing at me.

"What the hell do you do besides read music magazines and listen to the radio?"

I sigh again. I have a feeling this isn't a good answer, but it's the only one I have: "I build model cars."

John shakes his head in disgust, laughing even harder now. "Jesus. You are fuckin' pathetic, Yzemski man." He grabs the two cigarettes from inside *Eat a Peach* and then closes the door to his bedroom. "Here's what we're gonna do. First, we're gonna smoke this joint."

"Then what?" I say, afraid of the first thing, but most certainly afraid of whatever could come after that.

"Second, we're going to smoke the other joint."

Go Ask Danny

I haven't even tried it yet and I already feel high. Everything is in slow motion. Is it because I'm doing something wrong? Or because I'm actually doing something? Let's face it, John is right: I don't do much. My father knew it too. I go to school and work, do my homework, watch TV, listen to the radio or records, and take care of Mom. That's pretty much it. So maybe that's why everything has slowed down—because something is about to happen for once. I'm going to take drugs.

John puts on a fan and pops open a casement window. Cool air streams into the room. We sit on the carpet across from each other. I notice a loose toenail clipping embedded in the shag. I watch John as he lights the cigarette, takes a big puff, holds it, and then finally exhales. "This is primo shit," he says in a squeezed voice, as if he's holding his breath, which I guess he is.

The smoke is not as unpleasant as I would have thought. It reminds me of Fan Tan, my favorite chewing gum, kind of spicy and acrid and sweet all at the same time. When John hands it to me tip first, I grab it the same way, trying to ignore the sogginess. I put it to my lips and suck in. I hold the smoke there in my mouth. It feels like nothing. I blow it out.

"Did you inhale?"

"I don't know. I think so."

"A lot of times people cough when the smoke hits their lungs."

"Oh."

"Take a real toke."

"A what?"

He rolls his eyes at me. "A *toke*. Take it into your lungs, dickweed."

"Take it easy. I just told you I never smoked anything."

My mother, when I was little, when she acted more like a parent, got it into my head that any kind of smoking was bad. I know, strange coming from someone who smokes two packs of L&Ms a day, but she said that what she herself did was dumb. The fact that she admitted her mistake made me feel like she was telling the truth. When it came to pot, she did not make as convincing an argument, or any argument. But my father did. Every once in a while, something about drugs would come on TV, like an episode of *Mannix* where some kid gets hooked on heroin. He would look at me and say something like, *You've never done anything like that, have you?*

No, I'd say, scared by the threatening tone in his voice. I wasn't used to that from him.

Good thing. 'Cause I'll kick your ass from here to Timbuktu if you do. You'll be out of the house. He was not mean often, but I knew he wanted to make an impression on me. It seems funny now that he was worried about me taking heroin, when I couldn't even bring myself to try a cigarette. I guess none of it matters anymore.

Anyway, I was the one who was so worried that someone was going to make me take drugs when I got into high school. Yet John is my friend and a good guy, so I'm willing to give this a try, even though in *Go Ask Alice* I'm pretty sure she started on pot.

"Do you take other . . . drugs?" I ask, still holding the cigarette.

John wiggles his fingers back and forth in front of my face like he's hypnotizing me. "Oooooooh. *Drrrrugggs* . . ."

"Yes. Drugs."

He laughs. "Naw, man. I'm just messin' with you. I don't do any chemicals or powders. I don't like that shit. Pot is okay because it's organic."

"They make heroin from poppies. Isn't that organic?" I'd seen a special about it on educational TV.

John considers this. "That's true, but it's still processed, like a chemical. Pot grows in the ground naturally."

I have to give him this. "Yeah."

"Someone did dose me with angel dust once," he says, shuddering. "Man, I thought I was going to go fuckin' nuts."

This terrifies me. "They do that?"

"Sure, man. Someone gives you a joint and doesn't tell you there's animal tranquilizer and shit in it. *Fuuuck*. Next thing you know, you're so wasted you can't walk."

"Do people ever think they can fly?"

"What?"

"Like Art Linkletter's daughter. The guy from TV? His daughter took LSD and jumped off a building and died."

"Whoa," says John, shaking his head with a grin, for some reason amused at what I just said. "Kids do the darndest things."

"Does that ever happen?" I just stare at him as I hold the joint.

"This is fine. Relax, man. I wouldn't do that to you." He grabs his green Bic lighter. "Hey, dumbfuck, you let it go out."

I put the cigarette back between my lips and he holds the fire up to the tip.

"Now suck in the smoke and hold it in your lungs."

I do as he says and instantly start hacking and wheezing for the next thirty seconds. My throat burns and aches, like I inhaled fire, but it itches too. I feel stupid for coughing so much. I expect John to be mad, but he looks pleased.

"Right on. Now you're *smokin'*."

We smoke the entire cigarette and nothing happens. I'm relieved. I guess marijuana isn't as scary as I had imagined. No desire to jump off a building. No imaginary insects crawling under my flesh that I'll need to cut out with a rusty razor blade. No signs of me going schizo whatsoever. Good deal. Is it weird to be proud of myself for smoking pot? I kind of am. I look over at John. His eyes are red and slitty.

"Oh, man, I'm so fucked up," he says, his voice slower than it was before.

"I don't feel any different," I say.

"Yeah." He pulls a white can of something called Ozium out from under his bed and sprays all around us and on us. "Sometimes you don't feel anything until you smoke a couple times."

"Really?"

"Yeah." He reaches under the bed for an old El Producto cigar box, flips open the top, and pulls out a small bottle of Murine. I focus on the bright yellow liquid as he takes the glass dropper, leans back, and puts two drops in each eye. Apparently, smoking marijuana requires a lot of equipment. Then I remember the Mouse House and *paraphernalia*. Eureka! It's all making sense now.

"Are my eyes red?" I ask.

"A little. Not too bad."

"Are we going to smoke that other one?"

"Can't, man. I'm too messed up. We'll do it after dinner."

"Dinner?" I say.

"Yeah, dinner. My mom made some for us."

Oh jeez.

Spaghetti and Sympathy

"John! Could you please give me a hand in the kitchen?" his mother yells as soon as she hears us coming up the basement stairs.

"*Fuuuck*," says John under his breath.

"Hello, Danny," Mrs. Tedesco greets me when I walk into the kitchen.

"Hey, Mrs. Tedesco," I say as John heads down the hallway, away from the kitchen, I guess to the bathroom. She's smiling, so I smile back. She's dressed in a cream-colored blouse and wide brown slacks, kind of work-dressy, like she might be a secretary or something. I note the rocks glass on the tile counter. It's not amber-colored like my mom's, it's clear, so I'm thinking: *vodka*. But maybe it's just water or pop. It's possible.

"So glad to have you over and finally meet you. John talks about you all the time."

"He does?"

"Sure."

"Oh. Well, thanks for having me."

Unlike John, I'm pretty comfortable talking to his mom. As I've said, I like being around adults. Actually, I get along better with them than I do people my own age. (It occurs to me that I should probably try to work on getting along better with people my own age.) Mrs. Tedesco seems nice even though she scares me a little. Her reddish-brownish hair is helmety on the top, but bells out on the sides and never seems to move even when she turns her head. I also try not to focus on her eyebrows but it's difficult. I have never seen anyone with eyebrows that have been drawn on before. It makes her eyes seem very curious, like she can't wait to hear what I say next, but it may just be how she looks.

"John's just going to help me with dinner, Danny. Please go and sit down in the living room. It's going to be a couple minutes before we eat."

"Okay. Can I help?"

She cocks her helmet hair to one side. "*Ohhh*, that's so sweet of you to ask. No, dear. You just go have a seat."

As I leave the kitchen, John comes back. Right away I can hear them talking in whispers. It sounds like John's getting chewed out about something. I hope it's not me. Or the marijuana. I walk around their living room. It's different from my house, all decorated in some sort of black-and-red Spanish style. Hanging on the walls are big crests with swords crossed on them and oil paintings of bullfighters. The couch is upholstered with ripply gold velvet and covered with clear plastic. The tables and shelves are dark wood with gold accents and the candleholders on the walls look like tarnished gold. I don't know if they're rich or if they're what my mother would refer to as *ticky-tacky*. The only time I've seen furniture like this was when Mom took me into Lasky's Furniture to shop for a coffee table. After two minutes, we walked out. *Furniture for Polacks*, was what she called it. (An odd comment, considering she married one.) I don't know if the Tedescos are Polish, but I like the place.

John walks in and joins me, rolling his eyes. "She is insane," he says.

I just smile and keep looking around.

"She wants to know if you like spaghetti."

"Yeah. Sure. Whatever it is will be fine. When my mom makes dinner, I usually end up flushing it down the toilet."

Again, John seems surprised by what I say. It's pretty hard to surprise him and I've done it twice already tonight. Between that and his mother's eyebrows, I'm starting to think that I'm pretty interesting.

"Dinner's ready!" Mrs. Tedesco announces from the dining room.

John and I file in. We're going to eat in the dining room, which is furnished in the same fancy way as the living room. We all sit down at a thick dark-wood table. The plates have brown and gold flowers on them and the napkins and place mats are gold burlap. There's a big bowl of spaghetti that looks great to me—rich and reddish brown from all the ground beef in it and covered with a snowdrift of Parmesan cheese. There's also a fresh salad with tomatoes cut up in it and black olives. I realize just how hungry I am.

"Johnny, do you want to say grace?"

John exhales loudly. "Mom, why are you doing this? We never say grace."

"Maybe it would be nice for Danny."

John looks to me. "Do you care if we say grace? Do you ever say grace?"

I start to open my mouth, then just shake my head. It feels a little floppy on my shoulders.

"See?" says John, helping himself to the bowl of spaghetti.

"Hope you like spaghetti, Danny," says Mrs. Tedesco.

"Yeah, I was just telling John how much I liked it."

John piles a second spoonful on his plate, then shoots me a glance as if to say, *Brownnoser*. He's right. I guess I do like it when parents like me. And they always tend to like me. It's one of my talents.

He hands me the bowl. I'm so eager by now to get the food that I have to control myself. I take two giant spoonfuls, strands of it trailing off my plate, and it's all I can do to not take a third.

"You boys are hungry," says Mrs. Tedesco.

"This looks really great," I say.

Mrs. Tedesco seems pleased. John shoots me another look. I can't help it. It does.

She piles salad on our plates next to the spaghetti. There are bottles of Thousand Island and Catalina dressings. I've never had the Catalina dressing before, so deep, deep orange, and I take that and pour it all over my salad. I'm so excited to eat that I'm feeling a little dizzy. John is digging in, but I hold off until his mother serves herself.

John turns to me. "What? What are you waiting for?" he asks, his mouth full, a strand of spaghetti hanging from his lip.

I don't know what to tell him. I don't want to make him mad, but then Mrs. Tedesco jumps in.

"He's waiting for me to get food on my plate. Like polite people do."

John's going to kill me, I think. Instead, he just exhales and drops his fork on his plate. I can't look at him because I know it's not going to be good.

After his mom puts some salad on her plate, I start to eat. It's the best spaghetti I've ever had. Way better than my mother's, even when she used to use real ingredients, instead of catsup and old crumbled hamburgers like she does now. But instead of saying how good it is, I just stuff my face.

Mrs. Tedesco puts her fork down and wipes her mouth with her napkin. "I was very sorry to hear about your father, Danny."

That's when the spaghetti that I'm enjoying so much expands in my trachea and I start to choke. I cough into my hand and I strain something in my throat, which makes me cough more. I cough out spaghetti all over my plate and the place mat in front of me. I can feel my face get redder and I don't know if it's because of all the coughing before from the marijuana or because I'm embarrassed. Which is crazy, I know. It's not my fault that my father is dead.

Mrs. Tedesco runs into the kitchen and brings me back a tall glass of water. "Just see if you can take a sip." She puts her hand on my back and the cool feel of it there calms me a little. "Just take a sip," she says, and finally I manage to get a little water down my throat. "That's better. Just take it easy, dear. Probably just went down the wrong pipe."

"You okay, Yzemski?" says John. Even he looks worried.

I nod my head. Mrs. Tedesco moves her hand from my back to the top of my right arm and gives it a little squeeze and a pat. She sits down. I'm finally able to take a breath. I take another one. Then I notice the awful silence.

I'm so relieved when Mrs. Tedesco says something. "So, John tells me that you're a music lover too."

I nod again.

"John, what was that album I just got you that you like so much?"

He looks confused at first, then he thinks for a moment. "Steely Dan? *Pretzel Logic*?"

"That's the one. Have you heard it?"

"Not much of it," I say, my voice cracking the way it used to before it changed. "But what I've heard was good."

"John, maybe you should play it for Danny after dinner."

"Okay, Mom," he says, in a way that's nicer than anything he's said to his mother all evening long.

"Feel better?" she asks me.

"Yeah, I can breathe okay now. Thanks." My voice cracks a little again. "Sorry about the mess."

"That's all right. It'll come right out. Think you can eat anything else?"

"Yes," I say. "It's really good. I guess I was eating too fast."

She pats my arm again. "That must be it."

Listening and What Comes Before

After dinner, John and I go back downstairs to his room to listen to the Steely Dan album. He lights up the second marijuana cigarette, puts the record on the turntable, flicks the lever so the turntable starts revolving, then turns up the stereo real loud. He hasn't even lifted the needle onto the LP yet, but here's the crazy part: even this sounds good.

I stare at the ABC label revolving all pink and orange and yellow like the fog job on a model car and realize that I love this part. The moment before the needle touches the record, that spooky little hum of electricity hanging in the air. There's a heaviness, but a good heaviness, a prickly, alive feeling that's the opposite of how you feel when a song you love fades out.

It's all pure possibility. The amplified click of the needle as it's lowered onto a record you're hearing for the first time, the little sizzle as the needle finds its way into the groove. Time stops just then.

Until the music starts. It's no longer just possibility, but reality. If you're lucky, the song is good. It's really good. It's a really good song on a pretty decent album. It's Uriah Heep or Robin Trower or the first Montrose album. You did fine. Other times it's not so good. It's the bummed-out letdown of Wet Willie or UFO or Badger, your high-fidelity bad judgment lingering in the air like the scent of rancid lunch meat.

Then, once in a while, that moment after the click and sizzle is transcendent. (Another word from hippie Dale.) It's the opening searing slanted riffs of Led Zeppelin. It's the Coop. It's Sabbath. It's Iggy. It's a jam. And when it is a jam, it's like nothing else. That moment after the click and sizzle is a moment where anything is possible—incredible music, kind words, people getting along, good food, no tormentors, no one dying. It's the antifade.

Tonight, after that long moment, after the click and the sizzle, the air is thick with possibility and pot. Then the opening notes of "Rikki Don't Lose That Number" roll into the basement. Steel drum trickling into electric piano, which is when John turns to me. He smiles. He doesn't need to say anything because I'm smiling right back. He doesn't need to mention anything that happened during dinner or anything that will happen tomorrow at school. We just listen. We hardly talk at all. Maybe a word or two between tracks.

We just listen.

Dreaming of Nightmares

When I get back to my house that night (wobbly walk home, stars smeared against streetlights, opossum eyes glittering under driveway Oldsmobiles, buses glowing down Grand River like giant vacuum tubes), Mom is asleep in front of the television. It may have been the second joint we smoked but I feel kind of weird. I'm not sure if I like marijuana, but I did like that new Steely Dan.

I cover Mom with an afghan and hope she doesn't wake up for a minute, decide to smoke a cigarette, and then fall asleep. This is a worry of mine, that she'll burn down our house and we'll have nowhere to live. Or that the fire will kill us both, which I guess would solve the problem of nowhere to live.

When I go to bed, I lie there in the dark, my eyes wide open, staring at the ceiling of my room. I turn the light on and try to read *Crash Club* by Henry Gregor Felsen, but can't focus on the words. I switch the light off. Finally, I turn on my radio and keep it so low that I can just barely hear the DJ's voice. I fall asleep to Frank Zappa's "Peaches en Regalia." I think I do, except I'm not even sure if I'm really asleep.

I dream of bad dreams. I dream of when I was a little kid, six years old, the time when I had my long period of nightmares. Night after night, I would wake up terrified and crying. It happened so much that I became afraid to go to sleep. I'd stare at the ceiling and tell myself that I was never going to sleep again. The next thing I knew I was awake, screaming and sweating. The dreams themselves always had someone or something chasing me. I could never really remember what it was, just a faceless, nameless terror. It was a fear that I didn't understand, that I could only feel. I knew only that I had to run.

When I would shock myself awake, my mother would come into my room and say, *Did you have a bad dream?* I'd nod my head in that fast up-and-down way that little kids do, then she would sit on the bed, gather me in her arms, hold my head against her neck, and pat my back, shushing me until I calmed down. Tonight, in this dream, I can't remember what the bad dreams are about. Yet I still feel the fear.

Tonight, my dream of nightmares wakes me up in the same way. I lie there in my bed, breathless, staring at a quadrangle of light from the partially closed bathroom door on the wall of the hallway, hearing the gargled sounds of Mom snoring in the living room, all while a live version of the Stones' "Midnight Rambler" plays on the radio. Just then, I finally understand everything that happened during that period of bad dreams.

All the time you're a kid, your parents are hiding things from you. It's what they do. I'm sure they think they're doing you a favor, but they hide, they lie, they *forget* to tell you all the most important things. They build a bubble around you. They fill your head with tooth fairies and Easter Bunnies and Santa Clauses to distract you, and they tell you that what wakes you up in the middle of the night is just a bad dream, nothing to worry about, *just a dream*.

Though they mean well, I wonder if they wouldn't just be better off telling you that your bad dream wasn't really *just a dream*, but your own creeping awareness that you, six-year-old kid, are going to die. Maybe sooner, hopefully later, but still, you're going to die. And by the way, you're not going to wake up from that particular bad dream. Which makes me wonder, *What if parents did tell kids the truth?* I imagine my father saying: *Hey, buddy, it's okay. You just had a dream about death. I know it's scary, but you're just starting to understand it. It's coming in little waves of recognition, the whisper of an idea that you can't quite hear yet, but try not worry too much about it. It's the most natural thing in the world. In fact, someday I'm going to die on you. Not that long from now, as a matter of fact. How about that?*

What would happen if parents told the truth? Would kids go crazy or become depressed? Would they get angry? Would they become hippies and take all the dope they wanted? Or maybe kids would just take in the information like they do everything else.

Who knows what triggered my string of nightmares when I was a child. Was I somehow aware of what everyone was hiding from me? A suspicion, settling within my fragile kid bones, that our cat Charlie didn't really go to live on a farm. (Squashed by a neighbor's Corvair, my mother later told me.) Was it something I learned out in the world that brought about those knowing dreams? Who knows?

This is my theory: That bad dreams are really just the result of kids (who are smarter than everyone thinks) slowly figuring out how the world works. That people do bad things. They beat you up. They say horrible, mean words to each other, even when there doesn't seem to be much difference between them. That dads don't wake up and moms stop taking care of you and start going crazy. That nothing is going to turn out like you think.

A year ago, I was still living in that bubble world, even if I haven't bought the whole tooth fairy snow job in a long time. By the time my father died, I was building the bubble around myself, fooling myself in the way all of us do. And right there's the reason why the parents tell children all the lies—because they want, they need, they *have* to believe it all too, just to get themselves through the night.

Music Soothes the Savage Brain

An hour later, I still can't shut my mind off. So I plug my button earphone into my radio and turn it up. The DJ is playing King Crimson's "Larks' Tongues in Aspic, Part One," which is a righteous, crazy, jangly jam. I turn it up just as the tubular bells percussion segues into shimmery jingle bells and cymbals, then a searing violin section (yes, violins!) which raises the hair on the back of my neck just before it builds to a heavy buzz-saw guitar riff that slams my head into the pillow, blasting jagged coils of sound through my noggin even though I'm listening to it all through one crappy, tinny little earphone. Just then, my brain downshifts. I go from fourth gear to a steady idle. Mission accomplished.

Creem magazine says that the best rock is brainless. They're right, because music is the one thing that makes me stop thinking about everything (except music, that is). When I put an LP on the turntable, let's say Foghat's first album, and listen to "I Just Want to Make Love to You," with the boogie chug of that electric guitar and Lonesome Dave's phased vocals that sound like they're being moaned through a broken megaphone, it sends an electric current to my brain that makes me calm inside. It's not just about the words. It's about how music takes us out of ourselves, how it relieves our pains, lets loose something in our hearts, makes us feel better in ways we never knew we could.

Sometimes I sit in the basement with the headphones on for hours and hours, looking at album cover art or reading lyrics or memorizing who played the instruments on each song. Sometimes I pull a chair up to the turntable and just watch the label in the middle of the record turn, turn, turn, until I'm in a kind of trance. There's something about that movement that makes me feel less alone. Music is my language, the blasting soundtrack in my head, there to drown out my mother's anger. It's everything I tell myself to get through my shoving, taunting, insulting day. It's my security blanket, my force field, my loud, electric, screaming, bashing audio version of the bubble world. It's my Santa Claus, my tooth fairy, my Easter Bunny.

Except music is something that actually exists.

Sex, Drugs, and Rock and Roll

I wake up to my alarm with my earphone on the pillow beside me. I push it back in to hear the very beginning of "Hocus Pocus" by Focus, which is an excellent song. I roll over and reach down to the radio next to my bed to yank the earphone out of the jack. I spring out of bed, close the door to my bedroom, and turn up the radio for the guitar solo in the middle, which is really good.

"Danny!" I hear my mother yell from her bedroom. "Turn that goddamn music down!"

I guess it is loud. She must have gotten up and gone to bed during the night.

I open my door. "Sorry, Mom," I say, then close it again. I turn the music down during the weird Popeye scat-singing part of the song, so I can still hear while I get dressed. I put on a fairly clean T-shirt, my Led Zeppelin. I pick up the green flannel that I had on last night, and realize that it smells of marijuana. I don't know how I feel about that. I guess I feel different because now I'm officially a pot user, but I still feel like me. I don't suddenly want to take heroin or anything, but who knows? I'll keep an eye on me. I hang the shirt up in my closet, hoping that it'll air out so I can get a couple more wearings out of it. I find a red-and-blue flannel and look for some decent Big Yanks, but no one's done any wash. By that, I mean that I haven't done any wash. I'll have to do a load of laundry tonight, I think.

Just then, when I say the word *load* in my head, it makes me think of whacking off. Which makes me think about what John said. (I felt like a dummy when he made fun of me for not doing anything.) I asked my dad about it when I got to high school because I heard guys talking about loads and jizz and hand jobs and such in the locker room. I know parents don't always talk about that sort of thing, but my dad did, along with wet dreams and the reproductive process. He told me that masturbation was perfectly normal at my age and nothing to be ashamed of. I know. Crazy, right? But he said it. That's what made my dad so cool.

Still, I have to say that I haven't had a lot of luck in the whacking-off department. I feel behind in all this stuff, which shouldn't be surprising. My dad always used to say that I was a late bloomer. Then my mom would take a puff of her cigarette, blow out the smoke, and say that by the time Danny gets around to blooming, it'll be winter. I guess she kind of had a point. Anyway, I've only experimented a couple times and it kind of hurt, which makes me think I'm not doing it right. Then I hear the locker room guys talking about it and I figure if those Neanderthals can do it, I don't see why I can't. I decide that for the sake of research, maybe I'll try again tonight after I do my homework and take care of the laundry.

After I finish getting dressed, I head into the kitchen to make tea and toast. While the water's boiling, I discover that there's only one heel of Hillbilly bread left. And in the smallest owl canister, there are the last two tea bags. So now I've got shopping to do too, along with laundry, homework, and my, well, research.

"What the heck do you do all day while I'm at school and work?" I say under my breath, as I grab a spoon from the silverware drawer. "You do nothing. You just sit around. *Useless*." I slam the drawer shut.

"Danny!" Mom yells from the bedroom.

"Shut up," I yell back. I slam the drawer shut again, only louder this time.

The Wonder of Iggy

At school, before the announcements, I play "I Wanna Be Your Dog" by Iggy and the Stooges. It's the influence of John, I know, but I really like them too. In fact, he lent me the album to play. The feedback at the beginning of the song sounds great on the PA. By the time it cuts into the fuzz-box guitar and the tinkly piano and the jingle bells, I'm nodding my head so hard that I just about start jumping around in front of the microphone.

So messed up I want you here
In my room I want you here . . .

Mr. Beckler, speech teacher, AV club head honcho, and lover of sweater vests, who reminds me of Stanley Myron Handelman from the *Dean Martin Presents the Golddiggers* TV show, sees how excited I am and lets the song play longer than usual, before he gives me the signal that he's going to fade it out and that I should start the announcements. Today it's news about student council meetings, basketball games, and asking for volunteers for the yearbook committee. I make a slight flub during an ROTC announcement, but other than that, I get through them perfectly. Then more Iggy Stooge as outro.

"Nice job, Danny," says Mr. Beckler.

"Thanks."

"That's a good song," he says.

"Yeah it is," I say.

"I saw him at the Grande in '68," says Mr. Beckler.

I just look at him, not sure exactly what he's talking about.

"Iggy," he says. "The Psychedelic Stooges opened for Blood, Sweat & Tears."

"Who?"

"Not the Who, the Psychedelic Stooges. That's what they used to call themselves before they just shortened it to the Stooges."

"You saw the Stooges?" I don't know what to say. I always liked Mr. Beckler, but now that I know that he's seen the Stooges, I like him even more.

"Iggy blew them off the stage," he says, looking at the ceiling, kind of talking to himself. "He was dancing around like a spastic, throwing himself on the floor. God, that was a great night. My friends and I got so—" Mr. Beckler stops himself, turns, and glances at the studio door. There's no one there but the two of us. "It was—it was *fun*."

"Man, that's really cool, Mr. Beckler."

He takes a breath, then frowns. "Yes, well. Let's just keep that between us, Danny." He winks at me.

"Okay," I say, but I'm not sure I can.

I pull John's LP off the turntable, carefully slip it in the sleeve and cover.

John meets me after third period like he always does. I'm careful with his album, but I have to say that it makes me feel cool to walk around carrying the Iggy album so people know that I'm the guy who does the announcements.

"What's happening, Yzemski?" John says, holding out his hand for me to shake, thumbs-up, soul style. No one has ever done this to me before, but I get through it all right. "Man, I was so fucked up last night. After you left, my mother kept asking if I was all right."

I laugh. I still haven't made up my mind about pot, but I was happy to shower today in gym to wash off the smell. No heroin cravings yet, so that's good.

"I had a lot of weird dreams last night," I say.

"That happens." John leans in closer to me. "You want to cut class and get high?"

"Nah, let's save it for Thursday when we go to the Mouse House." I hand him back his album. "Thanks for lending me this, man." I discover that when you say *man* while handing someone a Stooges album, it actually sounds right coming out of your mouth.

"Shit sounded excellent," John says.

"I know, man. Thanks again." I look around to see if anyone's listening. "Hey, guess what?"

"What?" John looks at me suspiciously.

"Mr. Beckler saw Iggy and the Stooges at the Grande Ballroom."

"No fuckin' way."

"He just told me. I swear."

"Dorkler saw the Stooges? *Fuck you*."

"I'm telling you. He said they were the Psychedelic Stooges back then."

It takes John a moment to let this information soak in. "Fuck. That's really cool."

"I know." I feel a little bad telling Mr. Beckler's secret, but decide that it's okay since it actually makes him look good.

John looks at his watch. "Shit. I gotta book, Yzemski man. Later." He holds out his hand for me to give him five.

"Later," I say, slapping it. Another thing that no one has ever done with me before. I am breaking all kinds of new ground in coolness today. On top of that, I get through the whole day without anyone hassling me.

Iggy Stooge is my protector.

The War at Home

When I get home late after picking up some bread at the store, Mom is already in the living room with the TV on. I take a look at the level of the Canadian Mist bottle on the counter and it's definitely sunk since last night. I worry about her, but it's hard because there's so much other stuff to do. She hasn't attempted any dinner, for which I'm thankful. I had a Mr. Tony's roast beef sub on the way home. I don't know if she's eaten anything, but I'm still mad at her for being useless.

"I'm home," I say, not too loudly.

Mom makes a little noise acknowledging that she hears me. She's got on Walter Cronkite, which is nowhere near as bad as the local news. While *Action News* makes her angry, the national news just makes her sad.

"Dear god," I hear her say to herself, her voice clogged with phlegm, "all these poor boys."

I don't bother to look into the living room. I know what they're showing. It's pictures of the war. I hear Walter Cronkite giving the casualty counts for the week. I think about making myself watch with her, but it scares me too much. I think about having to register with Selective Service when I turn eighteen.

Then, as if she's reading my mind, my mother says loudly, "If they think that *you're* going to fight in this war, Danny, they've got another think coming. I'll drive you over the Ambassador Bridge to Canada myself."

"Thanks, Mom," I say, and I mean it.

I head into the bathroom to get my dirty shirts from the hamper and while I'm at it, I grab a couple of Mom's housecoats. They're all polyester and easy to wash, as long as I don't throw them in with my Big Yanks or something else that fades. Now that I'm doing all the laundry, it's strange to think that Mom is actually the one who showed me how to use the washing machine a long time ago. Despite not telling me about shrinkage or about putting darks and whites in the same batch (see the lesson of the pink shirts), that was a pretty good thing for her to do, teaching her son how to do laundry and sew buttons on his clothes. *I don't want you to be a helpless man, Danny,* she said to me once women's lib came along. *You need to take care of yourself. It's not some girl's job. They don't want to cook or clean anymore and I don't blame them one damn bit. I wouldn't have signed up for it if I had known there was a choice.*

So I guess I'm not a helpless man or whatever I am. I have a mom who wants me to be independent and doesn't want me to get killed in a war and a dad who took me to the drags and forced me to do stuff that was good for me. I guess I'm lucky. At least I *was* lucky. Right up until I wasn't.

I go into the living room. I stand next to my mother's chair holding a bundle of laundry. I don't say anything, I just look at her, at the glistening trails of tears on her face as she watches coffins covered with American flags on an airport tarmac. Then Walter Cronkite's voice fades into a commercial for Dristan.

I'm not mad at her anymore.

Research

Downstairs, I sort the laundry into two loads and then put my shirts and the housecoats into the machine. I'll do socks and underwear in a day or two. I throw in a cup of All-Tempa-Cheer and put it on warm. The lid still open, I watch the laundry fold itself into a clammy pinkish whirl and it reminds me that I was going to try whacking off again tonight. Thinking about it makes me feel strange and nervous, but excited too.

I head up the stairs, taking small, quiet steps. I tell myself to just make noise and act like nothing is going on. I hear the slosh and thump of the washing machine downstairs and the voice of Walter from the living room and think that the noise will be a good cover.

Upstairs, I grab a couple *Creem* magazines from last year that John lent to me. (I've heard that visual aids are helpful.) I close the door to the bathroom and casually page through the first issue. It's not until the fourth issue that I see it: an ad for an album called *No Secrets*. The ad is just like the LP cover, with a picture of Carly Simon walking down the street. She's really pretty and I can see her nipples sticking out from under her shirt. The song "You're So Vain" starts running through my head. That's when I lock the bathroom door.

My Research Pays Off

When I start to feel a little normal again, I hear Mom calling me, but I'm afraid to yell back right now because my voice might sound weird and shaky. I pick up the plastic cup next to the sink, turn on the faucet, and take a drink. I leave the water on. The song in my head shifts from "You're So Vain" to "Sunshine of Your Love."

I'll stay with you till my seeds are dried up . . .

I finally understand that dumb lyric, when Mom calls me again.

"Danny! What are you doing in there?" she shouts from the hallway.

Finally, I manage to get words out: "Sorry, Mom, I was just washing up. I couldn't hear you."

"It's the phone, for you. Some boy named John."

"Tell him I'll call him back, Ma."

"What?"

"Tell him I'll call him *back*."

I pull a long piece of toilet paper off the roll, get on my knees, and start trying to clean up the mess I made. It's not like the house is so spotless, but we certainly don't need there to be sperm all over the place, for crying out loud.

"I'll be right out!" I yell.

When everything is cleaned up and I've flushed the toilet, washed my face, combed my hair, and brushed my teeth (for some unknown reason), I finally unlock the door and walk out into the hallway. I ditch the magazines in my room, making note of which copy of *Creem* has the *No Secrets* ad for future research. I remember the laundry downstairs, but I'm not so annoyed about it now. I feel relaxed, which I haven't felt in a long time. I guess whacking off makes you feel less worried about things. Except maybe about whacking off.

Walter Cronkite Spies on Us

I walk into the living room, but my mother isn't there. I glance at the television. The war stuff is over and Walter is ending with something less depressing. I can tell by his voice. (As a fellow broadcaster, I notice things like this.) Yet that's not what really gets my attention. Over in the dining room my mother is struggling to move our heavy oak Danish modern dining room table.

"What are you doing?" I ask, not sure why I'm seeing what I'm seeing.

"Give me a hand, Danny," she says, sounding extra drunk. I don't know how she managed that in the half-hour since I saw her last. But then, I guess I do know: *by drinking*.

"Why? What's going on? Why are you trying to move our table?"

She looks at me like I've just asked a completely ridiculous question. "I've decided that I'm going to turn this room into a studio," she says, pulling at the table, separating the two sides. She's not all that strong, and even less so when she's been drinking. Which is to say, she's pretty much never strong.

"A what?"

"A studio. For artistic endeavors."

At this point, I just emit a long low-pitched groan. Imagine the sound of a door opening to a very tired haunted house.

"It can be for whatever we want," she says brightly, as she tries to shimmy the table toward the living room. "If you want to build your models here, you can. If I want to do my painting, I can do it here."

"Your painting? Since when do you paint?"

"I want to take it up again. That's what I was going to do in college—become a painter."

"I didn't know that."

"There's a lot you don't know about your mother, young man." She starts to tug at the table again. "Are you going to give me a hand?"

I stay right where I am. "Where are we going to put all this stuff?" Besides the table, there are four chairs and the china cabinet weighs a ton. "We just can't move it all out of the dining room. We've got to have somewhere to put it."

She stops tugging at the table and looks at me.

"Maybe we shouldn't do this right now?" I figure that I'll talk her out of it all later, when she's sober. "I have homework to do. How about we try to figure it out this weekend, okay?"

"I guess so," she says, pouting.

"Okay."

"Do you promise?"

"Yes," I say, sighing. I feel bad because I have no intention of doing any of it, but I have to say something. All my morals are flying out the window. It's probably the pot slowly taking hold of me. Back-alley death, here I come.

"Thank you, Danny. You're a good boy."

I go and refresh her drink. From the kitchen, I hear Walter Cronkite say, "*And that's the way it is.*" That's when it feels like everything my mother and I do together happens with the television on. Sometimes it seems like Walter or Bill Bonds or Johnny Carson are watching us at our very worst moments. I look up at them and I'm embarrassed. It feels that way now. I don't mean to lie to my mother, but turning the dining room into a Studio for Artistic Endeavors is not really at the top of my list of things to worry about. Ahead of it is: laundry, homework, grades, grocery shopping, getting caught skipping school, whether or not we have enough money to pay the mortgage (for short, the poor farm), Tim Riggle kicking my butt, the hippies at work, what I'm going to play on the air tomorrow morning, figuring out how to get into broadcasting school, and the fact that the Gilinskis next door heard about break-ins in our neighborhood from a real estate person.

I take a breath. Whatever calm I might have felt after my research is all gone. At least Walter Cronkite has stopped eyeing me. *Truth or Consequences* is on now and Mom has calmed down, as if she's been hypnotized by Bob Barker and his shiny hair. I want to sit down and watch it with her because I like this show and I'm worried about her, but my wash has gone through its cycle and I need to get everything into the dryer and get another load of darks going. I have to wash my Big Yanks in cold water. They're already too short and I don't need more comments in the hallways at school about the narc and his flood pants.

I'm on my way downstairs when the phone rings. "I'll get it," I call out as I head back up the stairs. I pick up the phone in the kitchen. "Hello?" I say, though I'm pretty sure I know who it is.

"Thanks for calling me back, dipshit," says John. "Too busy beating the meat?"

I'm glad that I'm on the phone so he can't see how red my face turns. *He can't possibly know*, I tell myself. But before I even get a chance to stutter any answer, he just keeps talking.

"Yzemski man, I scored two tickets for Iggy and the Stooges at the Michigan Palace next week. You wanna go?"

After this, I forget to be embarrassed. "Are you kidding? Iggy? Yes, I'm interested in going." I don't know what I'll tell Mom, but I'll think of something. "*Hell* yes!" More cursing. Continued proof of my imminent drug-fueled descent.

"Cool. You can pay me the five at school tomorrow. Later," he says, then hangs up.

Iggy.

Generation Landslide

After the laundry is done and Mom has fallen asleep in front of the television (I don't dare turn it off because it will wake her right up), I decide to forget about Johnny Carson because I don't need him staring at either of us tonight. So I close the door to my room, get into bed in my underwear (both pairs of pajamas are drying on the clothesline), and turn the radio on. I'm too excited about the idea of going to a concert to sleep so I just want to lie in the dark and listen to music. I don't know how we're going to get to the concert or how any of this is going to work, but I'm assuming John will handle it somehow. He's good that way.

They're playing Alice Cooper's *Billion Dollar Babies* album on W-4. So far, "Generation Landslide" is my favorite song, with its marching-band drums and cool twangy guitar, and the way Alice spits out the words with a sneer.

Brats in battalions were ruling the streets . . .

It's about anarchy, which I have again learned about from *Creem* magazine. They love anarchy and rebellion—breaking stuff, anger, changing things, sticking it to The Man (who cannot possibly be the same "Man" that Lou Reed is waiting to buy drugs from in the Velvet Underground song, right?). Unfortunately, I realize that I have a ways to go in the anarchy department. I'm getting better, but I'm still no rebel. I figure rebeldom is somewhere between Problem Teen and Back-Alley Death. After "I Love the Dead" fades out, the DJ announces the songs, but at that point, thoughts of my father win out over anarchy.

At midnight I hear, "*This is WWWW Detroit*," and commercials for all the usual sponsors: Mickey Shorr's Car Stereo, Dearborn Music, Full Circle head shop (for all your *paraphernalia* needs), and the very last one grabs my attention. It's for a place called the Specs Howard School of Broadcasting, which is an actual school to learn how to become a disc jockey. The announcer (Specs Howard himself) says the phone number of the place so fast that I don't get a chance to write it down. I'm sure it must be in the yellow pages, so I jump out of bed and run in my underwear to the front closet where we keep the phone books. My mother wakes up, but I don't even care.

"Danny, what are you doing?" she says to me, all groggy.

"Just looking something up, Ma. Go back to sleep."

She actually does what I say. On the television, Truman Capote snickers in a slimy way at something Johnny Carson says. I don't even care that the two of them see me in my underpants because there it is, right under *TRADE SCHOOLS: Specs Howard School of Broadcasting*.

It makes me happy just knowing such a place exists.

Tim and Jimi

The next day at school, everyone seems to be in a rotten mood. The various clusters of kids in the halls are shoving against each other extra rough today. I'm the only one in a good mood. My sonar is working and I actually find myself doing my old zigging and zagging between everyone, which is good since I need to be careful today. I'm carrying a precious copy of Jimi Hendrix's *Electric Ladyland* that I bought a few weeks ago. It's a double album. (By the Korvettes code, it was an *H* which made it extra expensive.) I've got it turned around and tucked behind my books for safekeeping, but you can still see psychedelic lettering, not to mention Hendrix's face, all cool and sullen and dead, peeking out over my English and algebra textbooks.

Still, trouble walks up to me as I'm on the way to second-period announcements. It's Tim Riggle and his friends, the Hollins brothers. (Am I forever doomed to be tormented by brothers?) The Hollinses were a problem in elementary school and I had so hoped they would go to a different high school, or better yet, both be dismembered by a psychopathic brother killer.

They stop in front of me. I try to zig around Bobby Hollins, but he squeezes close to his brother to block my way.

"Hey, narc. Where you going?" says Riggle.

I stop. I don't have a choice. He is much taller than I am. I am trying not to be scared, but I doubt if I'm doing a very good job. I tell him the truth: "I'm going to WRBG to do the announcements."

Tim Riggle laughs at me and the Hollins boys join in.

"That's right," says Riggle to his friends. "Faggot here does the announcements. When he's not sucking Mr. Beckler's dick."

I don't even know what to say to this, so I just say the first thing that comes into my head: "Mr. Beckler doesn't even have a dick."

To my surprise, the Hollins boys find this amusing. Even though they're idiots, I'm kind of pleased with myself for making them laugh.

"Shut up," says Riggle, who obviously feels betrayed by his friends. He tries to see the album I'm holding. "What are you gonna play today, narc?"

"Hendrix. I'm going to play 'Voodoo Child.' It's an excellent jam." I don't tell him that the song is actually called "Voodoo Child (Slight Return)." He's not worth it.

By the way the hallway is starting to clear, I can tell I've got roughly two minutes to get across the school to the radio station. "I've got to go," I say. Riggle scares me, but I'm not missing the announcements.

He leans in close to me and says, "I should have known you'd listen to nigger music." I notice that he doesn't say it too loud, there in the hall, where there are black kids who could hear him. He grabs for the album, but I hold onto it with all my strength and zig around him, busting between him and Ted Hollins. That's when I accidentally knock Riggle's books to the floor.

"You fuckin' asshole!" he yells at me. He starts to chase me, but a teacher opens the door to her classroom and stares at him. It doesn't stop him from shouting, "You're dead after school!"

Even with fear coursing through me as I rush down the hall, I can't help but think, *How cliché*. I've been hearing this from tormentors all my life. *Dead after school*. Why do I expect originality from them? Though I have to admit that it still works on me, which is probably why they keep using it. (It's an oldie but a goody.) I realize something about my particular brand of tormentor: not only large and stupid and unoriginal, but also a procrastinator. Frankly, I'd rather just get beat up right then and there—let's get it over with—but no, they're always postponing the poundings till later. *Dead after school*. But maybe they're not actually lazy. Maybe their schedules are so full that the only time they can really concentrate on their victims is after school. Maybe this is like extra-credit work to them or extracurricular activities. You know, something that will get them into a good bully college.

By the time I get to WRBG, a manhole cover of dread rests on my chest. I hand over the album to Mr. Beckler. "Last cut on side four," I say. Quickly, I review the announcements and look for the tough words that will trip me up.

Mr. Beckler finds the right cut and cues it up.

"'Voodoo Child.' Good choice," he says, pronouncing it *Chile* like Jimi does. I'm finding out just how cool Mr. Beckler is. Thankfully, he does not mention that Jimi Hendrix died of a drug overdose. I'm not sure what Ms. Lloyd might have to say, but she's not here.

Even through the crappy PA speaker, Jimi's funky wah-wah licks sound excellent. Just before the vocals kick in, Mr. Beckler pots down the music. I do the announcements and flub a bunch of times. I'm obviously shaken up about Tim Riggle. As bully magnets go, I don't actually receive many severe beatings. Beyond their tendency to procrastinate, my tormentors taunt and make fun of me, but often by the time they actually get around to violence, it's like, *Oh, what's the point?* A few slaps, a couple slugs, a bloody nose or a split lip, and they're done. Not today. I now admit to myself that Riggle was probably serious.

The fade slithers its way through my cowardly guts.

The Ticket

After second period, John finds me at my locker. He walks up, his usual army jacket flapping around him, holding my ticket in front of him.

"Check it out, my man," he says. "Iggy and the Stooges. It's going to be excellent."

"I can't wait," I say, happily forgetting my after-school fate for the moment. I reach for the ticket, but John holds it above his head where I can't get at it. "Come on."

He lowers the ticket slightly. "Think he'll do some Iggy shit?"

"You mean like roll around in glass?"

"Or fuckin' paint himself silver?"

"Or smear peanut butter all over himself?"

"Who the fuck knows, man," says John. "It's Iggy!" He holds out his left hand for me to slap him five, but my ticket is still in his right—he doesn't give it up until I fork over the five bucks. The feel of the ticket in my hand cheers me right up. It's a smooth, thin, shiny cardboard that really makes me feel like I'm holding something important. I stash it in my wallet. Even though it will get bent there, at least it'll be safe.

"How'd you get these?" I say. John doesn't have his license. His parents aren't allowing him to take driver's education. It's the only thing the two of them agree on, he says.

"Jerry Zabkiewicz went down to the Michigan Palace box office and I had him pick me up a couple."

"Cool," I say. Then John gets a weird look on his face. "What?"

"Gotta go," he says. He turns and just about runs back the way he came.

When I swivel around to see what's going on, I'm faced with my counselor, Mrs. Corbin. "We need to talk, Daniel," she says.

"I have to get to class."

"I'll write you a pass." She grabs my shirt and leads me to her office. Once we get there, she just says, "Sit."

I sit.

"I'm very disappointed, Daniel. I did not expect this of you."

Turns out Mrs. Corbin knows about me cutting class. She is not pleased. I'm surprised that I don't feel worse. A year ago, getting in trouble would have scared me more than getting beaten up by Tim Riggle.

As if sensing my lack of concern, Mrs. Corbin adds, "This is not good, young man."

I'm trying not to be a part of what's happening right now. I focus on Mrs. Corbin's hair, which is lacquered black, smooth, and bulbous like the 1940s version of the Batmobile that I've seen in some of the 80-Page Giants. Then I focus on her face, which is usually kind, but today seems disturbed and kind of PO'd. There's a splash of freckles across her upper cheekbones that I never noticed before because they're only a shade darker than her skin. I start to wonder what she and my father spoke about when he called her about getting me started in driver's ed.

"Daniel, are you listening to me? This is serious. I want to know why you've skipped English class almost every Thursday this semester."

I snap back into what's going on—that I'm actually in trouble. It's still sinking in. This has never happened before, so I'm not exactly sure what to do. Some kids are in trouble all the time, but not me. Me with the Citizenship Awards, up on the stage with all the girls, every tormentor's favorite target, Danny Narc. This is new territory for me.

"Well?" she says.

"I went to the Mouse House on Grand River to buy the *New Musical Express*. It comes in every Thursday." I don't involve John in any of this. He's my friend and I won't be a stoolie. Even though it was his idea, I'm glad we did it.

"Oh?" She looks a little bewildered by my answer, so I try to explain.

"It's a music newspaper from England. I'm studying it to help me learn about music for when I become a disc jockey."

Mrs. Corbin's face loosens up a little. "So you're interested in a career in broadcasting?"

"Yes ma'am."

"Well, that's something at least." She says nothing for a long, long moment. She looks away, as if she's examining the wall next to me, the pattern of shiny tan enameled bricks. Finally, she speaks: "I believe you, Daniel, because I know you're a decent young man and I know the last year has been very hard for you, what with the passing of your father and all."

Mrs. Corbin talking about my father is suddenly upsetting to me. I have to swallow a couple times to keep back the tears, but then I'm all right.

Her eyes narrow at what she says next: "And since you at least have a *slightly* educational reason for skipping class, I'm not going to bring this to the attention of Ms. Floyd, who would most likely suspend you from your duties at WRBG . . ."

Now I'm really worried. "Please don't do that."

Mrs. Corbin leans forward. "Daniel, I just told you I wasn't going to do that. Calm down."

"Okay."

"But I do have to tell your mother. She should expect a call from me tomorrow. I would advise you to bring it to her attention before I call. It's better that she hears it from you before she hears it from me."

"Okay," I say, thinking, *I bet I'm gonna get away with this*.

She sits back in her chair. "But there is something else I'd like you to do."

I Make My Getaway

After my last class on this crappy day (except for getting a concert ticket), I fly out of the school, grabbing my stuff from my locker as fast as I can, and head out the front door. I make it out okay, until I realize that I stupidly brought my copy of *Electric Ladyland* with me. I'm already too far to go back safely, so I just head for the bus stop. Other than my encounter with the group of black kids who were there that one time, the bus stop has been a fairly safe place for me. Until today. As my fellow students might say to me, *Your ass is grass and Tim Riggle is the mower*. Stupid, I know. How could anyone's ass ever be grass? It makes no sense.

The bus is taking forever. I stamp at the hard-packed dirt, clutching my books and album, keeping my head down, knowing it's the wrong thing to do, but unable to stop. Slowly, kids are coming up to wait for the bus too. Nothing is different from how it usually is. A hippie girl in patched elephant bells brushes past me, her long frizzy hair whooshing by inches from my face. She smells like the Mouse House minus the BO. It's intoxicating, but it doesn't take my mind off the problem at hand.

More kids show up. With a crowd of people waiting for the bus, I can linger in the middle of them. I know that hiding isn't really the way to solve this problem; my father would have told me that Tim Riggle will still be around tomorrow and the next day and I have to face up to him, but that doesn't stop me from wanting to escape him today. I really wish I had left the Hendrix album in my locker. If I get caught by Riggle, it will for sure get messed up. Of course the bus is late today. When there's a break in traffic, a lanky kid with acne wearing a CPO jacket takes a few steps out into Grand River to see if he can spot it.

Someone else asks him, "Is it coming?"

He holds his hand flat above his eyes like he's Magellan looking for the stupid Pacific Ocean. "I think I see it," he says.

That's when I get shoved from behind. I get pushed so hard, the books fly out of my hand, but I manage to hold onto my Hendrix album.

"Trying to get away before I found you, Yzemski?"

"I have to go to work," I say. I make a move to pick up my stuff, but Tim Riggle puts his foot on my algebra book and pushes it into the dirt. At least it's not muddy today. Then he shoves me again. Now the crowd at the bus stop moves back and forms a circle around us.

Riggle pushes me once more, but I do nothing. I just stand there holding *Electric Ladyland*.

"Not gonna fight? You fuckin' pussy. Come on, fight."

"Why would I fight you? I don't have a problem with you. I mean, I don't like you, but I don't see any reason to fight."

"Come on, you pussy. You little sissy."

"I'm not going to fight you, Tim."

He slaps me across the face. It hurts, but I just stand there with a death grip on my album.

"You're a little pussy, Yzemski."

"So what if I am. I don't care what you think of me."

"Fuckin' chicken."

"I don't care. I'm not going to fight you."

"Give me that fuckin' thing," he says, grabbing for my album.

I'm not exactly sure what happens at this point. I slip away from him, then without thinking, I grab the corner of the album and hit him in the throat with the hard edge of it. The album feels strange in my hand just then, like I can feel it sink in against his windpipe. He goes down without a sound. I just hear the thud of his body on the dirt. Then the gasping. That's when one of the Hollins boys—Ted, I think—slugs me in the chest.

Some kid in the back yells, "Fight! Fight!" This makes me angry. We should actually go beat that guy up.

I'm able to move out of the way for the second punch. I feel the whiff of his fist near my ear. I didn't sense a lot of conviction in the swing, but I don't know if I'll be able to do that again. His next blow hits closer to my forehead than my mouth or nose. It probably hurts him more than it hurts me. I hang onto my album. The third blow stings, but only for a second, and that's when I understand what to do. I stop moving. I stand and look at Ted Hollins. This is what I'm always afraid of, what I'm always trying to avoid, and I now finally realize that it doesn't matter. Getting hit doesn't hurt. When I don't flinch after the fourth time he hits me, he shoves me as if to throw me off my feet. That's the only thing I resist. When he shoves me, it's like he's trying to push a telephone pole. I don't give. I feel the blood inching down from my nose onto my Led Zeppelin T-shirt, but I don't care. I don't even have to tell myself not to cry.

"You can't hurt me," I say to him, sneering like the Coop.

He hits me in the face, hardest of all, but I just stand there and stare at him until the smile slowly fades from his face. A moment later I see the fear. That's when he stops.

I expect some closing taunt as he and his brother gather up a wheezing Tim Riggle, but he says nothing. The same with the kids around us. Eventually I hear the bus approach, and the doors gasp open. The crowd thins.

I wipe my nose with the heel of my hand, pick up my books, put them with my album, and step onto the bus, last onboard. As I drop my thirty-five cents into the till, I make eye contact with the bus driver, a grumpy old black guy who never talks to anybody. He looks at my swelling face, my bloodied nose, but it's not a look of pity. I would recognize that. He gives me a tiny, almost invisible nod.

There are no seats on the bus except toward the back. It's a long trip with everyone's eyes on me. I ignore them and just start walking. No one says anything; there are no attempts to trip me. I find a seat three-quarters of the way down the bus, next to an old woman. She moves her cane so I can sit down. Through bloodied teeth, I smile at her.

Fasthand

I wash up and button my flannel shirt to cover the blood on my T-shirt before I walk into the shipping department. No one says anything about the swollen scrapes and bruises on my face. They're starting to really ache now. Today at work, it's just me and Mitch and Dale. The Finney brothers are out for some Catholic school thing. Mitch has the radio roaring and W-4 is playing good stuff—Climax Blues Band, Seger, the Stones, Faces, Grand Funk, Frijid Pink, and a set of Zeppelin, so I just listen to the music. Mitch and Dale seem to sense that I'm in no mood for their nonsense.

A big bunch of orders for complete collections has come in, so I'm on my favorite detail. After I staple about a hundred boxes, I go into the back to get extra books to stack up in front of me. When everything is ready, I start making CCs like a wild man. My hands are a blur on the stacks. With the sweat and the glue, the pads on my fingers are just sticky enough. The slap of book on book is loud and somehow helps me ignore my throbbing cheek and forehead.

"Jesus, look at the fuckin' Crane go," Mitch says.

"He's like a speedfreak," says Dale. "Fuck *me.*"

"Go, Crane, go," says Mitch, like he's reading Dr. Seuss.

The music propels me. As the stacks of books steadily shrink, the rate at which the CCs pile up amazes even me. Then the DJ plays "Rock and Roll" by Mitch Ryder and the Detroit Wheels. The Velvet Underground originally did the song, but their version just isn't as good. Even Lou Reed thinks so. When Mitch sings it, Jenny, the girl in the song who has the rock and roll revelation, isn't from New York.

Then one day she hit the Dee-troit station
Couldn't believe what she heard at all . . .

It's just the kind of song I wanted to hear. Those chunky guitar riffs and soaring organ fills push me to go even faster. I'm slapping books into boxes, stapling them up, and stacking them next to me as fast as I can. My head starts bobbing with the bass line and Mitch Ryder's singing.

She started dancing to that fine fine music
Her life was saved by rock and roll . . .

"Check it out," says Dale, pointing at me. "Crane is jamming out to Mitch Ryder." They laugh, but not in a mean way.

"He's fuckin' diggin' it."

"Yeah!"

At the chorus, Dale turns up the radio way beyond the limit of where we're supposed to have it.

It was all right
It's all right . . .

It all sounds so good, especially the organ and cowbell. I glance up at Mitch and Dale without even thinking about it. Then the bridge of the song comes in with the scorching guitar solo and it's so good that I stop collating and twitch out the notes on the frets and strings of a make-believe guitar.

I open my mouth and it syncs up perfectly with Mitch Ryder's growl—"*Oh-ohhh*"—while I play guitar. I shake my head and realize that sweat is pouring off me. My flannel is soaked, my cuts and bruises sting, my cheek is burning, and I can taste blood in my mouth—but I don't care.

"Whooo! Go, Crane!" Mitch yells, bobbing his head himself.

Finally, the song ends and Mitch and Dale and I are laughing our butts off. We all look at each other, not sure exactly what has just happened. Then a wimpy song by Gentle Giant comes on. I take a breath, put my head down, and start making CCs again, worried that I violated my no-talking policy.

"What is this bogue shit?" says Dale, disgusted. "God, it's like getting kicked in the nads with music."

Mitch changes the station and just catches the end of "Crossroads" by Cream.

For the rest of the day, everything is all right.

Mom Goes Grocery Shopping

When I get home, there are bags from Great Scott! and A&P on the kitchen floor. I'm amazed that Mom actually went shopping for groceries. I guess even she noticed that we didn't have much in the cupboards. I think about telling her that I got caught skipping school, but decide to put it off for a while since it looks like she's having a good day.

"Hi, honey," she says, smiling.

"Hi, Ma."

Even though her eyes are dark and tired-looking, she seems twitchy, like she can't quite keep still. I'm thinking she got something from the doctor to give her energy. (If she didn't take Valiums all the time that would probably help.)

"How was your—" Then she notices my face, my split lip and swollen cheekbone and forehead. "What happened to you?"

"It's okay. I just had a little accident at work. I ran into a girder in the basement." Lying is getting so easy (the pot has obviously got its claws into me), but I can't tell her the truth, not today. I'm just too tired.

"You should be careful," she says vacantly. I guess she believes me or she's just not worried about it. Either way, it kind of bums me out.

"Let me give you a hand with the groceries," I say. That's when I look into the bags. There are at least ten boxes of cereal—Cap'n Crunch, Kix, Cocoa Puffs, Life, Heartland Natural Cereal, Trix, and a bunch of other ones. It's weird. I decide that I'm definitely not going to tell her about school tonight. Maybe tomorrow morning.

Mom sees me looking at all the cereal. "We're going to start having cereal more for dinner," she says.

"Oh. Okay."

"It's full of vitamins and minerals and it's easy to make and you can have it anytime you want."

"That's great, Mom."

This used to be a big thing with us. I always wanted all the sugary cereals and she wouldn't buy them for me. *You don't need that crap*, she would say to me when I begged for Trix or Lucky Charms at the supermarket. Now I guess I can have it whenever I want. Except I don't really like those cereals so much since I'm grown up. It's okay. I still like cereal and it makes me glad that she actually went to the market. I didn't have to go shopping and there's something in the house for us to eat. Best of all, I didn't have to go with her. She's a horrible driver.

I see that in some of the other bags are dish detergent and toilet paper and a few items that I had written on the pad of the owl list holder hanging up next to the cupboard. I see she also managed to get to the liquor store for a half-gallon of Canadian Mist, which is probably why she went out in the first place.

"Let's have cereal tonight," I say to her, thinking that this was her plan.

"Sure," she says, but she has already abandoned unpacking the groceries and is getting some ice for a highball. I leave my books and record on the landing, then walk up into the kitchen to take over the unpacking.

Mom lights a cigarette, pours a drink, and stares through the window over the sink. I don't know what she's looking at. There's nothing there but the side of our neighbor's house.

"I want to get going on the studio, Danny."

"The what?"

"The dining room. We need to clean it out."

"Oh, right." I sigh. I'd so hoped that she had forgotten about that. "I'll get to it, Mom."

"We need to do it."

I start to get annoyed now. "No, we really don't."

"Yes we do, Danny."

I'm tired of this subject, so I decide to change it: "Mom, have you thought about getting a job?"

She keeps looking out the window and smoking. "I can't do anything. I have no training. I'm just a housewife. Taking care of you is all I've ever done."

I decide to ignore this statement. "You could work at a grocery store or something."

"Nobody wants an old lady in their store."

"That's not true. Anyway, you're not old, Mom. I'm sure you could do something. We could sure use some more money coming in."

She stirs her drink with a fingernail, then walks into the living room, where I hear the television being punched on and channels being flipped. The tables have officially been turned. I'm the responsible adult and my mother is the sulky teenager. I hear the tinkle of ice and the voice of Bill Bonds and I know what's next. I rush to pack all the groceries away in the cupboard and fridge. My plan is to hole up in my room with a bowl of Cap'n Crunch while I do my homework, and then read the new *Creem* until *Kung Fu* is on, until I remember that there's something else I have to do. Something I don't want to do.

I put the ninth box of cereal away. That's when I realize that Mom didn't bother to buy milk.

Another Stupid Letter

I hate doing this. I'm just going to write whatever I feel like writing because it doesn't matter. I'm in the coal bin. I've got the radio on as I write this and the DJ is spinning an "All Night Album Replay" of the new Rolling Stones album, It's Only Rock 'n Roll. *I know you don't know who the Stones are, Dad. I'm sure you wouldn't like them at all, but I bet you'd be surprised at how many of their songs you've heard. Your favorite stations used to play them a lot, without the lyrics and guitars and with a bunch of violins and stuff, but it was still the Rolling Stones. Weird, huh?*

Let's get this over with. I'm turning into a problem teenager. I got into trouble today for the first time. I got caught cutting class and now Mrs. Corbin is threatening to tell on me to my speech teacher who runs the school radio station where I work as an announcer. (Apparently she doesn't know that snitches get stitches.) Wait, I just realized that I didn't tell you I was on the school radio station. Why do I feel guilty about that? What does it matter? I get to play music and read the announcements every day and even though I don't like to brag, I have to say that I'm really good at it. I don't want to mess it up. So when Mrs. Corbin asked me if I've been keeping up on my letters to you, I thought I better tell her the truth, that I hadn't.

When she asked me why not, I told her that it didn't make sense to write a letter to someone who is dead. They can't read it. She said that I wasn't really writing it for you, that I was writing it for me, to help me figure out my feelings about you being gone. Which still doesn't make sense to me. What am I going to write that isn't already in my head? What's to figure out? You're gone, that's the problem. I asked Mrs. Corbin how writing a fake letter to you was going to change that and she said it wouldn't, but it still might help, so I told her that I'd do it. Maybe I'll be in less trouble for cutting class. I know I could lie, but I've been doing that a lot lately. I guess my principles are changing.

I don't feel bad about cutting class either. It's been the most fun I've had since you died. I'm probably going to do it again if I can figure out some way to not get caught. Anyway, it's not like I'm stealing cars or robbing banks or taking dope.

Oh yeah. I forgot about that. I smoked marijuana awhile ago. I probably wouldn't even be telling you this if you were actually here, but then I probably wouldn't have done it if you had been here. That sounds like I'm blaming you and maybe I am. Nothing much happened. I didn't go schizo, I didn't jump off a building, and so far no heroin cravings. It was no big deal.

I just came up with another reason why I'm a problem teen! I got in a fight today. Maybe "fight" is the wrong word. Remember the kid you taught me to stare at? I guess I sort of beat him up today. He had it coming, but I feel bad that I hurt him. His friend beat me up right after. I wouldn't have felt like I won anyway because the whole thing was stupid. My lip is split and my face is throbbing right now in all the places where he slugged me. I've never been hit this much by anyone, but the weird thing is I'm okay. Getting hit isn't all that big a deal either. Were you trying to tell me that? Maybe you were. All I know is that it hurts, but it's nothing compared to the day you died. There's nothing Tim Riggle or anyone else can ever do to me that will hurt like that. I guess when the worst thing that can happen happens, there's a lot less to be scared of.

I know you didn't mean to die, but you really messed everything up good. I didn't realize how much you held things together around here. I was too dumb to notice and you didn't want me to have to worry because I was just a kid. That's what happened, isn't it? Thanks for that. I really wish we could have just kept on doing it, you taking care of Mom and me being a dumb kid who didn't know a thing about it. It wouldn't have been all that great for you, but it sure would have been better for me. I wouldn't be turning into a problem teen and at least you'd still be here.

Tyranny and Mutation and Top 40

In the morning, I chicken out and don't tell my mother what happened. I knock on her door and peek in, but she's dead to the world. I tell myself there's no way I could have woken her up, even if I had tried. So I didn't.

At school, the announcements go well, though Mr. Beckler decided to bring in some music to play. I didn't want to hurt his feelings so we played Jim Croce, which I didn't mind much, since I used to listen to that kind of music, but John wasn't so cool about it later. He was practically yelling at me.

"Yzemski man, how can you let him play that Top 40 crap on our student radio station? Nobody wants to hear that shit. Not the white kids, not the black kids, nobody!"

"There was nothing I could do about it," I shout back. "He's a teacher. He wanted to play it."

"But fuckin' Jim Croce!"

"It's not so bad," I say. John looks at me like I'm nuts. "What am I going to do? He and Ms. Floyd are in charge of the radio station."

"Well, it sucks the big one."

"I know. But he's always cool to me."

This does not go over well with John. "No, cop-out. Once you start playing 'Bad, Bad Leroy Brown,' everything falls apart. Entropy sets in. Next I'll be hearing ABBA. Then all will be lost."

"It'll be okay," I say, rolling my eyes.

"I thought he saw Iggy, man. You can't like both Jim Croce and Iggy. It's physiologically impossible."

"Just cool it. Jim Croce died and everything."

John shakes his head. "Thank god he's dead."

"Take it easy, man," I say, staring at him. (I discover that staring people down works better when your face is all cut and bruised.) We stop at my locker. Quickly, I spin the combination on my lock to open it.

John sighs, like he's not really sure he wants to say something. "Look, I'm going to lend you some albums to play on the station, but you have to be really careful with them."

"Really? Are you kidding?" John has so many great albums I'd love to get my hands on.

"Yes. But you have to be *careful* with them. I mean it. Keep them safe."

I think about my copy of *Electric Ladyland*. "I can do that." I grab my English textbook from the shelf in my locker. "I'll take them home every night so they'll be safe."

John narrows his eyes at me, not sure of my intentions. "Hmm. Maybe I should just meet you before the announcements, give you one record, then you could give it right back to me at third period."

"That sounds like a lot of work for you, man."

"Fuck you," he says, smiling. "You just want to take my records home."

"I don't know what you're talking about," I say, trying not to laugh. "But you should definitely bring Blue Öyster Cult, so I can play 'Cities on Flame with Rock and Roll.'"

"We'll see, fucker."

"John," I say, all serious-like. "It's for the good of the radio station. We have to undo all the damage done by Jim Croce."

He laughs, which is good. I need to distract him from thinking about this too much.

"Look," I say. "You want to go to Korvettes tonight? I can get the car."

"Really? Are you kidding? I didn't know you got your license."

"Yeah, sure. I could come pick you up."

"Fuck yeah, Yzemski. All right."

"You'll bring some records to play on WRBG?"

"Yes, but you better not let anyone else get their hands on them."

"Mr. Beckler runs the board and handles the turntable, but he's really careful. I taught him how to hold a record."

"I'm not talking about him. I'm talking about all the people that fuck with you."

"What do you mean?" I guess it was stupid to think that John didn't know about any of that.

"What do I mean? Look at you, man. I mean Tim Riggle and the rest of those dickheads. Do not get beaten up while you're holding my albums."

"Yeah. Okay." Like I have any say in the matter.

"*Yeah*, says the guy with a split lip and a shiner. What happened anyway? Did you do something to Riggle?"

I don't say anything to that.

"Why they call you a narc, man?"

"I don't know. They just started doing it and I couldn't stop it."

"They started calling me one because I hang out with you, so I told them that there was no way you were a narc since you had smoked weed with me."

"You did?"

"They didn't believe me, but I said it was fucking true."

"Wow. Thanks, man. That's really cool of you." This makes me kind of choked up. I can't believe anyone would do that for me. "Thanks, John."

"Shut up, fag. When are you going to pick me up?"

I better be able to get that car tonight. I decide not to think about Mrs. Corbin calling my house and what's going to happen after that. "How about quarter after six? We could get something to eat before if you want."

"Fuck yeah."

"Okay. See you then," I say, closing my locker, then locking it up. I feel different. All morning I'd been feeling the fade coming on, but now it's gone.

My Diabolical Plan

At home that night, there's no sign that anything is different. I'm not greeted by my mother with her hands on her hips, glaring at me the way she used to when I was a kid and I had messed something up. (I was such a good kid, that hardly ever happened.) When I announce that I'm home, everything feels normal: *Action News* on the TV, Canadian Mist on the counter, and Mom in the living room, griping about Detroit. Business as usual.

I got a reprieve, I think. Or Mrs. Corbin forgot to call. Or she doesn't think she has to because she thought she'd tricked me into telling her myself. The latter is a distinct possibility. She's still thinking of old honest, Citizenship Award–winning, un-school-skipping, non-dope-smoking Danny instead of the Danny who is currently riding the razor's edge between reform school and drowning in a pool of his own vomit. Either way, it's good for me. Except I had to work late, so I'm behind schedule to pick up John.

"Mom, I'm going to drive to the supermarket to get some milk for all this cereal, okay?" I call to her from the kitchen. The lies just keep on coming. I leave my jacket on.

"Why don't you just go across the street to Shrubland?" she says back.

"It's cheaper at the supermarket. It's on sale at Great Scott! I checked the circular." That part is true at least.

"Sure, fine," she says, paying more attention to the television than to me. "Oh, for Christ's sake, what is going on with this city?"

"Then I think I'm going to Korvettes, okay?" I say *sotto voce*, as we say in Ms. Floyd's speech class.

"*Um-humh.*"

Not sure if that's a yes or no, but it's good enough for me. Luckily, my Parent-of-the-Year candidate has still forgotten that I only have my learner's permit. Which is not going to matter soon since I'll be taking my final test next month, but it's still highly illegal. What with the lying, the fights, and everything else, I feel as though I'm definitely moving from Problem Teen to Rebel. I snatch the car keys from the key rack I made in elementary school by the back door (shaped like a big key, of course), and I take off before she can say anything else.

Once I'm in the *Hindenburg* and out on my street, I roll down the windows even though it's pretty cool tonight. I don't care. The air feels good and I feel free (which is a great song, by the way). I drive down the street, past the *FOR SALE BY OWNER* signs, past the house with blue windows where I used to turn left to get to elementary school. I head toward Grand River, up to John's house.

I turn on the radio and spin the knob around, not finding anything that I really want to listen to since the radio doesn't have FM. I punch one of the buttons, which are still tuned to all of Dad's stations. Without thinking about it, I switch to the Canadian station at the end of the dial. A swell of lush violins fills the car and it takes me awhile to recognize the song, but it's one I remember from my Top 40 days, a Beautiful Music version of "Blue on Blue" by Bobby Vinton. I listen and then the song changes to an instrumental "Get Back" by the Beatles. I hold my left hand out the window and drive one-handed. It's pretty easy.

When I hit Grand River, which is a busy road, I have to turn right to get to John's house. There are a lot of cars coming, so I just wait until it's clear. The Electra behind me is impatient and he honks at me, but I don't care. Finally, right after he honks again and veers out to go around me, traffic clears and I turn onto Grand River, cutting him off. It's an old guy and he pulls up next to me on Grand River and rolls down his power window like he's going to yell at me. I'm not in the mood to be yelled at by anybody, so I turn up the string version of "Break on Through" that's playing, flip him the bird, and take off with authority.

At John's house, I turn down the radio almost all the way. I think about honking, but it seems rude, so I moor the *Hindenburg* and walk up the porch to knock. Mrs. Tedesco answers. Today's office outfit is a shiny geometric-patterned jumpsuit with long pointy lapels. It's snazzy. I decide that Mrs. Tedesco is pretty, though in a spooky kind of way.

"Hey, Mrs. Tedesco," I say through the screen door.

She smiles. "Hello, Danny. So nice to see you again."

"You too." A mom who answers the door instead of just waiting until whoever's knocking gets discouraged is refreshing to me.

"John'll be right up. So, what are you two up to tonight?"

"We're just going to go to Korvettes."

Her penciled eyebrows climb even farther up her forehead. "Oh really? He told me you were going to Farrell's for ice cream."

"Isn't that for kids?" I say, even though I was going to Farrell's with my dad two years ago. I'd get the black and white with two ice creams and marshmallow. "We can go there if he wants." I kind of like that idea.

Mrs. Tedesco turns and calls to John: "Danny's here to take you to Korvettes." She says it in a sharp, singsongy way that does not sound cheerful.

When John comes up from the basement toward the front door, he's shaking his head.

"I wish you wouldn't lie to me, John," Mrs. Tedesco says.

John walks past her and pushes open the storm door. "Let's go," he says. I wave to Mrs. Tedesco and she smiles back at me.

Once in the car, he says, "Do me a solid and just honk the fucking horn next time, okay? I'm not supposed to be going to Korvettes."

"I didn't know. How was I supposed to know?" I start the car. "Why can't you go to Korvettes?"

John sighs loudly. "I'm already wasting too much money on records, according to her."

"Wish I had that problem," I say.

"She's pissed because my dad always buys me as many as I want."

"Man, that is so cool."

John shrugs. "Yeah, I guess so. But it's kinda fucked up too."

It's quiet for half a minute and then he starts talking again.

"He's trying to be a big shot and to make up for not being here, but mostly he's trying to make up for balling some black chick he picked up on Eight Mile and my mom finding out about it."

"Wow." Just then, I think about Ms. Floyd and the short skirt she was wearing in class today. I turn to John while we're stopped at a light on Grand River. "Is that what happened?"

John keeps looking straight ahead at the road. "Yeah, that's what happened," he says in a quiet voice. "Fucking dick."

"Bummer," I say, trying out this word. It seems to fit the occasion.

"Yeah, bummer." He takes a breath, then frowns and looks at the radio. He turns it up. An instrumental version of "Mother's Little Helper" is playing on the Canadian Beautiful Music station.

"What the *fuck* are you listening to?" says John.

"Nothing. It was on real low when I got in. I guess I forgot to turn it off." I don't look at him to see if he believes me. I just turn the radio off.

"Drag that we got no FM," he says. "Wish we had some tunes."

"I know."

"Wanna hit McDonald's?"

"Oh, yeah. Right." I had completely forgotten that we'd talked about that. I decide that I'm not going to worry about spending a little money tonight.

We go to the McDonald's near Grandland. We order our food inside, then eat in the *Hindenburg*. I get a cheeseburger, fries, and a Coke. John gets a Big Mac and a Filet-O-Fish sandwich, which he refers to as "Grease Ecstasy."

He washes it all down with a strawberry shake like it's nothing.

Afterward, as a shortcut to Fenkell, I drive through the parking lot of Grandland, which I didn't think about until it was too late. We're right where my dad gave me driving lessons. My eyes burn and my throat kind of closes up, so I take a big drink of my Coke. The cold helps. I turn onto Fenkell.

I peek over at John. He's got his elbow on the edge of the open window and his hand holding onto the roof of the car. He's bobbing his head and tapping his hand on the roof in time to some song that I can't hear. Seeing him do that makes me feel farther from the fade and its evil powers. I realize how good it is to be out on my own and in the car with a friend.

When I put on my signal to turn onto Outer Drive, John snaps out of his song trance and says, "Hey, keep going straight down Fenkell, would you?"

"What? Why?"

"Just go this way, Yzemski. It'll be okay."

"But what for?" I like to stick to the plan. I don't always have a plan, but when I do, I like to stick to it.

John senses my nervousness and lowers his voice. "Be cool, man. It's okay. I just want to make a quick stop, all right?"

"All right. I guess," I say, not sure what this is all about. My *Go Ask Alice* alarm is going off. Am I headed for a drug deal gone bad?

"Fuck!" John says after a few minutes. "This no-music is killing me." He turns on the radio and starts going through all the stations. He stops at CKLW, where the DJ is playing "Tin Man." "Ugh. America. Fuckin' wimps." John turns the knob. We hear snatches of music and talk, but nothing that sounds appealing to either of us. Finally, on a second pass through CKLW, we hear "Ain't Too Proud to Beg," the old Temptations song, but done by the Rolling Stones.

"Stones, yeah. This'll do," he says.

We just listen, nodding our heads and mouthing the words to the song. We drive up Fenkell, past my street, past Shrubland Market, past the Bird Cage bar, past the beige tile front of Checker Drugs, where Mom fills her prescriptions and buys Canadian Mist and where my father and I used to go for vanilla phosphates when he needed to get away from her. (I now realize this.) Above it is Brightmoor Lanes, where my dad and I used to bowl. I take a breath and try to fight off the fade.

"You know about Connie's Corner?" John asks.

"Isn't that a party store?"

"It's just up the way, near the Irving Theatre." "Ghetto Child" by the Spinners comes on. John turns it down, but leaves it on.

"Oh yeah. Okay," I say, relieved. A party store. No back-alley death yet.

I used to go to the Irving with Mark and Jim every Saturday during the summer. We would see horror films as well as the old Batman serials that they started showing after the TV show became popular. 1940s Batman was sort of fat and 1940s Robin had a small Afro. Both of them looked like they were wearing pajamas while they punched bad guys. We stopped going there after the riot. I wasn't allowed to go anywhere. Then Jim and Mark were gone.

"Pull over here," says John.

I steer the *Hindenburg* to a space in front of the store.

"I'll be right back," he says.

I don't know why John needs to go here. It's a dumpy place as I remember and the owner was mean. We could just go to the snack bar at Korvettes if he wanted a pop. But when John comes out of the store, I realize that he did not want to just get a Faygo or a bag of Better Mades. He's carrying a six-pack of Stroh's beer. When he sees me looking at him, he lets out a whoop.

"Time to party down!" he yells, holding up the six-pack like a trophy.

He gets in the car next to me. I'm not sure what to do at this point. He whoops again. "See why I wanted to go to Connie's Corner?"

"Not really," I say.

"I can fuckin' *buy* there." He lifts the six-pack again. "Beer. Let's party. *Whoooo!*"

I try to look excited about the beer, but John is not buying it. "What's wrong, man?"

"Are you going to drink that in the car?"

"No." He pulls up his flannel shirt to reveal a Coors belt buckle, which he disconnects from his belt. I watch as he then holds the bottle up to the back of it and pries off the cap. Beer squirts out onto the floor mats and dash of my father's car. "*We're* going to drink it in the car," he says, sipping off the foam, then handing me the bottle.

"Billy Don't Be a Hero" comes on the radio and John snaps it off with his other hand. "Wimp!" he yells.

"Stop spilling it, John. No thank you." I hand the bottle back to him, then quickly revise what I say to, "I'm cool."

"What? You're cool? Are you kidding? You know how hard this is to get?"

I shrug. "It didn't look hard at all. You were in there for two minutes."

"That's because I look eighteen. Normally, you have to find someone to buy for you. That takes a long time."

I remain silent.

"Don't you like beer?" he asks, all confused. "Come on, man. Let's get fucked up."

"Nah. I just want to go to Korvettes and look at records."

"We can still do that. It's just more fun fucked up." He looks at me like I'm nuts, which I'm realizing he does a lot.

"You can drink," I say, finally. "I don't care. Just don't spill it, okay?" I put the car into drive, and pull a U-turn on Fenkell back the way we came. I decide to head down Lahser and catch up with Outer Drive there.

"I don't get you, man," says John. "What's the deal? You smoked weed. What's the difference?"

I keep my eyes on the road. "I don't know. I just don't care about drinking. I've had beer lots of times. It's no big deal."

This is true. My dad used to give me sips of beer all the time. It's okay, I guess. I can't exactly say why I was willing to smoke pot, but I don't want to drink. Maybe it's because I have to watch Mom be drunk every night. After you clean up someone's stale bottles and glasses and their piling-up ashtrays, or even worse, their puke, drinking doesn't look like that much fun.

"You're fucking weird, Yzemski. You are *weird*."

"Shut up," I say.

"Why?" He takes a big drink of beer, then swallows and belches loudly. "I'm right. Fuckin' weirdo."

"I said *shut up*. Jerk." I feel the fade rising in my chest.

I concentrate on Mott the Hoople's "All the Way from Memphis" playing in my head.

"Fine," says John, taking another big swig. "More for me."

Neither of us speaks for quite a while. I'm not even sure I want to go to Korvettes with John anymore. I'm PO'd at him.

We follow Outer Drive through its various twists and curves. It's a crazy road because it sort of circles the whole city of Detroit like a necklace. It looks pretty much the same wherever you are. All the houses are nice and there are lots of trees and a big boulevard dividing the two sides of the road. There's something about this street that calms me down.

I turn the radio back on to CKLW. The end of "(You're) Having My Baby" is playing, and I leave it on just to annoy John.

He gulps down the rest of his first beer. He rolls down his window and chucks the bottle, which bounces once on the easement before shattering on the sidewalk in front of someone's house. "Whoooo!" he yells, then opens another bottle.

I wish he wouldn't do that. Someone's liable to see him. And just as I think that, the wide-eyed, bucktoothed front grill of a blue-and-white Plymouth Fury comes out of nowhere and lodges itself in my rearview mirror.

"Oh, man," I say. "A cop."

The cop hits the siren a couple times, just short bloops to get me to pull over. I turn Lighthouse's "One Fine Morning" all the way down until it clicks off. My hand is shaking.

"Fuck, man," yells John. "Fuckin' pigs. Shit!" He starts

stuffing beer bottles under the front seat. He slips the full one that he just opened behind his back. "I've got fuckin' weed too."

I turn around and watch the policeman come up to the car. He's a big guy and he's kind of waddling up. I get out my wallet. I'm really scared now.

"Just be cool, man," whispers John, looking straight ahead at the road as he speaks. "Act like nothing happened. Fuckin' pigs."

I'm too scared to even shush John.

I meet the cop's big round face, which is red around the forehead and blue around the cheeks and jowls. As terrified as I am, I can't help but to think, *He actually looks like a pig*.

"License, please."

I open my wallet and pull out my learner's permit, unfold it, and hand it to the officer.

He points to John. "Is he a licensed driver? You're not supposed to driving without one in the car."

I can't even speak at this point. Luckily, John says, "Yes I am, officer. I wanted to take Daniel out here for some practice." When he says this, he sounds just like Eddie Haskell from *Leave It to Beaver*, which is to say, full of baloney.

"Where's *your* license?"

John shrugs. "I forgot it, sir. That seemed like another good reason to let young Daniel drive."

"Oh bullshit," the cop says, moving in close to me, close enough to make me uncomfortable. "Have you been drinking?" he asks me.

"No sir, I haven't."

"Well, I smell beer somewhere. And I saw you throw

something brown out the window. If you make me go back and look around for it, we'll be leaving the car here and I'll take the both of you in."

I glance over at John with as mean a look as I can possibly muster. *Please don't make me snitch*, I think. I will if I have to. I will end up with the Mark of the Squealer, but I don't care.

The cop looks at John. John keeps trying to seem all innocent.

"I don't have all day here." He's still holding the piece of paper that my learner's permit is stapled to. "Of course, we'll have to search you too. God only knows what else we'll turn up."

Finally, John exhales loudly, his shoulders lower a little, then he leans down and pulls the scattered beer bottles out from under the seat, all four.

"Okay. Dump 'em all out," says the cop. "Start with that one behind your back."

John opens the passenger door and starts pouring out beer as the cop leans on my side window and watches. He's so close I can smell him. It's a combination of Aqua Velva and Coney Island chili. It takes forever because John has to use his stupid belt buckle to open each bottle. After the last one is empty, he places it into the six-pack holder along with the other four.

"You are very lucky tonight . . ." says the cop, looking at my permit, "Daniel Yzemski. No more driving without a licensed driver in the car and no more beer. If I catch either of you littering again, I will arrest the both of you."

After he leaves, I just sit there in the driver's seat. I'm really shaking now.

"Fuckin' pig," spits John. "Making me pour out good beer. For being a fuckin' litterbug."

I can barely speak. "Are you kidding me? We could have ended up in jail. I don't even have a real driver's license yet. We were drinking in the car. They would have found your pot."

"No they wouldn't have. I crotched it."

"I don't think you're the first person to ever think of that."

"Still, it's fuckin' bullshit. This happens all the time, man. I've heard about cops having people shake out their weed too. These guys don't care. They got a lot better things to do in Murder City than bust white kids for beer."

I lean my head on the steering wheel of the *Hindenburg* until the chrome strip starts to pinch my forehead. I try so hard not to cry, but a tear or two work their way out. I wipe them away with the back of my hand and hope John doesn't see.

"Come on, man, let's go," he says. "Everything's okay. We're fine."

I take a deep breath and nod. "Yeah, okay." I turn on the radio. It's middle of the Golden Earring song "Radar Love." It's a good song, so I turn it up.

We've got a wave in the air
Radar love . . .

We go to Korvettes, where I buy the new Humble Pie album *Thunderbox*, which makes me feel better.

There in the record department, which is crowded with kids our age, I exact my revenge on John. While he's over at the jazz section looking at Weather Report records, I sneak over to the pop section, pick up an LP, and yell to him, all the way across the aisles of the record department: "Hey, John!" I hold the record up over my head. "Here's that Olivia Newton-John album you wanted!"

Man, was he mad.

Freak Out!

I come in the side door at about 9:55, trying to make as little noise as possible, though I don't think Mom will even notice that I was gone for almost four hours instead of one.

I am wrong about this.

"Oh thank god you're home," I hear her say from the living room, all dramatic. The TV is still on, playing the music from *Love, American Style*.

The couch creaks when she gets up to confront me at the back door. She's half dressed in a pantsuit, but hasn't fully buttoned up the front yet. I wish she would. She does too much walking around half dressed as it is. She's not wearing a blouse and her bra has a smear of lipstick across the right side of it. It scared me because at first I thought it was blood. She's got an L&M 100 dangling from her mouth.

"Of course I'm home. What's wrong?"

"I was just getting dressed. I was going to go out looking for you. I thought you'd been mugged or murdered. There's so much going on out there."

"Where?"

"Detroit."

"Nothing happened, Mom," I say, which is my grand prize whopper so far, considering I drove without a license, got pulled over by the cops, and barely escaped getting arrested for drunk driving, possession of narcotics, and littering.

"Where the hell have you been?"

Her eyes are all bugged out. I don't know what she's on but she's scaring me with the tone of her voice. It's so high-pitched that it makes my voice quieter. I guess I'm trying to calm her down with it. "I told you that I was going to Korvettes, Mom. That's where I was."

As if for proof, I hold up the square Korvettes bag that contains my new Humble Pie album. (John: *Marriott was way better in the Small Faces.* Me: *Ha.*) After I listen to it four or five times downstairs, "I Can't Stand the Rain" will be played on WRBG, and possibly the title track, if I can sneak it past Mr. Beckler and Ms. Floyd.

That's when she grabs the bag from me and pulls out my record and examines it. I try to grab it back, but it's hard for me because I'm still standing on the landing by the back door, which is a few steps down.

"Goddamn it, Danny. What *is* this?"

"It's a record, Mom."

"Where's the milk you were supposed to get?" she says accusingly.

Oops. "Oh. I forgot."

She keeps looking at the cover, which has a big keyhole cutout with a seminaked lady behind it. "This is obscene. Why are you wasting your money on this garbage?" She shakes the record at me, bending the corner. I haven't even opened it yet and she's ruining it.

I reach up and try to take it from her again but she won't let go. "It's my money. I made it working. I can buy what I want with it." I'm getting angry now, but she won't let go. "Give it back."

"No. You've got to learn to be responsible," she says.

Now I've latched onto the record and we're both pulling at it. I'm in a tug-of-war over a Humble Pie album with my half-dressed mother. "I have to learn to be responsible?" I say, my voice getting louder. "What about you? You don't do anything around here. You sit around all day long. I'm the only one making any money. Why don't *you* be responsible?"

"How dare you, you little shit."

She's really pulling at the record now. I can feel the cardboard and plastic bending underneath the cellophane wrapping, which makes me madder.

"Oh, I forgot. You can't get a job because you're old and useless," I say, just wanting to hurt her. "Except it's really because you're drunk all the time and you don't even try."

The cigarette drops out of her mouth and falls onto the floor. Sparks jump across the linoleum. "Why don't you clean out the dining room like I asked you?"

"What?" Her and her stupid dining room. I pull at the album and almost wrest it from her. "What? For your stupid studio? For your make-believe artistic endeavors? Who cares?"

"Someone called from school and said you've been skipping."

"So what? What do you care what I do?"

"You're grounded for the next month."

I don't say anything. All I can think of is the Iggy concert.

I pull back at the record but that's when the tug-of-war kind of ends. She just takes her side of the record and bends it down. The vinyl snaps sharply and I stop pulling. My mother lets go and the album drops to the kitchen linoleum, like someone shot it out of the air.

I look at it there on the floor, bent and torn, still in its cellophane with a Korvettes price sticker on it, next to the smoldering L&M. I don't say anything at first, then finally, in a flat voice: "I wish you would die too." The expression on her face after I say this is pretty awful, but I don't care. "It'd be easier around here."

I feel bad as soon as she starts crying, but I said it and can't take it back.

She walks out of the kitchen and locks herself in her bedroom. I want to be as far as possible from her, so I pick up the broken *Thunderbox* off the kitchen floor and head downstairs to listen to something real loud on the earphones. It ends up being "Down by the River" by Neil Young. A song about shooting someone sounds pretty good to me about then.

Name That Tune

I have to work on Saturday and I'm happy to do it. I just want to get away from my mother. At work, Mitch and the Finney brothers are being their usual jerky selves, calling me names and whooping at me, but there's lots of work to do, so we all have to concentrate on getting orders out. The radio is blasting music louder than usual, which we can do because there's no one in the office side of the building. The W-4 jocks are keeping the energy high—Beck, Bogert & Appice, Blue Cheer, Nazareth, and Mahogany Rush.

At about two, Dale says, "Anyone want to play a little Name That Tune?"

"Sure," says Mitch, slinging a lock of hair behind his ear.

"Fuck yeah," says Matt Finney.

"I don't give a shit," says Andrew Finney, who is horrible at it.

I say nothing, which they're used to.

"Next song up then," says Dale.

"This goes to the winner," says Mitch, placing a mini-bag of Better Made BBQ chips by the stereo. He must have brought them with his lunch.

Right then, the radio is playing "Uncle Albert" by Paul McCartney. I wait for the song to end. After it fades, I can't hear anything. At first, I think maybe the DJ has messed up and that there's dead air, then I hear the very beginning of what sounds like a heartbeat. That's all I need.

"Pink Floyd!" I yell out, while I'm slamming together a complete collection. "'Speak to Me" segueing into "Breathe."

The song hasn't even become a song yet. Laughter and voices, then the sounds of an adding machine and a clock slowly fade up. Eventually a woman screeches like a bird, then the guitar and keyboards slide in and everyone realizes that I'm right.

"Jesus, Dan," says Dale, again using my real name.

"Fuckin' Crane."

I shrug and decide not to mention that Pink Floyd was coined by Syd Barrett (their crazy first guitarist) after two names he found on the back of an old blues album, Pink Anderson and Floyd Council. That would be showing off. After that song finishes, I hear two notes of the next one.

"'Vicious!'" I yell out. "Lou Reed."

"*You hit me with a flower,*" says Lou.

"Fuck," says Mitch.

I don't know why I choose this day to show off, but

I do and it's fun. After I get Leon Russell's "Queen of the Roller Derby," "Them Changes" by Buddy Miles, and "Angry Eyes" by Loggins & Messina, the DJ comes on, repeats all the same bands and titles as I did, then there's a commercial and no one feels like playing anymore. I'm glad they didn't play anything stupid like Tucky Buzzard or Bloodrock, which I might have missed. (But then so would everyone else.) Anyway, I don't like barbecue, so I leave the chips up by the radio.

I keep making CCs and don't say anything else to anybody. On the way home, I pick up some milk at Shrubland.

A Model Day and a Visitor

Sunday, after filling up on three bowls of three different cereals, I decide to stay downstairs, playing records and building the model cars. The one thing I'm *not* going to do is clean out the dining room. Yet before I can head downstairs, I do need to paint my model 1967 Chevrolet Impala. Since Mom gets mad when I stink up the house with spray paint, I decide to do it outside to avoid a hassle. I open the garage door and set up a card table on the driveway nearby. I give the body a couple coats of Testors #11 Blue, which dries quickly. After that, I paint the interior seats and dash #47 Gloss Black, then #46 Silver for the chassis.

While I'm waiting for everything to dry, some little kid keeps riding his bike past the house. Every time he passes, he looks toward the garage to see what I'm doing. He's a small kid, black, maybe about eight, but his bike is way too big for him, like maybe his mom and dad figured he'd grow into it. I'm bored, so after he rides by a fourth time, I wave him into the backyard. He looks scared at first and keeps riding, but then he changes his mind, wheels the giant bike around, and comes up the driveway into the backyard.

"Hey," I say to him. I've never seen him around. He's one of the new people moving into the neighborhood.

"What you doing?" he says, almost suspiciously, tilting his head toward the card table.

"I'm painting these parts for a model car. After they dry, I'll put all the pieces together with glue and it'll be a really nice car." I show him the AMT model box that everything came in.

He rolls his giant Huffy closer and takes a look at the picture on the box. "That an old car," he says, almost whispering.

"It's not too old. It's just from a few years back."

"Why you want to build that for?" he asks, scratching the side of his nose.

"I don't know. My parents had one kind of like it when I was about your age."

"A little one?"

I laugh. "No, no. A big one." I point to the *Hindenburg* to indicate scale.

I have to say, he doesn't seem impressed. We're both quiet for a minute.

"It's something to do," I say, finally. "It's pretty fun."

About then, I hear my name being hissed from the back door. I look up and see my mom's head with a cigarette dangling from her mouth, peeking out the side door at me. She does not seem happy.

"What?" I yell.

The kid knows something's up. He turns his bike around and rides down the driveway the way he came, probably afraid to look at my mother, who stares him down as he rolls past. I don't even know the kid, but I feel bad for him. I feel embarrassed for myself.

"Danny," she calls again, angrily.

I put down the model car box and walk over to her. "*What*?"

"What are you doing talking to that boy?"

"He was just curious about what I was doing. He'd never seen a model car kit before."

"Like hell. He just wanted to see what we had in our garage. If we get broken into, it'll be your fault."

"He's just a kid."

She exhales a quick puff of smoke, taking the cigarette almost down to the filter. "He obviously stole that bike."

"He's just a kid," I say again.

"A kid can't steal a bike? Just never mind. When you're done out there, you close up and lock the garage. Don't forget you're grounded."

"Fine."

"I mean it. And don't you invite—*people*—into our backyard." She throws her cigarette out onto the strip of grass between the driveway and our neighbor's house.

Back in the Bin

Back inside the house, I make up my mind to stay downstairs for as long as I can. I play records while I build the model cars in the coal bin. I stack them up to play one after another (though John has told me that this is bad for them), but I can't play anything loud since Mom will complain. Finally, I just give up and listen to my radio in the coal bin, which turns out to be a lucky thing. In the late afternoon, the DJ on WWWW plays an old Iggy and the Stooges show recorded live at the Grande a few years ago, to get everyone psyched for the show this week at the Michigan Palace.

No fun, my babe
No fun . . .

I look at the clock and discover that it's 10:15 p.m. and I've been working on this model car for the past eleven and a half hours. When I finally stand up, my legs almost give out from under me. I realize how hungry I am and how badly I have to pee. Upstairs, the television is on and Mom is snoring on the couch, scrunched up in a ball. Anyway, she looks cold and I'm tempted to leave her there since I'm still mad at her, but instead I go get an afghan. When I spread it over her, she wakes up a little.

"Danny?"

"What, Ma?"

"Come here."

"What?" I don't want to talk to her. I want to get to my room.

She pushes the afghan away and holds out her arms. "Give your mother a hug."

It's the last thing I feel like doing, but I kneel down on the floor in front of her. When I get within reach, she pulls me to her, so tight that I almost can't breathe and my bladder feels like it's about to burst. Turns out she's not cold at all, she's clammy warm. Her hair gets all into my face and I try to spit it out quietly so she doesn't hear.

"You little goofball."

This is something she used to call me when I was little. Dad called me that too, until they started calling me it in public. I put the kibosh on that.

"I'm right here, Mom." All I can think of is, doesn't she remember all the mean things we said to each other? No, of course she doesn't. She remembers what she wants to remember and the rest of it is lost in the Canadian Mist.

"I'm worried about you. I hope you understand why I had to ground you."

I guess she remembers.

"Love you," she says, her voice a cigarette slur.

It would mean a lot more if she would say it when she wasn't drunk, but I guess I'll take it. "Love you too, Ma."

She pushes her cheek against mine. Her breath is a boozy ashtray."Ma, let me go, would you?"

Finally, she lets me loose. I sit down on the floor right in front of her and look at her. Her face sideways, mine straight up and down.

"What are we going to do, Danny?"

I don't have the answer. But it makes me recall that we're coming up on the anniversary of Dad's death. It'll be a year on the day before Halloween. I think of that morning when I didn't want to wake him up to say goodbye and it's as if the air is sucked from my lungs. I can't speak, but it doesn't matter because Mom has fallen back to sleep. I get up from the floor, put the afghan back on her, and go to bed.

Dust in the Wind

In the morning, when I walk the long walk toward the front door of Redford High School, there's something going on. I mean, besides the usual gauntlet of freaks, smokers, sports-playing kids, hillbillies, hard guys staring at you, various flocks of tough, pretty, or hippie girls, and even a leftover pompadoured G-ball or two (who don't fit in at all but are committed to it because their older brothers were G-balls). Usually, there are also groups of black kids hanging out, pretty much ignoring the white kids. All of which makes getting into school feel like a long obstacle course, full of pitfalls and potential threats that someone is going to torment you, fight you, or jump you. Today, though, instead of the groups of black kids ignoring the white kids, there is some sort of miniprotest going on. A couple kids with signs milling on the lawn next to the walk. The signs say:

Equal Representation in the Student Council!
Redford Students for Equality!

As I walk by, I hear a snatch of conversation that pretty much says it all: "Detroit has a black mayor now so—"

No one seems mad at me, so I'm all for it, whatever it is they want. I actually recognize one of the black kids from speech class with Ms. Floyd. His name is James and he's always been nice to me, so I wave to him. He looks at me like he has no idea who I am. My hand just wilts in the air like one of those time-lapse films of a dying flower. I put my head down and walk quickly into the building, past a couple kids palming lit Kools. (I can tell by the menthol.)

I have just enough time to get to gym class without being late. I pass by Halloween displays made by the Spanish club. All the skeletons unsettle me, even though they're just cartoony cardboard bones riveted together at the joints. When I get to gym, the class feels thin today but it doesn't stop the coach from yet another Shirts vs. Skins game of basketball. As always, I end up a Skin.

I hurry out of the locker room, brushing past Tyrone Bennett, who looks at me like he wants to crush me for getting too close to him. He's a sports-playing kid, I think football. He's also good-looking with a big natural and clothes that always seem dressy for school, wide-legged plaid bells and silky polyester shirts, and a lot of the kids look up to him as an athlete and fashion plate. Luckily for me, he doesn't say anything, but I sense his eyes on my back as I race for the locker room exit. It's the eerie feeling of a situation barely avoided, but I need to meet up with John, who's going to hand off Bowie's *Aladdin Sane* to me so I can play "Panic in Detroit" at the second-period announcements.

When I get to my locker John is nowhere to be found. I start to freak out. I'm looking up and down the halls, but don't see him anywhere. Kids are flying past me, bumping into me as I stand there in the middle of the hall. I have to get over to the radio station. Finally, I remember that in my locker I have a cassette tape of some old Deep Purple, but it's not cued up. I grab it anyway, along with my books, slam shut my locker, spin the lock, and run for WRBG.

As I'm rushing there, sweat running down between my eyes, I know I'm going to be a minute or two late. But when I get there, I see that Mr. Beckler is not manning the board today. Ms. Floyd is there in a short skirt and platforms that make her look extra tall, and she's already got someone else in front of the microphone, Alonzo, the black kid who also tried out for WRBG. When I enter, she holds a finger up to her lips, which is when I accidentally drop the cassette tape and it flies across the floor, bouncing off of Alonzo's shoe and under a shelf of reels. They both ignore it as Ms. Floyd pots up the music, which I recognize as Sly & the Family Stone. The super-low bass note intro plays, then the wah-wah guitar comes in and then the vocal snaps in: "*It's a family affair . . .*"

After it repeats that a few times, Ms. Floyd pots down the music and Alonzo reads the announcements, devoting quite a bit of time to the student council inequality stuff that I saw people protesting about in front of the school. I hadn't heard anything about it before this morning.

Alonzo does a pretty decent job reading the announcements. He stumbles three and a half times, but all in all, he does okay. I have to admit, though, my feelings are hurt by getting bumped off the air. Especially since I could have made it in for the announcements pretty much on time, but by the time I got here, it looks like the decision had been made to use someone else for the day.

After the announcements, Ms. Floyd plays a little more Sly & the Family Stone. "And we're out," she says, lowering the fader.

I step up to her, barely even waiting for her to slip off her headphones (which she is wearing in a cool way, with the headband slung under her chin, probably to preserve her natural). "I'm so sorry that I was late, Ms. Floyd. Someone was supposed to bring me some music to play and they didn't show up. I'm really sorry."

Ms. Floyd just stares at me. It's like she doesn't exactly hear me so I just keep apologizing: "Alonzo did a great job taking my place." I look over at him like he's going to be on my side, but he turns away.

"Daniel," she says, "I'm sorry that you're not taking this job a little more seriously."

"I am taking it seriously. I *do* take it very seriously. I really do." I think I'm sounding like I'm begging, but I can't seem to stop myself.

"You're not showing it if you are."

"I'm so sorry. I'll be here extra early next time, I swear."

Ms. Floyd glances at Alonzo, who I now wish wasn't standing there watching this whole thing. She looks a little annoyed at him too. "Alonzo, could you excuse us, please?"

His shoulders lower a little like he's just been told he can't have his favorite cereal for breakfast. He slinks out of the room, leaving only the oily sweet smell of Jade East cologne in his place.

"Daniel, this is not just about you being late today. I've been hearing from some of the students that they're not feeling like they're being represented in a fair way by the radio station."

"What do you mean?" I say, trying not to stammer.

"I mean that you like to play a lot of rock music, but you don't seem to play much of anything else. Like black artists."

"Oh. I guess I didn't know I was supposed to."

"Actually, you did know that you were supposed to. I asked you to play music that all the kids would like. And now it's a problem."

"I can do that," I say. "I like Sly and Jimi Hendrix and—"

"And that's all you can think of, isn't it?"

"No. I, I like the Funkadelics and Screamin' Jay Hawkins and John Coltrane and Sun Ra . . ."

This is a little bit of exaggeration because I'm really just listing off some of the music that I sometimes hear on WABX. I do like a lot of it, but not really Sun Ra, who thinks he's some sort of Martian, but the mention of his name raises Ms. Floyd's right eyebrow in a way that makes me think she's at least a little impressed that I've heard of him.

"I know that you know a lot about music. I've listened to your speeches in my class. Almost every single one of them has been about music. Except when they're about zeppelins." She takes a breath then, and I'm afraid to hear what she's going to say after. "All of which makes this situation somewhat disturbing. *All* the kids need to feel represented. Especially right now. So I'd like Alonzo to take over the announcements and act as music director. I just think it would be a good idea for the time being."

I look at her, unable to speak.

"If you want, you can stay and help run the board or write the announcements."

I look at the edge of the cassette tape I brought in that ended up under the shelf. I wish I could crawl under there with it.

"Daniel?" she says, tilting her head down as if to tilt mine back up. "How does that sound to you?"

"I don't want to write the announcements," I say.

"News writing is an important part of any radio station. A future broadcaster should be able to do any job at a station."

She stops talking and I don't say anything for three or four seconds. Then I finally look up at her. "Is this because I'm white?"

Ms. Floyd locks her eyes right into mine. "It's because

of a lot of things," she says, her voice steadily deepening. "Not all of them have to do with you. Now it's time for you to get to class, young man."

I am dismissed.

The Fade Kicks Me in the Nads

In my head as I walk through the halls is "Rock and Roll, Hoochie Koo" and I don't know why it's there. It should be "Dazed and Confused" because that's how I feel right now, but I guess you can't always choose your own soundtrack, though that seems unfair. Mr. Koznowski, one of the hall monitors, approaches me.

"No announcements today, Danny?" he says. I know he doesn't mean anything by it.

I walk past him, not saying anything. I'm just so embarrassed about what just happened, I can't bear to talk about it.

"Danny?" he says quietly. He is not one of the loud, mean, or even crazy teachers we have here at Redford, who do things like jump in wastebaskets. He's a good teacher. "Where's your next class, son?"

I finally manage to get a word out: "English." Rick Derringer is playing guitar so loud in my head, I can barely hear myself speak.

"With Mr. Acitelli?"

I nod.

"You're going the wrong way," he says, putting his hand on my shoulder.

I stop and turn around and walk in the other direction. The fade is on me so hard now, I don't know which way I'm going.

"Are you all right, son?"

"I don't know," I say, meaning it.

"You look pale."

Mr. Koz puts his hand on my shoulder again, lowering his head to peer into my eyes to see if I'm pulling a fast one. Or if I'm high on drugs.

"Maybe you should stop by and see the nurse." Then he writes me a hall pass for it. "Get over there right now."

I keep walking and when I get to the nurse's office, I just keep moving until I find a door out of school. I go out the side door onto Westbrook, past the kids smoking cigarettes, past a couple tough kids who look at me like, *What is* he *doing cutting class*? Yet no one bothers me. I've noticed this same thing happen when I've cut class with John. All the kids who might normally give you a hard time leave you alone.

My head starts to clear a little, though the throbbing effects of the fade are still plenty strong. I walk up Westbrook to Grand River, not really caring if anyone can see me from a classroom. Up ahead is the stupid eight-ball car horn statue across the street. As I aim for that, I start to feel mad that I got fired just for being white. It doesn't seem fair. It isn't fair and part of me wants to say and think all the things that Mom says when she yells at the television, but somehow I just can't. I'm not even sure why, it's just that I made up my mind a long time ago that I wasn't going to be that way.

I was that way once. It was awhile back, when I still had friends in the neighborhood. Mark and Jim both hated the black people who were supposed to be moving into our neighborhood. (The weird thing was, back then, they really *weren't* moving into our neighborhood.) I suppose I did too, though I really couldn't have told you why if you had asked me.

My dad, coming home from work every night, worried about the blacks coming into the office, getting hired, and taking the jobs away from white people. My mother would complain about how Detroit was going to hell in a handbasket with the blacks moving in and property values going down, which got her started on the riot with the blacks burning and looting until the National Guard had to take control of the streets and how was anyone supposed to feel safe after that and what were we all going to do? My friends would say all the stuff they had heard from their parents and I would say all the stuff I had heard from my parents. Somehow the world was easier to understand that way. Then, within a couple months of each other, both Mark and Jim moved away. Their parents just up and sold their houses. One moved to Livonia and the other to Garden City. So I was suddenly alone on the block.

Later, I would watch *All in the Family* with my mom and dad and laugh at the things that Archie Bunker would say about the *coloreds* and *them people*. My dad would say things like, *Tell it like it is, Archie!*

We'd all laugh.

Yet inside of me, there was just some little hum of a voice saying something back to me. I pictured a family at home like we were, only black, with the television on—probably most of the time like at my house—and *All in the Family* coming on and them watching it. What if they had a kid about my age who heard the way Archie Bunker talked? I knew it would hurt my feelings to hear Archie Bunker talk about me and my parents as *coons* and *jigs* and *their kind*. On TV no less. And to know what a popular show it was all over the country—it would be sad to think about how everyone was laughing at you in a way.

It didn't stop me from watching the show every week with my mom and dad, but it did kind of ruin it for me, to the point where I liked it more when Archie got made the butt of the joke, which happened a lot, I was starting to notice. Still, my parents' favorite part was when Archie would say all those same things. *Tell it like it is, Archie!* my dad kept repeating, which was kind of a hippie expression at the time, so it sounded weird coming out of his mouth—he was nothing at all like a hippie.

It's not like I paid so much attention to that little hum of a voice, mostly I acted like it wasn't there, until my parents sent me to camp for a couple weeks. It was a Boy Scout camp, something Dad wanted me to do so I could meet other boys and learn how to do those things boys are supposed to do, like swim (you know how that turned out) and pitch a tent and tie knots and row boats and hike and get stupid fresh air, instead of staying inside the house to listen to CKLW or read *Drag Strip* by William Campbell Gault or build the model cars, all of which made me perfectly happy. I promised him I'd try the Boy Scouts for a year, which made me miserable. Troop 402 wasn't as bad as I thought it would be, but when you go Boy Scout camping, you're not allowed to bring a transistor radio, there's nowhere to build model cars, and everyone makes fun of you for reading a book even if it is about hot rods. So over that summer I was stuck camping for two whole weeks, with planned activities, craft classes, rifle ranges, KP, the dreaded swimming, and other unpleasantries. Of course you're also supposed to spend time trying to get a rank up from lowly Tenderfoot. (Action News flash: I didn't.)

Something else happened at Boy Scout camp, something that I'm ashamed of. At that time, Troop 402 was mostly from my elementary school, which was still all white. That year at camp, there were troops from all over the city of Detroit, which meant there were a lot of black scouts. This didn't please the kids in my troop. No one gave any real reasons why. They just didn't like it. It didn't matter much because really the only occasion all the troops were gathered at the same time and place was at the first day and at the closing ceremonies, where everyone got together for Indian rituals, speeches, and handing out awards.

I was so relieved that it was going to be over, I couldn't wait for the closing ceremonies. In a way, though, I was proud of myself for getting through it all. I hadn't been promoted to second class, but I could read a map and tie a decent half hitch. I had also gotten "initiated" a number of times—thrown in the water in the middle of the night, sent on *snipe hunts* or off to other camps in search of imaginary utensils like *bacon-stretchers* and *smoke-shifters*. But I wasn't the only one getting tormented, which was nice for a change.

The fact was, when camp was over, I was going to tell my dad that I didn't want to be a Boy Scout anymore—no more meetings, no more campouts. It had just been a year at that point, so I had fulfilled my end of the deal. I was done. But on this last night, me and a group of eight or nine other scouts from my troop were heading over to the jamboree area for the final ceremonies. There were other groups of boys walking the road as well, all on our way to the same place. Then I looked up ahead and coming the opposite way was another group of scouts, about the same size as ours, but they were all black.

After they passed us, I don't know why I did it, but I said, loud enough for everyone I was with to hear: "Fuckin' niggers."

I was surprised that I had said this, because I had never said that word aloud in my whole life, and haven't since, but it just came right out like it was nothing. Maybe I didn't say it all that loud, I don't know, but the words sounded so loud coming from my mouth. I didn't look at my fellow scouts because they didn't bat an eye at what I said, but I glanced back to see if anyone else had heard me. There was just one kid, one of the black scouts, who turned around at the same time as I turned around. He glared at me with such hatred that it took the breath out of me.

I still don't know why I said it. Maybe I was trying it out. Maybe it was being part of a group or being so sick of camp or something that I didn't even know was inside myself, but I said it. I'm not going to try to blame what I said that day on anyone else. It was me. I said it and nobody else.

It was horrible seeing that kid stare at me. I felt scared and ashamed and sick and alone even though I was walking with a group of boys my own age, who were from my neighborhood. Most of whom, like I said, didn't think for a moment about what I had just uttered. I think maybe a couple of them liked me more because I said it, but I didn't like me more. I didn't like me at all. In my head, I kept playing the whole thing over and over, that moment of me saying it, then turning back and seeing that kid look at me. I couldn't stop thinking of it the entire time I was at the ceremonies that evening, seeing all the different boys from all around Michigan. I kept looking around to see if that group of boys was there. I don't even know why they were headed the opposite way.

During the award presentations and the speeches, I still couldn't stop looking around. There were a lot of black Boy Scout troops there too and I kept thinking that I must seem different to them now, as if those kids knew they were observing someone who hated them. It was a horrible feeling. I wanted to get up on the stage during the rituals and apologize, say that I didn't mean it, that I don't even know why I said it. But I had said it and I couldn't un-say it. I had broadcast it out into the world.

After the final ceremonies were over, after the hot dogs and beans, we all trouped back to our campground. My stupid little tent felt even darker and hotter than it had for the past thirteen nights. A mosquito dive-bombed me all night, buzzing and whirring, never veering far from my right ear, always too fast for me to catch in my hand. I was miserable. When I finally fell asleep that last night, my ridiculous sleeping bag twisted around me, even more hot and weighted on my chest than usual, I decided that I just wasn't going to be that way anymore and that I was never going to say anything like that ever again. I know it sounds dumb to say, but I made a sacred vow not to do it, right there in my tent, as my last official act as a Boy Scout. I felt better almost right away. I actually got an hour or two of rest before Denny Pedilla blew reveille and woke me up.

I Seek Refuge

So I'm not sure how to feel about possibly getting booted off WRBG for being white. Instead I think about how I don't really know why it happened. I also think about how I wasn't really kicked off the station. I quit because I couldn't do the job I wanted to do, which is a babyish thing to do. I'd still rather work at the radio station writing the news or working the board than not work there at all. I worry about skipping school, yet it doesn't stop me from walking block after block down Grand River, the fade crushing in on me. When I finally look up, I see a familiar place.

Glimpsing the Mouse House makes me feel better, except for the fact that it's not actually open. It's not even ten a.m. yet. I don't have anywhere else to go, so I decide to wait. After about fifteen minutes, a beat-up aqua Volkswagen Squareback station wagon pulls up. There are faded bumper stickers all over the rear end that say things like, *Ban the Bra*, *War is not healthy for children and other living things*, and, *Is There Life After Birth?*

After sitting in his car in the parking lot shuffling through a bunch of papers and smoking a cigarette, Donnie finally emerges, holding a bundle of paper bags, a few small boxes, and a couple eight-track tapes. He pulls his keys out of his jeans pocket and looks at me.

"What's happenin', Jeff?" he says. "Where's Mutt?"

I smile as if I don't mind being called by that name.

He inserts the key into the grimy lock, twists it, then rattles the doorknob, unable to open the door. "You two up to some of your high jinks?"

"Not today," I say blankly.

Donnie laughs at his own joke because I'm sure not

laughing at it. I don't need any more nicknames. The only good thing about him calling John and me Mutt and Jeff is that now he's not so grouchy when he sees us, because he knows he can make fun of us. Even though he makes the same stupid jokes every time we come in, it's still better than him thinking I'm a narc.

"Hey, Donnie," I say, noticing that he's still fumbling with his keys at the lock. "Need a hand with that stuff?"

"Naw, I'm cool." One more rattle of the knob and the door finally opens. "Come on in."

I walk in behind him. He goes over to the counter where the cash register is. I head over to the table with all the magazines.

"You know we don't have the new *NME* until tomorrow, right?"

"Yeah, I know."

He gives me a look, then glances up at the old neon clock that's always glowing pink and buzzing up on the wall behind the cash register. "Kinda early for you. Not that I give a shit one way or the other, but aren't you supposed to be in school right now?"

Suddenly, I feel like I'm dealing with a parent, which annoys me at first, then it kind of cheers me up. Donnie actually sounds concerned.

"We're always supposed to be in school when we're in here," I point out to him.

Donnie gives a slight shrug, then pulls the band out of his ponytail and smooths the frizzy mess of his hair into a slightly tidier mess, then stretches the band back around it, twisting the two wooden balls around each other to keep it all somewhat in place. "Yeah," he says with a smirk, "guess you're right."

It's quiet in the store except for the buzz of the neon clock.

"I just got fired from the school radio station. That's why I left school today." I don't know why I say this. I guess I want to talk about it with someone. I'm sure Donnie couldn't care less about my stupid little problem, yet he doesn't make fun of me.

"Times is hard, man," he says, taking a small carton of milk out of one of the bags. "Drag."

This is more sympathy than I would expect from Donnie. He goes over to the stereo and inserts one of the eight-track tapes he brought in from his car. Jeff Beck blasts from the speakers right in the middle of a good instrumental from *Truth* called "Beck's Bolero." The fade inches a baby step away from me, but it's not going far.

I walk over to the magazines and examine the covers. Ian Anderson is playing the flute in a blurry photograph on the cover of *Creem*. I kind of want to pick it up and read some of it, but I don't because I shouldn't spend the money right now, and anyway, Donnie hates it when we paw the magazines.

Then he surprises me: "So what happened?"

I tell him about getting there late, and the protest, and Alonzo who was suddenly taking my place, and Ms. Floyd telling me I wouldn't be doing it anymore because I was playing too much rock music, and all the rest of it.

"Too much rock? Is that possible?" Donnie's actually smiling, which may be the first time I've seen him smile when he wasn't laughing at me.

"I know!" I say, kind of smiling too.

"It's prejudiced in a way," he says.

"I know."

We don't say anything for a few seconds.

"Still, she probably got a point," says Donnie, finally. "Spades gotta get theirs by any means necessary." He holds up his fist.

I nod at this. When Donnie says *spades*, he doesn't seem to mean it in a bad way. I've heard Mitch and Dale use the word in the same way. It's a hippie thing, I think. I'm learning a lot these days about hippies. I still don't really get them and they sure don't seem all that crazy about me, but it has been interesting. Regardless, I don't think I'll be using the word, and definitely not around black people. That seems like a good policy.

Just then, Jeff Beck's guitar goes up really high, almost screaming but not quite, just sweet and soaring as if it's taking off from the ground, all while Jimmy Page plays a beautiful rhythm guitar while the other instruments get louder, colliding and meshing as the song rises to a beautiful, noisy, raucous climax. Donnie and I just stand there listening, him behind the cash register, me in front of the magazines, both of us blissfully nodding our heads along with the music. Suddenly, the song just ends. There's a silence, then the *ker-chunk* of the tape changing to the next track.

"Fuck, man. That's a good jam," says Donnie. His eyes are a little bit closed, but he's still smiling.

"Yeah," I say.

I wonder why Donnie's talking so much today and a couple things occur to me. First, I don't have John with me. I always just assumed that it was me who he doesn't like so well, but now I wonder if it's John. Or maybe it's the two of us together that bugs him. The other thing that occurs to me is Donnie smoking that cigarette in the car. If it were marijuana that would probably explain a lot.

Pictures of Jilly

At work, Mitch and Dale act like jerks again, making fun of my Rod Stewart T-shirt, saying that once he blew so many guys that he needed to have his stomach pumped from all the sperm, which is bull since I heard the same thing about Mick Jagger, so I ignore them. I just try to work and not think about what happened at school. I focus on the radio. It's like the DJs are trying to help me fight the fade by playing upbeat jams like "Saturday Night's Alright for Fighting," "Keep Yourself Alive," and "You Really Got Me," but it's no use. Then, just like that, the radio gives up and, "*I'm being followed by a moonshadow* . . ." Wimp! Even thinking about the Iggy concert doesn't make me feel better since I know I'm grounded.

When I get home that night, something looks different about the house. Then I see that most of the furniture has been emptied out of the dining room.

"Mom?" I say, stepping up into the kitchen. I hear Channel 7 *Action News* coming from the living room, but quieter than usual. Bill Bonds's voice is slightly muffled. I walk through the kitchen into the almost completely empty dining room, which looks a lot bigger and brighter without furniture or drapes.

"Mom?" I say again, a slight echo to my voice. What I see in the living room reminds me of the forts I built when I was a kid with a bedspread draped over a couple chairs. All the dining room furniture is crowded into a pile. She's got chairs stacked sideways and upside down on top of the dining room table and drapes thrown over them. She's moved everything in there except the china cabinet. Bill Bonds says something about the mayor.

"Oh for Christ's sake," I hear my mother say from behind the wall of furniture. "He is out of his *goddamned* mind."

A narrow thread of cigarette smoke finally leads me to her. When I make my way around the dining room table piled high with chairs, I find her on the couch with her feet up, drinking a tumbler of Canadian Mist and Uptown, yelling at the television. My mother is sitting in her own adult fort of Danish modern furniture, highballs, and anger.

"What's going on, Mom?"

She looks up at me as Bill Bonds chatters away. "Good," she says, her voice shifting from angry to eager. "You're home."

"Yeah I'm home. Why's all the stuff shoved in here?" I ask, knowing very well why.

"I told you we were cleaning out the dining room," she says, way too cheerily. She tips back the tumbler, drinks until all that remains is the rattle of ice, then holds the glass out for me. "Could you freshen this?"

I inspect the glass. There is no freshening this drink. It requires complete reassembly. "This is a bad time to do this, Ma," I say, grabbing it.

She stares at me, eyes creepily unblinking. "Are you kidding? It's the perfect time to do it."

I can't tell if she's enthusiastic, drunk, or speeding. (Thanks to a special pharmaceutical-themed issue of *Creem*, I have discovered that what my mother takes is basically speed—that is, when she's not taking her Valiums, which are downners. I guess I should be thankful that she's not on 'Ludes yet. It's kind of funny that, after all my worrying about drugs, my mother turns out to be the dope fiend in the family. Well, whatever she's on, I'm not in the mood for any of it. And I'm definitely not in the mood to move furniture after the day I had. On top of that, this really bugs me so close to the anniversary of Dad.

"You'll have to help me move the china cabinet. We'll do it after the news."

"What are you going to do with all of this furniture? Where're we going to put it? There's no room in the basement."

She stares at me as if to say, *Why would you even ask that?* "We're just going to put it all at the curb."

"You're going to throw it away? You're going to throw away our furniture? You wanted all that stuff. Dad bought it for you and him and me to use."

"I don't need a dining room set anymore. I'm becoming a new woman."

This is all I need. "Why are you doing this?" I snap, really PO'd now. "You're not an artist. What do we need a stupid *studio* for?"

"I told you. For—"

"I know! Artistic endeavors. Who cares? Why are you being this way?"

"You shut your mouth, young man."

I'm getting *young man*'ed a lot lately and I'm growing pretty sick of it. "I'm not going to shut my mouth. He hasn't even been dead a year and you're emptying out our house like he was never here."

"We're moving it after the news."

Like fun we are, is what I'm thinking as I turn around

and walk through our now-barren dining room back to the kitchen, still holding her dumb glass.

From the kitchen, I hear an annoying commercial jingle telling me that I have an uncle in the furniture business, which really peeves me considering the discussion I just had. I decide to leave her glass on the counter and let her make her own drink. Then I think of something. I go to the freezer, get a couple of fresh ice cubes, and put them in the tumbler. Instead of measuring out a neat shot like I usually do, I take the half-gallon of Canadian Mist and glug it into the glass until it's about half full of whiskey and ice. Then I go into the bathroom and get one of her Valiums out of the medicine cabinet. Returning to the kitchen, I crush it up with the back of a spoon and dissolve it in her drink. I swish it around, then top it all off with Uptown.

I put the drink on the coffee table next to her, then head immediately into my room and turn the radio on loud. Even with Savoy Brown blasting away, I can still hear Mom calling me back to put more pop into her drink. I ignore her, knowing she'll eventually just drink it that way rather than get up herself. Lying there, I realize it's official: Bad Danny the Problem Teen has taken over. I feel horrible dosing my mother, but she's making me crazy. Not just the furniture, but because she's trying to act like my dad never mattered. I guess it's okay that she wants to become a new woman, but why can't she be a new woman and get a job? And take up painting *after* work?

Until she passes out, I keep the door to my room pushed shut to drown out her and the news. I lie on my bed, face shoved into my pillow, trying not to think about the day I've had. I listen to a commercial for Cosmic Circus. The announcer telling me that they've got all the latest styles—bell-bottoms, stovepipes, and Edwardian gear. I start to doze until I begin thinking about Jill Orr, my old lab partner, which gives me an instant boner. I kind of try to push it out of my head and ignore it as much as I can, knowing that even if I wanted to, I can't whack off in my bedroom with Mom watching television not that far away. Still, as if my body wants to tell my head to shut up, I start to rub myself against the mattress and it feels good, even better than the time in the bathroom, so I keep rubbing and rubbing myself against the mattress, all the while listening for the sound of Mom getting up.

It feels so good that I start not to care about anything. The commercial is over and the disc jockey begins talking about the Iggy show, but I have other things on my mind. Namely the time Jill Orr wore a see-through blouse to class. She had a velvet jacket on over it, but I could still see plenty. It was the day we had to dissect a cow eye and she wouldn't touch it so I had to do the whole thing and unfortunately the picture in my head is half Jill Orr's boob under her jacket when she would finally uncross her arms, and half the inside of the cow eye that looks like a melted gumdrop.

I keep rubbing against the mattress and after a while I don't really care about the song that's playing. Eventually, Jill Orr's boob wins out over the grossness of the cow eye and my head goes empty for the first time today, the fade lifts just enough, and I keep pressing and rubbing and rocking against the mattress, trying not to make the bed creak, and I think of Jill Orr and her boob and her glowy face with the feathered hair and the dangling earrings, but mostly her boob, and I moan pretty loud as the sperm comes out of me and I feel as though I'm flying. When I finally stop rubbing, my pants and underpants are soaking wet and my peter hurts, but I don't care.

I lie there panting for what feels like three or four minutes. The radio is playing Emerson, Lake & Palmer.

Welcome back my friends
To the show that never ends . . .

When I eventually get up the energy to turn over, my mother is standing in the doorway. I have no idea how long she's been there. She doesn't look shocked or mad or upset or anything. Just vacant.

I gasp because it's not what I expected to find—my mother looking numb, having possibly watched me whack off. "Mom!"

She's holding the drink that I made her, but the glass is empty. She doesn't look down, but there's a giant stain on the front of my jeans now and I scramble to pull my bedspread up and over myself.

"What do you want?" I say, voice shaking.

There's a long time when she doesn't speak at all, then finally she does: "That drink was delicious." She places the glass on my desk, next to the radio. "Would you make me another one?"

Is It Me?

After Mom falls asleep, I make sure she's okay, then I wash up, change into my pajamas, and sit in the dark and listen to music on my radio on my earphone. The disc jockey on WWWW is doing an "All Night Album Replay" and spinning the entire double album of the Who's *Quadrophrenia*. It's so good that I can't even believe it. I had read about it and just heard a few songs here and there on the radio, but all together, it's really excellent. I know just how Jimmy, the guy in the album, feels. Except, of course, he drinks, takes pills, gets in knife fights, belongs to a gang, and has a motorbike and a girlfriend. Other than those things, though, I think we're pretty much the same.

I hear the music of a heartbeat
I walk, and people turn and laugh . . .

I lie there in my bed, in the dark, with only Roger Daltrey's voice keeping me company. Listening to the album calms me down and makes me feel less weird about what happened with Mom, who didn't act weird about it at all. It's like she doesn't even know what happened. Maybe she was just drunk or high enough to not remember anything. She was probably already pretty messed up before I gave her the drink. Anyway, I've resolved to never whack off again, no matter what.

Is it me?
For a moment?

During the music, I watch the stripe of light between the door of my room and the doorjamb where it has popped open again. Though I've got my finger plugged in my other ear to hear the music better, I can still hear the television on in the living room where my mother is sawing logs in front of Johnny Carson. I can only catch bits of the show—loud parts, like when the audience laughs or applauds. I shove my finger farther into my ear, until I can feel my fingernail gouging the flesh. I want to focus on the music. I want to lose myself in it. I feel blood in my ear and I don't care. My eyes start to water. The line of light in front of me intensifies and lengthens and glows. I may be falling asleep, but I notice that the music has ended. There's complete silence. Nothing at all. *Dead air*. That's what I've learned it's called when no one says anything on the radio, when there's silence. It's a bad thing. Dead air is not supposed to happen. I don't know where the DJ is—maybe he's in the bathroom or in another studio or smoking pot with another disc jockey. I can hear the needle ride the end groove of the album over and over again, a *kush* of static every other second. I stare at the now-shimmering band of light in front of me, listening to the dead air, and I'm not sure if I'm asleep or awake, if I'm dead or alive, and it's then that I think it's finally happened.

I have become the fade.

Power of the Fade

The next day at school, the black kids are still out front, though everything looks a little less official, as if the school told them that they couldn't have a protest out there, but there are still black kids milling around, holding up signs and big pieces of poster board with slogans on them. In gym, we have a different coach because I guess Coach Tillman hasn't shown up to work for a couple days, so Coach Samuels has to cover his swim class. We have free play today so I just run laps by myself. I get so caught up in them that the assistant coach has to blow his whistle twice to get me to stop. At second period, I suffer through

Alonzo stammering his way through the announcements. I put my fingers in my ears toward the end of it and I can feel the aching crust of dried blood in one of them, but I don't care. It's better than listening. When I see John after second period, he says nothing about it, which I take as the sign of a friend.

"Hey, man, I meant to tell you, my mom's driving us to the concert."

I don't say anything about being grounded. "Wow. How did you work that out? I thought she was mad at you."

John rolls his eyes. "She's always mad at me. In fact, she wasn't going to let me go—" He stops suddenly.

"What happened?"

He sighs. "She said since I was going with you, it was okay."

"Really?" I say.

"Yeah."

Bad Danny the Problem Teen has a good hearty laugh at this.

When I get to speech class, Ms. Floyd isn't there either. The substitute has us read *Speech and Communication* quietly at our desks.

At work, the radio is off all afternoon. I don't ask why, but time goes slow.

When I get home, most of the furniture is still moved out of the dining room, though nothing else has happened. I see that some of her adult fort is down, yet she's still surrounded by furniture. Mom is watching the news as usual, but not talking to the television. She's dressed in a sweatshirt and slacks, with her hair pulled back by a scarf that I remember my father gave her for Christmas one year. She's got a drink next to her, but she doesn't seem drunk. I walk down the hall without saying anything. Bill Bonds is talking to the weather lady about the weather getting colder.

"Right after the news tonight, we're moving that china cabinet, Daniel," my mother calls out to me.

I go into my room and drop off my loose-leaf and books. I take off the flannel that I was wearing, put on the Blue Öyster Cult T-shirt from the bottom of my dresser. I had washed it but never worn it. I put it on and slip a different flannel shirt over it. Then I sit on my bed in my underpants with a single-edged razor. I start slicing the hem out of the right pant leg of some new Levi's that I bought awhile back and have been saving for a special occasion. The fringe looks great and my pants are long enough for once. Maybe a little too long, but that's all right. I'm just finishing off the left pant leg when Mom walks into my room.

"Did you hear me before? I said we're going to move the china cabinet and then we're going to paint the dining room."

"No we're not," I say. "At least I'm not."

My mother puts her hands on her hips. "Oh? And what are you going to do?"

"I'm going to a concert," I say.

"Like hell you are. No one said you could go to anything. You're grounded."

I'm putting on my All Stars by now. I tie the left one, then the right. I stand up and stare at her. It's been awhile since we looked each other straight in the eye. Not that it matters, but I realize that I'm taller than her now. I guess I've been growing.

"Bye," I say quietly. I walk right around her, grab my jacket as I head out the back door. She doesn't try to stop me. Outside, the cool fall air feels so good. I decide to walk all the way to John's house. I can smell a bonfire from somewhere in the neighborhood. I pass trees with toilet paper dangling from them and I notice a few cars with soaped windows or the remnants of broken eggs on them. There are always kids getting an early start on Devil's Night. I remember that tomorrow is the anniversary of Dad.

It's dark when I get to John's, but I'm right on time.

Night of the Iggy

Mrs. Tedesco drives us down Grand River in her Galaxie station wagon, with John and me in the backseat. Nobody says much until John points out the Grande Ballroom, which looks closed now. It's beat up and deserted, but I can't help but think about all the famous bands that played there: the Who, Zappa, Traffic, Cream, Jethro Tull, the James Gang. John's thinking the same thing, I guess. "Wish we could have gone there," he whispers to me.

"Please don't whisper, John. It's not polite," says Mrs. Tedesco from the front seat. "If you have something to say, just say it out loud."

John ignores her and I just keep looking out the window. Every once in a while, we pass the remains of a charred building or some random piles of brick and wreckage in the middle of a weedy lot. On the front of one building, I notice the faded words *SOUL BROTHER* spray-painted right on the brick.

Downtown Detroit seems dim and desolate. I'm surprised there aren't people walking around. I think of how it looked when I was a kid on Saturday mornings with my father. The sun was bright between the skyscrapers, the streets and sidewalks angled with light and shade. The buildings seemed so teeteringly tall, I would mash my face against the car window to try to see the tops of them. Yet when we get to the Michigan Palace, it's definitely not deserted. There's a long line of hundreds of kids that winds down the block. Mrs. Tedesco looks overwhelmed as she circles the venue, searching for the entrance.

"My god," she says. "This is really something. I don't know about this."

Uh-oh. Quickly, I decide that it's time to use my only superpower, the ability to make parents like me. "It'll be fine, Mrs. Tedesco. I think they haven't opened the doors yet so everyone's just waiting in line. It should be open soon." Luckily, I've learned about concert protocol from *Creem*. "Don't worry. We'll be really careful." There's a long pause. "Thank you *so much* for the ride," I add.

"Yeah. Thanks, Mom," says John.

The moment passes and she pulls the car over. "You're welcome, both of you," she says with a faint smile. I smile back at her.

John is almost out the door when she reaches over the backseat and grabs his jacket to keep him in the car. "You boys have a good time." She then lets go and pats John's face. He doesn't pull away as I would expect. "But not too good a time."

John nods frantically at her.

"We'll call you as soon as the show ends," I say.

As the car drives away, John just looks at me, his eyes wide, exhaling loudly, as if to say, *That was a close one*. We walk along the line, headed toward the back. "It's general admission," John explains. "So once they open the doors, there's a big fuckin' rush to get to the front. So just stay with me and run like a motherfucker once they take your ticket. Zabkiewicz told me to head for the front left section because everyone goes for the middle. So left side when we get in, got it?"

After waiting in line for forty-five minutes, that's exactly what we do. He and I run like crazy through this lobby that actually looks like a palace, all gold and red with checkerboard floors and brass rails and marble columns and twisty staircases and giant chandeliers, all of it dusty and kind of worn out, but still real cool. We get good seats about twelve rows back on the left side, just like John said. I feel a little bad because I saw a girl fall while everyone was rushing in. I know she got stepped on a couple times. I wanted to go help her, but John was pulling at my coat and I had to follow him. I'm hoping she's okay.

While we wait for the show to start, I turn around in my seat and look behind us. I can't stop doing it. All the flushed faces, all the flannel and denim and olive drab and black leather and T-shirts. All the hair. The auditorium is almost as cool as the lobby, with huge arches and curtains and paintings and mirrors and lights like glowing teardrops dangling from the ceiling, just on either side of a kind of window cut into the ceiling above us, beaming like a giant version of Iggy's *TV Eye*. It's like a church inside, except the PA is loud with Frank Zappa and Hendrix and some sort of crazy sitar music, and a few people are throwing around Frisbees. I see some guy get bonked by one so I pay attention. The light has a harsh brightness to it, the air hazy and acrid-sweet with the smell of pot.

There's a current of something else too. I feel kind of exposed and not used to being in the middle of this crowd (or most any crowd, for that matter) of hippies and freaks and cool kids, and while that excites me, it worries me a little too. But no one's giving me the *narc* look, so I feel like I'm doing okay.

"Fuckin' excellent, Yzemski man," says John, smiling after taking a deep toke off of the one of the joints he brought. "The fuckin' Stooges. *Whoo!*" he yells. I hear someone *whoo* back from behind us.

As I take a puff, I try not to think about where he stashed it. The joint goes back and forth a couple times, then I let John have the rest. I feel it more tonight, and that, too, excites and scares me. I keep glancing around, I don't know why. Suddenly, I can't stop smiling.

"You stoned?"

"I don't know," I say.

"Then you are."

"Maybe."

"This is fuckin' cool, huh?" says John.

"Yeah, it really is."

After an opening act called Elephant's Memory finishes, we wait for Iggy and the Stooges. "Those guys sucked," says John.

"They were all right," I say, even though I know they were kind of wimpy. It was just so cool to see people play music in front of me. We wait and wait for Iggy to come on. Finally, the lights go down and all we can see are a couple of small red lights here and there on the stack of amplifiers. The crowd is screaming by this time, some of them chanting, "*Iggy! Iggy!*" Finally, there's a screech of feedback and noise and Iggy comes onstage in tights and a kind of tutu, strutting around and sneering like a crazy person, swinging the microphone stand.

Raw power is sure to come a runnin' to you . . .

It's not long before the crowd starts throwing stuff at the band—ice, joints, bottles, coins, eggs, and what look to be pills. James Williamson's blazing riffs fly while Iggy taunts the audience.

"I don't care if you throw all the ice in the world. You're paying five bucks and I'm making ten thousand, so screw ya," he says to all of us. It's insanity. I'm scared for Iggy. I'm scared for me. And the band sounds so loud and raw and ragged and so great. I've never seen or heard anything like this.

I'm a streetwalking cheetah
With a heart full of napalm
The runaway son of the nuclear A-bomb
I am the world's forgotten boy
The one who searches and destroys . . .

"I am the greatest!" Iggy screams at us.

I think he might be right. During "Gimme Danger," John turns to me and says, "We made it, Yzemski man. Iggy! Fuck yeah!" He lays his hands down low for me to give him some skin. "Rock and roll!" he yells.

Shortly after that, during "Louie Louie," a beer bottle almost hits Iggy and the show ends. As he walks offstage, Iggy gives us the finger and says, "Ya nearly killed me, but you missed again. Keep trying next week."

Rock and roll.

Have You Seen Your Mother, Baby?

When I get dropped off shortly before midnight, the house is silent. No television, no radio, no nothing. Walking in through the kitchen into the hallway, ears still buzzing from the concert, I can see my mother waiting there in the living room for me. Before she even says anything, I can tell that she's drunker than I've ever seen her before. I don't know what else she's got in her, but her voice is both shaky and slurred.

"Look who's home from his rock concert," she says from her fortress of furniture. She's got one cigarette in her hand and another smoldering in the hubcap ashtray. "The boy who just does whatever he wants."

My ears are ringing and I'm still in a good mood from the concert. "Go to bed, Mom."

"I could just put you out of this house, Daniel," she says, smearing the syllables in my name. "I could do that."

Normally, this kind of talk would alarm me, but not tonight. "Yeah, you could, but you'd never survive."

"Oh, is that so?"

"Uh-huh. Who'd do the shopping, the laundry, the bills, the dishes? Who'd clean up the messes you make? Who'd make any money around here? I keep asking you to get a job, but you won't. We got Dad's pension, but that's not enough. You've pretty much drunk up the insurance money."

She looks at me like she doesn't know the person who's speaking to her. "What has happened to you?" The circles under her eyes are so dark. She's got her hair pulled back with a rubber band. Her housecoat is stained in the front. There are a couple of burns in it too. My mother is a mess and I don't want to fight anymore.

I meet her eyes, but they can't seem to focus on mine. "I'm sorry I skipped school, Ma. I'm not going to do it anymore." I wish I could say that I mean it, but I really say it to make her feel like she's won so she'll leave me alone and we can all go to bed.

She takes a sip of something from a tall tumbler. A giant jug of Canadian Mist was on the counter when I came in. I didn't even know they made them in that size. I guess she's not bothering to mix in any Uptown anymore.

"I never wanted to get married," she says, looking at the bottom of an upended dining room chair, the cushion resting on one of our end tables. "I never wanted to get married. I never wanted to have a baby. I never wanted to live in this city." She takes a deep drag of her cigarette and holds the smoke in her lungs like it's going to ease her pain. "I hate this place. I always have. I wanted to go to college and go live in New York or Paris or somewhere beautiful, somewhere instead of this ugly goddamned city where I grew up and where I'm going to die."

"Ma."

"It's my own fault. I just did what I was supposed to do, what everyone told me I had to do." She stops to stub out her cigarette and light another. "Everyone thought it was silly that I would want anything other than—" She holds up her wobbly hand and swivels it around. "*This*. Now it's too late and even the husband I didn't want—"

"Mom, please." I don't want to hear any of this.

I watch the end of her cigarette glow red, then lighten to ash as she inhales. "Your father and I—we got used to each other and got used to our life, but that was about it." She takes a long sip of her drink. "I don't know what happened. Maybe there were other women."

"Ma, if he wasn't at work, he was home, taking care of you and me or building something for the house. He never stopped worrying about you."

"He loved you very much, Daniel."

"I know," I say, holding back tears. "He loved you too. You don't know how much."

"Go to bed," she says in a half-whisper.

There's Got to Be a Morning After

When I wake up in the morning, the fade is on me so hard I'm not sure I can move. Even Iggy can't help me today. I decide that I'm not going to school and that I will call in sick to work. Then I start to think about what happened a year ago on this day and my mother calling in sick for my father. That makes me decide that I should get up, but I still can't even turn on the radio. Amazingly, what gets me out of bed is Mom, who for the first time in months is up before me. She actually comes into my room.

"Get up, Daniel," she says, not bothering to lower her voice. She sounds weird—peppy and grouchy and still drunk.

"I don't feel good," I tell her. My stomach is queasy and the whiskey smell coming off her isn't helping. I don't think she's been to sleep.

"You have to go to school. You *have* to go to school."

"All right, all right. Fine."

I get up and she disappears into her room. There's no mention of what happened last night. I wonder if she's decided that she was dreaming or that we should both act as though nothing happened. Or she just plain forgot everything. I turn the radio on low ("Train Kept A-Rollin'"—the latest Aerosmith). After I get washed and dressed, I notice a bowl of soggy, brown-milked Cocoa Puffs on the kitchen table that looks like it's been there for at least a couple hours. There's also a bag lunch waiting for me. I grab it and head out the door without saying anything, figuring she's finally gone to bed. The day is overcast, unseasonably warm and muggy, but it doesn't look like rain. The air is heavy and hard to breathe. On the way to school, passing more TP'ed trees and egged front doors, I look in the lunch bag and find a half-eaten apple, a box of Jell-O, and three cents folded up in a napkin. I haven't needed milk money since fifth grade. I pocket the three cents and toss the rest in a garbage can.

At school, the crowds are even bigger in the front yard around the kids with the signs about equal representation. There is chanting too, though it's not very organized, and since I'm rushing past I can't really make out much of what they're saying, but I do think I hear a few of them yelling, "*Equality now!*" There are some hillbilly-looking white kids milling around too, along with a few leftover G-balls. I don't know if they're for or against the protest, but I keep moving, doing more zigging and zagging than I've ever had to do outside.

I'm sick of all of them, to tell the truth. All I wanted to do was read the announcements and play music and everything turned into something that meant more than I ever intended it to mean. I feel so stupid and ashamed for not thinking of playing more music by black people for the radio station—besides Hendrix, that is. I would have happily played Buddy Miles or Earth, Wind & Fire or War. I think of the Isaac Hayes and Temptations and Graham Central Station albums that I'd seen at the library, that I never once thought about taking out to play on the air. I could have been the cool free-form FM jock who simply plays what's good, regardless of category. Instead I was just inconsiderate me. I wasn't trying to hurt anyone's feelings. I just like rock and roll.

The smoking kids are looking at the protesting kids, not in any particular way, just like they're watching to see what happens, but they're too cool to act like they care. When I walk past them, their eyes shift toward me and I wonder if they know I got fired. My face burns and I pick up my pace to get to the front door. The walk seems extra long today. All the good feelings from the last night's concert are gone. I feel clammy inside my clothes. My face is hot and tingling, so much so that I'm actually looking forward to a shower after gym.

Sly Stone Was Right

I'm at my locker putting away my books, getting ready to head to gym class. I still feel as though people are staring at me. But when I turn around, there's no one looking. In fact, there aren't even as many people in the hall as usual. I do see a couple of black girls running toward me, yelling kind of crazy-like. I can't understand what they're saying. I don't know why they're goofing around before class, and I don't really care. But behind them, I see more kids running and screaming, and it doesn't sound like anyone is goofing around. "And When I Die" by Blood, Sweat & Tears starts playing in my head. I haven't heard it in ages.

Just then, there's a hushed rumbling and a vacuum *whoosh* all at the same time. I think of the Doppler effect from my science class with Mr. Plasyk. The rush of sound as a train approaches the station. That's what I hear a moment later—a giant, deafening wave of noise, louder than any song in my head. More kids are running down the hall now and the looks on their faces scare me. I hear the voices of kids behind those kids. I feel something in my chest, the clatter of my heart, the quickening of my breath, the shrill static of blood rushing through my veins—all these noises increasing in volume, made louder from the echoing space inside of me. The first few kids pass and behind them is another crush of kids, but they aren't running. They're fighting. One of the hillbilly kids I saw out front is now using a picket sign to hit a black kid. The sign is bent and torn, with blood on it. There are white girls hitting black girls, black girls pulling the long hair of white girls. A couple of sports-playing white kids are hitting a black kid, then they get jumped by a couple of sports-playing black kids. I am in the middle of a mini race riot, yet it doesn't look so mini to me.

I realize that I have to get out of the way of this thing, this sucking cyclone of sound and violence and madness that's passing through the halls. All I can think of is how it looks in a cartoon when characters fight—a big whirlwind, all circular lines with the occasional fist or foot sticking out from the blur. I slam my locker shut, not bothering to put the lock on it. I glance around to see where I can hide. The bell for class rings, though I can barely hear it.

Around me most of the running kids look scared, but some of them are really after each other. In front of me, someone tackles a black kid to the ground and starts hitting him. Then someone pushes me into the pile of people. Black kids fall in on top of me. I don't know if they're after me or if they're being pushed. Then someone kicks me in the thigh and someone else slugs me in the back of my neck. Out of reflex, I swing my arm around. I hear a scream and I realize that I've hit a black girl in the head. I'm just trying to get away. I swing my hand the other way, attempting to get myself off the floor, but I hit someone else. Someone else screams, and I realize I'm still holding my lock.

"I'm sorry!" I yell. I let go of the lock.

Auburey Wimbush, a big black kid, picks me up from the pile and throws me a few feet straight into a locker, possibly my own. My head makes a loud noise when it hits the metal. The wind is knocked out of me so I can't breathe. It all hurts, I think, but I can't really feel anything. The good thing is that I'm out of the tornado of people and I can still stand up. As I'm wheezing against the locker, Auburey is about to hit me again, but a tall white kid with short hair socks him on the side of his head and they go at it.

I'm wheezing and dizzy and I start staggering, unintentionally doing my zigging and zagging, trying to avoid everybody, when I see the door to the boys' bathroom. Before anyone can hit me again, I run over to the door and try to push it open. I don't know why I think I'll be safe there, but at least I'd be out of this. The door won't give, but I'm too scared to stop now. I catch my breath and push harder, throwing my shoulder against it, which hurts really bad. Finally I put all my weight behind it until the door shoves open far enough for me to slide in. I crush through, feeling my stomach, then my rib cage, squeezing past the doorjamb. When I finally get my whole body inside, I right away fall over something, I think someone's leg. I'm in another pile, but it's just a pile of two. I can't see much at first since the lights are off and it's dim in there.

"Don't hit me," a kid says, covering his face with his forearms. His voice is high, but it's definitely a boy.

My side hurts and my head hurts and my leg hurts and I'm just starting to be able to breathe again. "I don't want to hit you!" I yell, panting. "Don't hit me!"

"Hold the door shut!" the kid says, frantic. "Hurry!" I can hear the tears in his voice. "They'll get in here!"

I realize he's right. "Yeah, yeah, okay!" I say, sliding around on the floor. I can hear the studs on the pockets of my new Levi's scratch the gold-colored tile that we're lying on as I push my shoulder against the door right where someone has drawn a big peter with sperm shooting out of it like bullets. The floor is gross, of course, like it always is, and I can't believe I'm sliding around on it, but I'm glad to be away from the madness out there. The echo inside the bathroom seems so loud, even though it's just the two of us, whispering. I guess we're not really whispering, because you have to speak up to be heard over the weird *whoosh* of screaming and hitting and slamming against lockers that's happening on the other side of the door.

The kid shifts himself on the floor, kneels at the door, and together we hold it shut. No one seems to be trying to get in, but every once in a while there's pressure against the door as if people are falling against it as they fight. We push against it as hard as we can. Hearing him sob makes me start to cry a little too. We stand there, pushing against the door, both kind of crying, but trying not to do it in front of each other, which is pretty hard since we're only a foot apart.

I look over at the kid now that my eyes are adjusting to the light. He's a black kid, maybe about the same size as me, but a little heavier. He's wearing a light-green shirt with a striped design on it, probably from Arlan's or Topps, which I'm sure was pretty nice this morning when he got dressed, but now it's dirty and torn at the shoulder. His dark-green plaid bells are scuffed and shiny at the knees like he slid on them. His round face is wet with sweat and tears. There's a big scratch on his cheek too. He's got a natural, but it's not big and cool like the other kids. It's lopsided and I can see a piece of light-blue lint on the back like it came from his blanket. I don't recognize him, but that's not so strange. There's a lot of us kids, black and white, who no one pays any attention to, who wander the halls of Redford every day. We're all trying not to be seen or heard, so is it any wonder that we don't see or hear each other? I'm one of them, even though I had my little period of notoriety when I was on the school radio station. Now that's over.

"What happened to your face?" I ask, trying to talk normal, but my nose is running and I have to sniff back the snot.

Finally, he looks at me. "Some white girl clawed me."

"Jeez." I wonder if I should apologize, but I didn't do it. "Auburey Wimbush threw me up against a locker. I never did anything to him. He doesn't even know who I am." I'm not trying to outdo him, I'm just saying what happened.

"He's big," the kid finally mutters.

Talking about it makes my shoulder ache, but I keep cramming it against the door. "I know. It really hurt."

"Who started it? Do you know?"

I think back on when I walked into school and I remember the hillbilly white kids around the protesting black kids. They didn't look like they were there to support the cause. But I don't really know. I just shake my head. "I'm not sure what happened. It's crazy."

The kid holds his ear to the door. "What's going on out there? It still sounds like they're fighting."

I listen as well. I hear yelling.

"I'm scared," he says.

"Me too," I say, not loudly.

I turn and put my back to the door, facing the inside of the bathroom. I look at the filthy towel roller sagging off its spindle, at the *Dirty Hoods* graffiti markered on the wall. I try not to use the bathroom while I'm at school. It's one of the areas to stay away from, a lair of tormentors. I learned that fast. If I have to go, I usually hold it till I get to work.

"You think there's any way we could get out of here?" I say, looking at the windows up over the sinks.

"Maybe. I don't know where those go."

"Go see if you can get one open. I'll hold the door." I put my ear to the door. Things are quieting down out there. Still, I'm not going out to check.

While the kid gets up, I push against the door extra hard, which hurts a lot. He walks over to the window and gives it a try. When it lifts right up, he looks at me all excited, but then we see the metal grating fastened over the outside of the window frame.

"Dang," he says.

"I forgot about that stupid grate." Then the door pushes against my shoulder and opens about two inches and I lean back as hard as I can. The kid runs over, shoves his shoulder against the door, and we get it shut.

"What was that? Did you see?"

"No," he says. Then he yells at the door: "Go away!" He looks at me, eyes wide, as if to say, *Where did that come from?*

"Boys," says a male voice on the other side of the door. It doesn't sound like a student. The voice says something else that I don't quite catch.

"What did he say?" I whisper to the kid.

"I don't know."

We keep our shoulders against the door.

We hear the voice again: "Boys, let us in. Everything's all right. You don't have to be scared. It's okay."

"I think it's Mr. Beckler," I whisper. Then aloud: "Mr. Beckler?"

Silence for a moment. "Danny? Is that you?"

No More Pencils

A black teacher who I don't really know takes the kid away. I am sent off the other way down the hall with Mr. Beckler. It doesn't even occur to me to say bye or anything since they split us up so soon after we opened the door. I guess we were distracted by all the cops in our school. Strange to see them walking around, guns on their hips, radios squawking, grim official expressions on their faces. I look over at Mr. Beckler and he seems shocked at what he's seeing too. The hallway is a mess. There are books and jackets and busted pieces of signs and broken glass and knocked-over trash receptacles, paper and garbage spilling out.

Walking along with Mr. Beckler, my internal soundtrack kicks in and guess what? Alice Cooper's

"School's Out." Finally, an appropriate song in my head for once. The excellent whanging guitar intro—*Do da dee, do da dee, do da dee daaah!* Then those stomping, walloping drums roll through my head. Even with the post-mini race riot headache coming on, it makes me feel better:

Well we got no choice
all the girls and boys
makin' all that noise . . .

With my foot, I push a girl's platform shoe out of the way as we pass and it's so heavy I almost trip on it. Up ahead, I see a shiny little dark puddle on the floor. It's not very big, but it feels big once I realize it's someone's blood.

School's been blown to pieces!

Don't get me wrong, all of this, except for the blood, is nothing that a good sweeping wouldn't take care of. (And even the blood could be cleaned up with some of that sawdust stuff they use when some kid vomits.) This is, after all, a high school, lined with metal lockers and thick reinforced doors and three-hundred-pound porcelain drinking fountains from the 1930s. It's built to be indestructible. It's what's in the air that feels different. I can still feel the anger, smell the fear and the hate and a little bit of pee too, as if someone got scared and wet their pants.

I'm not sure what I'm feeling right now, yet I pretty quickly realize that the fade has lifted. Which is weird since you'd think this would sink me even lower. Instead I feel just the opposite. I've never been in the middle of anything like this. Now I can say I've been in a mini race riot. It makes me feel older and cooler. I know it's crazy, but it's true.

"I'm assuming you boys were in the bathroom when it started," says Mr. Beckler.

"Oh no," I reply, almost bragging, "I was right in the middle of it."

His tone changes: "You were?"

"Oh yeah."

"Shit. I didn't realize. I thought you two just happened to be in there and stayed there. Are you okay?"

It throws me off to hear a teacher swear. "I don't know. I guess."

Mr. Beckler stops me in the middle of the messed-up hall. "Hold up, Danny. I'm asking if you got hurt."

"My shoulder really hurts, but it's okay." I move my left shoulder to show that it still works. "I did hit the back of my head, though."

He walks around behind me. I feel his hand up near my hair. "Does this hurt?" he asks.

An electric jolt of pain burns from my skull straight down my neck and Alice Cooper flies from my brain. My scream is answer enough.

"Christ. We're taking you to the nurse. You've got a great big goose egg back there."

I try to say, *Okay*, but I'm still gasping.

Mr. Beckler pats my shoulder. "Sorry about that."

Suddenly, I don't feel so cool anymore. Mr. Beckler allows me to catch my breath, which takes a minute because now my chest hurts too. After I get my senses back and he's sure I'm not going to pass out, we turn and head toward the nurse's office.

"What happened with that?" Mr. Beckler asks, his voice low.

Without thinking, I just say, "Auburey Wimbush threw me into a locker." I don't say it like it's any big deal, it's just what happened.

Mr. Beckler doesn't look pleased. He purses his lips and makes a small shushing noise. His eyes dart to either side of the hall.

I realize what he's doing here. "Oh, I'm sorry. I didn't mean to be a squealer."

"It's not that. It's just—you're still going to have to go to school here come tomorrow, Danny. We all are. You need to remember that."

I rush to explain myself, but Mr. Beckler holds a finger to his lips. "In a moment, Danny." He looks off to the side where some kids are talking to a teacher. "Okay."

I get it now. Mr. Beckler doesn't want the other kids to think I'm telling on anyone. We keep walking. Up ahead, two black girls are speaking to a police officer and my counselor, Mrs. Corbin. It's a light-skinned black cop with a thick mustache and puffy tufts of Afro sticking out of the side of his policeman hat. Luckily, neither of the girls is the one I accidentally hit. When we pass, they look at us. I wonder, *Is it a coincidence they're all black? Are the black teachers talking to the black kids and the white teachers talking to the white kids? Is that what's going on?* The girls look at me, but I can't tell if they're mad.

Mrs. Corbin separates herself from the group and catches up with us. "Are you all right, Danny?" she asks.

"I'm taking him to the nurse," Mr. Beckler says. "He may have a concussion." He points to the back of my head.

Mrs. Corbin takes a peek at my goose egg and makes a pained face. “My lord,” she says, shaking her head. She touches my hand. “We’ll talk when you feel better.” She heads back to the cop and the girls.

Once we’re a few steps away, Mr. Beckler says, “Now you may continue. Discreetly.”

I keep my voice down, but I’m in a hurry to explain. “Auburey thought I hit some girl with a lock. I mean, I did, but it was an accident. I forgot I had it in my hand. Everything happened so fast. Then when he threw me into the locker, some other kid slugged him and I got away into the bathroom. So Auburey sort of did me a favor.” I have to stop talking because I need to swallow.

Mr. Beckler puts his hand on my shoulder. “I understand. It’s okay.”

I don’t know why I’m sticking up for Auburey. I guess I feel that I could just as easily look bad too, hitting girls with locks and everything. Besides, I don’t need Auburey on my list of people who want to beat me up. Even though I may already be on it.

“I heard about what happened with WRBG,” Mr. Beckler says. “I’m very sorry. You were our best announcer.”

This is the nicest thing I’ve heard in the past two awful days. At first, I think I’m going to cry, but then I just get the hiccups. They come on so fast, it’s like I’m swallowing the air and can’t stop. I’m making a noise that’s kind of like a whooping crane. Maybe Mitch and Dale were right after all.

“Okay, take it easy,” says Mr. Beckler. We stop by some lockers and I realize I can’t catch my breath. The hiccups just keep getting louder. Some girls walk by and start laughing after they pass.

Mr. Beckler runs away for a minute and returns with a little plastic cone cup full of water. He hands it to me. "Go ahead, Danny. Drink it."

After spilling a fair amount on the front of my shirt, I manage to get the water down. The hiccups stop as quickly as they started.

"She just took my job away," I sputter. "I was late once. *Once*."

He puts his hand on my shoulder again. "She's in charge of the station, you know that. She's my boss too. Plus, it's more complicated than you just being late."

"I know, I know. It's my fault. I was playing too much rock music. I should've been thinking of all the kids."

He looks at me sadly. "It's *much* more complicated than that, son."

"Do you think you could get me back on?"

"I don't know, Danny. I'll do what I can. We'll see."

When we reach the nurse's office, there's a line of kids waiting to get in. No one looks too messed up. I go to the back of the line. There's another police officer standing on the other side of the hall. I don't know why he's here. Are we all going to be arrested after we see the nurse? Or is he here so there are no more fights? I'm hoping it's the second reason.

Dumb Questions from Dumb Adults

The nurse, Mrs. Srodek, a stern, thin woman with a nicotined crook between the index and middle fingers of her right hand, checks me out, asks me a few questions like if I feel dizzy, who the president is, what day it is, and stuff like that.

"That's a pretty good bump on your noggin," she says,

touching the area around it. I'm glad she's being careful. "What happened to you?"

"Someone pushed me against a locker." I keep Aubu-rey's name out of it this time. "I didn't see who."

She shakes her head and tsks. "*These kids* . . ." She doesn't say the rest of it, but it's there. I can hear it. I'm getting a lot better at hearing what adults are actually saying these days.

Mrs. Srodek holds up two fingers and asks me how many she's holding up. I tell her. She looks in my eyes, gives me a packet with a couple aspirin and another cone of water. I take them and she tells me to go home, put a cold compress on the bump, and rest, but not to take a nap. She doesn't think I have a concussion, but I should definitely stay awake until it's time to go to bed tonight.

"There are kids who go to sleep when they have a con-cussion and never wake up. You remember that."

I nod and it hurts.

"You need to go straight home, nowhere else. Do you hear me?" she says sharply. "Will your mother be home?"

"She's always home," I say.

"Good. We'll be calling her to let her know you'll be along. No lollygagging. Straight home."

I immediately recognize this as a lie. Mrs. Srodek writes out instructions on a piece of paper as well as a permission slip to get me out of the school.

As I leave the clinic, I overhear that they're sending most students home for the day, but not everyone. Some are being *spoken to.*

The main hall is quiet and mostly deserted now, though still a big mess. The front entrance is closed off for the rest of the day and when I walk out a side door onto Westbrook, there are no kids hanging around smoking or anything. There are still cop cars parked outside—bulbous light-blue-and-white Furys from the 8th Precinct across the street. I'm surprised that it took them so long to get to the mini race riot today. But then it all happened so fast, and I'm starting to think that although it felt like it went on for hours, like me and the kid were trapped in the bathroom forever, the whole thing was probably over and done in about ten minutes.

After a few deep breaths, a song by Spirit starts playing in my head.

It's nature's way of telling you
something's wrong
It's nature's way of telling you
in a song . . .

It makes my head hurt a little, but it's a good tune so I just let it play.

Mystery to Me

On the side streets, the only sounds I hear are a few birds in the trees and the hum of traffic from Grand River behind me. Then someone yells, "Yzemski!" The first person I think of is Auburey Wimbush, but it doesn't sound like him, and the voice isn't angry. I turn to see John running toward me. He's so tall it's like watching a film of a giraffe on *Mutual of Omaha's Wild Kingdom*, except the giraffe is wearing an army jacket. I can imagine Marlin Perkins saying something like, *Behold the majestic creature romping through the veldt*. Just watching John run cheers me up a lot.

"Hey, man, hold up," he calls out.

I start walking back toward him. "Hey, how you doin'?"

His eyes are wide and excited as he shakes my hand. "Holy shit, man, was that fuckin' nuts or what? That shit was *heavy*, man."

"Yeah, I know. I got caught up in it. I was in the middle of it," I say, almost with glee, though the mere mention of the fight makes the back of my head throb. My shoulder starts to hurt too.

"No shit? Really? *Wow*."

"Yeah!" I don't know why I'm making it sound so exciting. "I got hit in the head and bashed against a locker and everything." I almost mention Auburey's name so it sounds authentic, but decide against it. I point my finger up near the back of my head.

"Really? You did?"

"Yeah."

John cocks his head to take a look. "Whoa. That's a fuckin' knot, Yzemski."

"I ended up barricading myself in the boys' bathroom with some other kid."

"No shit?"

"Yeah. We were trapped there. It was like we were in a POW camp."

John starts laughing. "Only you, Yzemski man. We have a mini race riot and you're playing *Hogan's Heroes*. Fuckin' turkey."

I know John is kind of making fun of me, but I don't care. I laugh too. It's really good to see him.

"Sorry about the radio station gig, man. Blows."

He knows. I guess everyone knows. I want to tell him about what happened with WRBG, but I don't. I don't want to hear what he says about it, I don't want him to be angry for me, because I'm finished being angry for myself.

"Eh, it's cool," I say. And for the first time, when I say that something is *cool*, it actually sounds cool. Which cheers me up for some goofy reason. Anyway, I've already made up my mind that I'm going to go see Ms. Floyd tomorrow to find out if I can still work for the station, at least doing something. "Where were you when everything happened?" I ask, changing the subject.

"Aw, I was just about to geometry. Guess I was pretty far from the action," he says, pressing his hands into the pockets of his army jacket. I hear a little regret in his voice.

My head starts aching again, and I'm done making it sound like I was cool for being caught in the middle of a big stupid fight between white kids and black kids. "You were lucky," I say, tired now. "It was really scary."

He shrugs. "I guess."

We move along in silence after that. I don't really know why John is walking with me to my house since his house is in the opposite direction. He's got a pretty good walk ahead of him to get back home, but I guess he's in no hurry, and besides, we've all got the day off. I wonder if the kids who were fighting in the halls are still in school or if they've let them go. Will they all find each other again and continue to fight? I worry that here in Detroit we'll all be fighting like this for the rest of our lives. It makes me sad.

"I'd invite you over to my house," I say to John, thinking about the pile of furniture in the living room and the fact that I haven't cleaned the house in weeks, "but the place is a mess. My mom's kind of . . . redecorating."

Which is a pretty nice way of saying it, I think.

"It's cool. No problem. I'll just catch the Fenkell bus by your place."

And as if by putting a name to whatever it is my mother is doing, I end up making something happen. When we're about a block from my house, I can see that there's a blue car on someone's lawn up ahead. This is not so unusual on our street, since there's a lot of people moving in and out these days, and for all the same reasons. Even so, I start to walk a little faster.

"You in a hurry to get home or something?"

"No, no," I say, but I keep moving fast, not really even knowing why until I'm eight or nine houses away. That's when I realize that the car I see might very well be on my lawn, though I still can't tell. It looks an awful lot like the *Hindenburg*.

"Oh man."

"What's happening?" asks John. "Why you freakin' out?"

I'm just about to start running when I see the *Hindenburg* drive off the lawn, then the screen door snaps open and our china cabinet flies out behind it, being dragged by the car, gouging out ruts of grass as it bounces down the curb.

Stunned, I just stand there and watch it happen right in front of us. My mother, driving my dead father's car, screeches toward us, her eyes focused only on the road before her, as if she didn't have a large piece of Danish modern furniture tied to her bumper with clothesline. As she passes, I see that the legs are broken off, the wood is scraped white beneath the varnish, and the doors pop open every few seconds, releasing pieces of the china my family never used to shatter on the street.

"What the fuck was that?" asks John, more astonished than I've ever heard him.

I take a breath, squeeze shut my eyes for a second, then open them up. "My mother," I say.

Brokedown Palace

After she drives past us, I don't know what to do. I should run after the car but instead I just stand there. I'm still in shock from my day at school, so this is more than I can even try to understand.

"Mom?" I yell as she roars down the street. Yet even if she was paying attention, there's no way she could hear me over the grind and screech of wood against concrete and the breaking glass and porcelain.

Right at the end of the block, Mom hits the gas and the last big piece of the china cabinet slides around and slams right into the back of a Dodge Polara parked just a few doors down on the next block, finally breaking the clothesline that she had looped around the thing. After that we see only the taillights of the *Hindenburg* as they flash and swerve down the street, a spaghetti flutter of rope ends hanging from the back of the trunk.

I glance over at John and we both turn away and start walking toward my house like neither of us saw anything the least bit insane.

"That was your mom in the car?" John says after a few moments.

I nod, looking at the trail of debris in the middle of the street that leads right to my house. There's a stubby wooden leg, some pieces of dishes, silverware scattered everywhere, paper and cloth place mats littering peoples' easements. A couple of neighbors are out on their porches now, surveying the damage, avoiding eye contact with me.

"Fuck, man," says John, "I thought *my* mom was nuts—" He stops talking. "Sorry."

"It's okay. You might want to go now, though."

"You sure?" He says it to be nice, but I can tell by his voice that this is exactly what he wants to do. I would too, were it me.

"Yeah. The bus stop is just on Fenkell next to the Standard station."

"Okay. See ya, man. Good luck."

I watch him walk to the end of the block where he turns left on Fenkell and disappears behind a hedge. *I hope he makes it to* Melody Maker, I say to myself.

At my house, the front door is wide open. There are huge gashes in the doorjamb and curls of wood dangling from it. Our screen door, yanked back by the china cabinet, is hanging from only one hinge. Pieces of debris now rest on the front walk, near where the cabinet slammed down the porch steps. The bush next to the porch is half crushed. Our lawn is furrowed from the legs and corners of the cabinet. Broken dishes and silverware are scattered everywhere, along with candles, dainty cut-glass salt and pepper shakers, and oil cruets. Stuff we haven't used since my parents hosted pinochle parties years ago.

I wedge the screen door back into place. I pull out the screen where it is torn and throw it on the front lawn with all the other trash. With my hands and heels, I push the torn turf back into place as best I can and press down loose chunks of it into the bare spots. Then I go into the backyard and get both the trash cans. I pick up all the stuff on the front lawn. When one of the cans is filled, I haul it to the backyard.

After that, I go into the garage and get my Radio Flyer wagon from when I was a kid, put a broom and dustpan in it along with the other trash can, and pull that behind me down the street, picking up as much of the stuff as I can. I sweep up broken glass and pieces of china and trampled napkins, placing it all in the trash can. As I work my way down the block, I notice a couple people watching me through partially open front doors or from behind the shades in their windows. The only person who actually shows himself is the kid on his bike who visited me in the driveway that time.

"Hey," he says to me. He's on his bike again. He's on it a lot, I've noticed. He's stopped and for some reason he's got the back of his T-shirt pulled up over his head. I don't know why, but it makes me smile.

"Hey," I say.

"What happen?"

"There was a little accident."

His mother appears in the driveway. She calls to him: "Darrell, don't you bother that man."

I put a broken pink candle in the wagon and look up to her. "He's not bothering me, ma'am," I say. "It's okay."

Darrell rides up to where his mother stands. She puts her hand on the back of his head, then smiles solemnly at me. They turn and go back up their driveway.

I just keep pulling the wagon, cleaning up as best I can. I go most of the way down my street, picking up everything I find until I notice a blue-and-white Plymouth Fury driving toward me a block away. I'm too tired to be scared. I just don't care anymore. The cop car keeps heading in my direction until it's about half a block away, then it stops near the smashed-up Polara and pulls into a driveway. That's when I roll up to the sidewalk and turn around to head home. My block is clean. That's all I can do for now.

A Lighter Shade of Beige

I'm surprised when the police don't show up at the house. I assumed they would go door to door asking neighbors if they knew anything about a woman pulling a china cabinet behind her car, but I guess that didn't happen. When I cleaned up our block, I hadn't meant to get rid of the trail that led back to our house, but I suppose I did that very thing.

What worries me more than the police showing up is my mom *not* showing up. I call into work and let them know why I'm not in today. I tell them about the mini race riot and that the school nurse says I might have a concussion and that I need to rest.

Mitch says, "I don't care. You just better be in tomorrow. Fuckin' Crane." I hear the James Gang's "Funk #49" playing on the radio in the background. I focus on the cluck and grind of Joe Walsh's guitar instead of Mitch talking.

I don't know what to do with myself. After I finish the homework that I should have done last night, I decide to fix some of the mess that Mom made. It will keep my mind occupied. I bring my radio in and play it as loud as I like. In the dining room, there are gouges in the walls, so I find some Spackle downstairs and fill them in. I do the same with the gashes on the doorframe. An hour or so after the Spackle dries there's still no word from Mom, and I decide to repaint the walls. So I drag up cans of beige and white paint from the basement, along with a roller and a tray. I lay down newspaper on the carpeting.

I paint. It makes me feel a little better to cover all the mess on the walls. I cover it all with beige paint. It gets on my hands and I notice that even though beige is a light color, it's still darker than my skin. When Dad painted the room a couple years ago, I remember my mother telling him that beige was *tasteful*. She always wanted things to be tasteful, not *gaudy* or *tacky*. I remember Dad not having an opinion either way. He just wanted to make her happy, so everything got painted beige. I decide that it's funny that my mother loves beige so much because it's brown and white mixed together, which is just what she doesn't want to happen in our neighborhood. It's stupid, I know, but it makes me smile.

I keep on painting into the night. I have just enough paint to give all the walls one coat. After that, I paint the white trim around the door and some other places that got scraped or chipped. The radio is on the whole time, the DJs keeping me company and playing music I like—Zeppelin, Mountain, Tim Buckley, Dr. John. I get paint on my brown flannel and my new Levi's, but I don't care. When I'm finally done painting, I clean up the newspapers on the floor and put away the paint. I bring up my dad's toolbox and then I disassemble the dining room table. I stash it, along with the chairs, downstairs in the unfinished part of the basement, which is probably what I should have done in the first place. The dining room is clean and painted and perfectly empty, except I guess now it's a studio.

I don't really notice what time it is until I start to feel dizzy. My head has been hurting all day, but when I begin feeling like I'm going to pass out, I realize I haven't eaten anything since breakfast. Then I think of the bowl of disgusting Cocoa Puffs and I remember that I didn't eat breakfast either. I glance at the clock in the kitchen and see that it's almost midnight. I think, *At least I made it through the anniversary. Kind of.*

Once I realize how late it is, I really start to get worried. Mom hasn't driven anywhere other than Grandland or the doctor's office or Checker Drugs for the past year. I think about calling the police, but I've had my fill of them today, and besides, I can't tell them what she did, so I hold off. I don't know what to do.

In the kitchen, after turning down the volume on the radio, I stand there in front of the refrigerator for a good two minutes meaning to eat something, but I'm in a daze. I look in one of the drawers and find half a package of Oscar Mayer Olive Loaf I bought a couple weeks ago. It's old, but not green yet. In the cupboard, there's some stale bread. I put the meat on the bread, slather mustard on and a few pickle chips. I sit there and take a bite of my stale sandwich, my hands covered with paint. At first I think I'm going to throw up, but I keep chewing. Except then I can't swallow. I get up, put my head under the faucet, and drink from the tap. It makes my head throb, but everything goes down. I sit back at the kitchen table and finish the whole sandwich. I think about making another one. Instead, I close my eyes. The radio is playing "Thirteen" by Big Star. A pretty but sad song about being a kid, which is not exactly what I need to hear right now. Even still, I feel better when Alex Chilton gets to this part:

Rock and roll is here to stay
Come inside where it's okay

That's the last thing I remember.

Headache Song

Even though I'm sitting there at the kitchen table in my own house when the phone wakes me up at 4:25 in the morning, for a long moment I truly have no idea where I am. The radio is still on, playing some stupid fake-classical, too long, pretentious, boring Rick Wakeman song, which I don't like one bit. The air is thick with paint fumes, but my headache is better, though the sound of the phone ringing again and again is not helping.

I drag myself up from the table to answer it. When I press the receiver to my ear, I'm reminded of the lump on the back of my head. I concentrate on the pain instead of how scared I am about the phone ringing in the middle of the night with my mother still missing.

"Mom?" I say.

I hear a woman's voice on the other end of the line, but it's not my mom. "This is Jean Trascoma calling from the Detroit Police Department. I'm looking for a relative of Mrs. Eleanor Yzemski," she says.

"That's my mom," I say. "Is she okay?"

"Eleanor Yzemski of 15318 Stout Street?"

"Yes." This woman is scaring me now. "Yes. That's her. Is she okay?"

The woman starts coughing, horrible and loud, right into the phone. I can't believe it. I can only think that she's putting off having to tell me that my mother is dead. I hear her take a drink of something. "I'm so sorry," she says, her voice cracking.

The breath is sucked out of my lungs when she says

this. I stand there holding the phone, pressing it tight to my head, hoping the needles of pain will keep me from passing out.

She clears her throat. "Excuse me," she says. "She's fine. She's perfectly safe."

I can't speak just then. It takes me a couple seconds to get used to the fact that I'm not an orphan.

"Is this Mr. Yzemski?"

I'm so relieved that I forget to answer for a moment. "No. I'm her son," I finally say.

"I see. Is Mr. Yzemski there?"

"No, he's not. He's dead." As soon as I say it so casually like that, I feel bad. I'm not sure if it's for me or for my dad or for Jean Trascoma of the Detroit Police Department. "He died a year ago yesterday."

There's a long pause. I hear a *tink* that's probably a pencil on something ceramic, like a coffee mug or something. "I see. I'm so sorry for your loss." Another pause. Another sip of something.

"What's going on, please?"

A loud breath over the phone tells me this is all sort of a pain in the rear end for Ms. Trascoma. "May I ask how old you are?"

"Sixteen," I lie.

"Are there any other adults or guardians in the household?"

"No ma'am," I say, omitting the fact that I'm the only guardian in this household even when my mother is here. "I'm it."

"I see. Well, I'm afraid that Mrs. Yzemski was found asleep in someone's bushes on the 18000 block of Trinity. Some residents called us. Apparently, she had been walking around in the neighborhood for some time, disoriented and agitated."

"But she's okay?"

"Yes, she's all right. It does appear that she was intoxicated."

"Canadian Mist." It's all I can think of saying.

"Excuse me?"

"Never mind."

"It appears that she abandoned a car on someone's property not far from where she was found. It's registered to a Mr. Harold Yzemski."

"That's my late father," I say, using that expression for the first time.

There's no answer at first. I just hear shuffling papers on the other end of the line and the amplified chatter of a police radio in the background. "Are you able to come down to pick her up? She's being held here at the 8th Precinct. Do you know where it is?"

"Yes, it's right by where I go to school. Is she in trouble?"

"No, but your father's car has been impounded. You'll have to get it out tomorrow, but you can come get her right now. Just come to the front desk and tell them you're here to pick someone up. They'll know what to do."

"Okay," I say. "Thank you." But she's already hung up.

The drum solo in my head settles from Keith Moon to Ringo Starr.

A Hard Day's Night

I've never driven my mother's car before—she's always been weirdly possessive about it—but once I get it on the road, I realize that this was the car that I should have been driving all along. Turns out that even without power steering, my mom's Tempest is much easier to handle than the *Hindenburg*. It's a good thing that we didn't get rid of it, even though I've known for a long time that we have to sell one of the cars. There's the insurance, and with the gas shortage, we need a car that gets decent mileage, which is the Tempest. We'll sell the *Hindenburg* if it's still in one piece.

I can't help thinking of yet another reason to sell it as I pass the Polara at the next block. I get a good look at it now. The bumper has been pushed into the trunk (sprung, and still ajar) and the driver's-side rear fender is caved in pretty bad. There are still red and white bits of taillight on the street that glitter under my headlights as I pass. I feel ashamed, but I tell myself that their insurance will take care of it. Obviously, if these people see the *Hindenburg* drive down the street, they're going to know who did it. I make a mental note to avoid this block when I bring the car back. I will stash it in the garage until we can sell it. Planning this gives me a little thrill. Between all this illegal activity and being in a race riot yesterday, I really do feel like a tough guy. Then after a moment, the feeling is gone. I'm back to being me.

I've never driven at five a.m. before. My neighborhood is so quiet. Aside from the hum of the Tempest, I hear only the stirring of leaves under my tires as I glide through half-bright streets lit with yellow porch lights and harsh backyard floods (fear of break-ins) as well as streetlamps, crowded by the trees grown in around them, throwing fractured bright and dark patterns on the pavement. The air is still warm and I keep the windows of the Tempest open to wake myself up. I worry about what's going to happen after I pick up Mom.

No Hassle from the Pigs

Everything at the police station is easier than I thought it would be. I sign a paper on a clipboard and the officer at the desk makes a call. When he hangs up, he gives me a card with the address of the impound lot and tells me it will be a hundred bucks to get it out. It's liable to be there for a while, I think. At least until the heat is off it.

When Mom comes out from the back, she's wearing the same flowered housecoat she was wearing the night before when she was standing in my room, only it's really dirty now. She looks at me, but it's like she doesn't really even see me.

"Hi," I say to her.

She squints at me. "Danny?" Her voice is strained and gravelly. It doesn't really sound like her.

"I'm here to take you home."

She rubs her face with a filthy left hand, pushing the fingers into her cheek. "Good. I don't like it here."

"You're not supposed to like it in jail, Mom."

As I take her hand, I glance over at the lady who brought her out. She doesn't seem like a police officer, but she's got a uniform of some type. Her name tag reads: *Denetta*. She's a middle-aged black lady, short and round, with a face that reveals nothing until she speaks to my mother.

"You take good care, Eleanor," she says. "Glad your boy got here."

"Thank you, Netty," my mother says, smiling weakly.

Denetta looks over as if she's sorry, worried, and embarrassed for me all at once. "Whammer Jammer" by the J. Geils Band is blasting in my head at that moment. All that harmonica makes it hurt, but I can't stop it.

Mom doesn't smell good. Not BO so much, but like maybe she's been throwing up. Her elbows and knees are dirty too. I'm not going to ask about any of it for a while. Maybe never.

Morning Has Broken

I don't go into school that morning. I don't call. I don't worry about a note. I just don't show up. Things are probably still a mess because of the mini race riot, but it doesn't matter to me either way. I just lie in bed until about noon or so, the back of my head throbbing on the pillow and the fade weighing heavy on me. Finally, I get up, get dressed, then go to the kitchen, turn on the radio which is still there, and make myself a bowl of Trix. As I eat, the radio is playing the old Bowie track, "Space Oddity." When it ends, I turn down the radio till it's real low, then I have a couple more spoonfuls of cereal because I'm still putting off calling work. After I finish the bowl, I walk over to the phone. When Mitch answers for the shipping room, I tell him that my mom is not feeling well so I won't be coming in today.

"You should get your stories straight," Mitch tells me.

"What do you mean?"

"Yesterday you said *you* were sick, today your mother's sick. You should make up your mind."

"I was sick yesterday. My mom is sick today. I have to take care of her."

"If you want this job, you might want to show up once in a while. We're going to have some big orders coming in today. You better be here or don't bother coming in again."

"Go fuck yourself, Mitch," I say, slamming down the phone.

I turn the radio up and just sit there at the kitchen table. Even "Out on the Tiles" doesn't cheer me up and I love *Led Zeppelin III*. The fade pushes up from my belly until I feel like I'm about to throw up the cereal I just ate. I stare at the pinky-blue milk in my bowl of Trix and I guess I kind of start to cry. I don't want to, because I can hear my father telling me not to be a baby, like he always used to, but even that doesn't stop me. I sit there crying at our kitchen table, the ceramic owls from my mother's collection on the shelf staring down at me as I bawl. *Whoo? Whoo? Who's a big baby?* they say.

"Danny?"

I look up to see my mom there. I thought she'd sleep all day and night. I wipe at my eyes with the heels of my hands, embarrassed.

"Could you turn down that radio?" she says in a low voice.

I nod and turn it down. She's very pale. The dark moons under her eyes are deep, but she has a clean robe on and it seems like she washed herself up, I'm not sure when. Her hair is hanging in damp, stuck-together strips of gray-streaked blond, yet she looks better.

"Hi, Mom," I say. My nose is running now. I don't have a tissue, so I just use the back of my hand.

"What are you crying about, honey?" She sits down with me at the kitchen table.

I take a breath through my mouth because my nose is so stuffed up. "Nothing," I say.

"What are you worried about now?" she asks, smiling, and it's like she's her old self and I'm a kid again, worried about some dumb thing. "I'm sure it can't be anything too bad."

"You think?" I can't help but smile.

My mother sighs loudly. "I'm sorry, Danny."

"You are?"

"I don't know what happened."

"Neither do I, Mom." I'm not sure I actually want to know what happened. I just know that I'm going to have to keep an eye on her.

"I didn't mean to break your record."

Stunned, I stare at her. "Mom. I just got you out of jail and you're apologizing for breaking my Humble Pie album? How about for driving drunk and high through our neighborhood, pulling our china cabinet behind you? How about for smashing it into someone's car? Or for passing out in someone's yard and letting me worry all night? Maybe you should apologize for that."

Mom looks at me and shrugs. "Okay. I'm sorry." Her eyes start darting around the kitchen. She's searching for her cigarettes, I'm sure. I can practically see the lightbulb click on over her head as she gets up and walks over to one of the drawers under the counter, our junk drawer, where she usually keeps an extra pack of L&Ms. She finds half a pack, shakes out one of the long cigarettes, and puts it in her mouth. Then she goes back into the drawer for a matchbook and a beanbag ashtray. I watch her light up and take a deep, deep drag. She's still holding the matchbook, which is from a supermarket at Grandland and reads:

Great Scott!

We love you

I hadn't really noticed this before. It's weird, I don't know why a grocery store is telling me they love me, until Mom sets the matchbook on the table. Then I see what it says on the other side:

You'll love our prices

After a couple puffs, some of Mom's color comes back. The smoke swirls up around her face and she waves it away like she always does. She'll be looking for a bottle of Coke soon. I don't think we have any in the house, but I'll go get some for her. My stomach doesn't hurt so much anymore. I feel the fade start to lift. Neither of us says anything for what feels like a long time.

"You and your father always got along so well," she finally says. "Sometimes I felt like an outsider."

It had never occurred to me that she might feel that way, yet I realize something just then. "It seemed like you wanted that, Mom. It always did."

She stares at the glowing tip of her cigarette. "I thought that after he—" She takes a puff instead of finishing her sentence. "I thought maybe we would grow closer. But we didn't. You didn't need me at all."

"That's not true. I did need you," I say angrily. Then quietly: "I need you."

Mom considers this for a moment. Then she waves the hand that's holding the cigarette in the general direction of the other room. "The studio looks nice, Danny. You did a good job."

As confused as I am, it still makes me feel good to be complimented by my parents. Even if one is dead and the other is losing her marbles.

"I wanted to fix it up for you. For artistic endeavors."

"Thank you," she says, glancing down at the floor, then at my cereal, anywhere but at me. She takes another deep pull off her cigarette. I watch the ash sag from its own weight until it lands on the table where it is ignored. "Can I have some cereal too?" she asks, stubbing out her cigarette.

Gravely, I shake my head no. "Silly rabbit," I say, "Trix are for kids."

I know it's not a very good joke, I'm just repeating some dumb TV commercial slogan, but I laugh at it anyway. She even laughs a little too. I allow myself to think that everything is going to be okay, even though I know better.

On the radio, real low, I can hear "Future Games" by Fleetwood Mac. It's not the old blues Fleetwood Mac or the new Top 40 Fleetwood Mac, but the one in between. Without thinking, I turn up the radio. It's not a jam or anything. It's real quiet—all lilty guitars and Bob Welch's whispery singing, but I like the song a lot. Nobody plays it enough on the radio.

"This is pretty," my mom says.

All of the wild things tomorrow will tame
Talking of journeys that happen in vain . . .

I get up, I collect a bowl and a spoon, and make Mom a bowl of Trix. I shake a little more into my bowl while I'm at it.

And I know I'm not the only one . . .

We both sit there at the kitchen table and have our cereal while we listen to the radio. I guess it turned out to be a good thing that she bought so much after all.

Sounds of '75!

I Told You Once and I Told You Twice

For the record, I still think this is stupid, but I'm going to do it one last time. I haven't promised anyone that I'd write you and even if I had, it wouldn't matter. I don't care what I'm supposed or not supposed to do anymore. Too much has happened, man. I'm not going to tell you all of it, but trust me, there's been a lot going on.

I convinced Mom to go to the doctor after she went kind of schizo. Not Diane-Linkletter-jumping-off-a-building schizo, but bad enough. (Maybe none of it would surprise you. Then again, maybe it would.) The doctor's got her on some new tranquilizer. They kind of help, even though she's not supposed to drink while she's taking them, but she still does.

After things settled down some, I finally convinced her that part of being a new woman should involve getting a job, so now she's working part-time as a cashier at Great Scott! Mostly, I think she likes it. She gripes about the bosses all the time, but seems to like the other cashiers. She says she feels more modern, so I guess that's good. I'm just glad she's bringing in money. I'm still not sure we're going to be able to keep the house, though.

For her birthday, I got her a starter artist kit, so she's also been painting pictures. I just thought it would be good therapy, but she's not half bad, to tell the truth. When she's not working or drinking, she sits in her studio (you know it as our dining room) and paints pictures of bowls of fruit like Cézanne. (I suggested a bowl of cereal just for a change, but she didn't think that was very funny.) Some nights, when the pills are working and she doesn't drink too much, we watch TV together and sometimes we even make it through Johnny Carson. I like those nights, but they don't happen very often.

The neighborhood is still changing. Mom talks about us moving out and getting an apartment in the suburbs, but I like it here fine. Our new neighbors are nicer than our old ones. The old ones mostly treated me like a weirdo, which I know I am (I guess you knew it too), but that doesn't mean they had to be that way. When the news is on, I let Mom talk herself out, then I tell her that the world is changing along with our neighborhood and she damn well better get used to it. That usually quiets her down for a while. I don't mean to be a jerk, Dad, but the same goes for you.

Here's something else: I got fired from my job in the shipping department for telling my boss Mitch to go fuck himself. (I didn't think you'd mind the cussing since I was sticking up for myself, which you were constantly telling me to do.) Here's the cool part. Stan, the guy that hired me, gave me my job back. I even offered to apologize to Mitch, but he told me not to bother. The weird thing is, since I told Mitch off, my other boss, Dale, has been much nicer to me. I do not understand people at all.

We hardly ever have mini race riots at school anymore. I'm still working on the school radio station, though I'm not on the air right now. I belong to the future broadcasters club and am working hard to get an internship at the Specs Howard School of Broadcasting. Last week, I went on a tour of one of the Detroit rock stations. The DJ who showed us around told me I have a good voice for radio. (Then he told me I have a good face for radio too, but he was just kidding around.) I'm doing fine with my classes, but knowing about music is the smartest thing about me.

I know you wouldn't like rock music, Dad. It's really loud, not at all like what you used to listen to. It's all screeching guitars and crashing drums and singing that sounds like yelling. It's what you would call a bunch of racket. The musicians have long hair and take a lot of drugs and sometimes even die from them. You would hate it all, but I don't care. I love it. I want to be on the radio and play loud music for everyone. There's a lot of noise that needs drowning out—ugly words and nasty voices and dumb ideas. I'm sick of hearing it all. I'm going to do what I can to release something positive into the air. A wise man once said: "Let me be who I am. And let me kick out the jams."

There is one more not-great thing that I do have to tell you. We had to get rid of the Bonneville. I'm sorry, Dad. I know you loved that car, but it had to be done. Pete Madzik at the Standard station gave me a hand with the whole thing. He was really cool. I know he used to work on the car so I asked him if he knew anyone who might want to buy it. A couple days later, some guy came to the house and made me an offer. I gave him a good deal (less than Blue Book) for more of those reasons I won't go into here.

We really needed the money and we definitely didn't need two cars, even though I'm now a legal driver, but it still made me feel pretty awful to watch the guy drive it off down Fenkell. It made me think of you and me in that car, especially you and me driving home from Korvettes. The sun low in the sky, our record albums in their paper bags on the backseat, us still feeling that thrill from buying them. Maybe you'd be smoking a cigarette from the fresh carton you just bought. The radio would be on, usually to that Beautiful Music station in Canada, the one that used to go off the air when the sun went down. I didn't tell you back then how scared it made me feel when that happened. I still don't know why. Maybe it's just the feeling of being lost in that moment, in between what just ended and whatever comes next. Back then, I always hoped that you would just change the station before it went off the air. I feel less that way these days, but it still makes me ache right now thinking about it. I think about a disc jockey, broadcasting from a small radio station somewhere in Windsor, across the Ambassador Bridge, in another country, far from our neighborhood in Detroit. Sitting in a dimly lit studio, a record on a turntable spinning before him, playing the Canadian national anthem. And as the song fades, it all gets quieter, and there's only the sound of the disc jockey saying: "This is CBE Radio ending its programming day. We will resume broadcasting at sunrise tomorrow. Good evening."

The song ends. Then suddenly, static.

Special thanks to:

Rita Simmons, with my love and gratitude always.

Keith McLenon and David Bierman for the early readings and encouragement.

DeAnn Forbes for the kindness, the conversation, and never-ending help.

Andrew Brown, Tony Park, David Hughes, Nick Marine, Luis Resto, Eric Weltner, Holly Sorscher, Jim Dudley, Russ Taylor, Jeff Warner, Tims Teegarden and Suliman, Amanda and Duffy Patten, and the Detroit ad community for all the literary support over the years.

Jeff Edwards, Jim Potter, Barry Burdiak, Mark Mueller, and Michael Lloyd for the long, long friendships.

Johns Tjaarda and Niemisto for the listening parties and music talk.

Jud Laghi for the sterling representation.

Sally van Haitsma for the strangest journey of my life.

Susan Summerlee for Gene Pitney, Dion and Del Shannon.

Doc, Crow, Wimp, Jeffy-boy, the Rushes, Don, Lar, Jim, Craig, Ed, Wendy, and the rest of the HP crew for the education, musical and otherwise.

Rosalie Trombley and CKLW for shaping Detroit's soundtrack and culture.

And to all the legendary jocks at WABX, WWWW, and CJOM.

Kick out the jams, motherfuckers.